THE
VAGABOND
KING

Jodie Bond is a writer, dancer and communications professional. She has worked for a circus, a gin distillery, as a burlesque artist and has sold speciality sausages for a living, but her biggest passion has always been writing. *The Vagabond King*, the first in a trilogy, is her debut novel.

THE
VAGABOND
KING

JODIE BOND

PARTHIAN

Parthian, Cardigan SA43 1ED
www.parthianbooks.com
First published in 2019
© Jodie Bond 2019
ISBN 978-1-912109-37-1
Edited by Richard Davies and Carly Holmes
Cover design and map illustration by anneglenndesign@gmail.com
Typeset by Elaine Sharples
Printed and bound by 4edge Limited, UK
Published with the financial support of the Books Council of Wales
British Library Cataloguing in Publication Data
A cataloguing record for this book is available from the British Library.
Every attempt has been made to secure the permission of copyright
holders to reproduce images.

For Luke, with love

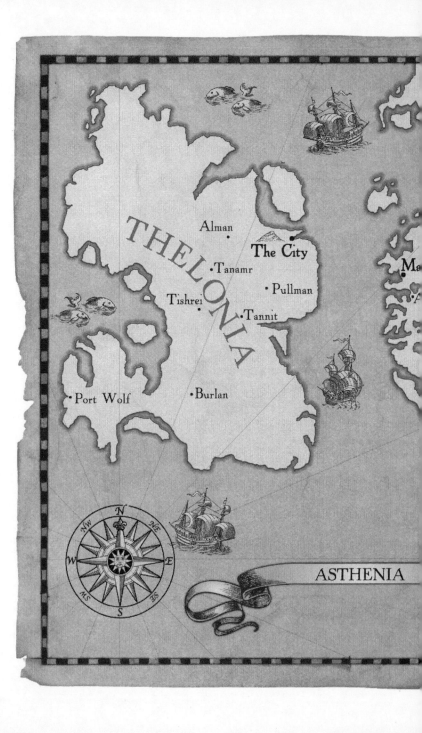

THELONIA

Alman

The City

Tanamr

Pullman

Tishrei

Tannit

Port Wolf

Burlan

Me

ASTHENIA

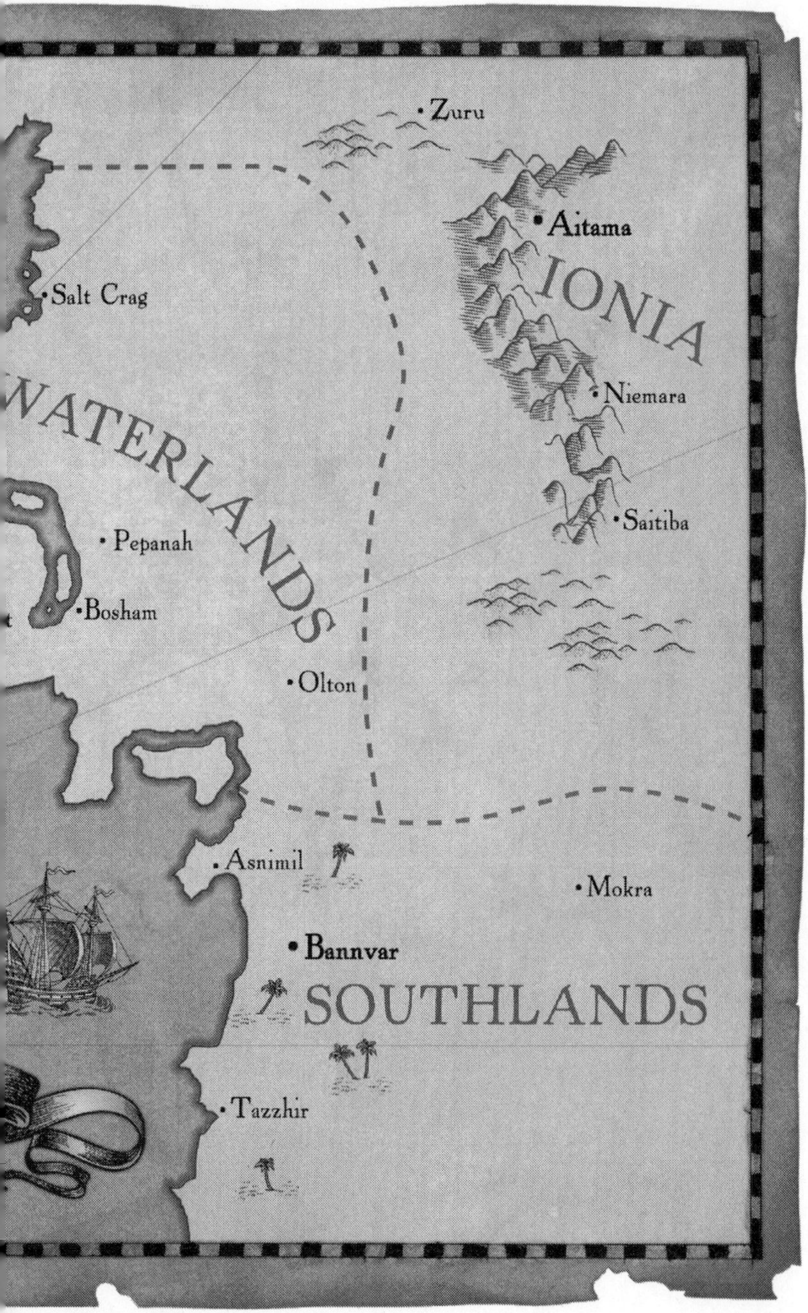

- Zuru

- **Aitama**

IONIA

- Salt Crag

- Niemara

WATERLANDS

- Saitiba

- Pepanah

- Bosham

- Olton

- Asnimil

- Mokra

- **Bannvar**

SOUTHLANDS

- Tazzhir

PROLOGUE

Even now, in the dark and after countless journeys across this stretch of ocean, the land ahead stole the attention of every eye on board the ship. Green and fat and arable, and ready for taking.

An orange glow nestled at the shoreline marked their destination: the city of Maradah.

Lleu breathed deep, rolling broad shoulders to warm his muscles. The night air tasted cold like calculation; the way it always felt before battle. Soldiers crowded the deck completing weapon checks and pulling on armour. Their silence betrayed a mix of apprehension and steady readiness. He reached a hand down instinctively to his sword, gripping the pommel with a sweaty palm.

This journey was familiar, but never before had he travelled to the Waterlands on a raid. It was necessary, they said. The country ahead gorged on fertile land.

The people of Thelonia were starving.

Lleu didn't feel starving. Most of the spoils of the raid

would go back to feed palimore soldiers like him. Maybe some would make it to the villages and the mines. Maybe.

It had been a long time since he'd seen combat. Real combat. The world of the arena was a far cry from battle. In battle you can taste fear in the air, feel adrenaline in your blood. He didn't doubt that the soldiers of Maradah would fight fiercely. He didn't doubt that they would give it their all. Nor did he doubt that there would be deaths. It had been long years since the last palimore soldier had died in combat. Strength and experience were on their side.

'Ready to fight at home, Blue?' Deryn elbowed him as she whispered the words.

Lleu ignored her, keeping his eyes on the horizon. Blue eyes. The feature marked him as an outsider. They didn't forget it either. It was said the prominence of blue eyes in the Waterlands was a reflection of their devotion to Athys, the water god. But to his fellow soldiers it was a mark of inferiority. Of impure blood. He didn't care. He'd proven himself their equal time and again in combat. Tonight would be another such opportunity as he faced killing his own kin. Shrugging the thought away, he wiped sweat from his palms and tightened the straps of his armour.

The ships anchored hidden among rocky crags, and the soldiers emerged on the shore wet and panting from the mile-long swim. Leaving the rowboats behind would help them warm up, promised the commander. Lleu paused for a moment, letting water drain from him as he regained his breath on all fours. He pulled himself to his feet. Swimming in armour had been tougher than he'd thought. He was cold but his heart beat hard. The workout made a pleasant change from training on the confinement of a ship deck.

Fellow soldiers were shadows in the pale moonlight, each

gathering themselves for the fight ahead. Behind him, horses were being led down a wide gangway to splash through waves and join them on the beach. Lleu spotted his own among them, but there would be no immediate cavalry charge. Tonight would be won by stealth. The captain waved instructions to move forward to the barracks. They stole silently through the town, dealing out quick deaths to beggars and dogs who might deign to raise an alarm.

It didn't take long to find the barracks. Lleu's company paused outside its large wooden doors. The smell of meat, alcohol and the sweat of undisciplined men stretched out into the night. It was the eve of midsummer and the city's soldiers had been celebrating. Drunk, asleep and unprepared. That's what the palimore hoped for. They would win this the easy way, honour bedamned.

There were fifty men in Lleu's party. They gathered in formation outside the door.

The captain held up three fingers. Two. One.

The company moved forwards with force. The main door yielded far too easily and beyond it they found the men at the heart of Maradah's defence. Startled from sleep, unprepared and stinking of drink. Just as planned. Some scrambled for weapons. Others fled like cowards.

Lleu's party spread out to fill the width of the room. No one would escape by the main entrance.

The Maradah army numbered just over two hundred men. A myopic number for a city of such size. Decades of peacetime meant they were unseasoned, never tested in battle. And they were young, so young.

Swords lined the walls. Several barracks men were quick enough to grab one, but it would do little good. Muscles still slack with sleep, blinking hard to clear their vision, these soldiers already knew they faced cruel odds. As Lleu drew his sword his pulse quickened with the dark excitement that comes from facing, and delivering, death.

His troop moved forward with fatal efficiency.

The palimore ceased being individuals. Long years of battle drills made their movements second nature. Matching stances, blades poised to attack, they encroached on Maradah's men, eating up the remaining space of the barracks. Fear paled the men ahead. A handful ran, scrambling to crawl through windows. They would soon be picked off by one of the other troops in town.

Those who held their ground had to be admired. They faced death head on. A large bearded man surged at the wall of invaders, arcing his sword through the air. His eyes singled out Lleu, marking him as his target. He brought the weapon down. Sword met sword as Lleu defended the blow. He pushed back where their blades touched and the bearded man staggered backwards. Before he could correct his footing, Lleu thrust his sword forward. It tore through the man's sternum and he jerked the blade up towards an astonished face, ripping him open. Lleu allowed himself a satisfied snort as the body fell backwards.

His party cut forwards through Maradah's remaining men in a similar fashion, with shameful ease. Some had failed to wake in the commotion. These Lleu killed with a grunt of distaste. A humiliating end for any soldier.

The last of them died backed up against the far wall with nowhere to run. Some dropped their weapons and begged. None were spared.

The mission was finished within minutes. Lleu hadn't even built up a sweat. Limp bodies filled the room, some groaning final breaths. Blood pooled around the far wall, where most had died. Lleu wrinkled his nose. He could handle the iron smell of blood, but it had been a long time since he had been faced with the earthy rot of torn innards.

4

'To the castle,' barked the lieutenant. Her words jarred against the quiet of the dead. Lleu was happy to turn his back on the scene.

It was a poor fight. The bastards hadn't stood a chance.

The road to the castle danced under Threon's feet, limbs ungainly with drink. An ingrained homing sense always dragged him back after a night drinking with the soldiers. On arriving at the front gate, he nearly walked straight into it. It stretched up far above him with a smaller door set into its thick wood. The guards usually remembered to leave it open until he returned. He cursed under his breath.

Bringing a fist against the door, he called out. 'Guards.' No response. 'Where the hell are you?' More silence. 'Guards! Open the gate.' He held out a hand to steady himself against the wood, then kicked the door in frustration.

Where was everyone? He looked around, listening in the darkness. No sound came from the stables, the kitchen, the guard room. The entire castle was silent.

Wariness sparked a little sobriety in him. He pulled a knife from his boot and levered it at the bolt on the door. It swung open with surprising ease.

Inside, the main courtyard was empty. No torches burned. The shadows of night-shift workers were absent. A lone horse snorted as it paced across the cobbles, loose from the stables.

He trod a careful path across the yard towards the main building, glancing around, eyes straining in the darkness.

Then he saw the guards. He froze. His heart quickened. Their bodies were piled against the stable walls, lifeless.

Death changed the way a body looked; the skin, where it wasn't bloody or bruised, was pale and waxy; the flesh hung heavier on their bones. And there was something about their stillness, their inert chests and unblinking eyes that made him shudder. He knelt down, shaking as he scanned the faces. Tonight's guards. Two young stable boys. A maid. Their throats gaped dark crimson.

Raiders. They had come at last.

And they might still be here.

He searched the guards' bodies for a weapon larger than his knife, but found none, then skirted around the wall to the cover offered by the stables. His drunken shouts were sure to have drawn attention.

Here the floor was slick with blood. Each of the horses lay dead in their stalls. The bodies of stable hands were clustered together, as though they had died fighting in unison. The smell of flesh made him retch. His head spun. Pressing up against the wall, he breathed deep, willing away his drunkenness.

A covered stairway ran from the stables to the top of the castle walls where he might get a better view of the devastation. Knife clenched in fist, he stepped into the dark tunnel. His heavy breath echoed in the stillness as he staggered up the steps, faint moonlight outlining the open doorway up ahead.

He reached the top and looked out over the city below where five thousand people made their home. Fires burned, cattle grazed, people slept. Would they wake to plunder? Would they wake at all?

A hand clasped over his mouth. An arm gripped his waist. A dagger pinched at his ribs. He had been immobilised before he was even aware someone was behind him.

Threon's eyes darted to the city alarm bell. It was ten strides away.

'Well, look at you in your finery,' a woman breathed in his ear. 'I'll wager you're someone important.'

The knife moved from his ribs to his throat. The flat of the blade pressed hard against it, stifling his breath. Unable to move, he could see nothing of his captor, just feel her grip tighten as she pulled him back to the tunnel.

'Geran,' she called.

Another figure dropped down from the roof of the corridor and stood before them. This one a man, and huge. Threon had heard stories about the palimore, broader than gladiators and stronger than bulls; it seemed they were an understatement. This one had arms twisted with sinew, chest broad as a prow and a face gnarled and square with muscle. A quick glance down showed the woman's arms were equally thickset.

'Must be the prince,' the man said. 'Careful, he's got a knife.'

Threon cursed himself for not being quicker to move with the weapon. The woman laughed quietly. 'He's probably better trained to slice oyster shells. And he reeks of booze.'

Threon's hand shook as he gripped the handle of his paltry weapon. If he was going to die, better to take one of these bastards down with him. He stabbed backwards quickly, aiming for his captor's side, but missed. They both laughed. The man drew a blackened sword. Threon met his eyes. There was no malice in his gaze but the soldier's calm was chilling. Threon tensed, heart punching his ribs.

The man lunged the blade forward.

Risking his throat, Threon put all his weight into forcing the woman over the edge of the wall. Taken by surprise, she let go of both him and the knife to catch herself from falling.

It was not enough to stop the other soldier's sword.

The length of metal plunged through his side. A stab of cold, and then burning pain. It was quickly drawn back out again for another swipe. He clutched at the wound, eyes wide. A stumble towards the ground. But then, pulling on a reserve of strength, he forced some momentum into the fall, pushing past the soldier with the raised sword. His vision blurred, but adrenaline gave him the strength and sobriety to reach the alarm bell. Falling on the rope, he used his weight to pull it to chime. He hoped it was enough to wake the city.

The shock of the wound sapped all his strength. Too weak to run, too weak to fight. Pain seared through his body. As warm liquid spurted from his flesh, the edges of night closed tighter on his vision.

Both soldiers were in front of him now. He wouldn't give them the satisfaction. With a marathon effort he pulled himself up onto the wall and let his body fall back into the courtyard.

The cold wind felt soothing as he fell. In that fleeting airborne moment, he thought of his family. Maybe they had escaped. The thought seemed wistful.

Then the cobbles hit.

'Get down there. Finish him off.'

The voice was distant. Threon was on the edge of deep sleep.

Eyes fixed on the cobbles. Short shallow breaths. So much pain.

It felt an age before the soldier's shadow loomed over him. Threon tried to raise his head to meet the eyes of his killer, but moving only caused black to bloom in his vision. A boot in the ribs. He groaned and managed to roll onto his back, retreating a whole foot from where the soldier stood. A grunt of contempt. Then another boot, this time harder.

Another distant sound. The thud of steel on wood. People at the gates.

'Quick. Call the others.'

Shouting. Banging. Wood shattering. Rushed feet pounded the floor. More screams, more cries, and the sound of death.

He closed his eyes, unable to help, unable to care, and slipped into oblivion.

The light of dawn was blinding. Threon closed his eyes again. How long had he been out? His head jostled against stones as he was dragged across the courtyard. Vaguely aware that he should be in pain, his body felt numb and a foreign heat burned his insides.

Through blurred vision he cast his eyes around. A figure in dark robes was pulling him across the courtyard towards the now broken gates. He could smell burning and his stomach churned when he saw pillars of smoke rising from the town.

Where were they taking him? He was helpless. A limp body, bleeding and frail. Perhaps they'd dug a mass grave. Wavering on the edge of consciousness, he lacked the capacity for fear. So was this it? Unceremonious, compassionless death?

He was dragged for a long while. Out of the gates, past mounds of corpses. Past the servants' entrance. Down the slope towards the miller's cottage. Then the palimore stopped and propped him against the miller's barn. The miller's wife and dog lay dead on the grass nearby, her once familiar face changed by a concave blow to her skull.

The hooded figure looked around before taking out a flask from his robes and putting it to Threon's lips. Water. He grabbed it with shaking hands, forcing the cool liquid down. It left him spluttering.

The man removed his hood revealing the hard, muscled face of a palimore soldier. 'Ranar ardell,' he said in greeting. *Peace to the Waterfolk.*

Threon tried to speak but no words came, just a piercing cough. Blood filled his mouth with a sharp tang.

Ranar ardell? Maybe this man wasn't going to kill him after all.

'I can't guarantee your safety,' the soldier said, standing over him. He was broad, tanned and stern-faced. This close, Threon could appreciate the size of these born fighters, a force

9

his people could never hope to face and win. His eyes were cold and unnerving, but they were as blue as his own. Palimore never recruited soldiers from the Waterlands. Who was this man? He crouched down so he was at eye level with Threon. 'No promises, but I'll do what I can for you.'

'Why?' Threon's voice was a whisper wet with blood.

The palimore ignored him and ripped one of Threon's trouser legs, revealing bone that pressed up against the skin at a grisly angle. Threon felt dizzy and looked away. The soldier growled in annoyance. Broken. Threon touched a hand to his chest, wincing at the tenderness. Broken ribs too, most likely.

The palimore strode to the miller's log stack and picked out a straight branch. He knelt and bound it to Threon's leg using strips of fabric torn from the prince's cloak. Threon tensed, gritting his teeth in anticipation of what was to come. 'Ready?' He didn't have a chance to respond. A grinding snap and pain seared up his leg, forcing a tide of black over his vision. The palimore tightened the bindings over the straightened bone as Threon squeezed his eyes closed, trying not to cry out.

'Your ribs will heal themselves in time. If you can avoid infecting that gash in your side, you might live.' The soldier reached into his robes and pulled out a glass vial. 'This will help.'

Vish'aad.

Threon had never seen it before. Even royalty in the Waterlands couldn't afford such riches. The soldier must have seen the expression on his face. He grunted, amused, and handed him the small bottle.

Threon held it to the light. The violet powder was packed down tightly in the container.

'Don't take it yet. The first time can induce shock. Let me fetch my horse first.'

He disappeared behind the cottage and gave a loud whistle,

which was soon followed by the sound of approaching hooves. Threon opened the vial with shaking hands and breathed in the smell. Sweet, earthy, with a hint of decay.

'I said wait,' the soldier commanded as he came around the corner of the building, leading a horse by the reins. The beast was jet black and enormous, more than eighteen hands high. His muscles rippled under a shining coat. A Thelonian stallion. He was magnificent. 'This is Bloodbringer,' said the soldier. 'He'll get you out of here.'

Threon screwed the vial shut. He tried to push himself forward to stand, but weakened muscles betrayed him and blood rushed to his head to steal his consciousness. He fell back and opened his eyes again on the floor.

The palimore grabbed him under both arms and lifted him like a child. Threon groaned. The wound at his side released more blood as he moved. He was pushed up on top of the horse. Unable to sit upright, his face lay in the beast's mane.

The soldier pushed his feet into stirrups and tied them down. His leg pounded horribly. Then a rope came around his waist which was secured about the horse's neck. 'You're going to fall unconscious again. This should keep you steady.'

He ripped Threon's shirt around the gash in his side. 'My horse will take you south. He knows the roads that lead to Bannvar.' Threon knew of the aptitude Thelonian horses had for unaided navigation, but he'd never expected to experience it himself. 'You've been?' Threon shook his head. 'It's a long journey. Far enough, I hope. You should be safe there for now.' The soldier eyed Threon's side critically. He took the vial out of Threon's hand and emptied the powder into his palm. 'Brace yourself. I'm going to put it on your wound; it'll go straight to the bloodstream.'

Ice shot across Threon's body as the vish'aad touched the lesion that was already halfway to killing him. It fired lightning through his bones. His eyes widened and he snatched in air. The throb in his side, his leg, his head, fell away instantly. He jerked up to sit, but the rope held him down. He dug his fingers into the stallion's mane as his heart raced. The colours of the world brightened. Sounds and smells and touch magnified a thousandfold. His senses were on fire.

'Gods be with you,' the palimore said. His voice was like crystal.

He slapped the horse's rear and the distance soon stretched between them.

With sharpened senses, the prince tore through Maradah, tied to the back of the stallion. He saw death, smelled blood, heard the final cries of the dying. With his heightened senses, he could *feel* the life being torn from his city. It was agonising. The horse skirted burning buildings, dashed along unwatched alleys. When they reached the slopes of Mount Anthor, Threon could see the full extent of the devastation. Palimore ships filled the harbour, and more approached in a pillar of wood and sails that stretched from his home to the horizon.

A new flag flew from the castle.

He wanted to stop. To take the whole horrifying scene in. To grieve. But the horse pushed on.

As his body began to adjust to the drug coursing his veins and his heart slowed again, the pain began to return, thudding and persistent. Each step the stallion took no longer felt like floating on water, but jarred his body like a knife. It wasn't until the vish'aad had fully worn off, hours later, that he was granted respite in unconsciousness, speeding away from his home.

CHAPTER ONE

'We did it. We bloody did it!' Savanta rushed into her mother's arms, forcing a burst of joyous laughter from the old woman.

Her mother hugged her tight. 'You're back late. Thank the gods you're okay.'

Her father followed Savanta through the front door, and a scampering of feet heralded little Erin's appearance at the bottom of the stairs. Savanta turned to meet her daughter's eager greeting. The four of them nearly filled the small room that made up the ground floor of their home. They lived in a modest terrace house, three generations squeezed into undersized accommodation. Their ground floor comprised one room that was mostly kitchen, but they had managed to cram in a dining table fit for all four of them to sit together.

'You did us proud, love,' said her father.

'We're going to be rich.' Erin jumped up and down and Savanta placed a kiss on her copper-haired head, unable to hide her smile.

'Calm down,' said Savanta. 'Nothing's certain yet.'

'She's not wrong to be excited,' said her father. 'The island's first flying machine. Imagine.'

'Dad! It was just a test flight.' Savanta had been trying to control her expectations all the way home. Her machine, which she had named Windracer, had flown for a whole five minutes, and she was confident she could fly it longer. The Empress was throwing money at projects like hers. If she could take it to the city… gods knew, they could do with the money. 'We've no idea what will happen tomorrow. Maybe they won't buy it. Maybe Windracer won't be able to sustain the flight.' Her family shone with hope and she didn't want to dampen spirits, so stopped talking.

'Can you really fly, Mummy?' Erin was still wide-eyed with excitement. 'What was it like?'

Savanta threw her head back. 'Scary,' she said to her little girl with a grin. 'Scary and extraordinary. I felt like a bird.' This seemed to please Erin and she clapped her hands, giggling.

Savanta collapsed onto a chair, the adrenaline of earlier leaving her tired but elated. Today was just a test. The real challenge would come tomorrow.

The next morning Savanta and her father took the long walk to her workshop on the far edges of town. She hadn't slept all night.

Their route took them past the slums on the outskirts of the town, and then up a steep grey hillside. It was here that she'd discovered an abandoned barn and adopted it as her workshop. The place overlooked an old open pit mine and must have once been used as storage for the mines.

Now they stood together in the barn, making final checks. Shafts of light fell warm on the machine's wing-like

14

structures, a thin metal frame clasping enormous fabric sheets. Years of work had gone into the thing, and now this modest rig held the weight of her future fortune.

A breeze stirred in the windows of the workshop, ruffling tattered curtains. It played along the wings, and the thing looked, not for the first time, as though it lived. As she pulled open the barn doors, letting fresh air flood the musty room, her father circled around to the front of the machine.

'Are you sure you're ready?' he asked, wrinkled brow pinching above a neat silver beard.

She nodded. 'I'm sure. Today's perfect. Just feel that wind.'

It was evident he was apprehensive, but he tried to hide it with a smile. 'I'm so proud of you,' he said.

No point in putting things off. She clapped her hands together. 'Okay. Let's do this.'

She unwound a rope that hung on the nose of the machine and pulled it towards the doors. It rolled behind obediently.

Outside, bright daylight caught on a landscape swirling with dust. The hill they stood on fell away to a steep cliff face revealing a grey vista from here to the horizon. The mine that once tore into the hill now lay deep and dark, abandoned below them.

She looked out beyond the mine, to the only colour in the scene; a faint blue line on the horizon. The sea.

Her father helped her unfold the fabric wings until they stretched out so far that the thin metal bent and kissed the ground.

Savanta hugged him tightly. 'Thank you. For everything.'

He kissed her auburn hair, clinging onto her like he didn't want to let go. 'Are you sure you want to do this? The city is so far.'

'You saw how it worked yesterday. Don't sound so worried.'

15

'You made Erin stay at home.' The warning in his voice was justified; if she was certain she would make it, she would have brought her daughter too.

'The workshop isn't suitable for children. She'll have plenty more chances to see it in action once I'm commissioned.' She broke off the hug. 'Wish me luck.' Despite the excitement in her voice, she felt her stomach turn. It would all be fine. It had to be.

Windracer consisted of two large wings with thin metal wires connecting them to handlebars at the nose of the machine. There was a sling of fabric for her to lie on set beneath the wings, from which she could reach the controls.

A gust of air pushed past them, and lifted Windracer a foot from the ground. It crashed softly back down as the breeze passed. She grabbed hold of the rope to hold it still and ducked under the wings, climbing onto the fabric sling beneath. 'Ready, Dad?'

'Be safe, love,' he said, and she could see his knuckles pale under the force of clenched fists.

He took the rope from her and pulled hard, running down the hill, towards the cliff. The wheels of the machine bounced against the uneven floor, scattering dust until a cloud formed around the pair. Another gust of wind came and the bounces doubled in size as Windracer took air under her sails.

The cliff edge neared. Savanta struggled to keep her eyes open through the dust, but she could sense her runway was nearly over. She clung to the handlebars and glimpsed her father let go of the rope. He fell flat to the ground, Windracer bounding over him.

The wheels touched the ground once, twice, and then the dust stopped. She was away from the ground, over the cliff. It began to plummet nose first and she pulled up sharply on the heavy controls, forcing the wings against the wind.

16

Buzzards circled ahead, and she guided the machine in their direction until Windracer rose on the same thermal air as the birds. Slowly, the machine began to edge upwards. The ground spread out far beneath her. She laughed. Another success.

She nudged the controls around until she could see her father on the ground ahead. He waved both hands in the air, joyous laughter filling his face.

As she rose higher, more of the island came into view. Thelonia's dull, grey landscape stretched out for miles. The extent of the abandoned mine spread out below, and beyond it many more operating mines scarred the land. Ahead of her lay the town of Tishrei, plumes of black smoke rising from the vish'aad purification process. To her right was her hometown, Tannit.

Angling the wings in its direction, she was soon above the slums where she watched in delight as people stood shock still, eyes fixed on her machine. The slums melted into suburbs, tiled roofs and crooked brick buildings squeezed tightly together. She could see her street. Her mother would be playing with Erin in the kitchen no doubt. She soon glided past her home, and past the wealthier city centre.

If the Empress granted her a commission there was a chance she would be invited to work in the capital. Her parents wouldn't need to worry about where their next meal came from. Her daughter could go to school, have a real future.

The palace lay at the coast in the east. She pushed on toward it, willing Windracer to make the journey.

Following the lines of the main road, she watched groups of slaves and their ponies pull carts of waste material from the mines. They never looked up, plodding on with solemn determination. The grey landscape below stretched on and on. As the land sped below, she grew more accustomed to the machine, daring to glide higher and to take sharper turns. She lost track of time, but when a glimmer appeared in the distance she realised how far she must have come. Rumour had it the palace was made of gold. The capital was in sight. She was going to make it. She ran through her pitch again in her head, reciting the practised words over and over.

Then the calm sky was torn with a sudden sharp wind. It slammed into her wings and threw Windracer sideways. She let go of the controls with one hand to keep herself steady on the sling.

The delicate balance keeping her airborne was broken. The craft began to spin at an angle. Her body was thrown from the sling, and she clung desperately to the handlebars as Windracer sped towards the ground. She was tossed like a feather in the air, the land beneath growing ever nearer. Her heart raced as she tried to re-balance the craft. Hooking a leg back into the sling, she tried pulling her body back into it. Another gust of wind forced the wings over again, this time tipping the craft past the point of return. She hung upside down from Windracer's belly, her whole weight on the bars at the nose of the craft. Unable to reach the sling again, they plummeted down.

She struggled to haul herself up, thinking all the time about how foolish this was.

The gamble hadn't paid off.

She hit the ground.

A tangle of metal. Fabric dashed across rocks. And the body of a woman sprawled on the surface.

Savanta had landed in a working mine. She opened her eyes, afraid to move. A dozen slaves ambled past, sullen eyed, apathetic.

She was alive. Miraculously.

Propping up on her elbows, she noted scrapes, blood and deep bruising. But she could move; nothing broken. The fall should have killed her.

The wind picked up again and she shielded her eyes from dust that stirred from the mine's surface. She mustn't be caught here. Punishment for trespassing was enslavement or death, and she knew which she would prefer.

She stood, glancing around, looking for a way out.

Where do you think you're going? The voice arrived on the wind.

'Who's there?' It was not the voice of a slave. Nor the voice of any man. It rang in her skull, bypassing any means of hearing.

Oh, come now Savanta. I think you know, it said. The voice was male; musical and darkly playful. It arrived in her mind like an invading thought. She picked up a stick that lay on the ground, ready to defend herself. *You wanted to be me,* it continued. *You wanted to play god.*

She dropped the stick. Bile rose at the back of her throat.

Colours began to manifest on the wind, and they outlined a male form. His skin was opaque and his slender body shifted with the moving air as though he had been drawn with ribbons that played in the breeze. His long pale hair streaked out like cirrus clouds in the wind.

She fell to the floor in prostration. 'Lord Zenith,' she said, face against the ground.

The voice laughed quietly, the sound now reaching her ears. 'You are the first human to conquer the air. I'm impressed. It takes a lot to impress me. The first to join the birds and the stars in my domain.' She kept her face to the ground, eyes clasped shut. Drawing a Vyara, one of the three gods, into the living realm was seldom met with reward.

19

'Stand up.' She glanced up, uncertain. 'I said stand.' The air under her body seemed to swell and grow in pressure, and she was forced to her feet.

'Pretty thing,' he said. As he circled her, a cool wind ruffled her hair and shirt. 'So you were seeking to make a profit by giving the key to the skies to your race. Who gave you the right?' The humour left his voice as he bit off the last words. She couldn't read his face, transparent and wavering against the grey sky.

She wanted to say something, to ask for forgiveness, to beg for mercy, but no words came.

'I am the canopy above, the night and the day, the air you breathe. And what are you? A peasant from Tannit, with no deference for the gods who keep this world. You dare to defy the natural order.'

Tears streamed down her face. Her body shook. She wanted to run but found herself immobile.

Zenith stopped circling and moved closer. He stood several feet taller and his pupilless eyes bore down on her. 'You want to know what I'm going to do next.' A cruel smile played on his lips. 'I can see the anticipation is killing you.'

He reached a hand forward and she saw it slide through her chest. She more than saw it. His translucent fingers disappeared under her skin. Her insides froze, and she felt pressure on her organs as he twisted his fingers around them. The breath was squeezed from her lungs and a dreadful sickness filled her.

His hand pushed to the back of her chest and she could feel his palm between her shoulder blades.

'Wait for it…' he teased.

Savanta let out a cry. An unbearable pain. Like two knives forcing themselves from her spine, into the cool air. The pain lengthened, and she felt new bones growing out from her back. Like new branches stemming from a tree, two stumps of flesh pushed up and out of her body. They grew to her left and right, beyond her peripheral vision.

She gasped for air.

More thin bones branched down from the protrusions, forming a pair of skeletal wings. Thin fronds of flesh weaved between them and she could see veins entwining with the new skin.

Zenith removed his hand and stepped back.

Savanta collapsed to the floor and vomited. She retched until her throat was raw, and nose and eyes streamed with water.

Her body felt false, unnatural. A new weight pulled at her back.

Then a sharp tingle spread across her shoulders and spine making her shudder. The new appendages moved with her. Fist pounding the dirt, she tried to will the sensation away.

It spread from her back, along her limbs and through her chest. Hot and cold pinpricks. She saw the colour drain from her hands as they turned from tan to a deep grey. They matched the stone on which she cowered. Her red hair turned black.

A scream forced itself from her throat. In the distance a handful of slaves looked up, but didn't stop.

'There, there,' Zenith said, above her. 'You didn't think I was going to kill you, did you?' She didn't meet his eyes. Every slight movement felt unreal.

'What's happening to me?'

'I couldn't let you go totally unpunished. But to waste such a fine mind as yours… that would be madness. You really should be more grateful that you're still alive.'

He proffered a large, formless hand. She daren't offend him now and went to take it, surprised to find it solid, and warm like flesh. He pulled her to her feet.

Two large bat-like wings framed her small body, her skin now the colour of slate. Her shirt fell in tatters about her shoulders where it had been ripped by the wings.

'You look marvellous.' He gripped her by the arms. 'Now, this is a creature that belongs in my sky.'

Savanta shuddered as chills wracked her body and sweat blistered on her forehead. The skin on her back felt strange. Tightly stretched. She found she could control the wings as easily as any other limb, but the alien movement made her nauseous. Zenith was watching her. His translucent face wavered in the wind, flickering between amusement and impatience.

She felt currents of air billowing around her. They forced her wings open to a staggering span. She looked down. This wasn't her body. Grey skin like soft leather, a tapered waist and legs that were garishly thin. Her ribcage was rounder and she could see the light imprint of thin bones there. She felt light and delicate, like a twig easily snapped. The winds made her unsteady on her feet, and she worried that the fragile wings would break if she resisted against the mounting air pressure.

Fly. The word echoed in her skull.

Impulse drove her to beat the wings down, once, twice, then again and again. Her feet left the ground.

That's it. Beautiful! Zenith's form had swirled away with the wind, and she heard only his voice now. *Let me take you higher*.

Another few beats of her wings, and Savanta found herself high above the mine. She could see the Greylands stretch out for miles around.

This way. The wind changed direction, and she was forced east towards the capital.

Her eyes grew hot with tears. Fear and shock had hijacked her mind. She allowed Zenith to carry her on the wind with no knowledge of where he might lead her. She had never been overly devout, and the few offerings she made to the Vyara had always been for the Earth, never the Sky. The thought was chilling. But she also felt a sense of wonder growing as she acclimatised to the wind in her wings, the steady beating, the freedom of the empty sky.

She soared on through the blue. It was a long while before she gained the confidence to try forcing her wings against Zenith's guiding wind. When she did, a harsh gust nearly knocked her from the air. She spiralled downwards for a few seconds before regaining her form.

You're mine now, Savanta. You do as I say. Don't play games.

'What do you want from me?' she shouted into the air. Her question went unanswered.

She endured the rest of the journey in silence, allowing his current to lead her directly to the capital.

The sun was low on the horizon when they neared, and the landscape faded from the harsh grey of the mines to a patchwork of lush green. She saw farms. The first she had ever laid eyes on. People toiled in the fields, just dots on the landscape from where she flew. Ahead were gardens. Verdant patches of land, filled with flowers, with the wealthy classes strolling, sitting, contemplating life. There were more birds here too. They gave her a wide berth, this strange new hawk in their sky.

By now she was feeling more secure in the air. The sickness had abated. She was curious and wanted to see more of this rich landscape. She swooped down to get a better view, prepared to meet resistance from Zenith. But he let her.

Houses began to appear below. Grand houses with vast tiled roofs. Servants scurried in the streets and in the gardens. Some saw her and pointed skyward, some ran, fearing the dark figure overhead.

She flew over the largest building in the city. Its plain walls and four turrets marked it out as the palimore's barracks. The size of the centre courtyard took her breath away. A thousand troops practised their art in the evening air, shooting bows, engaging in swordplay, wrestling. She had heard new recruits would train here for fifty years before seeing combat.

The palace emerged from the city ahead, golden and shining brightly in the last of the day's sun.

Beautiful isn't it? She had nearly forgotten that Zenith was with her.

'More than I imagined,' she said.

Head for the top window in the eastern tower. The one overlooking the sea. Oh, and look out for arrows from below. I can't guarantee you'll be a welcome sight to the guards.

'And if I turn back?'

Try if you must. I think you'll find it's an impossibility. She pressed on towards the tower, curiosity overriding any desire to flee.

Sure enough, there were shouts from the guards on the walls surrounding the palace, and these soon transformed into a volley of arrows. A sharp gust of wind sent most off course.

But one hit. It flew through her right wing. She was surprised to find it didn't cause much pain, but it did disrupt her balance in the air. She veered to the right and flapped hard to correct her path. She was nearly at the window but flying too low.

The golden wall came up to meet her fast, too fast. The window was just above her head. She pushed her feet against the palace walls and reached up quickly, grabbing the ledge and pulling herself up.

Two pairs of hands grabbed her and hauled her through the window. They forced her hands behind her back, squeezing her wings together painfully.

As her eyes adjusted to the darkness of the room, she recognised her restrainers as palimore soldiers. She had never seen one up close before. Both men had dark hair, dark eyes, and shoulders as broad as a doorway. Between plates of royal armour, she could make out bulges of muscle thick as tree trunks. Their size and power was staggering. She didn't resist.

'What are you?' one of them barked. 'And what is your business?'

'Zenith,' she whispered, half in answer and half in a call for help. None came. What was she doing here?

'Let it go,' said a woman's voice from across the room. They released her.

The room looked like it had been chiseled out of rock. Exotic plants climbed the walls, and the floor was rough stone, swirled with lichen in intricate patterns. She had never seen anything like it. Flowers were rare in the Greylands, but here, even in this dim room, they flourished in a collage of colour.

The woman stepped towards her on bare feet. She wore no fabric, but her body was heavily ornamented in gold, silver, copper, iron and stone. An intricate metal belt sounded musically as she moved. Her arms and legs were ringed with bands of multi-coloured stones and metal. A heavy slate torc sat about her neck and chestnut hair curled down to her hips. The Empress expressed her devotion to the Earth god even in the way she dressed. Her close relationship with the god Deyar was known by all on the island of Thelonia. She had married him.

Savanta dropped to one knee. 'Empress,' she said.

'What a marvellous creature,' the woman said. She knelt down to Savanta's level and stroked a wing, pulling it out gently to reveal the thin flesh between her bones. 'What are you?' she asked.

'My name is Savanta, Empress,' she spoke into the floor. 'I come from Tannit.' She faltered. What *was* she? A question she didn't have an answer for.

'Get up.' Savanta rose. 'What brings you here?' The Empress circled her, looking her up and down.

'Zenith brough–' She was silenced by a sudden tightness in her lungs, as if all the air had been snatched from the atmosphere. She couldn't speak. A light wind swirled the room, and Zenith appeared before them. She gasped in a deep breath as he released the hold on her lungs.

His translucent appearance became more solid this time. His outline formed a regular sized man, long blond hair, a flowing blue courtier's outfit stitched with a large sun, and a black cloak which glinted with jewels like stars. His face was handsome, androgynous features offering a singular beauty.

The guards behind her knelt as they recognised the Vyara.

'Ah, my Lord Zenith,' said the Empress. A note of displeasure played just under the surface of her voice. She did not kneel.

'Keresan,' he replied, and flourished a bow matched with a mocking smile. 'I bring you a gift. This is Savanta. A loyal servant to the Empire. I plucked her finest details from my dreams and weaved them into this beautiful tapestry for you and your dear husband.' He smiled broadly. 'She was on her way to present a gift to you when I found her. But I thought it much more fitting that she should give her whole self to you.' He gave a magnanimous wink. 'Consider her a gift of friendship; put her to good use for my brother's sake. Her wings are far more swift than ships that cross the sea, and her reports more fluid than notes carried by birds.'

Savanta shifted uneasily on her feet. She had wanted to come to sell her design, and now faced being gifted like a slave. She gauged the distance to the window behind her to be about two metres. Both soldiers stood blocking the way. She would have to find another means of escape.

'I'm sure my husband will be delighted,' the Empress said. 'Your brother was beginning to worry that he had fallen out of your favour?'

'Oh, never, my lady. I wouldn't *dream* of giving dear Deyar offence.' Scathing sarcasm radiated from his smile. 'My powers dwindle here since you so wisely outlawed my worship. I bow to him on your shores. For now, at least.'

'I wouldn't want you to forget it.'

Savanta saw his face twitch in anger. She had long known the power their ancient Empress held, but to see her speak down to a god made her skin shiver.

'No, no. Impossible. Especially since you gave him that title. King of the Gods. How resplendent!'

'I sense envy, Zenith. You deny his title?' She flexed her fingers with the impatience of one speaking to a peevish child. 'His worshippers far outstrip those who follow you and your sister. His power grows daily as yours fade.'

'Does an Empress outrank a King, I wonder? It's hard to know if you're his puppet or if it's the other way around…'

'Enough!' He seemed amused by her anger, but still fell into silence. There wasn't a man, woman or child who didn't know the Empress's devotion to the Earth god was all-consuming. It had shaped their land, their laws and their history. Zenith's accusation that she might be using him seemed to have struck a nerve. She met his eyes in confrontation and then released a breath, calming herself. 'Enough,' she said, more quietly. Then, changing the subject, 'Any news from your sister?'

'None, my lady. She hasn't left the water for some time. Honestly, I think she prefers the company of fish to our family. But who could blame her?'

'It's about time she came to pay tribute to the Earth. Her absence hasn't gone unnoticed.'

'I'm sure my brother will find some way to dry up the seas if she continues to offend.'

'Don't doubt that he couldn't. It's entirely within Deyar's power.'

'I'm sure.' He nodded vigorously, with a patronising purse of the lips.

'I don't need your petulant attitude, Zenith. Need I remind you what happened the last time you overstepped your mark?'

The smile dropped from Zenith's face. 'Some people show all the gratitude. I was leaving anyway. Enjoy the gift.' His form shattered into dozens of singing starlings. Savanta ducked as they flew at her and streamed past the guards, out of the window, into the sunset.

Keresan looked pleased. 'Wyn,' she said to one of the guards, 'take her to the Minister of Secrets. Ask him to find something for this creature to do.'

'Yes, your grace.' Hands like iron took hold of her, and thoughts of escape were replaced with fears of the damage a man this size could inflict. She stared around wildly and allowed herself to be led out of the chamber, deeper into the palace.

It was late that night when Savanta was shown to what would be her new home. A room in the House of Eyes. The palimore who escorted her gave a gentle push at her back when she hesitated going through the door. She stepped in. A simple room, small and undecorated; a single bed, a wooden chest and a chamber pot. There was a bowl of food at the foot of the bed. She turned to say something to the guard, but he was already closing the door. The bolt slid across. When the sound of his footsteps had faded, she forced her shoulder against the door. It wouldn't budge.

She was both physically and emotionally drained, and soon lost the energy to continue beating herself against the door. She picked up the bowl of food. Rice and vegetables. Real, fresh vegetables. And rice from across the sea. She devoured them in moments and sat down on the bed.

Tracing a finger along her arm, she was unable to identify the grey skin as her own. Falling back onto the bed with a sigh, she landed painfully on one of her wings, then rolled onto her side and pulled the wool blanket over her head. The bed was far comfier that the one she had at home. But it was missing something vital. Erin. She clutched the blanket in one hand, willing herself not to cry, but her bottom lip was already trembling and she let out a sob. How long would they keep her here? What would Erin think when she didn't come home? She would have given anything to hold her little girl.

She reached out to Zenith with prayers for forgiveness and prayers of mercy, until tears soaked her pillow and sleep took her.

CHAPTER TWO

Five years after the raids, the land was beautifully familiar and bitterly changed. Threon shifted the weight of his pack and straightened his stance. The weather was colder in the north, colder than he remembered it to be, and he pulled a stolen sheepskin close around his shoulders. It hadn't been cured properly and the fleece was oily, the strong ovine smell punctuated with growing rot.

The South was dry and hot, dusted umber by desert sands; five years there had bronzed Threon's skin and bleached his sandy hair bright blond. More than that, his time away from home, from the comforts of a princely life, had changed him. Dropping over the cliff edge of royal privilege into the life of a refugee felt, at first, like an insurmountable adjustment. Life became a constant stream of the unimaginable: stealing, sleeping rough, begging, prison, hunger. He lost his physique, growing thin, and he buried his sense of self deep within.

His last copper went on a piece of shit mule that had carried him for almost a month. It had limped and stumbled as often as he did before it keeled over and died. The break to Threon's leg and hip had healed badly, the old wound accosting him throughout his years in Bannvar and now growing more painful as he slumped north through the harsher climate of home. But it didn't bother him now. In the distance the city gates rose, flooding him with a renewed energy.

A hulking figure stood at the gate, watching his approach. A palimore soldier. Threon had seen more and more of these soldiers as he grew closer to home. They had spread across his country like a disease. Seeing one here, guarding the gates to his home city, made his heart pound. He clenched his fists.

'What business?' the soldier called. Threon slowed his pace and tried to relax, doing his best to look non-threatening. An easy task given his current physique. The man towered a full foot above him and bore a figure twice the width of his own. Eyes flicked across his clothing. Stained and battered Bannvarian robes. 'You've travelled far.' Gods, it had been a long journey; it had nearly broken him, destitute, penniless and far from the life he had built in the South. But he was home. He had to force a smile down. Palimore soldiers favoured the meek.

As of yet, his worn clothes, haggard appearance and uneven beard had made a rather fitting disguise. Though his face wasn't familiar to the palimore, he thought locals might recognise their prince. In Bannvar, he had told everyone he met who he was. Some foolish part of him believed that the South might offer a kinder welcome to a foreign royal in need. How wrong he was. His arrival was preceded by news of the raids and few wished to harbour a man who was a target of the palimore army.

The people of the Waterlands would remember him as an arrogant young prince, draped in fine clothing. So far the beggar he had become had gone unrecognised. After five years' absence they likely thought him dead. He was grateful for that, wishing to keep a low profile. A royal welcome from the palimore would prove deadly.

He gestured to the instrument on his back. 'Musician. Come to play for a coin or two.' The six-stringed kestro had saved his life in Bannvar. As a child, Threon had never been a scholar, his only academic pleasures were the pursuit of swordplay and music. After months on the streets, the theft of this instrument had changed his fortunes. It wasn't long before he began to earn a meagre but honest living playing at inns across the city. His repertoire was fresh and exotic there, and though perhaps they didn't believe it, locals enjoyed hearing about how a prince had escaped death to live a peasant life in their city. He was easily recognisable, standing out against dark skinned locals, and soon won a name for himself. They called him the Vagabond King.

The soldier snorted. 'Must be down on your luck. You won't find much coin here.' Threon shrugged in agreement and the man gestured for him to come through the gate.

The city was empty. The throngs of people who would beg, barter and brawl at the gates were gone. Half the wooden houses had been eaten by fire in the raids and never rebuilt. In their place were canvas shacks. Two small children played at the end of the street. Their clothes were oversized, hanging on emaciated frames. It was a familiar sight. The further north he had travelled, the thinner people became. And the fewer they numbered. He hadn't wanted to believe the rumours that reached the South, but they had all turned out to be true.

It had been a long and hungry journey, punctuated with reminders of the danger he was walking into. Even as far as the Southlands border he encountered villages marked by the raids. Many had one, sometimes two, palimore soldiers posted to a village. They stomped out any whispers of rebellion and kept a stranglehold on the markets. Farmers in these towns were forced to sell entire harvests for a pittance to the army. At first Threon heard grumbles from market stallholders about being short for the coming winter. As he continued north, the grumbles became more and more desperate. Storehouses were depleted, wealthy houses were forced to trade in fine meats for soups. Poorer houses lived on bowls of grain.

The towns that had already been captured teemed with palimore, and for those who had not been enslaved or killed, a hard life on the land ensued. Taylors, bakers, smithies, stable hands and potters all gave up their crafts to farm or forage the land in search of food. Their long days toiling in fields were rewarded by the soldiers collecting their harvests and shipping any decent food across the sea.

His first instinct was to head to the castle, to find old friends. Five years away from home and he was desperate to find out what had happened here. He longed to stand in the courtyard again, to feel the hearth-warmed slates against his feet in the hall, to gaze out to sea from the highest point in the city. But he knew he could not go there. He tore his gaze away from the place. It would be swarming with palimore. Instead, he turned down a side street in the direction of the Honeydew. It was the largest pub in the city, considered the heart of Maradah for many of its citizens. He had never been inside, and balked at the memory of how his former self considered the place beneath him. He couldn't even afford a bed there now.

He knocked on the closed door, praying to Athys that someone still ran the place. A soldier paced past him on the street, eyeing Threon suspiciously. He knocked again, eager to get out of sight.

The door opened a crack. 'What d'you want?' In the darkness beyond he made out a grey-haired woman, slim and deeply wrinkled, her voice a grindstone.

'I'm looking for a room.' Her eyes narrowed. Renting rooms was a thing of the past. No one had money to waste on such inessentials now. 'I can't pay much, but I can play.' He gestured to the kestro. 'I'm good.' He offered her a smile.

She began to close the door. Threon jammed a foot in it.

'*Ranar ardell*. Please, let me in.' She studied his face and a vague look of recognition passed her eyes.

'Do I know you?'

'Please. Can we talk inside?'

She looked up and down the street, then pulled the door open.

No candles burned inside, no customers sat and drank. It felt eerie, abandoned. Threon moved towards the dim fireplace and rubbed his leg in the scant warmth. The woman kept her eyes locked on him, arms tight across her chest.

'What d'you want?' she repeated.

He wondered how much to say. 'I've been away from home for a long time. Since the first raid.'

'You're from round here then? Looks like you've taken on the southern style.' She was eyeing his clothing, traditional blue robes worn by men in the South, now tatty and stained from travel. She kept her distance, holding herself rigid.

'I ran when the raiders came. I've spent half a decade away from home.'

'Didn't stay to fight with your kin, eh? Can't say I blame you. If my sons had done the same, they'd still be here now.' She paused, the suspicion returning to her voice. 'I don't recall you ever singing here before the raids...'

'No, I never did.'

'New to the trade?'

'Necessity made me take it up. I've had a bit of a fall from grace.'

Suspicion dropped in favour of offence. 'You call playing kestro a fall from grace?' She started moving towards the door to usher him out. 'You don't know the half of what's been going on here. How dare you.'

He cursed his choice of words. 'I only meant… A lot has changed since the raids.' She softened slightly at his tone and moved away from the door again.

'Yes. And I bet this weren't the welcome home you was expecting.' She came to join him by the fire and sighed. 'You got any family left here?'

'Not anymore.'

'Same club as me, lad.' She held out a hand. 'Orna.'

He took it. 'Threynar,' he said, catching himself before revealing his name.

'Well, welcome home, Threynar. Five years away deserves a drink.' She scuttled behind the bar and poured two glasses from a bottle and passed one to him. '*Ranar ardell.*' They clinked glasses and drank. It hit the back of Threon's throat like fire and made him splutter.

'Gods! What'd you put in this?'

She laughed and patted his shoulder companionably. 'My moonshine. Locals call it dragon piss. Does the trick most times.' She guided him over to a table near the fire. 'Come sit, come sit.'

'I need to know what happened here. The people? And my family…' He trailed off. His picture of what had happened after the raids had been painted by rumours and stories made colourful and gruesome by a hundred different tellers and a thousand miles of distance.

'Your family? What's the name? I hear most of what goes on with people in this city.'

He shook his head. 'They lived on the edge of town. Didn't ever come this way. You wouldn't know them.' He sighed. 'I fear they can't have survived.'

She touched his arm, shaking her head sadly. 'We've all had a terrible time of it. That night you left… Gods, I still wake from the nightmares.'

'Tell me what you remember. Please.'

She looked down at her glass, pursing her lips as if considering her choice of words. 'It was a dark time. I hates to think back on it. We all lost a lot that night. As far as we can tell, they started in the castle. The raiders. I don't know much about what happened in there.' She paused. 'They brought out three heads after and mounted them on the castle walls. The king's eyes had been removed, they'd shaved the queen's hair. The poor prince's face was so beaten he was hardly recognisable.' Threon swallowed. He'd known deep down that they couldn't have escaped, but hearing confirmation of his parent's deaths brought on a fresh wave of grief. He didn't need to ask if they had been given a water burial. Their corpses probably rotted away with the mounds of dead. And the bastards had let the city think him dead too.

She watched him closely as she continued. 'By the time the alarm rang in the castle, they'd reached the barracks. Our men are brave, but against the palimore… Only one survived, sleeping outside. They musta missed him. He ran into town, shoutin' the whole city awake. We either barred ourselves in or took to the streets with whittlin' knives and meat cleavers. I watched my two boys sliced in half that night.' She shook her head and swallowed. 'They were a fearsome sight, I tell you. Biggest men I ever saw. Shoulders broad as houses. And so calm. They strode into town, cutting through our folk like they was reapin' wheat.

'The fires started in the early hours. I dunno if it was us or them what started it. My poor barmaid, Darcy, and her two babes couldn't get out the house, and was swallowed by flame.' She gazed into the fire, memories flickering across her eyes.

'Athys keep us,' said Threon quietly, his voice nearly cracking on the prayer. He had come home hoping to assess the reality of the city's situation. In the hope that he might help. Things were worse than he feared. Orna's words filled him with guilt for running that day. What if he hadn't gone drinking with the soldiers? If he'd stayed in the castle and celebrated midsummer with his parents?

He realised they had fallen into silence. She was watching him closely, suspicion back on her face. 'When I mentioned the royals then... Did you know them?'

He swallowed, trying to bury his emotions. He didn't want to give himself away. She stepped closer and peered intently at him before reeling backward, recognition finally dawning.

'No!' She slapped her thigh and laughed out loud. 'I knew I'd seen that face before. Threynar, my arse. You're the prince.' Her smile made her look ten years younger. He lowered the glass and expelled a long breath. He saw little point in denying it. She poured another healthy serving of dragon piss in their glasses and raised hers in toast. '*Ranar ardell*, my lord. Back from the dead.' They clinked glasses and drank again. He swallowed bitterly.

'Innkeepers know all the secrets, I suppose,' he conceded. 'Keep it quiet, yeah? Wouldn't want those brutes to know I'm back.'

'I'm sorry. I just – your face when I mentioned the King and Queen.' Her face dropped in solemnity. 'Did you not know?'

'Heard rumours. Guessed. It's little consolation knowing that they missed the fall of the city.'

She offered a sympathetic smile. 'Times is worse now. 'stead of moving on to the next town, they've set up shop in the castle.

Palimore march the streets and Thelonian merchants have arrived to squeeze us dry. They commands us all to work the land and they take all our hard-earned crops and ship 'em back to their precious Empress. There's no more meat. I ain't eaten proper meat in two and a half years. My carveries was the best in the city back in the day. We live mostly off of parsnips and taters and what we can forage off the mountain now.'

He knew the feeling. The markets and restaurants of the South felt a lifetime away after his journey north. For weeks he had been forced to eat like those around him. Hunting skinny songbirds and foraging leaves and berries. Supplies of game which were once plentiful in the Waterlands were near exhausted. Inns serving warm meals were few and far between. Those he did find, charged tenfold southern prices.

'Will you eat mule?'

Her eyes brightened at the thought. 'I'd eat a rat if I was fast enough to catch one.'

'I've got most of a mule leg in my pack. It's on the turn, but it should be good to eat tonight.'

'Athys bless you.' Her bright smile was back. 'Meat. Imagine! I'll cook us a feast tonight, lad. You don't mind if we share? There's some out there who needs it more than us.' He nodded, knowing she would be right.

'How many dead?' he asked, and the smile dropped from her face again.

'More 'n half. But they didn't just kill us. Us who were left were forced to rape the land of everything it had. When the first merchant ships arrived to take our meat and crops, they piled some of our folks in too. Boat after boat, they took them over the sea. None's ever returned.'

'Slaves for the vish'aad mines.'

'I don't wanna know. It can't be nothing good. They've stopped taking us now. Too few left, I figure. I hear stories they're taking folks from towns south of here. Slowly eating up the Waterlands.' It was true, he'd seen it, but he said nothing. She took a large gulp of the dragon piss. 'Bet you're glad you're back, eh?'

Threon gripped his glass to his chest and let his voice drop to a whisper. 'I should have come back sooner.'

'You did what you had to to survive. We all do. We've still got our lives, that's something,' she said. 'And now our king has returned.'

Threon prickled at the title. 'They call me the Vagabond King now. King of Nothing. The Greenbrooke legacy burnt to cinders.'

'Aye, but from cinders tall oaks can grow. If we don't have hope, what've we left?' She leaned forwards with a gleam in her eye.

'How is it I stumble upon such an insightful woman?' he teased.

'Us innkeepers are wise and we know how to comfort. In times of trouble, folks come to this place. Our people need hope and you can offer it. I know it.'

Threon wasn't so sure. He hardly cut an inspiring royal figure, but the new look of confidence in her eyes stopped him from saying so. 'The raiders can't know who I am. My head would be on a spike before morning.'

'True. But I knows who to trust.' She scraped her fingers through horse-like hair. 'Say, you're looking for a way to help? I've been looking for a man about the house to help me with a little project.'

'Oh yeah?'

She leaned forward conspiratorially. 'How'd you fancy yourself a smuggler?'

Orna advised sleeping out of sight. She left an old horse blanket in the attic for Threon, claiming it would be safer than sleeping in the guest rooms. He dragged the blanket up against the chimney breast and collapsed onto it, pressing his back up against the fire-warmed stones.

Hot food in his belly, the gentle haze of alcohol, and a bed in his hometown. If it weren't for the realities that loomed beyond the inn's walls, he might be happy.

Threon worked hard through the winter.

He adapted to a nocturnal life, bringing the inn alive with music in the evenings and, under Orna's guidance, smuggling food into the city at the darkest hour. By day, locals were searched on returning from the fields, and any food they carried confiscated. Now, by cover of darkness, Threon would make his way out of the city to gather up anything he could from surviving farmland and sometimes, when he was lucky enough to encounter a sleeping guard, steal from the storehouses. Groups of locals came to the Dew to hear Threon's songs, to sip Orna's moonshine and to take a share of the smuggled supplies.

Threon liked to play the old songs, songs that the whole town knew. At first the music made them lament for what they had lost. But a whisper of hope began to stir among them as they toiled in the fields. The prince had returned. Was it a sign?

As the days grew shorter, talk of rebellion grew stronger. The Dew grew full to bursting each evening, and when Threon sang, the people joined in. They sang of their history, of their heroes, of their landscapes and traditions. Pride returned to the townsfolk, and a little strength too.

As their hopes grew, Threon's eyes lingered ever longer on the castle.

CHAPTER THREE

It was three weeks before the ringing of New Year, and Threon paddled a small boat along a shallow stream. The water, used as the town's sewage way, was the only unguarded route into the city. Getting so close to the runnels of shit that ran through the city made him gag at first, but making this journey two or three times a night had conditioned him against it.

He wore a black cloak to hide in the shadow of night. Beside him in the boat sat five sacks of vegetables stolen from palimore supplies and the rare boon of a pair of pheasants from the forest. Orna would be overjoyed at the sight of the meat.

He was at the edge of the city, around a mile from the inn, when there was a scuffle of boots on the ground. It was after curfew and unlikely to be a friendly face.

He stopped paddling and held his breath in the silence. The footsteps were heading his way. A flash of lamplight caught his eye as a figure appeared the other side of the bushes that hid the stream. He caught a glimpse of the man's feathered hat. A Thelonian merchant: softer than a soldier, only here to steal resources, not to kill and maim. He relaxed a little.

The footsteps grew closer still.

Threon sunk his paddle to the bottom of the water, and gently pushed his boat to shore. He wanted to be able to make a quick escape if needed.

The merchant appeared ahead, pushing past the undergrowth at the edge of the stream. He began to piss into the water. As his eyes followed the urine's path downstream, they alighted on Threon crouched in his boat.

'Hey,' the man shouted. He stepped back, startled, and fumbled for the crossbow that hung at his hip. He took aim at Threon.

'Steady, friend,' said Threon. 'I'm unarmed.'

The merchant stepped down into the foul current and paced towards him, the crossbow shaking in his hands.

'What are you doing here? It's past curfew.'

'My friends and I are hungry.' He kept his voice level, reasonable. This man was one of the reasons for the city's impoverishment. 'I've been foraging in the forest.' He gestured to the pheasants.

The merchant was very close now. He pulled the edge of the boat towards him, eyeing the sacks piled at the prow. Now he was closer, Threon could see him better. Overweight, and expensively dressed in velvet and fur.

'You've been doing an awful lot of foraging.' The merchant grabbed the nearest sack and opened it. 'Parsnips. These don't belong to you.' He pressed the bolt of his crossbow to Threon's chest. 'Guards!'

Threon was not going to be taken. He thrust upwards, forcing the bolt up and away from his body. It tore through his clothes and left a red streak down the middle of his chest.

In his panic, the merchant fired and the bolt flew into the air.

Without giving him a chance to reload, Threon reached into his belt and drew out his hunting knife. He jerked it into the merchant's round belly. Shock filled the man's face, his eyes widened as he looked down to the weapon.

He clutched his gut, crying out in panic as blood spilled over his hands. Threon leapt out of the boat and knocked the man's feet from under him. He fell heavily and began to cry louder. An alarm bell sounded in the town. He didn't have long.

Bubbles burst from the man's mouth as Threon pushed his head into the foetid water. His body thrashed in the shallow stream.

End it.

He pulled the knife from the man's stomach and pushed it through his throat. He felt the neck bones give way under the pressure, and the merchant stopped moving. A final glut of air left his lungs and bubbled through his ruptured throat to the surface.

He heard footsteps and the baying of dogs in the distance. Grabbing the knife, he turned to run just as one of the palimore appeared at the edge of the stream. Their eyes met and for a split second Threon felt immobilised by fear. Then his senses snapped back with a wave of adrenaline and he took flight downstream, leaving his boat, his cargo and a floating corpse behind.

Threon could barely hear over the sound of his heart thumping in his ears. Behind, he could make out the palimore's pursuit, crashing through water. Threon had never dared try outrunning them before and just hoped that the soldier's bulk would slow him down. Then a large splash and the soldier's cursing. He must have tripped and fallen in the

43

water. Threon breathed a prayer of thanks and kept running, away from the city.

He spent the night hidden in the forest. Foetid water soaked his clothes, and the winter air bit cold against his skin. But he couldn't light a fire. They would be looking everywhere for him. After walking near-blind in the dark, he found shelter made by a fallen tree and collapsed. The man's blood stained his robes. He had committed murder. Yet the sensation of killing had felt no different to slaughtering an animal. He wondered that he didn't feel remorse. Instead a dreadful energy and determination swelled in his heart. If he could kill one, he could kill more.

He was unable to sleep that night. Plans consumed his mind, and hopes for what could be if he succeeded.

One way or another, he would have his home back.

It was in the evening of the following day, at the change of the guards, that Threon made his way back into the city. It was too risky to return up the waste stream, so he climbed an unwatched section of the city walls then picked his way over roofs and through quiet alleyways back to the inn.

A feeling of dread filled him when he found the front door thrown off its hinges. Inside, furniture had been smashed against walls and floors. The ground glittered with broken glass. The neck of his kestro smouldered in the dying fire, the body turned to ash.

The few sacks of smuggled food they had kept hidden in the cellar had been brought up to the bar and torn open.

'Orna!' He ran to the cellar, the kitchen, the rooms upstairs. There was no sign of her. 'Orna!'

'Shut it.' A skinny boy peered in from outside. Threon recognised him; he often came to collect supplies, orphaned with his younger sister over a year ago. The boy glanced around nervously before stepping in. 'You need to get out of here,' he said. 'They're looking for you.'

'Where's Orna?'

'They took her to the castle. You have to go. They know you're living here too. After they found the stores–'

'What are they going to do with her?' Guilt screamed in Threon's mind. This was all his fault.

'They've already done it, sir.' He spoke to his feet. 'She's hoisted in an iron cage above the temple. They want us to watch her starve.'

Threon pushed past the boy into the street. The youth grabbed his arm and pulled him into a side alley. 'Please. Don't let them catch you too.'

'I've got to go after her. If it weren't for her, you lot would have starved.'

'She couldn't have done it without you… we can't lose you both.' He spoke urgently, round eyes pleading for him to slow his anger. 'Some of the field workers are planning to storm the castle tonight. No one will forget how good she was to us, or the risks she took. They don't stand much of a chance against the palimore but I don't think anything will stop 'em from trying.'

'I know the castle better than anyone.'

'They're meeting where the old bakery used to be, after sundown. But, please, stay hidden till then.'

Threon nodded and began to haul himself up a drainpipe, back onto the roof. 'Tell them I'll be there,' he said to the boy.

Threon found three men, around five years his junior, waiting at the old bakery come nightfall. Their faces were set with a grim determination that must have mirrored his own. He recognised all three from the Dew. The youngest was Tom; a pink-faced lad who suited his perpetual grin. He had a great

45

voice and was always the first to join in when Threon played a tune at the pub. The other two were Dan and Maus, two of the stronger men in the town. They had helped Threon with smuggling food on more than one occasion.

They quietly hummed songs of rebellion as Threon led them towards the castle through heavy rain. A shaft, wide enough to fit a grown man, led from the kitchens to a point on the western wall. It was used for disposing of scrap food, back in the time of plenty. They scrambled up the shaft in single file, emerging in the darkened room.

The party followed Threon through the empty servants' quarters and they arrived in the courtyard unnoticed. Threon felt his stomach knot. He was finally home, but the place had never felt so unwelcoming.

They hid in the shadows at the edge of the yard. Above, on the walls, palimore soldiers manned guard posts, shadows against the night sky.

The rain beat down hard on the cobbles and the creaking of iron travelled across the yard on the wet wind. It came from the temple at the centre of the courtyard. The temple was open to the elements and consisted of nine pillars in rows of three. The Greenbrooke flag had flown from the centremost pillar, and the temple was headed by a dais which had once borne a fountain in tribute to the water goddess, Athys. The fountain was gone now, as was the flag. Now, a bare flagpole jutted from the marble column and a cage swung from it on a metal chain. Orna's naked body was hunched within it. The bars were close to her body, enveloping her so tightly that she was forced to stand. Her long grey hair was slick against her body in the rain and she held her arms tightly for warmth, head hanging low.

Threon motioned to the party to wait in the shadows. He stepped out briefly to determine the position of each of the

46

guards. There were four of them, one to each wall. He timed their pacing, and when he judged it most safe, sprinted to the temple. The sound of the rain hid his footsteps and he lurched behind a pillar before he could be noticed.

From where he stood he could see the chain that held Orna's cage. It had been nailed into the base of the pillar to keep it in place.

He looked back at the men. They were all young farmers, thin, but strong from a life on the fields. None were soldiers, but a fierceness burned in them that gave Threon courage. Dan and Maus carried large hunting bows, and Tom carried a crow bar and an axe.

He nodded when it looked safe and held his breath as they darted across to him. The archers ran to the pillar opposite and Tom joined him at his post.

Threon had brought his own hunting bow and knife, still marred with the blood of the merchant. He nocked an arrow and pulled it back, keeping two of the soldiers in his sight. Dan and Maus followed suit, tracking guards on the far walls.

Tom raised his eyebrows in question. Threon watched the guards until they were looking away. He raised a hand in signal. When the other archers had done the same, Tom sprinted to the centremost pillar. The guards were looking out over the walls, but Tom was in full view now if they deigned to gaze back at the courtyard.

He dug the crowbar into one of the chain links and lifted the axe up, ready to strike it.

There was no quiet way to do this.

He kept his eyes on Threon, who gritted his teeth and nodded.

The axe came down. A metallic clang rang through the yard. The guards swung their gaze inwards.

'Now,' shouted Threon.

His first shot sped through the rain to land square in the chest of one of the guards. It glanced off his armour like a pebble skimming water. Threon ducked back behind the pillar. If they caught sight of him, he was dead. Palimore didn't miss.

The axe came down on the crowbar once more. Orna's cage jerked under the force. She cried out. Threon thought he heard her call his name.

A third swing of the axe brought the chain free. The cage plummeted to the ground and Threon saw the look of fear in Orna's eyes as her elderly body came to meet the ground. 'You were meant to catch the bloody chain,' he yelled. He ran to where the cage had fallen as Dan and Maus loosed more arrows at the guards. He dragged it to cover behind a pillar.

'Orna?' The cage had broken open and she lay on the ground, unmoving but conscious.

'Threon, you stupid bastard.'

'Are you okay?'

'Fine. Get outta here.'

'Not without you.'

He helped her get to her feet, her skin ice to the touch. An arrow flew past Threon's ear. He spun around, arrow nocked, to find a soldier charging towards them. He loosed it at the man's face as he bounded towards them, sword outstretched. The arrow flew true, but the Thelonian knocked it aside mid-air with his sword. The speed at which he had moved made Threon's bowels churn.

Another soldier had reached the other side of the temple. Dan and Maus had drawn knives, sharpened implements taken from the old butcher's place. Threon didn't hold out much hope for the weapons, or those wielding them. There was a chime of metal as they struck out at their opponent's armour, and then a shriek and thud as Dan fell dying to the floor. Maus screamed in fury, leaping at the soldier, knife clenched in his fist. He jammed the blade deep into the palimore's eye and his assailant staggered backwards, but not before he had skewered his sword through Maus's body. Both men fell to the ground and lay unmoving.

'Run,' Threon screamed at Tom. 'Take Orna and go.'

He poised his knife as the soldier he'd shot at ran into him. Metal clashed as sword met knife and the weapons slid against each other until they met at the hilt. The palimore forced Threon backwards until he was against a pillar with nowhere to go.

Then the pressure eased against his knife. The soldier nodded discreetly to him.

Peering into the darkness of his opponent's helm, Threon recognised those blue eyes.

'You…' he said.

The soldier kicked the legs from underneath him and sent Threon to the floor, silencing any incriminating words. He angled his sword at Threon's throat.

'Halt,' the guard called. The other soldiers paused in their advance on Tom. The lad picked up Orna in the respite and held her shivering body close.

The other three soldiers gathered around, all eyes on Threon where he lay on the wet ground.

'Run,' Threon called. The sword pressed harder against his throat.

'What's this then, Lleu?' one of the soldiers asked.

'Maradah's most wanted,' replied his captor. 'This is the singer we've been looking for.'

'Well, well,' said the first soldier. 'Today just isn't your day is it?' He spat down at Threon. 'You killed one of our own. That merchant was Stellor Arntree of the Imperial Council. He owned half this city. You will regret this.'

'You failed to protect him,' said Threon, a dark smile curling on his lips. 'Did I get you in trouble?'

The first solder lurched his sword towards Threon. Lleu batted it away. 'Cain, stop. We need to make an example of him. Of all of them.'

'Fine.'

Cain stamped on Threon's wrist; pain forced him to release his knife. The soldier pulled him to his feet and dragged him over to the central pillar.

'Pass me that chain,' said Cain. Lleu picked up the chain that was once attached to Orna's cage. He placed it in the other soldier's hands with a frown.

Attaching the end of the chain to a crossbow bolt, Cain cast it into the air. It soared up in an arch and fell to the ground, having looped back around the flagpole.

He pinned Threon down with a boot on his back as he tied the chain around the prince's feet.

With a sharp jerk, Threon felt himself lurch into the air. The soldier pulled him higher and tied the chain to the pillar once more. Blood rushed to his head as he hung there. Reverse hangings were an old Thelonian tradition. Growing up, he had been told about them to illustrate the barbarity of the ancient civilisation across the sea. Blood would build painfully in the head and the lungs, until it overcame the body. Threon thrashed against the chain, trying to get free, but as he did so the metal only bit harder into his ankles.

'It's a quicker death than starving, but less pleasant,' said Cain. 'I bet you can feel the pressure building in your skull already, can't you?' The soldier slapped Threon's back, making him swing in the air. 'Where's the woman? There's still a bit of chain left.'

Tom held his axe aloft, looking around nervously as the soldiers' attention returned to him. Orna was no longer with him.

Cain addressed the other two soldiers. 'Find her.' They moved to the castle walls in search of the innkeeper. Cain turned to Lleu, nodding at Tom. 'Let's finish him.'

It was a mercy when the wind rotated Theon's swaying body so that they were out of view. But still the screams came, loud over the sound of his heart pounding in his ears. As he gazed at the reflection of the moon on the wet ground, it bloomed red with Tom's blood.

When the last scream died, he heard Cain say, 'Go help them find the woman. I'll stand guard.'

Cain stood beside Threon for what might have been hours. It was frightening how quickly he had lost the strength to try and free himself. His head was a fog of pain and his vision became nothing but shadows. The sensation of pounding blood in his head, in his hands, in his arms was overpowering. To twitch a finger, red and swollen, was agony. He faded in and out of consciousness and his breath began to rasp with effort as his lungs struggled.

He allowed his mind to drift and take him back to his childhood, chasing dogs around the courtyard, practising swordplay, going to temple with his parents. He thought of Orna. Had she escaped? Why had he been so impulsive? They should have been better prepared. They should have planned.

Cain woke him from his reverie. Two large hands around his chest lifted him slightly, then the chain was released and his feet fell to the floor. He cried out as the blood filled his legs, feet feeling as though they might burst, hot with pain. His head swam and he gasped in air.

'That's it, get your breath.' Cain's voice was monotone, a man enacting a regular routine. Threon blinked, but black blots filled his vision. A small voice at the back of his mind was screaming for him to run, or to fight, but his body would not, could not, obey. 'This just helps extend it a bit. Most men

51

only last three turns, but one as skinny as you might go sooner. Could be over before the next rotation.' Threon was still rasping in breath when the chain was hauled up again, and he swung back into the air. The blood rushed back to his head. This time he was unable to cry out. His stomach heaved, and then he passed out.

He came to again when the moon was lower in the sky. A series of shouts had roused him. He opened his eyes but his vision was gone, a blur of shades of black. Amid the commotion he heard Cain and Lleu talking urgently. He was vaguely aware of the smell of smoke.

'She set fire to the munitions store. There were some barrels of cathfire in there. The place went up in seconds.'

'Mother's balls! I told you to find her. I meant fast.'

'I've sent the men to fetch water, but – I mean, look at those flames.'

'The merchants?'

'Evacuating to the ships.'

'And the woman?'

'Dead. She went up with the fire.'

'Any other casualties?'

'Could be.'

'What about the stores?'

'The merchants have the vish.'

'Thank the gods.'

'Cain, the men need your leadership. I think we're going to lose the place.'

'Yes, yes, I'm going.'

'What about the singer?'

'Finish him.'

CHAPTER FOUR

Savanta perched on the eastern tower. From here she could see most of the city.

The Minister of Secrets had assigned her the role of Watcher. She spent her days monitoring the streets of the city and reporting suspicious behaviour. On a couple of occasions she had been assigned to watch at the mines. A little more of her old self died each time her pointed fingers gave up the paths of the slaves brave enough to attempt escape.

Today she watched from the safe heights of the palace roof. The less she was able to hear of the city's rumours, the better she felt.

The winter sun shone wanly onto the roof tiles. She opened her wings wide to feel the cool rays. Heavy winter clothing made flight difficult and she resigned herself to thin, backless dresses and a perpetual feeling of cold.

When she was alone like this, for a moment, she felt free. Below her, rich merchants, politicians, soldiers and those graced with the Empress's favour scurried like rats. She had spent a good portion of the morning entertaining herself by watching a woman recently outcast from the circle of ancients begging at the palace gate. She screamed and wailed, pleading with anyone who would listen. Her access to life-prolonging vish had been rescinded. Whatever she had done to deserve her fate, Savanta couldn't summon the energy to pity her. So what, she couldn't take any more vish? The rest of the world managed pretty well without it. Mortality wasn't so bad.

An arrow embedded itself in the roof, cracking the slate beside her hand. Startled, she jumped away from it. From the ground, a palimore soldier saluted to her, bow in hand.

A note was tied to the arrow.

Our Holy Empress demands you in the species bank.

She threw the note to the wind and stood up. Spreading her arms and wings in the air, she leant forward and over the edge of the tower's roof and let herself drop. The thin skin of her wings grew taut under the pressure of the air. She soared.

Five weeks after her arrival at the palace she still drew attention wherever she went. People on the ground pointed up at her, some ducked into buildings in fear. She dove closer to the ground, enjoying the reaction she elicited.

The species bank was built on top of the city's only hill. Circled by tall white walls, it was filled with every plant and creature imaginable. The Empress Keresan had lived for over a thousand years and she had used her time to breed magnificent beasts and perfect nature's flowers. Her finest examples grew and roamed within the walls, a living tribute to her divine husband.

Flying over the gate, Savanta dropped within the walls. She glided over canopies of trees bearing strange fruits until the orchards gave way to open ground. A carpet of tall green-gold grass was bordered by plants with fat shining leaves and yellow blooms the size of fists. It was here that she spied the Empress reclining on the ground with her favourite tyger. The animal was beautiful; white, with black stripes and golden eyes. When he stood tall his back reached higher than Savanta's shoulders.

She alighted gently, careful not to disturb the pair.

Keresan lifted her head from where it lay in the cat's thick fur. 'Savanta. Welcome.'

'You called for me, Majesty,' she said.

'You really are a wonderful gift. Calling anyone here on foot would take an hour. You command the skies and arrive in minutes.'

Savanta bowed her head. 'I am at your service.'

'How are you finding life in the palace?' She smiled.

Terrifying. Stifling. She wanted to go home to her family, to hold her daughter. 'I'm enjoying my new form, Empress. The palace is more strange and beautiful than any of the stories ever hinted at.'

'I haven't lived a thousand years without being able to read people. I can see you're unhappy.' Savanta was about to object, but the Empress waved her quiet and continued. 'I can't let you go home, you're too valuable to me. But perhaps I can offer you some solace in sanctification.' She rubbed the tyger's ears. 'I expect Zenith was your first encounter with the Vyara?'

'Yes, Empress.'

She scoffed. 'Then I pity you. Zenith has no more right to his divinity than a beggar in the street. He's mischievous, cunning and has a terrible sense of humour.'

'Yes, Majesty.' Savanta would call him far worse than a mischief. He'd stolen her life away.

'You've been going to temple since you arrived?'

'Since I was a young girl, Majesty. Earth, my body.'

Keresan looked pleased. 'Good. Have you ever left the island?'

'No, though I've always wondered what it's like overseas.'

Keresan smiled at her. 'The Mainlands are filled with heathens. Many give equal credence to all three Vyara, with very few recognising Deyar as the Mother's true heir. He rules the ground they walk on, the food they eat, the body they live in. We are creatures of the Earth. Their lack of faith is unfathomable.'

Until recently, the notion of polytheism in the Mainlands had intrigued Savanta, but the thought of people building temples to Zenith now made her shudder.

Keresan continued, 'I want you to watch there. I want you to feed back to me, and to find the niches that will allow Deyar's reign to prevail. Our soldiers have made great progress in establishing civil rule there. The time for conversion is ripe.' She gave Savanta a bright smile. 'You'll go for me?'

'How could I refuse?' An edge of sarcasm escaped with her voice. She quickly corrected it. 'You offer me a great honour, your Majesty.'

'Those who show Deyar loyalty are always rewarded. Serve me well and you could find yourself among the ancients some day.'

She couldn't imagine living another year here, let alone centuries. Still, she bowed her head in thanks.

'You leave at dawn. The Minister of Secrets will give you a compass and instructions to guide you across the sea to our foothold in Maradah.'

The tyger woke and got to his feet. Keresan was dwarfed by his size. He stretched and yawned, revealing rows of sharp teeth. His fangs were as long as Savanta's hand.

Keresan grabbed a handful of fur and pulled herself up

onto his back. 'We'll be using these in battle before long,' she said, patting the creature's flank. 'The Waterlands is nearly mine. We'll soon have the full force of the Mainlands paying homage to Deyar. They'll learn the error of their ways. A little suffering for the greater good. They'll thank me one day.'

She nudged the tyger with her legs and they turned away into the dense vegetation.

It was not weather for flying.

Savanta had never flown long distances, and despite the dark clouds that loomed over the sea she had been told to leave. Rain was now falling in sheets and she was two hours into her journey with no land in sight to give her respite.

Her hands were numb with cold. She clutched a brass compass and a map stitched into sodden leather. Neither were any help to her; the sea gave no landmarks.

She flew low, allowing herself to be dashed with salty spray. Her wings, her back, her shoulders, all ached. She fought to beat her wings against the weather. Every beat burned.

'Zenith,' she breathed.

The response was immediate. *Hello. I wondered how long it would take you to beg for help.* His musical voice appeared in her head. *Don't you like the rain?*

The effort of keeping airborne was making her pant for breath.

'I don't – think – I'm going to – make it.'

Such a shame. After all those nice promises you made to that bitch Keresan. Now you don't really think I gave you to her to serve my brother, do you? I heard you talking. She's enlisted you as one of her dreary missionaries. Surprised it took her so long if I'm honest.

'Please. It's – not fair.'

Life's not fair. His voice grew dark, his tone matching a bolt of lightning that flashed in the clouds. *I made you. You belong to me.*

'I'll do anything.' She was sinking closer to the waves. 'Please. Help.'

The rain eased a little.

You've become embroiled in a dangerous game, my girl. You know the tales of the Vyara and our battles for power. The next one is just warming up, and when it ends I will have my brother's crown. You, my Watcher friend, are going to help me get it.

Savanta said nothing, still panting for breath.

Savanta? he probed. *You won't get far without me. I doubt you'd even make it back to land.*

'Anything. I'll do anything. Help me. Please.'

The rain petered out. Ahead, the clouds parted and a warm breeze picked up, allowing her to glide.

CHAPTER FIVE

Threon fell to the ground, the chain clattering to the cobbles behind him.

His head spun. Pain shot down to his feet as blood rushed away from his head. He tried to cry out but his breath was too shallow and it came out as a groan.

'You're going to get me killed. I told you to stay away. Now is not the time for vengeance.' The soldier pulled the chain from around his ankles and helped Threon to his feet. 'There. Can you stand?'

He felt dizzy and his feet screamed with hot, throbbing pain, but he nodded. 'Thank you.'

As Lleu let go of him, Threon stumbled, just managing to stay upright. His vision began to clear and he gulped in air as his lungs adjusted to being upright once more. He spat blood on the floor as a wave of sickness passed over him.

Dark plumes of smoke were rising in the sky, and an orange glow flickered over the castle walls.

'Here.' Lleu passed him a tinderbox and a small box of

catchfire from one of his pockets. 'You want to destroy our biggest defence? Use this on your way out. Burn the castle. And watch yourself. I won't be able to save you a third time.'

'Tell me why you're helping me.'

'It's complicated. I'll find you again soon, when the time is right. Now go.'

Lleu drew his sword and rushed back to the main body of the castle.

As Threon half fell, half ran, from the courtyard he passed his friends' corpses. All three of his companions had been killed, in part thanks to his rescuer. He bent down and closed Tom's accusatory eyes before stumbling on, back in the direction of the kitchen.

Before he left through the kitchen shaft, Threon piled wooden furniture in the middle of the room. He dusted it with catchfire and lit it with a spark. The wood flared into flame so fast it knocked him back.

Making a quick exit, he headed for the blacksmith's house, where he spent the night hidden in bushes beside the barn. He spent the remaining hours of night watching the fire burn, and watching his home reduce to ash and rubble.

At noon he woke to the sound of hooves on the ground.

A woman looked down at him from her horse. It was a Mainlands horse, smaller and stouter than those ridden by the Thelonians. She wore a simple white dress with a hooded white cloak. She didn't look like a merchant, and she was far too small to be a soldier.

'Are you Threon?' she asked, an Ionese accent spilling over her words.

'Who's asking?' Threon dragged himself to his feet, reaching for his knife.

She pulled down the hood of her cloak, revealing short

dark hair and a striking, serious face. Delicate features, a slight figure and fair skin marked her as coming from the Ionese mountains. 'You have nothing to fear from me. My people heard rumour that you had returned home. I'm glad to see it's true. I am Azzania, a Guardian of the void.'

He eyed her suspiciously. 'My father told me about the Guardians. He would never allow you into court. He said you displeased the Vyara.'

'You might question your loyalty to them if you knew them better.' She dismounted and came closer. 'I know you have suffered. The people of the Waterlands have all suffered greatly. The pain all stems from the Empire, and from the woman who commands it in the name of a god. Do not let the Vyara rule you. They bring chaos into this world.'

'My faith has kept me alive so far.'

She sighed softly, a frustrated sound, as though she were explaining something to a child. 'There are other ways to get what you want. Look at the fortune your gods have delivered so far.' She gazed up at the castle, which still smouldered. She turned her dark eyes back to him and placed a hand on his chest. She smelled sweet as she pressed close.

'You can choose the void.' As she spoke the words, a ripple of energy ran from her hand and through his body. He felt the pain in his legs and feet disappear, and the anger in his heart melt. His muscles relaxed. He felt a calm resolve settle over him.

He watched her lips as she spoke. 'The void removes pain, removes passion, removes all turbulence in our lives. The Guardians live unscathed by human emotion and the games of the divine.' She removed her hand.

The pain returned and his sadness and anger welled up again, leaving him feeling all the more bitter after the short break from his misery. 'The Guardians seek to restore balance to this world. The inequalities delivered by the Empress and her life-giving vish have driven deep divides in the people.'

Threon slumped against the barn wall. 'So, how do you hope to do that?'

'We aren't the most trusted sect in the Mainlands. We know this. We can't do it alone. I've come looking for a champion to unite the people.' She held his gaze. 'Help us, and we can help deliver the revenge that I feel your heart burning for.'

Azzania left Threon with his thoughts, asking him to return to her when he had made up his mind.

He stumbled through the wreckage of the castle, painfully kicking at blackened stones. He had watched the soldiers retreat to the harbour in the night. It was a risk to be out in the open like this, but he was past caring. His home had been demolished, he was responsible for the deaths of three innocent men, and Orna was gone.

He made his way to where the great hall once stood. The carved marble throne stood up from the wreckage, its gleaming white surfaces painted black with flame.

Threon cleared the rubble from the chair and sat in it.

He felt so alone.

Gazing out across the ash, he counted human bones littered across the ground. Not all the palimore had escaped in time, then. In the distance he could hear the Thelonians tearing through the town. Whips cracking. Children crying. Crossbow bolts being loosed.

He wondered where they had buried his father and his mother, what had become of his maid, his squire, of the cook that always made him laugh.

His parents had tried to bring him up to be a good leader. They hired the best scholars to teach him about the kings of the past, about military strategy, about the laws of the

Waterlands, about appeasing the Vyara. He had wasted the opportunity, evading lessons whenever he could to play his kestro, or practise swordplay. And here he was, sat on a throne amid the ashes of his family's legacy. Would his parents be proud?

A glimmer in the ash caught his eye. He walked over and picked up a tarnished circle of gold and cinders. Embedded crudely in the heat-deformed object were sapphires and emeralds. It was his father's crown.

Holding it in his two hands he gazed out across the town, to the sea. Thelonia had taken everything from him.

Time to take something back.

CHAPTER SIX

The pillar of smoke led Savanta to Maradah like a beacon. Shards of emerald pierced a flat blue horizon as she grew near, revealing the most luscious landscape she had ever laid eyes on. Fierce mountains stretched up from the water, cloaked in green. Two high ridges of land stretched out from the city like enfolding arms, nestling a large sheltered bay. Savanta had lived her whole life in monochrome. This place was a dream compared to the grey landscape of home.

No wonder they had chosen this country for the first raids. She could only imagine the riches that must grow in the fields.

Arriving in the mid-afternoon sun, she circled the town, assessing the situation. The remains of what must have been a castle were smouldering at the highest part of the city. Below, she watched palimore soldiers charging through the streets. In Thelonia City she had always seen them as a wise and efficient policing force. Here, they dealt out angry violence on the locals.

She watched streams of people load bags of food onto ships with the same listlessness shown by slaves in the mines. They were preparing to leave. On board the ships several merchants paced nervously, their faces worn and tired. One took short snorts of vish, another splayed drunkenly on the prow, a bottle of plum wine in hand.

Coming closer to the ground, Savanta perched on top of one of the taller buildings, out of sight from the people below. She stretched her wings and folded them around herself. She was exhausted.

Leaning against a chimney breast, she let the cold stones cool her sweating skin, and closed her eyes.

The harbour was chaos. Orders were screamed for the city to be stripped of all goods, for the merchants to steal them across the sea. It was as if they had forgotten the soldiers were staying behind. What were they expected to eat? Grass and peasants?

Lleu had been ordered to keep the townsfolk moving, heavy goods strapped to backs and balanced on heads. He cracked a bullwhip overhead as they hurried down the harbour road, the sound motivation enough to speed their way.

His incessant thoughts kept returning to the prince, eating at the calm exterior he was fighting to maintain. Twice Threon had been caught, and twice Lleu put his life on the line to save him. He didn't trust the man to stay out of sight a third time.

Crack. More locals flinched from the whip.

He was a fool for helping. The risks were too great. If they found out… the penalty didn't bear thinking about. Even these peasants would pity him.

Crack.

What difference did he think the prince could possibly

make anyway? A runt of a beggar. Foolish, indiscreet, alone. Certainly no warrior. And without a plan.

Crack. This time the whip's tail coiled bloody against a young girl's arm. She cried out and looked back at Lleu with a face that screamed injustice. 'Move along,' he barked. Her mother pushed her forwards, hushing her cries.

It was a fool's errand. What did he hope to achieve going against the palimore? Betraying his own, those who raised him, men and women he had fought with for over a century. And the chances of success? Next to nothing. His gaze drifted to the surrounding mountains. Iced peaks cool and timeless, home to shepherds and ancient song. Their sides sloping to crystal fjords where the finest shipbuilders learned their craft. And beyond the mountains, a hundred towns and villages rich in culture and people who deserved their freedom. He was the only one who could see it and it would be his undoing, he was sure of it.

When the stream of goods began to thin out the Commander gave him a signal from the harbour. Off duty. Lleu gave a salute of acknowledgment and made his way up the hill, glad to get away. As soon as he was out of sight he changed direction, hurrying down a side alley that lead to the Honeydew. He needed reassurance that the prince wasn't still hiding in the city.

The Dew's door was off its hinges; the place was a wreck after the old woman's arrest. A thorough search of the rooms, basement and attic satisfied him that the prince hadn't returned. Not here at least. His nerves were wired and a quick rifle behind the bar uncovered a bottle of Thelonian brandy. The cork came free with a satisfying plomp and he breathed in the familiar spirit. A taste of the simple luxuries the raiding parties left behind when they sailed east.

The bottle was at his lips when a shadow filled the door.

'I thought I might find you here.' Cain's voice was dark with anger.

Lleu lowered the bottle and tried to read the man's expression. Did he know Threon was free? 'Come to join me for a drink, brother?'

'There was no body, Lleu. You let him escape.'

Lleu's blood ran cold, but he hid his fear. 'His body must have burned in the fire with the others.'

'Don't take me for a fool.' Cain stepped further into the room. 'I escaped through the courtyard. A broken chain, no blood, no prince. You let him go.' Lleu took a small step backwards, shrinking from his anger. 'Your incompetence is astounding. How did he get away?'

Incompetence? Not betrayal then. Perhaps he might get away with this after all. 'I—'

Cain didn't give him a chance to finish. 'You were meant to kill him there and then.'

Lleu did his best to look taken aback. 'I thought he was dead, Cain. I only left him alone for a moment.' Cain's anger did not diminish. 'Please. The Commander can't know.'

His plea unleashed manic laughter in the soldier. The stress of last night seemed to have put the man on edge. 'Funny, Lleu, funny. He'd forgive you anything, but he's still going to find out. I'm not going down for your mistakes.' He kicked a chair over, eyes wide with anger as he marched into Lleu's personal space.

'I left him for a moment. Just a moment.' He kept his voice low and flat, trying to restore calm. 'Nassa called for help and I got caught firefighting. When I got back, he was gone. I fucked up, Cain.' Yeah, he'd fucked up. Dragging Nassa into this, damn fool. Another soldier who could disprove his story. 'You haven't told anyone he's missing yet, have you?' Concern leaked into his voice unbidden.

67

'You keep fucking up, Lleu. Not a man or woman among us has a record of mistakes as long as yours.' His hands were gripping the edge of the bar, knuckles white. 'You just wait till the others hear. Just confirms what they say.'

'What they say?' The words came out in a low growl. He knew what was coming.

'Rotten blood.'

No one had had the gall to say it to his face. Lleu felt his lip twitch.

'Those blue eyes of yours got you slow. I can see by your face you know it's true. Weak blood.'

'You dare—'

'What you going to do? Cry to Daddy? It's time the Commander saw your failings. You're not like the rest of us.'

Lleu breathed hard.

'Or maybe your links to this dump have got you sentimental. Haven't got the balls to kill your own countrymen?'

That struck too close to the truth. Lleu's fist swung at him before he could think. It sent Cain reeling back into one of the tables. He pulled himself up, eyes widening in understanding. 'I'm right. I'm bloody right. You'd put these peasants before palimore?'

He would, it seemed. And he was about to prove it. There was no coming back from this now. Silence the bastard. Lleu felt rage burn through his veins unchecked and he lunged at his fellow soldier. They plunged into the table, its legs shattering under their weight.

'How fucking dare you.' Cain hissed contempt like venom. Lleu had no time for words. The man's incredulity had slowed his response. Only for a second, but it was long enough. Lleu grabbed one of the broken chair legs and smashed it into Cain's face. It hadn't been enough to knock him out. Blood spilt from his forehead and a newfound fury exploded from him. 'Traitor!' he screamed, crimson.

It seemed clear now. No witnesses. A bold step into betrayal. Cain had to die.

Another swing of the table leg. But this time Cain caught his arm. They were equals in strength and the makeshift weapon shook in Lleu's grip, edging neither forward nor back as both men gritted their teeth in effort.

Lleu let go of the wood and their stances changed instantly. Cain stepped back, dodging Lleu's fist. He kicked out, knocking Lleu to his knees. But as he fell he grasped hold of his opponent and swung him to the floor.

Lleu pinned him down and forced a hand over his mouth. No screams. Cain desperately tried to dislodge the hand, but Lleu put his full weight into it. He tipped his chin backwards, exposing the throat and reached for another leg of splintered pine.

Cain's pupils were black with horror. He moaned muffled cries and attempted to bite his way free as his arms frantically beat Lleu's chest and searched for weapons that were out of reach. Lleu took a steady breath. A thousand thoughts ran through his mind. There would be no going back from this. He had chosen to side with the enemy. A killing blow would make it official.

He held the weapon lifted high above his head, out of the soldier's reach. Cain was reaching up now, trying to grasp Lleu's neck.

Don't think. Do it. Do it now.

Lleu brought the leg down fast, crushing through the windpipe. The jagged wood pierced flesh and released a tide of red. Cain's eyes bulged. His breath bubbled through blood in a horrifying rasp. It began to pool around them both.

Cain's flailing hands fell, weak. Not long now. Blood surged under Lleu's hand and he struggled to keep it from slipping from the soldier's jaw. He closed his eyes as his brother's skin grew paler, his breath shallower and more rapid. He couldn't bear the accusation in his face. Killing came easy to him, but this was like killing family.

The remaining seconds felt like an age. Eventually the gurgle of breath fell silent.

'I'm sorry,' Lleu whispered.

He exhaled and stood up. It would be another minute or two before the blood stopped flowing. There was no time to wait for that. With shaking hands he set about piling broken furniture around the body. 'It's far from the way you wanted to go,' he said, more to himself than the corpse. There was a quaver to his voice. 'Not by a long way.' He wiped sweat from his palms and his brow. Cain was one of the first to look out for him in his early days, fresh out of training. 'Do you remember that first time we fought each other in the pit?' When his question hung in the silence, unanswered, he began to laugh. What was this madness?

There was enough wood now. He dried tears with a sleeve and took a deep drink of the brandy to settle his nerves. The rest he doused on the firewood. 'A parting drink,' he said, splashing a measure on the dead soldier's mouth which had fallen open in his dying cries.

He lit a match from beside the fireplace and touched it to the wood. Blue flames flickered along the pyre. He wanted to say something meaningful. To mark the death. To send his spirit on. To beg for forgiveness. But the words wouldn't come. They were caught, strangled in his throat.

Instead, he turned from the mounting fire and ran.

Savanta waited until evening, when the merchants had finished evacuating and the soldiers had quieted, before making her appearance.

From her vantage point on the roof, she could see across much of the city. The remains of a large building, likely the castle, smouldered at the top of the hill. The buildings in the town were large and many had gardens. She imagined that at one time this place must have been wealthy. It seemed so much better ordered than Tannit. She could pick out buildings that looked like an indoor market, a hospital and a theatre. Pity the place had been stripped so bare by the raids. To her, it seemed a haven. A place rich in food, wild landscapes, and a society that didn't appear to abandon the poor to a life in the slums. It might have once been a place she would have loved to raise Erin.

She had remained undiscovered long enough to recover some of her strength. Now she listened to a group of soldiers mumbling discontentedly to one another, sat on the cobbles of the high street. She crawled cat-like across the rooftop until directly above them.

Spreading her wings out to their full width, she launched off the roof and landed crouched in the centre of their gathering. They startled to their feet. Several swords hissed out of scabbards. They eyed her like a dangerous wild animal. She lifted her head and looked around them slowly. Not many could hope to inspire fear in these ageless soldiers. She forced herself not to smile.

'Who's in charge here?' she demanded, coming to stand with a confidence her former wingless body would never have mustered.

One of the larger men came forward. He wasn't wearing imperial armour, instead he wore a simple robe, cut Waterlands fashion; billowing trousers and a thick, belted tunic. 'Who and what are you?' He scowled at her under thickset eyebrows.

Savanta produced the compass and showed him an

engraving on the back. 'I'm here on divine business.' That ought to shut him up.

'You've come from the Empress? What kind of sinister creatures is she breeding these days?' His tone matched his sneer.

She snapped the compass back into her belt. 'To disrespect me is to disrespect the Empire. As Watcher, I could have you reported for a comment like that. Is that what you want?'

The soldier took a step back and looked her up and down. 'Alright, alright, I meant no offence.' He extended a hand to her. 'The name's Khan.' She looked down at his hand but didn't take it.

'Where is your armour, Khan? And what of the castle I was promised to find standing here? I was told you were sent here to take the city, not destroy it.' She was rather enjoying this newfound authority.

'Careful now,' he growled. 'I'm sure it wouldn't take much for a pretty bird like you to lose those wings.'

'We both know you wouldn't dare harm a Watcher. I need your report. Tell me what happened here.'

Khan relented. He sighed and picked up a wine cup. 'Here,' he said, pouring her a glass. 'We needn't fight.' She took the cup, taking several quick gulps, thirsty after her flight. Khan gestured up to the smoking rubble. 'Some bitch rebel escaped us and set fire to the castle. She died before we could get to her. The building was half wood and went up in a flash. We evacuated the merchants travelling with us and lost three soldiers in the blaze. Our vish supplies are already on their way back to Thelonia.'

'All of them?'

'The merchants thought it a suitable punishment to leave us without for a time.' A spark of anger tinged the edge of his otherwise calm voice. 'Our armour lies in melted heaps among the ash. Only the four on guard duty were lucky enough to be wearing their kit at the time. Most of us were sleeping. We could only save the weapons we had to hand.'

'So you intend to stay?' A couple of soldiers were watching her keenly, circling her to get a better view of her now-folded wings. She shot them a glare.

'Ignore them. Halor! Lleu! Sit back down.' The men sat. 'We must stay. There'll be riots in the towns and mass deaths in the mines by spring if we can't keep the food supplies running. The merchants will send for more troops, weapons and armour. We'll easily keep any upstarts at bay in the meantime.'

Savanta raised an eyebrow. *Upstarts like the ones that have already stripped you of your castle and your defences?* She bit the words back before they could leave her mouth.

The soldier he had called Halor spoke up. 'Send her. With wings like that, she could reach the city faster than any ship.'

Khan silenced him with a wave of his hand. 'He's right. The merchants' ships will take two to three days to reach the island – likely longer with the winds as calm as this. How long did it take you to fly? I assume that's how you got here.' Though more discreet than the other soldiers his curiosity was evident, eyes flicking over the wings.

'I left at dawn and arrived after noon. The wind was on my side.'

A smile broke out on his face. 'You and I could be very good friends,' he said. 'Take a couple of hours to rest and eat with us, then fly back with a message for the barracks.'

She began to bow her head in acquiescence but felt a ripple of cold air around her face. The wind blew gently on her lips and Zenith's words came out of her mouth. 'No.'

The Commander looked shocked. 'You defy me?' His hand moved to his sword hilt in threat. Savanta's eyes widened.

She fought to bring words of defence to her aid, but the air in her lungs felt too thin to make a sound. Khan frowned. 'I will not stand for insolence.'

She began to beat her wings to make an escape, but he grabbed her wrist before she left the ground. He pulled her face close to his. 'What are you really here for? If you really are a Watcher, it's your duty—' he spat this '—to send word. The Empire is in danger, and you say "no"?'

She tried to plead with him using her eyes. Still no words came. Her lungs and throat felt strangled and her mind screamed out for Zenith to release her voice. What game was the god playing?

'Fine.' He looked over to one of his soldiers. 'Rhianydd, bind her wings. Lock her in the gatehouse until I decide what to do with her.' A tall, muscled woman pulled a belt from her waist and looped it around Savanta's wings. She pulled it tight. Painfully so. The woman drew her sword and held it to Savanta's back.

'Move,' she said.

The room was stiflingly hot. A large fire blazed against the room's only stone wall. Savanta was tied to one of the gatehouse's supporting wooden beams. It was dark and dusty, and the smell of stale ale rose sickly sweet from the baking wooden floor.

As soon as she had been left alone the hold on her voice had been released. She had screamed Zenith's name more times than she could count, but he did not answer. Her throat was raw, her mouth dry as ash.

She had tried to sleep in the night, but being tied in an upright position denied her much rest. She had watched the sun set, and now it was rising again. Zenith wasn't going to help her this time.

The soldiers would pay for this. She was mortal, and they may look down on her for it, but she held the power to destroy them with the right words. Watchers were not to be trifled with.

A shadow crossed one of the windows as someone walked past.

'I need water,' she shouted. To her surprise, the latch on the door flicked up and a panel of light spread across the floor as the door pushed open.

A soldier stepped in. One of the ones who had been paying such close attention earlier. He had unruly dark hair and a thick layer of stubble. His face was that of a man in his late twenties but his sharp blue eyes revealed him to be much older. He picked up a water skin from a table by the door and brought it over to her. She drained its contents in one as he lifted it to her lips, not pausing for breath. 'Thirsty, huh?' he said, raising an eyebrow. She was rarely so close to the palimore, usually watching from above, and she had to stop herself from shrinking away from his intimidating size.

'What are you going to do with me?'

The soldier drew a knife out of his belt. Savanta stiffened.

He smiled at her reaction as he reached behind her, cutting through the ropes holding her in place. She stepped forward, rubbing her wrists and lower back.

'I'm getting you out of here,' he said. 'Turn around.'

'Why are you helping me?' She offered him her back and he unbound her wings, dropping the belt to the floor. She stretched them out, feeling the ache in her muscles. Gods, it hurt to hold them tight for so long. 'Thank you,' she said.

'May I?' He nodded towards her wings. She extended one out to him and he ran a hand along it. 'Incredible. Did she breed many like you?'

Savanta withdrew her wing curtly. 'I am not one of her wild animals, bred to entertain.'

'I meant no offence. The palimore are bred for purpose just like most of the Empress's pet projects. Well, most of us.' He smirked.

'Why are you helping me?' she asked again.

'Taking a chance on a hunch. You risked death to defy my father like that. And if you're not here to help us… I figure you have other ideas about the right of our glorious empire to rule the world.'

The look on his face gave her the sense to nod in agreement. She'd say anything to get out of this room. 'You plan to betray your army?'

He seemed to wince at that. 'Betrayal is a strong word.'

'Strong enough for a nasty execution.'

His face darkened. Not something he wanted to hear, apparently. He paced to the window and looked out. 'We can't be seen together. You'll have to move fast. Can you fly?'

She flexed her wings, stretching the muscles, tight after their confinement. 'I'll try.'

'You're going to have to make a quick exit. When I give you the all clear, run out of the main gate and fly for the forest. With a bit of luck you might find Maradah's old prince there. He's on our side.' Savanta didn't have a side. This guy was a fool to trust her. But if he could get her out… He walked to the door and placed his hand on the latch. 'We're at our weakest now; there's a chance he could take the city back if the gods are willing. Don't let him come back until he has a plan.' He began to pull the door open. 'Ready?'

She nodded, heart beating faster in anticipation.

He walked out of the door casually and was out of sight for several moments before he swung it open again. 'Go. Now.'

She bounded out of the door and away from the city, bringing her wings up and down as she ran. A cry rose from the city walls as she was spotted by a soldier on guard duty.

'Stop her!'

As she left the ground, an arrow thudded into the grass beneath her, narrowly missing her calf. She beat against the air furiously, rising as fast as she could. She soon hit a current of air and was swept up, out of reach of their arrows. The forest lay to her left, the sea to her right. She could turn back, go home, report the commander. But no. Her word against a palimore soldier? Suicide. If she even got that far. It seemed more likely that Zenith would leave her to drown in the waves if she went against his will.

You know me too well. His voice streamed back into her mind and she shut her eyes tight, trying to block it.

'Where were you when I needed you?'

There was no reply. Only the sound of the wind in her wings as she beat on towards the forest.

Lleu left the gatehouse by a rear window and slunk between shadows on his return to the city centre. His ears pricked up at a sound behind him. Someone was following him. Little point in trying to hide. He turned to face his pursuer.

Khan stepped out from the shadows, spreading his hands. 'What do you think you're doing, son?'

Lleu let his hand drop from his sword hilt. 'Father?' Dread curdled in his stomach.

Khan came closer. 'I saw you go into that gatehouse and I saw that creature fly free.' His voice was heavy with displeasure. 'You better have a good explanation. Your actions are treasonous.'

'Look, Father—'

'You've always been soft. Too much of your mother in you. In the last century I've seen many things I like about you, and some I've grown to be wary of.'

'Father, she was on a mission for the Empress. I went to give her water. She told me she's been sworn to keep her purpose secret. Keeping her there was obstructing royal decree.'

A dark frown creased Khan's brow. 'Yet you free her without consulting me.'

'Would you have freed her?'

'No. And you know it. You have no place to act without my command.' His voice rose in anger. 'Our blood bond makes you bold with me, but you push the boundaries too far. Your trust in her is misplaced.' He turned to go. 'Or maybe mine is in you.'

Lleu waited until he was out of sight before leaning heavily against a wall. He pounded his fist against the stone. He was being too careless. They were beginning to see through the cracks.

CHAPTER SEVEN

With the castle gone, the palimore set up lodgings in the town. Scattering themselves among tired buildings they turned local homeowners out onto the streets. There were less than quiet grumblings about whichever fool had torched the Honeydew and its plentiful guestrooms. Canvas awnings were hoisted across every alley, creating shelter like a sea of fallen sails for the newly homeless.

Lleu didn't plan to join his fellow soldiers in town. He had a promise of a warmer bed with sweeter company beyond the city walls.

The moon was rising as he made his way out of the city. The night guard gave him a salute as he approached. 'Going out?' she called from the city walls above.

'Hunting,' said Lleu, and returned the salute and passed through the gate without another word.

The night was still and mild. He walked for a few minutes before cupping his hands to his mouth and calling out into the darkness, rising and lowering his voice in a tribal cry. He waited for two or three minutes before giving the cry again. He was answered by the sound of hooves beating the dirt path. His black stallion melted out of the night and came to a stop before him, whinnying in greeting.

Lleu scratched the beast on his forehead and was met with an appreciative headbutt to his chest. The beast's loyalty was undying, having returned to him all those years ago after delivering the prince to safety in the South. His tack had burned in the castle stables, but Lleu was no stranger to riding bareback. He pulled himself up onto Bloodbringer and nudged the horse on, away from Maradah.

It was a relief to get away from the city. He rolled his shoulders, trying to ease the tension in them. His father had seen through him. The thought made him tight with anxiety. How could he have been so careless?

And Cain. Cain. His brother. The sight of his spilled blood and the smell of his burning flesh were hard to keep at bay. Cain may have been the first but he was unlikely to be the last. He let out a tense breath, focussing on the stars to drive the thoughts from his mind.

He nudged Bloodbringer on, eager to distance himself from Maradah and more eager still to reach Ramsridge.

It was an eight-mile ride, and on his journey he passed through several abandoned hamlets that surrounded the city. They were eerie in their silence. Doors were left hanging open on their hinges, children's toys left scattered outside houses, and washing left out to dry many moons ago still swung in the light breeze. They were running out of villages to raid for slaves. He prayed Ramsridge would remain safe.

As he gained distance from the city, he began to feel more himself. The hamlets and villages began to show some signs of life. Candlelight flickered in windows, though it was quickly extinguished as soon as his presence was noticed.

An hour later he reached Avonmar, the last town before his destination. He was relieved to find the place untouched. Even the town's pub was open. He paused outside to listen. No music, and only a handful of people inside, but at least there was a little laughter. Ahead, he saw two teenage girls chatting by lamplight. They were making paper lanterns, for new year, no doubt. They looked up at the sound of his approach and he nodded in greeting. The sight of him caused them to jump to their feet in fear, gathering their things hurriedly. By the time he neared them they had already escaped into the safety of their home and locked the door behind. It wasn't so long ago that he would have been warmly welcomed here. How times change.

He nudged his horse on again, passing through the town at a trot, not wishing to cause any more alarm to locals.

As Avonmar petered out, he turned east onto a narrow path that would lead him to the lake. The moon was nearly full and the stars sparkled in a cloudless sky. Ahead, ice mountains reared up, painted shades of silver and grey. He followed the path alongside a fast-flowing stream which tumbled into miniature waterfalls as the landscape climbed. Bloodbringer's breath clouded in the cool air as he powered up the slope.

When the ground levelled out, the lake came into view. It stretched far into the distance, a mirror to the night sky. Where the stream began at the lake's edge, a statue of Athys stood. Where once tributes of food would have been left at her feet, now there were only flowers. The palimore, like all Thelonians, devoted their worship to the earth god, but Lleu still remembered the prayers his mother offered to the water goddess. He dismounted and bowed his head to the Vyara as he passed.

Beside the statue stood a long line of graves stretching out along the waterline. The resting place of his family. He walked past the graves of his siblings. Of their children, and their children's children. Mortal lives were cruel in their brevity. He paused before one of the graves and knelt. A small pyramid of quartz spheres formed a traditional Waterlands headstone. He pulled away some of the weeds that grew between the stones.

'Mother,' he said softly. Unsheathing his sword, he drew its edge across his index and middle fingers. Blood pooled up under the metal's touch. He let it drip on the topmost stone of the pyramid. 'Earth my body, air my breath, water my blood. Athys guard your rest.'

It was a brief ritual, but he completed it without fail on coming home. It had been over a century since he had lived here, but he would return to visit his remaining family whenever he could. He watched a drop of his blood flow down the side of the topmost sphere. She had died a lifetime ago and now he struggled to picture her face or recall the sound of her voice. His father had never been to visit the grave. She had simply been another encounter on a state visit to the Waterlands, long ago.

He stood, sucking the remaining blood from his fingers, eager to continue.

He left the horse grazing and walked further along the lake's edge. Ahead lay the house he was born in, a large stone farmhouse, now home to his great great nephew and his family. No lights burned in the windows. It was late. They must be sleeping. Lleu pulled a bag of coins from his belt and left it on the doorstep, keen not to wake them. His regular donations were the only thing keeping the family going since their flocks were liberated by merchants.

Beyond the farm stood a small wooden hut, built at the end of a jetty that stretched out over the water. A smile stretched across his face as he walked towards it. Home.

He stepped carefully across the jetty's slats, hoping to take Raikka by surprise. When he reached the door, he lifted it slightly to avoid its usual creaking. No lights burned inside. He stole up the narrow wooden stairs to the bedroom. Moonlight spilled across the bed, lighting up her sleeping form, huddled under mounds of silk. Coming closer, he snuck a hand under the corner of the bed sheets, his smile widening the whole while. With a quick movement he pulled the sheets back and reached out to pull her into his arms.

But she wasn't there.

The bed was cold and empty. Just mounds of fabric. A sudden chill took him. He glanced about in panic. 'Raikka,' he shouted, bounding back down the stairs. He was sure the raiding parties hadn't been this far. He had been sure she would be safe here.

Downstairs he cast about for evidence of what had happened. There were no obvious signs of a struggle. Her half-embroidered fabrics were piled in one corner, unstolen. A plate of food sat on the table unfinished, flies buzzing around it.

'Raikka,' he called again. His heart was pounding. Where could they have taken her? The Pullman mines? The Great Bays?

He barged through the door and ran back across the jetty. Had the farmhouse been raided too? A cold sweat prickled on his skin. His mouth went dry.

A shadow caught his eye in the trees behind the house. Something or someone was coming towards him at speed. He drew his sword.

The shadow reached the edge of the thicket and burst into the open, arms outstretched. Raikka tumbled into him, knocking his sword to one side as she reached her arms around him. The surprise and relief of seeing his wife put him off balance and the pair fell to the ground together.

'Lleu,' she breathed excitedly, kissing him up and down his face.

'I was ready to kill you. Gods, don't do that again.' They were both panting.

She sat up in the grass and took the sword out of his hand, laughing. 'I only wanted to surprise you. It was easier than I thought.' She was wearing one of the dresses she was so famous for making, the silks ripped and muddy from dragging them through the thicket.

He pulled her towards him again. 'I thought they had taken you. I thought –' He broke off and kissed her.

She pulled back from him, still giggling. 'I was only checking the crayfish traps. Couldn't sleep. You're always so paranoid.'

He sighed. 'It's been a hard two days. I'm so glad to see you.'

Her smile waned to concern. She ran a hand along his jaw. 'You look tired… What's happened?'

Cain's flailing body flashed into his mind. He shook his head. 'Later, later.' He took a deep breath, his heart beginning to slow. Apprehension shone in her dark eyes. 'Don't worry, it's okay.'

'We're still safe here?'

'I hope so. For now. The raids for slaves haven't moved beyond the outer limits of Maradah.'

'No one followed you?'

'No. They've got other things to worry about at the moment. No one could suspect I was coming here.' Other than his father, perhaps. He kept the thought to himself.

'Why are you wearing armour?' It chimed metallically as she rapped her fingernails against his chest. He loved the way her accent tripped over the word ar-moor.

'Just keeping it safe. There was a fire. Most people lost

theirs. I don't intend to let anyone swipe mine while I'm away.'

'A fire?' Worry still creased her face.

'Later, I promise. Look, help me get this off.' He unstrapped his arm braces, and she seemed to relax. She helped him unbuckle his breastplate, and he tossed the shell to one side. 'That's better.' He stretched his arms up and rolled his shoulders. 'Come here.' He pulled her close. 'I've missed you.'

'You should visit more often.'

'It's too risky. You know the penalty for marriage.'

'I could come back with you. Work in the fields—'

'No.' He regretted the edge to his voice. 'No,' he said, softer this time, 'I couldn't bear it. The townsfolk are worked to death.' And she would see the true monster he was as a working soldier. 'I worry enough with you this close to the city.'

'Then quit. Stay with me. We could run away. I'd take you back to Ionia. You could meet my family.'

Lleu sighed. He wished she would stop asking him to leave. 'I'd like nothing more.' He cupped her face, her long black hair falling over his hands, soft as the silks she peddled for a living. 'And I promise we will, soon. I have things I need to get done first. The Waterlands will never be free if no one stands to fight for it.'

'Soon, you say? By your timescale or mine?'

He kissed her forehead. 'My age doesn't make the minutes I spend away from you pass any faster. Listen, let's not argue. I can only stay a few hours.'

She sighed, looking up at him with eyes that matched the black of the lake. 'It gets so lonely here.'

'I know. I miss you too.'

She leaned over and kissed him, tender lips embracing his

own. He rolled onto his back and pulled her into his arms. It felt good to hold her. The tension seemed to melt out of him and into the cool ground.

She pulled his shirt open. The night air was cold on his bare skin but he didn't mind. She traced her fingers along the jagged scar that ripped from his navel to his ribcage. He'd earned that one in the battle of Seal Bay. To save him, his fellow soldiers had given him a near-lethal dose of vish. He had been lucky. Remembering their kindness through that time released a flare of guilt at his plans of betrayal, but Raikka kissed him again and he let go of the thought.

She had a way of doing that. Of drawing the soldier out of him. She made him feel like the boy he'd been, long before he was enlisted to palimore training.

She pulled the shoulders of her dress down around her arms, revealing her modest breasts and bud-like nipples.

'Cold?' he asked.

She grinned back at him. 'Warm me up then, soldier.' She let the dress drop down.

He matched her smile and pulled her down towards him, and for a sweet, brief moment, all thoughts of the palimore were forgotten.

CHAPTER EIGHT

Savanta's body ached from where the ropes had held her captive in the gatehouse. The wind rolled in from the sea and carried her fast from the city. She struggled over the forest, casting her eyes down to the carpet of green below, unsure of where she was going or why she was here. She began to glide down, needing to rest, needing to sleep.

As she descended, a magpie flew at her and they nearly collided. She tumbled in the air to avoid it and straightened out her flight. It turned and swooped after her.

'No rest yet,' it cawed. 'He's not far.'

She gawped for a moment and the bird eyed her as if to say, what did you expect?

'Zenith?'

The bird dipped his head. 'I'm always here.' A trace of the Vyara's smooth tones chimed through the bird's rough throat. 'You'll find the prince over the next hill. He's with a Guardian under that large holly ahead.' The word Guardian seethed from his beak.

'I'm too tired for another confrontation. Everywhere you send me I end up…' She trailed off. 'Just let me rest. Please.' She began to descend again. The wind grew stronger, forcing her up. She beat harder. It was an effort to bring her wings forward under such strong gusts. She was determined to win this. He would not have control over her will to go where she pleased.

The bird didn't seem phased by the winds. 'You'll only tire yourself out, honey,' it said.

'Fuck you.' She threw herself downward, flapping faster and harder, throwing everything into fighting against him to reach the ground. The wind changed direction, tossing her in the air, and then it dropped completely. Panic gripped her. She began to plummet backward towards the ground.

Twisting her body in the air, she righted herself just as the first twigs scratched her skin. Her thin wings caught on the branches. She beat hard and gained control again, narrowly escaped falling through the canopy.

'You're getting better at flying,' remarked the bird.

'You nearly killed me!'

'Think of it more as a life lesson. Never disobey me.' The bird cawed. She pulled herself higher into the air, panting to catch her breath. 'Now, as I was saying… on to that holly tree.'

The prince and the Guardian sat at a small campfire. Savanta watched them from the safety of a tree beyond the light of the fire. Neither figure was what she had imagined. The prince was rough-looking. He was skinny, with unkempt hair and a scruffy beard. He drank from a flask, and his occasional outbursts of laughter and the longing way he looked at his female companion told her that it wasn't water he was drinking. He struck her as a beggar.

She had heard about Guardians before, but mostly from

childhood stories, where they were portrayed as villainous witches from the Ionese mountains. The tales were meant to serve as a warning to young children; practicing the void in Thelonia meant a death sentence. This woman looked nothing like the witches from the stories. Her whole being was in contrast to the prince; graceful, elegantly dressed, serene in her conversation. She sat alert, speaking confidently, and looked as though she was constantly calculating her thoughts.

'I can't make out what they're saying,' whispered Savanta to the magpie, who was perched on the branch above her.

'They're making plans for their journey south.'

'South? Are they running away?'

'They're in need of allies if Threon wants to liberate his home. The Guardian wants him to seek help from Vituund, the King in the Southlands. Her people have already pledged support to the Waterlands.' His magpie voice scraped over the word *Guardian*.

'You don't like the Guardians?'

'They have their uses.' He ruffled his feathers. 'For now.'

'Bad history with them?'

'They didn't teach you much in history class, did they?'

'I didn't go to school.'

'I see.'

She rolled her shoulders, easing the pain in her muscles. She strained her ears to hear, but the wind hissed through the mostly-bare trees and kept her from catching their conversation. The prince was an intriguing figure. He seemed so coarse, so different from the polished figure of the Empress. He commanded no deference from his companion, but this didn't seem to bother him. She wondered what he must have been through to lose his grace, his castle and his people. It was staggering to think of the complaints back in the Greylands; the raiding parties were labelled idle for not providing enough provisions. Seeing this place for herself had been shocking. The palimore had picked this kingdom near bare to feed her people back home.

The prince stood up, stretching loudly. He turned away from the fire and walked towards them.

'Now's your chance,' said Zenith. 'Time to introduce yourself.'

Threon came to the edge of the clearing where Savanta sat, and began to piss against a nearby tree.

'You're the prince,' she said. Startled, he turned towards her, grabbing a knife from his belt. 'Up here,' she said. 'I'm coming down now. Don't be afraid. I'm here to help.'

She scrambled down to the ground and walked towards him. He held out his knife to her, mistrust on his features. 'Who are you?'

'My name's Savanta. I think we may have a mutual friend. Please, put the knife down. Do I look like a soldier?'

It was near pitch black. She could tell that he hadn't seen her for what she was. She opened her wings, revealing her silhouette.

He took a step backwards. 'What are you? Who sent you?'

The Guardian was on her feet now, and took a few paces towards them.

'I have the Vyara to thank for my appearance. I'm not as evil as I look.' She had meant it as a joke, but the words fell flat in the tension. 'I was held captive in what remains of your city. A soldier freed me and told me to seek you out. And here I am.' Not out of choice, she thought to herself, but it wouldn't help her to say so.

'A soldier?'

'He had blue eyes. Unusual for a Thelonian.'

'That makes two of us he's risked saving.' The prince's frown softened. 'Can you fly?'

'Yes.'

'Could be useful.'

'It is, sometimes.'

The witch had come closer now. She looked Savanta up and down, her face unreadable. 'This one is godstouched,' she said, warning in her tone.

'She has wings,' countered the prince.

'You say you're here to help us?' the witch asked.

'If I can,' said Savanta, bristling. There was something about the Guardian that put her ill at ease.

'Why?'

Because she was told to. Because she had no choice. But there was one honest answer she could give that might satisfy. 'I thought Thelonia was importing goods fairly. The Empress sent me here as Watcher. I had no idea what our soldiers were doing to your country. If I can help make amends, I will.'

'Which Vyara do you serve?'

Savanta's eyes flicked up to the tree. The bird was gone.

A whisper of anger broke through the Guardian's composure. 'The sky god?'

'To my misfortune,' she said. 'I didn't choose this.' She met the Guardian's eyes.

'Threon, we can't trust her. She's under another's influence. Zenith is a trickster and a deceiver.'

'Hang on,' he said, waving the comments away. He was frowning and looking closely at her wings. Savanta stretched them out again, and a smile played on his lips. The Guardian stepped back, her face heavy with displeasure.

'She's remarkable.' His eyes met hers. 'What's it like? Flying?'

'Like freedom,' said Savanta. Most of the time.

He turned back to his companion, awestruck. 'She could be so useful to us.'

'She's dangerous.'

'She said herself, she didn't choose to be this way.'

'Yes, and she doesn't have a choice in how she's manipulated either. If you bring her into this the consequences will be on your head, not mine.'

'Zenith wants to support you,' said Savanta. 'He would make a powerful ally.'

Threon cocked his head at his companion. 'She's right. And we need all the help we can get. We have to give her a chance.'

The next morning, Threon set off on the road with Azzania. With no other animals available to them, the pair shared the Guardian's mare. Azzania insisted on taking the reins and thwarted Threon's attempts to hold her around the waist with a scowl. Travelling had been slow along sheep trails that ran far from the main roads. It was late in the evening when they reached Getty's Falls. The waterfall was narrow, but fell from an enormous height, roaring loud as the waters tumbled to join the river below. Threon and Azzania made camp at the edge of the water and busied themselves foraging for their supper.

Above them, at the point where the river rippled over the cliff, Savanta stood, staring into the distance. She had flown ahead, growing tired of the slow pace. At her side stood Zenith, in human form. His star-stitched cloak billowed behind him in the wind.

'He's an interesting fellow,' he said, gazing down at the couple below. 'I do rather enjoy backing an underdog.'

'That strategy seems to have worked out so well for you,' she remarked.

'You grow too familiar with me, my dear.'

'What are you going to do? Ruin my life again?'

'Oh, don't be so dramatic.' He put a hand on her shoulder

and joined her in looking out across the jagged horizon. She shuddered at his touch. 'If you had your own free will in this little game of ours, would you still be going with him?'

'If I wasn't mixed up in this "little game", I'd be living peacefully at home, contentedly oblivious to the problems of the wider world.'

'"Contentedly oblivious." How foolish. You only get one life. It surprises me how often mortals are happy to waste it. At any rate, your ambition to explore the skies is what made you a player in our game. You only have yourself to blame. So, now you're in it, what do you think? Would you have chosen his side of the fight without me? Really, I am curious to find out.'

'What does it matter? Without you, I wouldn't be here. With you, I seem to have no choice in the matter.'

'Ah, this bitterness will fade… I can feel your joy when you stretch those wings in the air. I've shown you places you would never have seen and gifted you a role in the palace. The life I have given you is brimming with excitement, and we've barely even begun on our journey. Do you know what most people would give up just to see the Vyara?'

'What do you expect to happen? The Waterlands has no army – just farmers and a distant hope of support from the south. Have you seen the palimore? They'll be slaughtered like animals.'

'Ah. But this ramshackle army is backed by a deity.'

'Fighting an immortal army, backed by the King of the Gods.'

'My brother won't hold that title for long.' He smiled, but there was a hardness to his voice.

She sat down at the cliff edge, allowing her legs to dangle over the side. She sighed. 'I don't know what to think.' She certainly didn't agree with the way the palimore treated people here. And before she had reached Thelonia City she had never imagined that so many could live in such wealth, while the rest of the island lived in such squalor. A change might not be such a bad thing.

Zenith picked up a pebble and skimmed it across the smooth waters at the top of the waterfall. He must have heard her thoughts. 'I'm glad you have some morals at least. You'll see, things will be better when Deyar and his puppet Empress fall.'

'But you want to rule. Wouldn't the world be a more harmonious place with a united Trinity? "Three forces rule life; Earth your body, Air your breath, Water your blood. Devote yourself equally to their graces to reward the soul".'

The air went cold. 'You dare quote scripture at me?' His voice was deep and low. A dark cloud passed in front of the sun. 'You are mine. I could extinguish the life in you in the blink of an eye.' He stepped towards her. She stood and backed away from the cliff edge. 'You work for me, or you die. Do I make myself clear?'

'Yes, yes.' She bowed her head to him, flicking her eyes up to keep him in her sight.

He stepped closer so that he was looking down on her. She found she was unable to take another breath. A burning sensation built in her lungs. She looked up at him, eyes wide with panic, clawing her hands at her throat. He lifted a hand to her face and placed his finger against her lips. 'Don't you forget it.'

A bolt of lightning flew from the sky and enveloped his form. In a flash he was gone.

She inhaled a deep breath, and another. Tears stung at the corners of her eyes. Rain began to fall. She shook herself and turned back to the cliff edge.

Both Threon and Azzania were looking up at her, their attention drawn by the lightning. Threon called to her, waving, but she couldn't make out what he was saying. She launched herself off the cliff, gliding down towards them.

She felt no joy as she did so.

The journey took nearly three weeks.

Savanta flew for the most part, scouting their route and advising them to change path when palimore could be seen ahead.

When the winds were calm she would walk beside their mare. Threon was full of questions, keen to learn more about her island home. Azzania said very little. She emitted an aura of calm, but Savanta found her silence unnerving.

She enjoyed watching the pair from the air. Threon would lean back discreetly on the horse so he could watch the witch's face. Azzania's frown gave it away that his attentions were not as discreet as he perhaps hoped.

Savanta grew to like Threon. He was good-humoured, and she enjoyed his stories, and his singing even more so.

When it felt safe they would spend the night at a local inn, paying with Azzania's modest funds, which had been supplied by the Guardians. As they travelled further south, more and more people began to recognise him. Known for his busking, they called him the Vagabond King. At one inn a tradesman presented him with a battered old kestro. For the rest of their journey his playing bought them the best food available, and the softest beds.

Everywhere they went, Savanta was eyed with a mix of suspicion and awe. Many mumbled chants for protection under their breath as she passed. On one occasion, Threon had reached for a knife to protect her from a group of drunks. Even Azzania had stepped forward in her defence.

By the time they approached the border of the Southlands, Savanta had come to feel an affinity for her new companions.

The first time she had felt true kinship since she left her father on Windracer.

Inns were different in the South. The stone buildings of the North made way for earthen structures more suited to the drier climate. This one was cool inside and gave pleasant respite from the sun that shone warm here, even in winter. Azzania had grown up in the mountains of Ionia and felt better suited to snow. This climate made her sluggish and the long days of travelling wore hard on her.

Threon had bartered with the innkeeper for a light meal, stabling and a room for the three of them in return for an evening's musical entertainment. Azzania was impressed by how many people recognised him as they travelled further south. His reputation preceded him and she was beginning to see why. Tonight he sat on an upturned wooden crate and played a repertoire that spanned the whole mainlands, even making a go of songs from as far away as the mountains of her home. Local drinkers were enthralled.

He finished his song and gave thanks to the crowd, promising to play again after a short break. He put down the kestro and came to join her and Savanta at their table. A grinning local followed quickly behind with a tray of drinks for the three of them, professing his gratitude for the music before leaving them be. Azzania ignored the drinks and sipped at her water. Savanta was poring over the inn's map and picked up one of the ales.

'Not far now,' said Threon.

Savanta traced a finger along a path that looked to join a wider road in around five miles. 'We'll be there tomorrow,' she said. Threon nodded.

'Have you thought more about your address to the king?' asked Azzania, not for the first time.

He sighed. 'I honestly don't know. Things are so different here.' He gestured around them at the inn, bursting with happy, prosperous locals. 'How can they even begin to imagine what it's like at home? Where's the threat?'

'They have to see,' said Azzania flatly. 'If you don't win their support...' She met his eyes. He understood the gravity.

Her kingdom had the foresight to protect their neighbours. An immortal society was unlikely to stop after running one country dry. The Southlands had to see sense. Without them, she feared the Ionese army would go back on their promise of defence. And if she couldn't enact this campaign, her position in the order of Guardians would remain stagnant.

'Could your magic help?' Savanta asked her.

'The void isn't magic,' she said patiently. 'It's a path to access a deeper part of ourselves – and others.' She could see the Thelonian didn't really understand, but how could she blame her? The poor woman had grown up with indoctrinated ignorance on that island. 'I can only take away any strong emotion the king holds onto. I'm unable to influence decision making. I cannot control free will.'

Threon reached his hand across the table towards her. 'It felt like magic before,' he said. 'Try it again?'

A senseless use of the void, but there was something that made her humour him. She had grown surprisingly fond of this vagabond. The first day she had found him beside the rubble of the castle, her heart had sunk. He was a beggar, not a king. And yet, as they travelled together, as he told them stories of his past, as she saw the way he inspired others through song, she began to see a flicker of leadership and the man he could become.

He smiled and grabbed her hand. Her instinct was to pull away from him, but she didn't. Such a brazen move would be highly disrespectful in Ionia, but he had little knowledge of their customs. She shook her head and returned his smile. 'The void isn't a triviality to play with.'

'Come on,' he said impishly. She bit her lip to tame her smile. He was so naive. Her touch had the power to lay bare his emotions. In a moment, she could curtail his confident showmanship and leave him with stagefright. She had the power to take everything from him, leave him a hollow shell lacking all sentiment and passion. But he didn't fear the void, and for some reason she humoured him. She intertwined her fingers in his. He sat alert, eyes bright with anticipation.

She sent a ripple of void through her palm and into his. His body slumped, muscles relaxed. Savanta prickled at the sudden change in him.

'He's okay,' said Azzania. The last time she had touched him with the void, he had been in physical and mental pain. Her touch had been a relief. Now he was healthy and confident, enjoying the attention this evening had brought. The void drained his energy. It made him neutral. Serene. It also laid him out to her like a canvas, his being painted in emotion and fragments of memory. She was careful to hold back from delving too deep, prying where she might not be welcome. 'How do you feel?' she asked.

'Relaxed. Peaceful.'

She held his mind lightly in hers, feeling his presence; this man was generous, proud and loyal. She felt a spark of his attraction towards her too, and hoped the heat rising in her cheeks didn't show. That was a thread of emotion she daren't pull. She let go of his hands.

Threon straightened his stance again. 'Magic,' he confirmed with a grin. 'Like the peace of deepwater swimming.'

'You should be careful offering your mind freely to a Guardian like that. We're not all nice.'

'No?'

'No.' Her mother, for one. The only person standing between Azzania and her rightful place as High Priestess.

'Well, you're hardly palimore.' Threon was being jovial, stuck with the misconception that a Guardian's placidity meant they were harmless. Guardians weren't soldiers, but they had other ways to kill. Azzania's own ambitions within the order had taught her that harsh lesson.

She aspired to reach the very top of her order and take her mother's place as High Priestess. Azzania was better practised with the void than any of the senior Guardians. Her mother's jealousy of her powers had nearly proved Azzania's undoing. Ambition within the order was a quick way to win lethal enemies, whether they were family or not. The queen had promised to grant Azzania her mother's title if she could successfully unite the Mainlands against Thelonia. When her mother heard the news that her daughter had been granted an opportunity to take her place, she had tried to poison Azzania. It had been a narrow escape. Her mother's plans had been foiled when Azzania sensed the nerves of the servant who had delivered the lethal dish.

She offered him a small smile. 'Be careful who you trust.' She stretched out her back and stood. 'I think I'll retire to bed. It's been a long day.' He protested that she should stay until he had finished playing, but they both knew that when he got into his performance he was likely to keep going until the ale stopped flowing. Savanta stayed with him, and Azzania pushed through the crowd to seek solitude.

Threon carried an air of confidence about him as he approached Bannvar. Like he was coming home. It felt good to feel warm sun on his skin and desert sand in his shoes. This city had transformed him from cosseted young royal to a streetwise man, and seeing the place appear at the horizon had brought a thousand fond memories rushing back.

The enforcers on the city gate left their posts to come out to greet the party. There were four of them. Two in front with swords, and two behind, bows strung with arrows ready for loosing. They stopped several metres from the gate and the archers trained their sights on Savanta.

'Greetings, namsan,' said Threon, after dismounting from the horse. He wore his ragged Bannvarian robes, and the greeting in local dialect softened their expressions.

'Wait, is that the Vagabond King?' said one. The guards in front frowned as they studied his face, then recognition flashed in their eyes. 'We thought you were long gone.'

'All this recognition will do wonders for his ego,' muttered Savanta to Azzania. Threon shot her a glance.

'I'm back,' he told the guards, beaming and gesturing to the kestro strapped to the back of his saddle. 'A little worse for wear than last time I was here, admittedly.' He pulled at his threadbare robes and straggled hair. 'Please,' he said, speaking to the archers, 'put those down. This is my friend, Savanta.' He took her hand and brought her forward, closer to them. She extended her wings and flourished a bow. 'She is godstouched. An insult to her is an insult to the Vyara.' The Southlands still observed equal worship of the three gods; as they had neared the city on their journey, devotion to Zenith had made it easier for people to accept Savanta's strange appearance. The guards gave her another suspicious glance before lowering their bows.

'Alright then. Welcome back.'

'Thank you,' said Threon.

The guards let them pass and they strode into the city, an island of architecture amid desert sands. Most of the city was built from bricks of red pise, a mud-clay, that required maintenance whenever a rare rainstorm fell. Buildings lined either side of the wide high street which was dotted with hawkers and market stalls. Ahead, the high city rose above these buildings, red earthen towers stretching into the sky. Threon breathed in the familiar smells of the city and his stomach rumbled as he took in the market's toasting spices, aromatic stews and honeyed pastries.

His return was an entirely different experience to his first visit, when he had arrived a wounded beggar. They had tried to drive him out of the city. This time he was welcomed. A couple of people recognised him, asking where he would be playing that night, keen to hear news from the North. But his foreign companions drew even more attention by their exoticism. People stopped and stared.

They made their way through the bustling city to the palace gates.

More heavily armoured enforcers guarded this door. They held long, ornamental axes diagonally in a cross over the entrance. They didn't move as the three companions approached.

'We seek an audience with the king,' said Threon.

'On whose authority?' asked one of the enforcers.

'They obviously don't recognise me,' he whispered to Savanta out of the corner of his mouth. 'I'm Threon Greenbrooke. Surely you've heard of me? I come with important news for your kingdom.'

'Not without prior authority from our lord. Move along, bard.'

Azzania stepped forward. The axes twitched in the guards' hands.

'You can't possibly be afraid of me?' she cooed.

Looking slowly from one to the other, she held their gaze. Both relaxed their stance. She stood between them and put a hand on each of their chests. The tension visibly melted away from them.

101

'We mean your king no harm.' Her voice was a whisper. 'You would be doing no wrong by allowing us to pass. Do you understand?' The guards looked at each other. One shrugged.

'Sounds reasonable,' he said. The other joined him in pushing open the heavy wooden gate.

Threon and Savanta shared a look. Azzania offered them both a small smile. Threon had never met anyone quite like her.

'Don't look so surprised,' she said, walking forwards. The entrance to the palace was highly decorated and the wooden doors reached up twenty foot from the ground. As the doors parted, acres of beautiful gardens were revealed to them. A tiled path led up to the palace itself. They passed sighing fountains, neatly clipped labyrinths and towering palm trees. In the distance a peacock called. The smell of jasmine filled the warm air.

Despite living in the city for five years, Threon had never been granted access to the palace. The place was incredible. Instead of the mud buildings of the main city, here everything gleamed marble. Walls and floors were artistry, painted bright by patterned tiles. They entered the main hall through a large ornate arch. Servants scurried through the vast, cool rooms.

Threon grabbed the arm of a passing serving boy. The boy's eyes grew wide with excitement as he recognised the singer. 'We seek an audience with the king.'

The boy bobbed his head. 'Yes, sir. The throne room is just past the centre courtyard.' He pointed.

'But you won't find the king there.' A deep voice came from behind them. Threon turned and the young lad hurried away.

'Your Majesty.' Threon smiled and bowed low. Savanta and Azzania followed suit.

'Stand,' the king commanded. Threon stood to greet him eye to eye.

Vituund's black beard hung in a single heavy plait, his

robes the same traditional blue that most men in the city favoured. Threon caught his own reflection in the ruby that shone from the king's turban and wished he'd made time to tidy up his appearance.

'My lord, my name is Threon Greenbrook. We met once before—'

'I remember. You were in my prison. What was it? Stealing? And I know what you want. The answer is no.'

'My lord, if you'd let me explain.' Threon was silenced as Vituund waved a hand in his face.

'If I was interested in the politics of the North, don't you think I would have invited you into my home when you first moved here?'

'You didn't have me thrown from the city,' he countered, playing to the man's better nature. 'You were willing to risk harbouring an exiled royal. It saved my life.'

'I'm no barbarian. But I won't be drawn into your fight. What's more, you bring a Guardian into my home, and if I'm not mistaken, that one has been godstouched.' His eyebrows lowered as he looked into their faces.

'My fight will soon be yours. I've travelled the land at the border of our kingdoms. The raiders are moving further south. When they have stripped my country bare they will come for yours.'

'More reason for me to retain my troops to defend my city walls. I've heard tell of the smouldering ruins that you claim kingship over. I've no interest in rushing to the defence of a king who rules over nothing but ash.'

Azzania stepped forward to address Vituund, breaking the unsettling glares the men were giving each other. 'This man is a true ruler. He has the full support of my county and its army. He speaks the truth when he tells you of the enemy's plan to move south.'

'Silence, witch.' The king turned to Threon. 'How dare you bring this evil magic into my home?'

Azzania continued. 'Let him prove himself to you.'

Vituund met her eyes and looked thoughtful for a moment. He pulled at the end of his beard.

'I don't think she knows what that means here,' he said quietly. 'But you do, Threon. You've lived here long enough. *Prove* yourself to me and I will hear you out.'

Azzania looked at Threon quizzically. 'The fighting pits,' he explained. Vituund was smiling now, amused. She moved to speak, but Threon cut her off. 'How would you have me prove myself, Lord?'

A look of excitement passed across the King's face, before he brought it under control. 'The triad of beasts,' he said soberly. 'You're here just in time for the new year fights and I have been waiting for an opponent worthy of them. I dare say the people of the city would go wild for a fight with their Vagabond Bard. The offer is there. Take it, and I will give you an honest hearing with my council. Refuse, and I will have you banished from the city.'

CHAPTER NINE

Empress Keresan breathed deep and slow. It was the eve of new year, and the time for sacrifice had come around again. Despite performing the ceremony each year for centuries, the feeling of nausea still bubbled to the surface. Ancients filled all available space in the underground temple. She could hear them beyond the gateway, shuffling on their feet, muffling coughs, whispering to one another. Those who hadn't managed to find a place inside the temple lined the streets outside.

Her first ceremony here was so distant in her memory that it nearly evaded her. Back then, the palace had not been built, and this temple was nothing more than a cave. She held no title and was yet to build her society of immortal courtiers and soldiers. Back then, she had just been a young woman with burgeoning ideas for a mineral she suspected to have enormous power. She took a moment to savour the atmosphere, to savour the world she had built for herself, and gave a prayer of thanks to Deyar for everything he had helped her win.

She pulled her thick white furs closer, shivering against the cold. The priest was waiting for her. He began the ceremony by breaking into a deep, low hum. The ancients around him joined in harmony, some raising the deep sound to tribal chorus.

Keresan's sons and daughters stood in line before her, and they began to move forward at the sound of the song. She waited at the edge of the crowd, and once they had all taken their place in a circle around the priest she marched into the chamber.

Pillars of gold and silver held bowls of bright fire which danced shadows and light across the smooth, domed ceiling. The air was damp and thick with the smell of earth and vegetation. Fresh flowers and whole trees had been brought into the room for the ceremony. The floor was laid deep with soft green moss.

This priest was new. She had cast the last one out after he suggested cutting vish rations. He stood at the centre of the round room, surrounded by the congregation. He looked nervous. Plump and grey-haired, he wore dark brown robes adorned with leaves and flowers. On his head he wore a crown of ivy, and his face was smeared with earth.

Heavy bands of stone and metal chimed together at her wrists and ankles as she walked. Her crown was shaped to include images of earth-bound animals in a circlet around her long hair.

She came before the priest and knelt on the soft ground.

The priest ceased humming, and those gathered to watch lowered the sound of their singing so they could hear his words. 'Empress,' he said. 'You come here before our god to represent your people.'

'I do.'

'You come here before our god to give thanks for his mighty works.'

'I do.'

'You come here before our god to plead for fortune in the year ahead.'

'I do.'

Matton, her eldest son, brought a silver bowl to the priest. The bowl was half a metre wide and piled high with vish. The chanting and humming faltered briefly and the eyes of those watching widened to see such wealth in one place.

The priest took the bowl and held it above her. She swallowed, slowing her breathing again to prepare herself. 'Lord Deyar, you bring us the gift of life eternal.' As she spoke, the priest lowered the bowl to the ground and mixed the drug with water from a silver pitcher. 'You gift us our bodies, you gift us the land on which we live, the land from which we eat. Today I pay tribute for my people.'

The priest handed her the bowl of thick liquid. She put it to her lips and began to drink. It tasted bitter as poison and was strong enough to kill a dozen members of the congregation. She prayed her millennia of overuse would again grant her immunity from overdose.

The chanting around her grew louder, faster. The first sip filled her body with warmth, sharpened her vision, made her feel strong. But as she forced back more of the cocktail her stomach lurched. She paused for respite. The priest pushed the bowl back to her lips with a shaking hand.

She continued to drink, retching between gulps. Saliva streamed down her chin. Tears streamed from her eyes. Her sinuses stung and her head began to throb.

When she had taken all of the drug, she fell forward onto all fours. The priest removed the bowl and retreated to the back of the assembled crowd, leaving her alone in the centre of the room.

Where she stared at the floor, her vision danced. She

attempted to push herself back to a kneeling position but fell again, dizzy. Her stomach began to heave, and she vomited hot liquid onto the mossy ground.

The purple-red bile stained her furs and she wiped the remainder from her mouth using her sleeve.

Looking up, the sea of chanting faces blurred. Their features all looked the same. Deep black eyes, and jaws that moved in unison to the chanting.

They parted, giving a wide berth as the priest came through them again, leading Neyleen, her most prized tyger. The beast was shackled at all four paws, pulling heavy chains between them. A metal muzzle circled her head and she walked slowly, drowsily, head hanging low. The priest locked the chains to a series of metal rings that protruded from the moss. Lastly, he drew the animal's head down and locked it to the floor, forcing the beast to the ground. Her agonised growl rose in harmony with the room's swelling song.

Matton was beside Keresan again. Her son helped her up and placed a dagger in her palm. She stepped towards the beast and staggered, crawling the last few paces to where her head lay. The tyger thrashed, and several ancients rushed to hold it down.

Keresan lay a hand on the beast's head. Her eyes were narrow and her breathing came short and fast. She kissed the soft fur between the animal's eyes and felt the growl rattle through her chest.

She held the dagger above her head and looked up to the ceiling. 'Deyar, we thank you for all that you give us.' Her mouth felt dry. Her vision faded in and out. 'With the time you have lent us, my people have crafted fantastic works. Breeding beasts such as this is just one of the wonders we have achieved with longevity.' She paused again, her stomach heaving once more. She took a steadying breath and managed to keep it down. 'Take her life as tribute to your awesome power. In return, we ask that you grant us life, peace and security until the end of time.'

She cut the knife through the tyger's thick white fur. The drug had leached away her strength but she managed to force the knife in to the hilt. The beast yowled through her muzzled jaw and beat her head and paws wildly, but to no avail.

The room seemed too bright. Keresan was wet with sweat. Her heart beat too loud, too hard.

Blood pooled into the moss. It stained her hands, her legs. The fur she was wearing was wet crimson.

'Deyar, accept our sacrifice!' As she cried the words, darkness flooded her vision and then she passed out.

Keresan awoke some time later to an empty room. The fires burned low.

She lay against the still-warm body of the tyger, covered in blood. Someone stood behind her. She turned, head throbbing.

The man before her was tall, broad, and muscular. His pupilless eyes shone milky white out of a dark face. She reached up a shaking hand to him. 'Deyar.'

The Vyara knelt and helped her come up to a sitting position. 'You served me well today,' he said, his voice deep as an earthquake.

He peeled bloody furs from her, leaving her bare skin streaked with red. 'You found the sacrifice pleasing?' she asked.

He lifted one of her hands to his lips and sucked the blood from it. 'Most pleasing.' She closed her eyes at his touch. 'You are ever my loyal servant.'

'I would break the Trinity a thousand times to make you king.'

He swept her bloody hair over one shoulder and traced a finger down her spine. 'My brother came to you recently.'

'His powers here diminish. My people do not serve him.'

'No. But across the water? The trinity remains strong, and in the Waterlands my sister holds great sway. I hear murmurings of discontent from my subjects across the sea. Famine follows in the wake of your raids. They blame you. And they lose faith in the god that you serve.'

'No, my Lord —'

'Don't contradict me.'

She shook her head, looked down. He stood again, paced around her and lifted her head with a finger. His white eyes bore down into hers.

'How can I best serve you?' she asked.

'There is a rebellion rising. Three kingdoms unite to crush yours. You must put a stop to them.'

'Yes, Lord.'

'When they are defeated, I want you to put an end to all those who serve Zenith and Athys. Repopulate the Mainlands with your people. We will begin again.'

CHAPTER TEN

T hreon paced the palace corridors with Vituund, running a hand along the smooth tiles that lined the walls.

'You were quick to accept the challenge,' said the king.

'You didn't give me much choice.' Threon followed him into another ornate room. The walls were lined with wooden cabinets, and Vituund made his way to the nearest one.

'Threon, I don't want you to think ill of me. I want it to be a fair fight.' He slid a cabinet door open, revealing a suit of armour. It was magnificent. Threon reached a hand out and ran his fingers over the boat that had been imprinted in gold on the breastplate.

'My sigil,' he breathed. No detail had been spared in the design of the suit. 'This is… It's incredible. It must be worth a fortune.'

'Priceless. But it doesn't really belong to me – not anymore.' His eyes shone as he spoke. 'This used to belong to your ancestor, Amel the First. He gifted it to Bannvar as a token of peace after uniting the Waterlands. I'd like to give it to you.'

He reached into the cabinet and lifted the breastplate out, handing it to Threon. It was surprisingly heavy in his hands. 'Heavier than you're used to?'

'It's been a long, long time since I've worn anything like this.'

'Well, I hope it brings you luck in the arena, and in the future, whether we fight the palimore side by side or alone.' He stepped across the room to another cabinet. 'There are these, too.'

Weapons. A longsword, shortsword, two daggers and a bow. Threon's eyes widened at the sight.

'Go ahead,' said Vituund.

His fingers nearly trembled as he reached for the longsword. It was broad, beautifully weighted, perfectly balanced. It sighed as he freed the blade from its sheath.

'It's been so long…' said Threon. He dropped the sheath on the floor and flourished the blade through the air.

'It suits you.'

A grin had spread across Threon's face. 'For the longest time I thought I'd never hold a sword again.'

'You hold it as if you haven't missed a day's training.'

'I practised a lot, back in the day. My parents were always disappointed that I spent so much time fighting.'

'Well, let's hope your lessons serve you well tomorrow.'

'It's been a long time.' Threon was almost speaking to himself.

'You're welcome to use the courtyard to train. I'm sure any one of my officers would be happy to spar with you.'

Threon was barely listening now, stepping through old drills, rousing memories from what felt like a lifetime ago. 'I have other things to attend now, Threon. I'll leave you to it. Three days until the games. Be ready. We want to see a good fight.'

The air was stifling beneath the fighting pits. The banks of seats above Threon shuddered as feet shuffled along them. The noise of excited crowds roared through the air.

He checked the edge of his sword against a finger. It pierced his skin as if it were the surface of water. A thin trickle of blood seeped out and he sucked it clean. The iron taste reminded him of many a wrestling match in the old barracks. He had the feeling today would prove to be rather more of a challenge.

Sweat dripped from his forehead, but not from nerves. He felt good. Strong. He wiped at his face and rubbed the sweat into the leather on the thighs of his suit.

A hush fell over the audience.

A closed door stood between him and the arena. He heard Vituund's voice echo from beyond it.

'I know you're all very eager for our special guest today. Who here has heard the tales and songs of the Vagabond King?'

A loud cheer went up from the crowd.

'He lost his kingdom, and all he has now are songs of a failing nation.' A pitiful 'aww' came from those gathered. Like being at the bloody theatre. 'But today! Today, we have given him a chance at glory. Today, he comes before you in the spirit of the Valiant King of old, bearing the sword of his ancestor, Amel the First. Today, he fights!' The crowd erupted in cheers. Feet stamped along the banks of seats and sand dropped on Threon from between the floorboards. Then the doors swung open.

Time to give them a show to remember.

Light pooled into the dark corridor and he stepped out onto the hot, sandy floor of the arena.

The pit was small. Perhaps thirty foot wide. Banks of seats rose steeply upwards from the circular space, protected from any pit violence by a mesh wire overhead. In the nearest row of stalls a group of five women lifted heavy ox horns to their lips and blew. A deep, ominous sound.

Vituund sat in a box that overlooked proceedings, his wife and children behind him. He leaned over the balcony, calling to the crowd. There was a brightness to his eyes, and his teeth shone behind a grin that spoke clearly of his zeal for a fight. 'Here he stands, a glimmer of the Valiant King emerging from this Waterlands soul. The Vagabond faces the Triad of Beasts; a challenge of earth, air, and water; of body, breath, and blood.' He puffed up his chest and looked around the audience with narrowed eyes. 'Now: earth!'

Silence swept over the crowd.

A door opposite Threon burst open as a large bull stormed into the pit. He didn't have time to think. He dived to the left to avoid the charging animal, and rolled back to his feet, sword at the ready.

The bull was enormous, with a shining black coat and huge curved horns, painted gold. The beast ploughed into the far wall, the impact of a tonne of muscle making the arena shake. It righted itself and turned to look at Threon. A mad fear shone in the animal's eyes. It hoofed the ground, head thrashing.

Threon stepped slowly sideways, eyes locked on the animal. It lurched at him again and bowled him over with a sinewed shoulder. As he fell, Threon hefted his sword at the bull's front legs. He drew a crimson gash in the black pelt.

The bull screamed and stamped backwards, almost trampling him. Threon stood once more, catching his breath. He ran at the beast, sword grasped with two hands, held high above his head. The bull swivelled, horns lowered. As Threon brought the blade down the animal twisted around, avoiding his blow. The sword hit the sand and the bull arched its head, catching him on the arm. The horn glanced his armour, scoring a line into his golden arm braces.

Threon backed away. The bull tossed its head, stepping sideways, watching him warily. Those horns could kill a man.

If he got caught head on by them… He needed a clear shot at the animal. His sword caught a glint of the hot sun as he raised it again, ready to attack. The bull snorted, sides heaving with feral anger.

The creature began to charge. Gods, the speed on it. Threon's heart quickened. He forced his breath to slow, gripped the sword steady. The animal was three paces away. Its head lowered. Two paces. One. Threon lunged forward with the blade as the bull's skull met his chest. He stabbed down on the back of the beast's neck. The animal cried out but didn't slow. It charged into Threon, forcing him up into the air. He tumbled over the animal's back and landed heavily in the sand.

He stood as the bull turned back, its whole body thrashing under the pain of the blow. It staggered at him but didn't have enough distance to gather much momentum. Threon rushed to get his sword in position then swung down and around in a sharp arc. He stepped to one side, avoiding another blow from the bull's horns. The blade slashed into the beast's neck.

Blood pooled out onto the hot sand.

The bull staggered.

It turned to charge again, front wet with blood. As it lurched towards Threon, horns lowered, it began to slow, and collapsed forwards onto its front knees. The blood continued to pour from the wound and the beast's head lolled. It fell to one side.

Threon walked towards the dying creature. He rested a hand on one of its golden horns. It tried to twitch away from his touch. 'You didn't ask for this.' The animal was still panting, eyes wide with fear. The crowd were cheering again.

He placed the tip of his sword between two vertebrae on the bull's neck and pushed down hard.

The bull's body spasmed and then lay still.

It was a poor way to end an animal, but Threon knew how to work a crowd. He sliced off one of the animal's ears and turned to them with a broad smile. They cheered as he tossed the bloody ear to the stalls and raised his red sword to the sky in victory.

The crowd turned to the royal box as Vituund stood. He stepped to the edge of the balcony and waited for silence before calling: 'Now: air!' So, there was no time to rest then. Threon had half expected they would move the bull's carcass, giving him a chance to prepare for what would come next.

The sun was blotted out momentarily by a swarm moving across the sky. A flock of birds descended on the arena. He sheathed his sword and fumbled to grab his bow. He'd never been much of an archer. His attempts on the road with the hunting bow had been unpredictable.

As they neared, he could make out the silhouettes of buzzards. Three dozen of them dove down towards him. He loosed an arrow randomly into the flock, hoping it would hit something. He reached for another, but they were already very close. He let it loose before he could fully draw the arrow back.

The birds filled the arena, smothering him with beating wings, pecking and ripping at his armour with their claws. He raised an arm to shield his eyes. His ungloved hand blazed with pain as sharp scores were etched in it.

He grabbed his sword again, flinging it from left to right, blind. As he did so he felt the blade catch several birds, but the smothering cloud of feathers didn't seem to abate.

He stepped backwards, edging himself against a wall, and felt the bodies of those he had hit crush under his feet. Peering through raw fingers, he swung at the flock again. The birds were quick and most dodged his attacks. He could feel them clawing beneath his helmet, drawing blood at his neck. Huge wings beat frantically against him. His chestplate shook as they battered against his body. He sank down into a protective ball.

A strong gust of wind swirled around the arena, driving some of the birds off course. He took his chance and leapt free of his attackers.

'Threon!' Amidst the buzzard cries he heard Azzania call his name. She leant over the stalls, holding a burning torch in his direction. He ran to her, birds swarming around him still. She pushed the torch through the mesh net that protected the audience and he grabbed it.

Waving the flame wildly about his head, he saw that several of the birds had caught fire. Feathers smoked and flickered in flame, compromising flight. They panicked in the air, darting like hell's fireflies.

The buzzards avoided the flame where they could, and he held the torch in front of him. His face ran with sweat from the heat, but he could now see the birds beyond the fire. With his sword he aimed more purposefully, taking one bird down after another. Cheering began to build again from the stalls.

The birds gradually reduced in number. Threon's arm ached from swinging the blade with one arm. When only three birds remained, they fled, leaving Threon alone.

He flung off his helmet, breathing heavily as he watched them go. He pulled out his bow once more and took aim, not feeling any of the compassion he had for the bull. The bastard creatures had torn him to ribbons. Blood dripped from every bare patch of skin. He flung one arrow, then another, then another, rage building all the time as each shot missed. His last shot broke the string of the bow and when they were out of sight, he hurled it to the sand with a cry of fury.

A nervous applause began to build. He had forgotten his showmanship. 'I will write a song for the one who can bring me those birds in a pie!' he laughed, pointing after them, breathing heavily through the gritted teeth of his smile.

Laughter broke out from the crowd and the applause came more freely now.

Threon wiped sweat from his face and stretched his limbs as the king stood once more. Another minute. Just a moment to catch his breath, that was all he needed.

The ground shifted suddenly, and Threon adjusted his stance as he saw the floor of the fighting pit slide open from the centre.

'Now: water!'

A large circular area opened up in the centre of the pit. It narrowly missed swallowing the bull's bloody body. Threon walked to the edge, kicking sand over the cusp. Beneath him sat a vast tank of water.

The shadow of a mernad swam just below the surface. Murmuring rose from the audience. He looked up to Vituund, who smiled and took his seat once more.

The creature rose to the surface. Its wet skin shone like that of a seal. Two large black eyes stared into his from a human face. Beneath the creature's torso, his fishlike body writhed to keep him afloat. In one of his webbed hands he held a dagger. In the other, a net.

'Amel,' said the mernad. They were simple creatures, native to the Waterlands, and spoke rarely.

Threon looked back up to Vituund with a scowl. The king gestured for him to proceed and leaned back in his chair to watch.

Threon began to pull off his armour, piece by piece. 'I'm not Amel,' he said to his opponent.

'Amel,' the creature repeated, its unblinking fish eyes on Threon as he undressed. Mernads were said to live longer than the lives of five men. Could this one remember the old king?

'No, I'm Threon. Do you understand why you're here?'

The mernad bobbed silently in the water.

118

Threon had stripped naked, now drawing whistles and calls from some of the women in the stalls. He hesitated before entering the water and looked again to Vituund. 'Proceed, Valiant King,' he said. 'We want to see how the story ends.'

He walked to the edge of the pool. 'Water my blood,' he muttered. Picking up his knife, he dove into the cold pool.

His eyes stung as he opened them in the salt water, but not nearly as much as his newly torn skin. The sound of the crowds was muffled by water in his ears. He watched the shadow of the mernad circle him, becoming clearer as his eyes adjusted to the water.

The mernad circled faster, spiralling to the bottom of the tank. Threon rose to the surface to take another breath, before kicking down hard to meet the creature on the sandy floor of the tank.

They watched each other for a moment, those large fish eyes staring intently. Mernads were not creatures to fight. They were celebrated in the legends of the Waterlands; a peaceful, simple people, usually only seen by fishermen as they were saved from drowning. They lived under the protection of Athys.

Instead of attacking, the creature dropped his dagger and net. He placed a hand on his chest and bowed low in the water. As he did so he descended lower into the tank, until his tail curled under him and he sat peacefully on the bottom.

They continued to watch each other through the water. After a moment Threon held out his dagger, offering it to his opponent. The mernad hesitated before reaching for the hilt.

He opened his webbed fingers and let the knife sink to the ground.

Threon bowed his head.

He kicked back to the surface and took in a deep breath, pulled himself out of the water and stood before the silent crowd, water running down his body. He pulled on the tunic he had been wearing beneath his armour, and it clung to his wet skin. The crowd watched in silence.

Vituund stood, coming to the edge of his balcony again. Before he could speak, Threon addressed the crowd.

'I stand before you now as the man you know. The Prince of Melodies, the Vagabond King… the King of Nothing. I am not my ancestors.' He nudged the armour that lay on the ground with a bare foot. 'King Amel founded the Kingdom that raised me. He liberated the people and creatures of the land from a century of tribal wars.

'My mernad friend here remembers. He honours the memory of my ancestor, just as you cheer at the thought of seeing a legend come to life in your arena. As he honours my blood, so I honour his. I will not kill those my family were pledged to serve.' A murmuring rippled through the crowd. At least they're listening. Threon took a deep breath and continued. 'Everything Amel, and his sons and daughters after him, fought to maintain has been at risk from the rising power of Thelonia. It is no longer at risk. It has been destroyed.

'My homeland has been defeated. My friends and family, and the people I was raised to serve are slain, enslaved or starving. I ran from my home when the raiders came. Your city took me in. Not as a royal seeking refuge, but as one of your own. I drank in your taverns, bartered on your streets, and loved your women.' A wry smile elicited a gentle laugh from the audience.

'You made me more of a man than any scholar, swordsman or priest ever could. You gave me humility, and an understanding of those I once hoped to call subjects.

'I came here to ask your king to help fight back against those who have destroyed my home and now encroach on yours. But standing here before you, I realise the decision is not his to make.'

He turned to the royal box. 'My Lord, you command my

highest respect, but I must withdraw my request from you.' He turned his back on the royal box and addressed the crowd again. 'Instead, I put it to you, the people of Bannvar. I have seen the soldiers from the West and fought against the immortals. It nearly killed me when I did, so I know that what I ask of you cannot be taken lightly. I ask you to risk your lives to bring peace to the Mainlands.

'Join me and you may face death, but stand and idly wait for this force to land at your door, and you face a more certain outcome. You will lock your doors, man your defences, but the forces will keep coming. An immortal army is patient, strong and doesn't give up. Our only chance of success lies in fighting on our terms. Together. We take them by surprise. We raid their lands as they do ours. We take their weapons, their strongholds, their vish. Only then can we face a fair fight.

'Stay comfortable for now if you wish. But I warn you, they are coming. The forces of Ionia and the Waterlands are uniting to take on this foe for the sake of our shared continent. Please don't leave us to fight alone.'

He stopped and looked around the faces looking down at him. He had their full attention. Some held tightly onto their children, others gripped the hands of their partners. So, something got through.

'Are you with me?'

Savanta and Azzania stood up in the crowd. There was a stunned silence. Nervous glances left and right.

'Are you with me?' Threon clenched his fists tight. This had to pay off.

Then more stood. A handful at first. Murmurs turned into hushed chatter, which grew louder and louder as more and more people came to their feet.

Vituund's voice cracked the atmosphere and brought everyone to silence. 'Quiet!'

Behind him, three of his four children were on their feet.

He turned to Threon, a twitch of anger on his face. 'It seems, my Lord, that democracy has won out.' He turned his head to look at his family, noting his children standing for Threon. He sighed and seemed to let go of his anger. 'You have my sword, and the allegiance of any man, woman or child who wishes to stand for your cause.'

He sat down, and the audience burst into cheers. 'Threon the Valiant!' cried one, and it echoed around the arena.

Threon was carried away to celebrate his victory in Bannvar's great hall.

Savanta could hear the cheers and strange music travel through the warm night air to where she sat with Azzania. They had been caught up in the crowds, and although they had tried to join their victorious friend, the hall was packed shoulder-to-shoulder with people and they couldn't get in.

Instead they found themselves in a small, crooked tavern in the centre of town. The mood was high. It felt like most of the city had watched the fight and the air was full of chatter about the future. Young men bragged about how they would defend their home, whilst others fretted about the dangers. But most of all, it seemed the city had enjoyed watching an underdog outstep a king.

The tavern was hot with the press of bodies and the warm evening air. Savanta had wondered at the architecture of this place, how a city could be built from mud. She loved the exoticism of the South. The people were as warm as the sand they built on, and the drinks were strong and sweet. Tonight she let herself relax, and Azzania had seemed to do the same.

After a couple of hours soaking up the atmosphere both women had grown quite drunk.

Azzania hid it well. Her tranquil composition prevented her from drunken outbursts, but her speech had become softer, slurred, her eyelids heavier, and when she stood, her gait became meandering rather than purposeful.

It had been a while since Savanta had had a real drink. Not since she left home over two months ago. For the first time in a long time, she felt at ease in her grey skin. Rather than feeling threatened she felt entertained by the strange stares she drew.

She sat now with Azzania, eyes locked on each other, a tray of mast, a strong local spirit, between them. A crowd had gathered to watch.

Azzania threw her head back, knocking back a shot of the spiced liquor. She placed the small clay vessel back on the tray, empty.

Savanta's turn.

She rested her chin on her hands, swaying slightly. The floor felt like it rose and fell like the deck of a ship. She exhaled, swallowing hard, and hovered her hand over the tray of cups, before selecting one that was full to the brim. The crowd cheered. She lifted the cup to her lips and finished it in two sour gulps. Her eyes returned to Azzania's. She smiled wryly.

'I wouldn't go for those big ones.' Azzania picked up another over-full cup. 'You're wavering already. I can see it in your eyes.' She drained the cup and lined it up on the table with the others she had finished.

'Don't underestimate me,' said Savanta. She finished another shot and slammed the cup on the table with a burst of drunken laughter. 'I'll drink you under the table.'

Money changed hands in the crowd. It hadn't escaped Savanta's notice that the bets locals were placing on their little drinking game were largely in favour of the Guardian.

Azzania finished and lined up another shot. Savanta slammed another to the table.

'You think your precious void will help you beat me?' She grinned.

Azzania took another drink. 'I know it will. And your Vyara? Will he help you?' She smiled.

Unlikely, she thought, raising another cup. 'Water my blood.' A wicked sense of profanity gripped her as she acknowledged a god her homelands had taught her to reject.

'Foolish child.' Another drink.

'I am living proof of the power of the gods.' She spread her wings for effect. 'Can you say the same for your void?' A few of their gathered audience stepped back, making the sign of protection across their hearts. As she reached for another drink, Azzania grabbed her hand.

At the Guardian's touch, Savanta's grey skin retreated. She stared down at her hand, watching the dark skin disappear, and pink flesh blossom up her arm. She pulled her hands away in shock. As Azzania released her, the grey returned again.

'Witchcraft!' The voice came from the crowd. A tankard was thrown in Azzania's direction, but missed, spilling the mast over the table. Those placing bets held onto their money and slunk backwards.

The bartender pushed his way through those gathered. 'None of that shit in here. Out. You're banned.'

A hand grabbed Savanta's arm and she was pulled out into the street. She paid little notice. The whole time she kept staring at her hands.

Outside, the fresh air hit her hard. Her head reeled and she fell back against a wall. Azzania helped her steady herself again. The Guardian's eyes had a sharp clarity to them. She now looked clear-headed; totally sober.

'How?' Savanta managed.

'Would you like me to show you?'

The next day Savanta woke on the floor. Her face was flat against cold, painted tiles, and her head throbbed. Opening one eye, she was surprised to find herself in an ornately decorated chamber. Two carved wooden beds stood at either end of the room. The walls were painted with intricate patterns and a large gilded fireplace was laid into one wall. This had to be the palace.

'Are you awake?' said Azzania from behind her.

She pulled her wings over her head with a groan.

'Get up. We're having breakfast with the king before making plans for the trip back north.'

She heard Azzania pace towards her and felt her shadow come over her. She lifted a wing to see her companion. 'I'm never drinking again.'

Azzania offered her a hand to get up. Savanta went to take it, but pulled back, remembering her touch from last night.

'Come on,' said the Guardian. Savanta took her hand. Nothing happened.

Azzania pulled her to her feet and Savanta slumped herself at the foot of one of the beds, head in her hands. 'What happened last night?' she asked.

'You challenged a Guardian to a drinking competition. Not a wise move on your part.' Azzania looked sufficiently smug, beautifully composed and completely sober.

'No, I mean…' Savanta trailed off, holding her right hand at the wrist, turning it over and over.

Azzania came to sit next to her on the bed.

'I'm sorry to have taken you by surprise like that. It would have been better to show you in private. And less drunk.' She offered a sympathetic smile and took both of Savanta's hands. 'Here. May I?'

Savanta felt sick and the world was horribly fuzzy. She nodded anyway.

Azzania closed her eyes. This time Savanta didn't pull back. Her hangover melted away at the Guardian's touch, and then her grey skin retreated to her wrists and up, past her elbows, her shoulders, her chest. She stared at her skin in wonder. As the void spread to her back, the edges of her wings began to retreat. It was an odd sensation, her bones retracting into each other. The thought of losing her ability to fly struck her with a sudden panic. She let go. The grey returned to her skin like a drop of dye to a thimble of milk. Her wings returned to their former shape. Her eyes met with Azzania's. She now felt even more nauseous.

'Zenith did this to you. But it can be undone. Learn the void and you can control his influence on you. You can be human again.'

Human again. It was something she had never dared hope for. Savanta longed for her old life, free of the Vyara with Erin in her arms. She often worried about how poor Erin would cope, growing up with a monster for her mother. Would the other children tease her? Would she even recognise her own mother under this skin? But the thought of losing the gift of flight now made her shudder.

'The void requires a pure mind. You're in no state today. We'll begin your lessons on the road.' Azzania stood. 'Come, some food will do you good. I hear the palace is home to some of the Mainlands' finest chefs.'

Honey-baked figs, butter-rich pastries, spiced sausages and sweet fruits laden with cream. It was a breakfast for kings and Threon ate ravenously. Savanta and Azzania had joined him and Vituund on a palace verandah several storeys above the city. He was grateful for the warm morning breeze. Back at home the colder climate would have knotted his muscles, worn from yesterday's fight. Despite the soreness in his limbs and the freshly scabbed scratches, he felt good. There was a sweet pleasure in besting a king, and Vituund had been uncommonly good-natured about the outcome in the arena. Perhaps he was beginning to understand the threat the raiders posed.

A servant leaned past Threon and poured steaming coffee into his silver cup. He was finishing off his third plate now, licking his fingers clean of honey and sausage fat. Vituund watched him with thinly veiled amusement.

'I'm glad to see you enjoy your food,' said the king.

'I'd be round as a hog if I lived with these kitchens.' Threon grinned and waved his cup in the air until a servant swooped in to add sweetened cream to the coffee. 'Besides, you'll get to see the kind of harvests we've been suffering at home when we go north. After a winter living on swede and rabbit, anything would taste good. But this, this is divine.' He leaned back in his chair and kicked his boots onto the table. If Vituund was perturbed by his behaviour, he hid it well.

'It was an impressive show, in the arena,' said Vituund. 'You have quite a set of lungs on you.'

'You won't find a man, woman or child who isn't at home in the water where I'm from.'

'So I've heard. I'm glad to see your brother's accident didn't put you off. You must have been quite young, after all.'

'It only pushed me to become a stronger swimmer.' Threon bristled at his comment. He had never fully healed from his brother's drowning. Threon had only been twelve at the time, his brother four years older. They had been very close and Threon had looked up to him; Thrandon was older, wiser, stronger. He was destined to be king, and being second-in-line, Threon had avoided the strict royal education that was enforced on his brother. Thrandon's death destroyed their father. He became fiercely protective of his only remaining son and indulged Threon's every wish. Threon grew distant from his mother, who remained pragmatic and insisted that he study as an heir should. Years of his father's doting meant that Threon only ever pursued the education he desired: music and swordsmanship. Now he found himself dealing in politics and war. Now he was racked with guilt for resenting his mother. She had only been trying to prepare him.

'Such a shame… They tell me he was quite the scholar, your brother.'

'He would have made a better king, you mean?' Threon snapped the words before he could stop them. Vituund looked taken aback and Threon held his hands up in apology. 'Sorry. It's been a long few days.'

'Not at all, not at all. There are other virtues beyond the wisdom to be gained from books.'

Threon let out a breath, cursing his lack of control. Vituund gave a placating smile and stood. 'I'll leave you to enjoy the rest of your breakfast. I should attend to the matter of gathering our troops for the campaign in the North.'

Threon nodded. 'Thank you. If you need any help…'

'I'll be sure to call for you.' A servant rushed to remove Vituund's half-finished breakfast as he made for the door. 'Make yourselves at home. I'll see you later for dinner.'

When he had left, Azzania said, 'You have a quick temper.' Threon shrugged.

'You mustn't let the past haunt you.'

'What would you know about my past?'

'When you share the void with a Guardian, there are some things that spill over from one mind to another.' She watched him closely. He couldn't hold her gaze and looked away. 'You worry that you're not worthy of leading your people. You can't let it hold you back.'

'I was never meant to be king.' He knocked his empty coffee cup over with the tip of his boot. He stood up from the table and pulled himself up to sit on the balcony's stone railings, looking out over the city below. His presence disturbed a pair of pigeons who flapped from the balcony into the pale blue of morning.

'You seem comfortable enough with a sword in your hand,' said Savanta, looking up from her plate for the first time. She looked rough, having pushed the food around her plate all morning, not speaking and barely eating. Threon was glad she had found time to enjoy herself last night.

'You should eat up, Savanta. We won't get another meal like this back on the road.' He arched his back and rubbed his belly. 'I feel fat as a babe feeding at the breast of the Mother herself.'

'The Mother?' asked Savanta. 'Who is she? I've heard her mentioned everywhere here.'

Gods, there was a lot they didn't teach them on the island. 'She's Mother of Thelonia too, whether Keresan's happy with the fact or not.' He came back to sit at the table. 'Your priests never mention her?'

'They're all for Deyar. Polytheism is a punishable offence.'

He had heard as much and wondered how much the Empress kept her people in ignorance.

'Even Deyar had a mother once.'

'Zenith too?' She looked nervous as she spoke his name, eyes flashing up as though her words might summon him.

Threon nodded. 'And Athys. All the same mother.'

'What happened to her?'

Azzania pushed her plate away, finished with her food. 'She left,' the Guardian said. 'It's said she bequeathed the world to them to share in harmony as they had done when they were young. Earth would work in harmony with water and create mountains, valleys, glaciers. Air and water would make tempests, snowflakes, rainbows. And air and earth together could spark fire. When all three came together, they made life.'

'Earth my body, air my breath, water my blood,' said Threon. 'You don't have this mantra?'

Savanta shrugged. 'We've heard it. Just seems the body's the most important bit.'

Azzania brought her fingers together in a steeple. 'The Mother charged the Vyara with protecting and providing for life across the world, and then she left. Deyar's claim to be some sort of king of gods – and Zenith's desire to take his place – is a direct contravention to their duty. They were born to work together, in harmony. None of this hierarchy and demanding exclusive worship.'

'But if Zenith can help us win in Thelonia…' said Threon.

Azzania sighed. 'Yes, it's got to be worth a shot. But at what cost?'

CHAPTER ELEVEN

They maintained a brisk pace to keep the cold off. The hooves of Lleu's mount slid through leaf mulch in the heavy rain. He was on duty with his acquisition group, scouting the borders of their territory. Wind hissed through bare trees as they rode the forest path that wound between villages. They were trekking back to Maradah following a short raid.

Deryn, a dark-haired woman who was taller than him, rode in front beside Anna, a small but fierce soldier. He rode at the rear with Fey, a soldier of a similar age to him who had replaced her front teeth with gold after her face had been smashed in during battle. He had once thought her attractive, but her scarred face and unsettling smile now just made her look dangerous.

On days like this, cold and wet, with rough company and unpleasant work, he longed to be back with Raikka.

'So what do you miss most?' said Deryn. They were talking about Thelonia.

'Oh gods, the people,' said Fey. 'How did I end up stuck out here with you miserable bastards?'

'Nah,' said Deryn. 'People are better here. No mincing ancients, barely any merchants now, just us palimore. A soldier can talk straight, not like them tossers.' She spat into the mud. 'Lleu?'

'Aside from missing sleeping under a solid roof? Got to be the food. Give me barracks rations any day. I'm fed up of rabbit stew.' They murmured in agreement. 'I don't miss the work though. Give me this any day over working in the mines.'

'Mines is easy work,' said Deryn.

'But you don't get this view.' He looked up at the soaring mountains above the treeline, still impressive behind a veil of winter weather.

'Yeah, if you can see it through the pissing rain.'

'Anna,' said Lleu, 'what about you?'

She turned around, leaning a hand against her horse's rear as she looked at him, a smirk playing on her lips.

'What?' he said.

'I miss it all. But I'll be seeing it again, long before you sods ever do.'

'What? How?'

'Deryn knows.' Deryn was smiling too, in on some secret.

'Knows what?' Fey was looking at the women suspiciously.

'She's pregnant,' said Deryn. Lleu was speechless for a moment. Infertility was rife among those who took vish. It was the reason the palimore breeding programme had been set up.

'Pregnant?' Fey's jaw hung open. 'Since when? How?'

'It must have happened just before I was posted here.' Anna was grinning. 'I've missed three cycles.'

'Gods, that's amazing.' Fey jumped from her horse and

wrestled Anna to the ground, gripping her in a tight hug. They laughed together as Anna fought to get free.

'Careful, Fey. She's carrying precious cargo,' laughed Deryn.

'Who's your partner?' asked Lleu.

Anna got free and pushed Fey into the mud, panting. 'Matton.'

Lleu raised his eyebrows. Matton was the Empress's eldest son. He must have lived more than seven centuries, but Lleu could only think of three other children sired by him. Each of the palimore was matched with one of Keresan's children, hoping to keep their gene pool strong with Deyar's blood. 'Congrats, I guess,' he said. She grinned back at him. Her status had just gone up in the world.

Lleu was jerked back by a sudden pull on the chain he was holding. A line of ten newly recruited slaves stretched out behind them, tethered to the chain he held. A couple of them had taken the interruption as an opportunity to break free, and they put their body weight into ripping the chain from his hands.

One of the upstarts called in encouragement to the others. 'Pull, now!' Lleu grunted in annoyance and pulled back. All ten fell forwards into the mud. One of the youngest, who had been crying the whole way from his village, sobbed out loud as he hit the ground.

'Fuck's sake,' said Deryn. 'Keep them under control, Lleu.'

'Get up. No messing,' Lleu barked at them, gripping the pommel of his sword. The look he gave was warning enough, and they stood. A woman, presumably the boy's mother, quieted him urgently.

'Who's your partner, Blue?' said Anna, ignoring the interruption.

'Oxayra.' He grumbled quietly, winding the chain around his wrist again.

'You don't like her?'

He shrugged.

'Don't like em big, eh?' teased Deryn.

'She…' She wasn't his wife. 'She's very enthusiastic.'

'Can't handle her?' said Deryn. Fay and Anna sniggered. 'Grow some balls, mate.'

The slaves were looking around nervously. 'What is it?' Lleu asked them. They didn't answer. Then he heard it too, they all did. Horses. All the horses in the area had already been commandeered. These must have travelled far. Deryn put her fingers to her lips and gave the signal for Anna to wait with the slaves. She took the chain from Lleu and he dismounted quietly, following Fey and Deryn as she led them up a steep, wooded bank. As they got closer, Lleu could hear the squeak of leather and clink of metal. Armour, maybe. Could be soldiers.

The rain fell hard, covering the sound of their movement through the trees. As they reached the top of the ridge the land plateaued out into the wide eastern road that led to Ionia. Deryn motioned down with her palm. All three crouched in the shrubs, hidden from the road.

It wasn't long before figures emerged in the distance. Their armour was black and red, fashioned from leather and sections of wood and steel. Ten Ionese scouts. Lleu's heart beat harder. The army were coming. The prince had bloody done it.

Deryn motioned them to draw weapons, signing directions. They would attack from the rear. Lleu had to think fast: kill the scouts or attack his comrades? Returning home with his group dead would raise too much suspicion. He would be more use to the rebellion from within.

The Ionese rode fast, surveying the route for what he hoped would be a sizeable army following behind. They were damned foolish to be travelling on open roads. He hoped this hard lesson would inspire more discretion in future scout parties.

The palimore reached for their bows. Lleu stepped to his right, angling around a tree trunk. They were strides away now. As the scouts came level with them, Deryn made a silent signal. Fire.

Three scouts fell from their horses, skulls pierced through by arrows. The others spun their horses around, suddenly alert. Lleu followed his sisters as they burst through the undergrowth onto the road. Their next arrows were notched and loosed before the scouts had even drawn swords. Three more fell. Just four to go.

One charged at him. A slender horse, but agile-looking and fast. Even the horses were armoured. This boded well for the quality of the army that followed, even if these men were blind to their surroundings. The scout wore more anger than fear on his face as he spurred towards Lleu, sword raised. That was good.

Lleu waited until the horse was one pace away before he stepped across its path, cutting deep into the beast's unarmoured knees. The animal fell and the soldier flailed as he rolled to a stop at the edge of the road. Lleu jumped on him with his sword, but this one was fast. He sat up quick, and their blades met in the air. Fair play. Maybe he would give this one a chance. He stepped back, giving the boy a second to get to his feet. The Ionese soldier launched all his fury at Lleu. He was good, but nowhere near good enough. Lleu parried his cuts with a well-practiced ease. Behind him, he could hear the remaining soldiers dying under the knives of his sisters. 'How far is the army?' he asked the boy quietly. 'I can help.' It was worth a shot. The boy spat and went in to stab him. Lleu forced his blade aside again. He could see

Deryn approaching at the edge of his vision. She was wiping bloody hands against her trousers.

'Lleu,' she said. Quick, time to finish this. He pushed the boy's sword out of the way and kicked him in the stomach, sending him sprawling onto his back. Lleu darted his sword into the boy's chest and through the heart.

'Damn it, Lleu,' shouted Deryn. She ran over and kicked the body to check he was dead. It was her responsibility to ensure they had someone to question. 'What do you expect me to report to the Commander now?'

'You were too quick to finish off the others.'

She glared at him. He shrugged back, but that only stoked her anger.

'You're on scout runs until we find the rest of them.' She kicked the body again, hard. He heard the ribs break under the force of the blow. 'Damn it.' She took a breath and regained her composure. Fey was sneering at him with those ugly teeth. 'Come on, let's get back. We need to report this.'

It was a slow ride back to the city, leading the scouts' horses piled with weapons and armour pillaged from the dead. The slaves were more wary than they had been in the morning. Seeing the three soldiers return, clothes smeared with blood, made for silence and compliance.

Deryn instructed Lleu to take the horses and new slaves down to the harbour. Another merchant boat had arrived that morning and was being loaded with goods throughout the day. Lleu found himself in a queue as more groups returned with their spoils: slaves, farmed goods and stolen valuables slowly made their way on board. He leaned against a pillar on the jetty, cursing the wet weather. His captives had crowded together on the floor, holding each other tight. He took a drink from his waterskin and offered it to them. They must be parched, but none dared to take it. He wanted to tell them that it would end someday, that there were people on their side. They'd find it pretty hard to believe after the shit he'd put them through today. Instead, he looked out over the water with them while they waited.

'You lot know where you're going?' he asked. One of the group looked up at him, her face exhausted from fear, eyes sullen. 'Hm?' She turned her head slowly back to look out at the sea as though she hadn't heard a word. 'You're going to Thelonia, to serve the Empress Keresan, in the mines. You'll be doing important work, helping to keep devils like me alive longer than we deserve.' The young boy was crying again. He buried his head in his mother's chest as she wrapped her arms around him. Lleu sighed. This was shit work. 'Listen,' he said, voice lowered so only his prisoners could hear. 'I've seen the mines. I know you've heard the stories, and they're true. It's not pretty. You'll be going there – nothing's stopping that – but there are things you can do to make it easier. First, don't run. Those that run are cut down and publicly executed to make an example for the rest. Quick deaths are rare.'

They were paying attention now, but his words had only served to drain more life from their faces. 'Second, look out for each other. You won't find allies in your new masters. Share your rations fairly, help the weak and the sick with their work burdens. The better you work together out there, the fewer people will be dragged from their homes here. And thirdly, watch out for guys like me. Soldiers get bored in the mines. Brutal games are played for fun. Don't get caught up – ' The last word stuck in his throat. Something had caught his eye. The next group of slaves was being marched up the gangway. Her dress caught in the wind, throwing furls of coloured silks against the grey sky.

Raikka.

Lleu dropped the chain that held his captives. He pushed his way through the crowds to get closer. Her clothes were torn and tears streaked through dried blood on her face. She was looking around wildly. She was looking for him.

Lleu barged past more people, forcing his way to the ship.

'Fuckin' hell, mate,' said a soldier as he was knocked aside.

Then their eyes met. Fear. Love. Betrayal. Her emotions screamed to him across the distance, and the greatest was fear. Ivor, her captor, yanked on the chain and she toppled onto the floor, sprawling face first on the gangway, her hands bound and unable to break the fall. He jerked on it again, before she had a chance to get up, and she was dragged across the wooden planks.

Lleu couldn't bear it. 'Raikka,' he called. She snapped her head towards him and struggled to her feet. Her eyes widened in a warning and she shook her head discreetly. No. Don't give her away.

She followed the other slaves up the gangway and they were chained to one of the iron loops that lined the ship's deck. She turned back to look at him, silently mouthing words to him: I love you.

Lleu's heart beat fast. He had to go with her, to stop this. But his feet remained on the jetty. Exposing their relationship would mean death for both of them.

'I'm coming for you,' he said. She was crying, still mouthing those three words. They must have ventured further south. How had he let this happen? 'I'm coming for you.'

'You what?' Lleu's lieutenant stood shoulder to shoulder with him in the crowd.

Lleu blinked at the man. 'You alright, Lleu?' Lleu said nothing. The lieutenant looked up to the ship in time to see Raikka shift her gaze. Lleu's stomach turned, panic gripping his body. The lieutenant slapped him jovially on the arm. 'Ah, I get it.' He grinned conspiratorially. 'Had some fun with one of the pretties up there? Aye, we miss 'em when they're gone. But there'll be plenty more where she came from.'

Lleu moved his lips, trying to respond. Something to say to hide the anger and heartache, to keep her safe. But no words came, just a choking sensation in his throat. He wanted to be sick. 'I have to get back to my slaves,' he murmured and pushed back through the crowd, face dropped to hide his pain.

CHAPTER TWELVE

Threon shifted uncomfortably in his armour. The heat of Bannvar caused him to sweat under the heavy plates of metal. Vituund had organised a procession to celebrate the departure of the troops, and he, Azzania and Savanta formed a central part of it.

A new dress had been made for Azzania, more elaborate than her traditional Guardian attire. This one was studded with gemstones and the long hem had been embroidered with the Ionese mountains. She helped Savanta adjust her costume to fit more comfortably under the wings. 'I think you got the raw deal here,' she said. The Thelonian had been presented with a bare slip of clothing. A jeweled chain bra and a wisp of blue silk for a skirt that revealed both her grey legs from the hip down. She looked like a courtesan.

'I don't know,' she said, shrugging her wings up and down. 'I quite like it. Makes me look exotic.'

'That it does,' said Threon, holding back a smile.

They were half-way through the city. Vituund rode at the

head of the procession, sitting cross-legged on his black camel. His magenta-clad servants threw coins to the crowd, and in return they paved Vituund's path with flowers. The honour guard rode camels behind their king, and behind them Threon and his companions shared a horse-drawn chariot. The army followed behind, and then a contingent of servants: cooks, tent bearers and the king's personal attendants. They flowed through the city like a florid snake.

It may have been elaborate and unnecessary, but Threon was enjoying himself. He waved to the gathered crowds. They must barely recognise the famed busker in these princely clothes. Savanta finished adjusting her bra and joined him in looking out over the chariot. She spread her wings abruptly and snarled, eager for a reaction. Those watching jumped and shrank back. Threon elbowed her in the side. 'Leave them alone, bully.' She laughed.

Something caught Threon's attention. He could hear someone calling his name. He scanned the crowd and spotted a man jumping up and down, waving enthusiastically.

'Hamza!' The first person to offer Threon a room in this city in return for his music.

'Threon! Look at you, back south.' The innkeeper grinned. 'You never wrote, sly bastard.'

'Too busy and important now, my friend.' They both laughed.

'Don't forget your old employer when you're a king, eh?' Hamza put both hands to his mouth and blew an exaggerated kiss, chuckling louder still. The chariot carried them on and Threon waved goodbye to the man, looking ahead to the city gates that would take them away, and north. Home.

Three days on the road led the army through swathes of desert hills under temperate skies. Travelling north with

Vituund's army brought with it many more comforts than they could afford on their initial journey. It was a welcome change to have meals prepared for them and to feel the comfort of a tent bed at night.

The travellers stopped that evening on the outskirts of a village to rest. Azzania headed away from the busy camp seeking solitude.

She made her way along a goat trail that twisted up a scree-strewn hillside. Splinters of stone skittered down the slope, tinkling like china as she walked. The noise of camp was soon behind her and she perched on a sun-baked rock, crossed her legs and breathed in the quiet. Life outside Ionia was so brash, so loud. A daily retreat from the caravans helped her feel centred. It wasn't the first time she'd envied Savanta her ability to spread her wings to escape. The riot of several hundred men moving to war required some adjusting to. She drew on the void and felt the pressures of the day flow out of her. Her mind cleared and she immersed herself in a meditative state.

Just as peace settled on her, she was forced to open her eyes. A stone hit her back. Then laughter, and not the kind sort. She turned around. Two soldiers scrambled up the hill towards her.

'You woke her up,' chided one as he caught his friend around the head. He was tall and wore a plaited beard; his friend was a similar height, but broader at the shoulders and rounder at the belly.

'Can I help you, gentlemen?' Azzania swung herself around, bringing her feet straight out in front of her. They had reached the top of the hill now and stood either side of the rock she was perched on.

'Help us?' said the slimmer one. 'You can help us by walking straight into the desert and not turning back.'

142

She tilted her head to one side. 'And what would that achieve?'

'You're bringing us bad luck. It's bad enough marching with women, let alone a witch.'

'Ah, I see. You've come to this enlightened conclusion all by yourselves, have you?'

''S not just us,' said the larger man. 'No one wants you here.' He rested a hand on the pommel of a knife that hung from his waist.

'Well, that does seem rather unfortunate. Especially as you've all signed up to join forces with the Ionese army. We have women fighters too, you know.' She spoke to them like they were children. It wasn't appreciated, but then it wasn't meant to be.

Anger flicked across their faces. 'Grab her, Rami,' said the larger one. Rami clambered onto the rock and seized Azzania's wrists from behind. She didn't flinch, and this seemed to worry him somewhat.

'She's not gonna do her magic on me, Rab?' he asked.

'Shut it.' Rab pulled himself up so he was kneeling in front of the Guardian. He let out a lascivious growl. 'We'll show her what happens when women step out of line on our turf.'

Azzania met his eyes. He reached for the front of her dress and ripped it open. She fought to remain calm, grasping hold of the void in the sleeping part of her mind. 'Think this makes you more of a man?'

He struck her across the face. It stung, but she still didn't fight back. He unbuckled his belt and let his trousers drop.

'Too bad,' she said. 'I suppose the anger's got to compensate for something.'

He hit her again. 'Shut up, whore.'

'Witch or whore, which is it?' The words came out with venom. She took a slow breath, fighting down the emotion, channelling the void, seeking calm. Rab pushed her down flat against the rock and Rami let go of her wrists, jumping out of the way. Rab leant his forearm against her neck. It held her down as he fumbled to lift her skirt, pressing his body close. She held still, waiting for the opportune moment. He stared down into her face and snorted with sour-breath. His hand reached between her legs. That leer broadened to reveal blackened teeth.

Now.

She reached up with both hands and grabbed his face. He froze. She let out a steady breath and forced the void into him. His muscles relaxed as she held him in the meditative state. She could feel his lust; the excitement and the power. She saw herself through his eyes; an untrustworthy occultist who would lead them to ruin.

'You really enjoy this, don't you?' she said, feeling her way through his emotions. 'Makes you feel good to overpower a woman.' She glanced down. His manhood had shrivelled up. 'Not much use now, is it?'

Rami was backing away, small noises of fear rising from his throat. She turned her head to him. 'Wait, Rami, you should see what happens to men who think they can get away with this kind of behaviour.'

She looked back into Rab's eyes. The lust was gone, as was the sudden fear. Now he gazed back at her blankly. Harmless as a baby.

'If I can just latch onto your desire...' She waded through his mind and gathered hold of his lust, then visualised it boxed up. His desire flowed between them and she felt her hips give a small involuntary thrust as she struggled to contain it. 'There we have it. Can you feel it? Cordoned off, ready for truncation.' He nodded, face still vacant. 'You won't miss it, I assure you.' She searched his memories. 'No wife.

144

Good. We won't be depriving her of anything then.' She pictured the box pulling away from the rest of his mind. A man who didn't know how to control his libido didn't deserve to keep it. She amassed the void and flooded him with it. The box collapsed on itself. His body spasmed briefly and she rolled him off her.

'Mental castration. Easily done. You won't be hurting any more women from now on.'

Emotion returned to Rab and he scrambled to his feet, fear flooding his features. He and Rami backed away, both reaching for their knives. 'What have you done to me?'

'Nothing you don't deserve,' she said. 'Don't be surprised if you can't get it up again. Run along now, boys.' She waved a hand at them and they both flinched in fear. Rab pulled his trousers up and they ran down the hillside, tripping and skidding to the bottom.

Azzania looked down at her dress and sighed. He had made a real mess of it. She pulled the tattered fragments together. Nothing a needle and thread couldn't fix.

She leaned back and looked up at the sky, which had settled to a darker blue. It felt good to challenge the mind and she felt more refreshed than if she'd meditated all evening. She pulled herself to the edge of the rock and let herself drop to the scree.

When she got back to camp she was greeted with dark looks from some of the soldiers. They gave her a wide berth. Rab and Rami sat at one of the campfires, the former staring into the fire as though he were missing a part of himself.

'Alright, Rab?' she called cheerfully and he shrank away from her.

'There you are.' Threon strode over from another fire pit. 'I was looking for you. I've made tea.' He stopped in his tracks. 'What happened to you?'

Azzania's dress had flapped open where it had ripped and she reached up to hold it back in place. Threon rushed over and touched her face. Rab had a nasty punch to him, and she could feel a bruise developing. 'Who did this?' he asked.

'It's fine, Threon. I dealt with it.'

'Dealt with what?' he asked anxiously, and then his face darkened as he understood. His gaze shifted to the soldiers. 'Who did this?' he said, pacing towards the nearest group of men. He scraped fingers through his hair, eyes widening. 'Who did this?' This time he screamed the words with a startling anger. 'We're going to settle this here and now. Be a man – admit your crime.' He spat on the ground and unsheathed his sword. A few soldiers shifted uncomfortably in their seats. All avoided his accusatory eyes.

Azzania caught his arm. 'Really, Threon, I'm fine. Leave it.'

The prince marched to the nearest fire pits. A few of the soldiers backed away, and he kicked a log on the fire, shooting red embers into the air. 'If any of you dare lay a finger on her, you're dead, you hear?' He slashed his sword through the air. He was going to have to learn to control that temper. 'Understand?'

Mumbles of ascent were spoken into the ground. Rab flinched as Threon walked past him and Threon gave him a long, calculating glare.

'Threon,' said Azzania. 'Stop it now.' He was overreacting, but she felt a flush of pride at his protectiveness. He lowered his sword and puffed out a breath, face red with anger. She took one of his hands, and without using the void, her touch seemed to calm him. 'Tea heals all ills,' she said. 'Tea would be lovely.'

Threon scraped the borrowed razor against a leather strap. It gave out a pleasant ringing as the edge honed sharp. He picked up a mirror and watched the man who looked back at him. He ran a hand over his face. It might have been a year since he last saw himself in a mirror of any quality. A line or two more around his eyes, skin baked darker than it had ever been in his youth. And older. He still imagined himself as the prince of his youth; bright eyes, fresh skin, cocksure smile. The man who looked back at him now was weatherbeaten, tired, thinner. The water bowl between his knees was already foul from washing his face. He dipped the shaving brush into it and lathered soap onto his jaw. As Vituund's razor revealed fresh skin, he guided the blade with caution, out of practice after wearing a beard for so long. When he had finished he sported three red nicks on his skin, but a flicker of his old self looked back at him.

Vituund had left him a set of new robes too, which Threon unfolded, fresh fabric soft in his hands. They were cut Bannvarian style, a close match to those the king wore himself. He began to pull off his stained old robes, and then paused. He had grown accustomed to the man he had become, a beggar and a busker, one of the people. He put the clean fabric down and smoothed his blood-mottled robes. They reminded him of how far he had come. He remembered his brother telling him how a beggar knows much a king can only guess. How he would laugh to see him now.

He pushed through the tent flap into the early morning sunlight. Most of the men were still asleep, but he was sure Savanta and Azzania would be awake. He called to one of the soldiers who was warming a pot of thick, southern coffee. 'Seen the Guardian?'

'They went that way, sir.' He pointed off, away from camp. He followed the soldier's directions and several minutes later found the two women sitting together behind the kitchen tent.

'Graces, you're clean,' mocked Azzania. 'You just won't let me out of your sight, will you?'

'Just looking for some company.' He sat on the ground beside them. 'What's going on?'

'Shh.' Azzania nodded to Savanta. She had her eyes closed and was breathing slowly. 'She's channelling the void.'

The Thelonian had her two hands stretched out in front of her, fingers quivering as she concentrated. Her fingernails were pale pink instead of their usual grey. A breath later and more pale flesh revealed itself along her fingers and the backs of her palms. She opened her eyes, a smile crossing her face, and then it reversed, grey flooding back to her skin.

'You had it,' said Azzania, 'until you looked, you had it. You let emotion in. Excitement when you had a taste of success. It undid the work you'd put in. You have to keep your mind clear.'

Savanta sighed and threw her hands down. 'It's too hard.'

'Nothing worthwhile comes easily. But let's try something different.' She looked sidelong at Threon. 'Try to force the void on him.'

'What?' said Threon, putting his hands in the air.

'I'm game,' said Savanta. 'You scared of me?'

He rolled his eyes and held his hands out to her. 'Do your worst.'

She placed her warm palms in his and stared intently into his eyes. He couldn't help himself and let out a chuckle. 'I'm not feeling anything.'

'You've got to take it seriously,' Savanta complained.

'Alright, alright.' He took a steadying breath and left himself open to her. It seemed to grow warmer where her hands met his, and a feeling like static began to grow. The humour of the situation vanished and he could feel his muscles start to relax.

'That's it, Savanta,' said Azzania. Her voice felt far away. 'You've got him there. Now, focus on bringing him into the void with you. Feel your heart slow, your breath steady. That's it.' Threon felt time slip slower, felt his aches from travelling subside. 'Do you *see* him? He's in your hands now. Memories, thoughts, emotions. Yours to glimpse.'

Feeling flooded back as Savanta let go. She was blushing.

'What?' said Threon. Savanta covered her mouth to try to hide her laughter.

Azzania smiled. 'You saw something?'

'I saw how he sees you.'

Threon felt his cheeks grow hot. 'I'm bored of this game,' he announced, and got to his feet. If Azzania was embarrassed, she hid it well.

She caught his hand to stop him. 'Wait. Stay, Threon. There are no secrets in the void.' He let her pull him back to the ground but couldn't help feeling there was a touch of smugness about her. 'I'll let you try on me.'

He made himself comfortable and faced the Guardian, curious. She held out her hands to him and he took them. 'Here,' she said, 'let me start you off.' He felt a stillness rush over him, a clarity and tranquillity far stronger than when Savanta had touched him. 'Feel that?' He nodded. 'Try to push it back to me. Share it with me. Concentrate on our touch.' He did as she asked. Picturing the void like a ball of light in his mind's eye, he tried to send it out through his palms and into hers. There was a moment of heat where their skin met and he felt the calm ebb from him to her. 'Good, good. Can you feel me?' He could more than feel her. It felt as though their skin had melded, as though her words were his. A vast expanse of consciousness lay ahead of him. Memories that weren't his flashed through his mind like darting silverfish. 'I'm an open book,' she said. 'See me.' He

149

felt as though he could be swallowed by her, consumed by a myriad of memories, tangled forever in her mind. 'Focus, Threon. Focus on a part of me, or you'll drown.' He felt a love for her mother, saw the cat she adopted as a child, remembered her first kiss, recoiled from her schoolmaster's cane, enjoyed skating on ice, tasted her first bitter ionberry, felt her serenity in the temple of the void. 'Slowly, slowly,' she said. 'Focus on this.' The tumult of thoughts and memories subsided, and he was faced with one clear vision: how she saw him. 'It's only fair, after all.' He nearly broke the connection in his surprise, but her fingers gripped his tighter and wouldn't allow him to let go.

He was a prince; a warrior; brave; handsome, even. She saw him as a leader of people, as a beacon of hope. And more than that, there was a warmth to the feelings. Attraction and affection. A tenderness that was overwhelming.

He felt her fingers intertwine with his, and then she broke the void off and he opened his eyes.

'No secrets,' she said.

CHAPTER THIRTEEN

After a month marching with the army Threon had grown accustomed to early starts. Waking before sunrise he walked away from camp, up a small ridge that overlooked where six hundred soldiers slept. Dawn paled the dark horizon as he watched the first of them rise. They seemed so hopeful. Full of valour, eager to prove themselves, to return home with stories of great heroism. He wondered how many would.

He reached the crest of the hill and sat down with his back against a tree. Taking out his whetstone, he set about sharpening his sword. It felt good to own steel again. It had been too long.

The ritual cleared his mind. With each stroke along the blade, the dawn shone brighter on the steel. The journey back north had been slow. A crowd of hundreds hauled itself along at the pace of a walrus, weighed down under the burden of its own muscle and weaponry, but a rollmat bed under canvas was a welcome change to sleeping in the open, and more than made up for their slow progress.

As they travelled further north, occasional confrontations with palimore soldiers presented themselves. Threon was glad. Most Bannvarians had never come across palimore before. Now they knew just how wary they needed to be. Though they defeated every enemy who stood in their way, the ageless soldiers defended themselves well. Two dozen Bannvarians were killed on the journey.

His concentration was broken by a dark shadow looming behind. He jumped to his feet, brandishing the sword.

It was a horse. Bigger than any Mainlands beast, black coat gleaming in the morning light. A Thelonian steed. The beast snorted and stepped towards him. Threon brought his hand up to the animal's muzzle.

'I'd remember you anywhere.' He scratched the horse between the eyes. The stallion that had carried him to safety all those years ago. Could the soldier have sent the beast back to him?

He put his sword away, pulled himself up onto the horse's back and rode back down the hill, ready for the day's march. They were nearly home.

Camp was busy, foul-smelling and overly masculine. Savanta needed some space. Flight granted her swift distance, and she was soon a mile away from the army, hovering above a lake made silver by its clay banks.

She took a moment to watch her reflection, wings beating around her grey frame. Flight was a miracle, but it bought enormous freedom while trapping her inside a god's cage. She tried to summon the void again, staring at her hands, willing away the leathery grey skin. Without Azzania's guidance nothing changed. Would she really give up flight to stop being a monster? A hard trade-off.

She alighted and perched beside the lake, drawing a knife

from her belt. She had liberated the thing from one of the weapon trailers, sure no one would miss it. She needed to do something with her hands. A sodden piece of wood bobbed in the gently rippling water at the lake's edge and she picked it up, feeling its curves and divining what she could make of it. A horse, she decided. Erin loved horses, and it had been long since she had devoted any time to making her a toy. Her life in Tannit had been consumed by her pursuit of flight, much to her daughter's disappointment.

It was noon by the time she had finished. The army would have moved on by now, but she could soon catch up. She regarded the horse. It was a little rough; she was out of practice with carving. But still, it was a fair enough toy. All it needed now was a pair of eyes. She held the blade between her fingers and began to etch them out.

'Not bad,' said a voice behind her. Zenith.

She turned around. He was in his human form again: lithe, blond hair and a star-stitched cloak. 'It's for my daughter,' she said.

'Oh yes, sweet little Erin. You still miss her?'

She turned her back on him again and returned to working on the horse. She felt his hand run along one of her wings and he came to crouch beside her on the bank. He plucked at the moss between his feet, flicking it out towards the water. 'You know I miss her,' she said at last.

'I know you know I know.' He smiled impishly. 'I know *all*.' She clenched the knife tighter. Why ask such questions when the only answers would cause her hurt? But there was nothing to be gained from quarrelling with one of the Vyara. She hunched over her work, trying to ignore him. The knife slipped and she cut a finger. She raised it to her mouth to suck the blood clean. Zenith continued. 'I know all about your unconventional little family. About your hopes to drag them

153

out of poverty. About your guilt for spending so much time working, instead of mothering. About your anxieties when the other children taunt her for being a fatherless bastard.'

Savanta clenched her teeth. 'You have no right—' she started, but he stood up and the look on his face made her stop. She shuffled away from him, ready to get to her feet and run.

'I have *every* right. You are mine, Savanta. Mine.' He roared the last word, and then drew a breath, composure returning to his features. 'You are only alive because of my good graces.' He bent over her, reaching out for the horse. She looked up at him as she placed it in his hand. He smiled, his usual humour back. He ran his fingers over the carving. 'It really is rather good. Shame to have used such wet wood, but still, very nice. I wonder if Erin wouldn't prefer a little more colour?' As he spoke, the wood turned piebald and the mane and tail she had carved grew out as chestnut hair. His power still astounded her. 'Better?' She didn't answer.

'Some consolation for that poor girl. You know she would sit waiting at her bedroom window for you to come home? She would be there for hours, hoping she meant more to you than your work,' he continued. Savanta's work had all been for Erin. Every minute in the workshop had been spent in the hopes of a better life for her. 'And after all those years wondering who her dear father is… you're too proud to tell her that she was nothing more than a back-alley dalliance, his fun forgotten before light touched the next day.'

She was on her feet now, fists balled. She forced back angry tears. 'How dare you,' she said, but her words were more hesitant than she intended. Fear strangled her threat. He tossed the toy back to her and she grabbed it, clutching it so tight that one of its legs broke off. She marched closer to him, wanting an apology, needing him to take his words back.

He cocked his head to one side and gave her a quizzical

smile. He was amused by her anger and it made her want to burst. His outline began to fade against the sky. She flung a fist and it passed right through him. His blue eyes bored into her as his face dissipated. '*Mine,*' he said, and vanished.

Savanta cried out in fury. She hurled the toy horse into the lake. It bobbed in the water, refusing to drown.

She fell to her knees.

That night, when they made camp near the border of the Waterlands, Threon called Vituund from his tent to join him at a campfire.

'We're getting closer,' he said. 'This many soldiers won't make an inconspicuous approach. We don't know whether the Thelonians are aware of the Ionese moving west either.'

The Bannvarian nodded. 'We must be prepared.'

Across the fire, Savanta lay on the parched grass, watching the flames. She seemed lost in thought. A little sad, even. He had often seen her look that way when she thought no one was watching; and no wonder, who would want to be a prisoner of their own skin?

'Savanta.' Threon motioned for her to join them. The sadness buried itself deeper and she got up, eyes brightening, and crouched beside him.

'Let me guess. Another scouting favour?' She tilted her head to one side, unimpressed.

He spread his palms appeasingly. She had been a saint and he owed her a lifetime of favours for the safe passage her scouting had offered them so far. 'Please? It's important.'

She dragged circles in the dusty ground using a toe. 'What do you want?'

'Fly ahead to Maradah. Perhaps you can find our blue-eyed friend.'

'Lleu?'

'He sent his horse to find us. Might be a sign he wants to talk. Ask him what the soldiers know. We need to find a safe route to join with the locals.'

'Alright, but you owe me.' She flashed a smile.

'Fly by night. Tonight, if you have the energy.'

She stretched her arms and wings and took the tankard of ale that Threon held. 'I'll go now. I could do with getting away from camp again.' She took a swig of his drink, and handed it back before running into the darkness, wings spread. They saw her bat-like shadow block out the moon for a moment and then she was gone.

'We're nearly home,' said Threon.

'Yes, you are,' said Vituund.

'I can't thank you enough for helping.'

'You didn't give me much choice. Leaders who disobey the will of the people don't last long.'

'If you were in my position—'

'Doubtless, I would have done the same, yes.' He stoked the fire with a stick. 'You're a good man, Threon. Perhaps if I'd seen what I witnessed in the pits and what I've seen since on the road, I would have given you a warmer welcome when we first met.'

'A prisoner in a new city. I doubt I was at my most charismatic. I was a spoilt young prince back then, lost and confused. It was living on the streets of your city that made me who I am today.'

Vituund smiled. 'There's something in you that I'll always lack. The people – *my* people – they respect you. They think you're one of them. I could never hope for them to look at me the way they see you. I'm glad to go with you. It's been too long since our countries stood as allies.'

'Yes,' breathed Threon. He just hoped he wasn't dragging this man's people to ruin.

Lleu had worked long past the end of his shift. The idea of rest, of socialising with the other soldiers, was deeply unappealing. Too many people had stopped recently to ask if he was alright, and he couldn't face another evening of forced smiles and laughter. It was too hard with Raikka gone.

The sun had long since set over the mountains and it was a strain to see by moonlight, but Lleu continued with his work, clearing the rubble on the castle site. The job would take weeks. In places the castle had crumbled to boulders, and in others large sections of walls and turrets had collapsed, making the ground uneven. They would need to clear the site in order to rebuild another fortress of the Empress's devising; likely a keep for the palimore to maintain a permanent base. Later, who knew, perhaps she intended to set up an extension of government here too.

His hands were rough and blackened by digging through the ashen remains of the building. He threw another rock to the side of the site and stood up, stretching his lower back.

'Lleu.' He pretended not to hear, but the voice came again. 'Lleu!' His father jogged to join him; his features, nearly as youthful as Lleu's own, were shaded in the darkness. 'Son, you've been up here hours. Come eat.'

Lleu grunted in response. Khan put a hand on his shoulder and Lleu shrugged away from his touch. 'I'm not hungry.'

Khan frowned. 'No one wants this shift. Moving rocks? Hardly work for soldiers. You've been here since morning. What's going on?'

Most of the palimore thought such work beneath them, but Lleu found it highly preferable to stealing people from their homes on slave raids. He had joined the palimore when he was ten, far older than the other soldiers who had been born to the role through the breeding programme. Some said that was what made him soft. He remembered his first glimpse of the soldiers. His mother had brought him to Maradah during a Thelonian state visit and, while watching the military parade, she stepped out in front of Khan, saying *you have a son*. Lleu had been captivated by these soldiers. Bright uniforms and gleaming armour. They looked twice as strong as any blacksmith. His mother had never hidden his parentage from him, despite the fact she had only spent one night with his father. She married when he was a young boy, and five younger siblings followed. Lleu was taller and stronger than any of the other children. He was proud of his palimore blood and seeing those soldiers for the first time filled him with awe.

Khan didn't rebuke her for interrupting the parade. Lleu never forgot the way he looked at him the first time they met. This look of wonder crossed his face. The man had lived nearly three centuries and had never sired a child. It was nearly unheard of for soldiers to have children outside of the breeding programme, and was usually something that was punished. But his position as Commander and his favour with the Empress meant that he was given dispensation to bring Lleu home to join the palimore. It was an offer no ten-year-old boy would refuse. His mother was torn in two seeing him leave on the ship but let him go in the hopes of a better life.

If only she had known the things they would make him do…

Training was tough, but not as tough as the constant reminder that he was an outsider. He was years behind the other children, who made him feel clumsy and weak. When he reached the age of twenty-two, when he had toughened up, when he had made alliances, when he began to look and feel like a soldier, this was when he and his fellow trainees got their first taste of vish. It had felt like vigour and courage and fire in the blood. And it had preserved his youth ever since.

That was the day Khan had seared him with the brand.

His training group had lined up and Khan, perhaps out of kindness, made Lleu go first. His father lifted the metal from burning embers, and flames flickered along the white-red steel that formed the Empress's emblem. Being so young and so unaccustomed to pain, Lleu had started to back away. Soldiers held him down as the brand was pressed into the flesh of his back. He could still remember the smell of his own blistering skin and the pitiful scream he had failed to hold in.

That was the only wound he had acquired in the army that had not been treated with vish. They wanted the scar bold. It marked him as the Empire's property.

The mark was dehumanising. It made him feel like a slave. It had been a sore point between him and his father for a long time. But years later, when he finally graduated from training, real life as a soldier began. His anger at the branding faded fast as it was replaced with the distress of orders that ate at his spirit.

Threaten. Bully. Whip. Beat. Raid. Kill.

Lleu released a breath and threw another stone to one side. He looked his father in the eyes. 'It's nothing,' he said. 'Just need some space.'

Khan watched him cooly, unimpressed by his answer. Lleu was known for his quirks of nature. The sensitive one. Often found alone, often brooding or repentant.

'You know you can talk to me, son.' Lleu looked away and threw another rock into the night. 'You've been distant lately.'

'I'm fine.'

Khan stared at him a while longer, waiting for more. When Lleu said nothing, he sighed and threw his hands up. 'I give up,' he said. 'I'll tell them to leave you some supper. Come eat when you've come to your senses.'

Lleu ignored him and threw another rock onto his pile. He squeezed his eyes shut and kicked the rubble at his feet.

It was two hours before dawn when Savanta reached Maradah in the pouring rain. Guards stood sentry on the walls as she approached, but people never looked up during a downpour. She flew higher, masking her grey skin and black travelling dress against the night sky.

From high above, she surveyed the town. The castle was gone, left unrepaired, and beside it a wooden structure had appeared. It was surrounded with canvas tents. She gauged the moored ships in the harbour were capable of carrying several hundred slaves. Or delivering several hundred soldiers.

She made a line for the wooden building, hoping the sound of the rain would mask her landing on its roof.

One candle flickered silently against the inner wall of a canvas tent, but there were no sounds of movement. She watched the campsite for over an hour before the first soldiers began to wake. The first was just before dawn. A woman got up and relieved herself at the fringes of the camp before waking servants to begin cooking breakfast. By daybreak the cooks had several fires going, and the smell of sizzling meat had roused the rest of the camp.

Savanta lay flat and motionless against the roof, hoping not to be noticed. From beneath her the door of the wooden hut creaked open. A stream of soldiers emerged, and one she thought she might recognise, though she couldn't see his face.

He stretched his arms up and emitted an audible yawn, before moving towards breakfast. 'Let me guess, more rabbit?' Her ears pricked at that voice. It was him.

She watched the soldiers eat, growing hungry all the while. When he had finished, Lleu stood and walked back towards the hut. She wrestled a loose nail out of the wood, and as he passed beneath, threw it at him. He looked up. Their eyes met briefly and he continued into the hut without missing a step.

She waited. He didn't come back out until most of the soldiers had moved away from the camp into town, where they were given orders. Most were sent scouting east, into the hills.

A pebble landed on the roof beside her. Looking behind, she saw he was waiting for her at the rear of the building. She slid down the wet wooden tiles and dropped to the ground, keeping her back to the wall.

The soldier looked around nervously.

'What are you doing here?' The horse hadn't been a summons, then.

'The Bannvarians have joined the rebellion. They're travelling north now, just three days' ride from here. We need a safe route. Somewhere we won't be seen.'

His frown dropped in favour of keen interest. 'How many?'

'Six hundred. And a force of Ionese are joining us from the East.'

'They're aware of the Ionese. Scouts are looking for signs of the army all around the eastern hills. Safe passage is difficult. The mountain pass isn't regularly watched. Stay on the east side of the mountain and gather south of the city for your best chance.'

She nodded. 'Once the forces are united, we plan to attack your stronghold here.'

'You're putting a lot of trust in me.'

'You saved me once; Threon twice, I hear. Consider this returning the favour. Be ready to run or switch sides when we attack.'

His eyes twitched around, making sure they were still alone. 'Attack from the castle. One of the city walls was destroyed in the fire. It's the easiest breach point.'

'Good.'

He gestured for her to stay where she was and walked away from the hut, then glanced around. After a few

161

moments he turned to her and nodded. Time to go. She ran and was airborne in seconds. By the time she heard the cries from the guards, she was beyond the range of the arrows that hurtled in her wake.

There was somebody watching them. Threon could feel eyes on them as they marched. Shadows moved in the forest, only to disappear when he turned their way. They were nearly home now. He knew the hills they skirted, recognised the farm houses spied through thinning trees. He nudged his horse on to the head of the column to ride abreast with Vituund and Azzania.

'You sense them too,' said Azzania without looking at him. 'There's someone watching us.'

She nodded.

Threon glanced around again, nervous.

'Be on your guard,' said Vituund. He had a hand on the pommel of his sword. 'We don't want any nasty surprises.'

Threon wrinkled his nose. 'I'm going to check it out.' He reined his horse back and trotted to the edge of the forest.

'Threon,' barked Vituund in rebuke. From the corner of his eyes, he saw Azzania place a hand on the king's arm to hold him back.

The forest was too dense to investigate by horse, so he dropped from his saddle and pushed through layers of leaves and snaggling branches. In summer, light would mottle shades of green and white onto the flowering forest floor, but now in winter, the place was monochrome.

'Show yourself,' he called. A crow took flight, startling him. He pulled out his sword to slash at the undergrowth.

Then he saw it. A shadow running between trees. He brandished his sword and made after it. Brambles caught on his robes and scratched his face. His feet tripped through a tangle of young plants, but his momentum carried him

162

forwards, pushing after the figure. Threon was faster and soon caught up. The man ahead was slim, poorly dressed, no palimore. Threon landed on him, tackling him to the floor. The man tried to escape but Threon caught hold of him, nettles brushing heat across his hands and arms. The man was young and slight, and Threon managed to force him against a tree trunk. He held the sword to the shaking man's throat. His captive shrank back as far as he could to avoid the blade. The two men locked eyes.

'Who are you? Why are you watching us?' Threon pressed the blade harder against his skin. The man's blue eyes widened, but not with fear, instead with a mix of surprise and recognition.

'Prince Threon?' he whispered.

Threon lowered the blade.

'It's you, isn't it? I didn't recognise you until you spoke.'

Threon frowned, keeping hold of the sword.

'I'm Alhain. I worked in the library. Before.'

Threon didn't recognise the man, but there was honesty in his voice.

'I never spent much time reading books.' He sheathed his sword and stood, helping Alhain to his feet.

'No point starting now. The library's gone. The history of the Waterlands gone, lost in one night of fire.'

All that knowledge that Threon had evaded as a child, gone forever. He cursed the palimore. 'Why are you following us?' Beyond where they stood, he could make out at least two other figures, watching from a safe distance.

'We were worried. An army approaching home. We thought Bannvar had come to pledge itself to the palimore. If we'd known you were with them...'

'We?'

Alhain smiled. 'The resistance.'

CHAPTER FOURTEEN

'Your timing couldn't be more fortunate,' said Alhain. He was showing Threon, Savanta and Azzania around the resistance camp. 'Your people are nearly here,' he said to Azzania. 'A pair of scouts found us only three days ago. They're taking the long route to avoid the watched hills, but they'll be here within a day.'

'At least some scouts made it through,' said Savanta. Threon was glad to see a rare smile brighten Azzania's face.

The encampment was hidden deep in the forest. A natural clearing in the trees had been felled wide. Makeshift wooden structures had been erected, and crude defences of stakes surrounded the area. They had worked fast after the fire. He was pleased to see that hundreds of Waterfolk had escaped to gather in this temporary home. Few of the elderly and very young had survived the raids, but those who had were here, cooking or helping to make rudimentary weapons out of old farm equipment. The more able-bodied were sparring together or shooting arrows at targets of old rabbit skulls. The

Bannvarians had filtered into the camp, and some of them now took to showing the townsfolk how to hold their weapons and how to hold themselves.

'This is incredible,' said Threon.

'We began work the day you left for Bannvar. There aren't many left in the town now. Most of us escaped here. They haven't found this place, not yet. They've been looking, looking hard, and we worried they'd discover us before any help came. But you're here now, thank the gods.'

'They're ready to fight?' Azzania was eyeing the guerrilla army with doubt.

'No, not ready. Not ready like your people, or the Southerners. None of them are soldiers. But they're willing. The palimore have taken everything from us but our spirits; we'll fight with everything we've got.'

'I don't doubt it,' said Threon. He was grinning, and clasped Alhain around the shoulder. 'Let's send those bastards packing.'

The next evening, as the sky turned from silver to lead, the camp could hear the hiss of moving leaves growing louder. Something was pushing through the forest towards them.

A hush swept over as more and more of them heard it. Everyone's attention was grasped by the sound as it grew nearer, louder. Threon drew his sword. Beside him, he could see even Azzania held her breath.

And then the forest edge parted. Figures in white flowed through the trees, skirting the rough defences to enter the clearing.

'They're here,' whispered Azzania, breaking into a smile. The Guardians were ghostly apparitions, filing silently into the camp. Their tranquil demeanour meant they were not greeted with the same enthusiasm that the Southerners had received. Instead, the gathered armies watched them join the camp as if it was part of some sombre ceremony.

Behind them followed a column of soldiers. Five hundred men and women marched into the camp in regimented columns, four abreast.

Their armour was black and red, fashioned from leather and sections of wood and steel. At the head of each column a mounted rider gave hand signals. Each of the columns came to the centre of the camp and stopped in formation between the wooden huts.

The last to arrive were four men bearing an ornately carved litter. They strode to the side of the fire and placed the carriage down before standing to attention, right hands raised to their brows in salute. The door to the litter opened and a plump, aging Ionese woman stepped out. She wore red silks embroidered with gold. Her once black hair was thick with grey and slicked into an intricate bun, surrounded by a circlet of gold.

Threon joined Vituund who was already waiting at the fireside to receive the queen. Threon couldn't hide his grin. This army looked more disciplined than Maradah's soldiers had ever been, even on Unity Day. 'Most impressive,' he said.

Azzania was close behind. She handed the woman a cup of wine. 'Your Majesty,' she said, dipping in courtesy.

The queen's eyes were hard as stone. 'Azzania, well met again. So, these are the men we are to be fighting with?'

'Yes, Majesty.'

She looked Threon and Vituund up and down, lips pursed. 'Both of them?' She raised an eyebrow.

Threon was filthy from travelling. His beard had grown back unkempt, and he hadn't bathed properly since Bannvar. He wore his old Bannvarian robe, torn and ragged. In patches it was dark where blood had refused to wash out. Beside him,

Vituund stood tall, clean, regal. He had ridden in his armour all the way from Bannvar. It couldn't have been comfortable, but at least he looked the part.

'It is an honour to meet again, Queen Aya,' said Vituund, taking the woman's hand and kissing it. 'You must excuse Threon. His appearance echoes only the tribulations of his kingdom.'

Threon bowed low to her. 'It is a delight to meet you, My Lady. You have my deepest gratitude for joining our cause.'

'We have met before, Threon. You were only a small child, so I forgive you for forgetting.' She smiled, amused. 'And my, how you've grown up. How different you seem to your father.'

He had not missed the language of court and its veiled insults. 'My Lady, it is not outward appearances that make a man.' She held the smile, seeming satisfied with the response.

'I was very sorry to hear of his death. Your mother was a wonderful queen. I regret not knowing your parents better.'

There was sincerity to her words. 'Thank you,' he said. 'I hope we can get to know each other well enough.'

'Come now, my men need feeding and a good night's rest. We were attacked on our journey and news of our arrival is sure to reach the forces in Maradah soon. We must catch them unawares. We attack tomorrow at dusk.'

She stalked past them and called to her mounted soldiers. 'Make camp, men.'

Threon shared a look with Vituund. He smiled. 'I like her.'

Lleu let his reins hang loose, allowing the stallion to find his way through the forest. Bloodbringer had come at his call and now, he hoped, would lead him to the camp. If Savanta had followed his instructions they wouldn't be far.

He needed to see this army. To understand their power.

More and more his thoughts had returned to the raid on Maradah, to that first night when they had cut through drunk and inexperienced soldiers. It was hard to imagine that starved farmers would fare better. Would the Ionese and Southerners make the difference?

Bloodbringer snorted and came to a stop. Lleu strained his hearing, eyes scanning the undergrowth. Certainly no army here. But wait. He made out the snap of twigs ahead. Someone was forging a path. He lowered himself from the horse and trod silently after the figure, keen to go unnoticed. He may have doubted the power of this cobbled-together army against his own, but he wouldn't stand a chance if they all turned on him alone. Nothing could disguise a palimore soldier. His hulking frame would scream *enemy* at the Mainlanders from any distance.

As he drew nearer he picked up on sound. The distant clatter of swords and conversation. The camp was near, then. The figure he tailed was male, slim, with ragged hair. It might have been the prince, but he couldn't be sure. The man swept a nocked arrow through the undergrowth, probably hunting for birds.

Lleu grew closer still, but the figure didn't notice. Not until Lleu wrapped his hand over the hunter's mouth and pulled him to the ground.

It was Threon. 'You need to learn to watch your back.'

The prince struggled free of Lleu's grasp and threw a fist at him. Lleu caught it and forced him against the floor. Brambles tore thin streams of red across his face. 'Let me go.' Threon fought to gain control and kicked Lleu in the shin.

'Threon, stop. It's me.' He either didn't hear the words or he ignored them. 'Quiet,' he hissed. 'I don't want the whole camp to find me here.' Another kick. Lleu groaned in frustration and pulled the prince up, pinning him to a tree.

Now they were eye to eye. 'It's me. Stop.' The struggle died out and Lleu released him.

Threon rubbed his shoulder. 'What are you doing here?'

'I need to know I can trust you with the fight ahead.'

Threon looked affronted. 'Trust *me*? This isn't your fight, it's ours, all of ours.' He gestured broadly back in the direction of the camp.

Lleu picked up the hunting bow Threon had dropped and passed it back to him. 'I know the palimore. You're not just risking your neck and mine. If you misjudge this, you could wipe out every man and woman in that camp.'

'You think that hasn't been keeping me up at night?'

'I've waited decades for this moment,' said Lleu. 'We can't misjudge it. If you're not ready, you will be throwing away your only chance of success.'

Threon bent down to re-string his bow. 'Don't lecture me. I know what I'm doing.' But Lleu still wasn't convinced. With bow back intact, Threon stood and threw it around one shoulder. He regarded Lleu with an uneasy trust. The two men knew little of each other.

Lleu took a levelling breath. 'Just look at my eyes, Threon. My mother was of your kin. My family still live south of the city.' Or they had, until recent raids. He stopped the thought short as his mind flicked to Raikka again. What had happened to her? Threon had to succeed, for her sake. If the palimore were defeated, they could no longer control the mines. The slaves would go free. 'Blue eyes mark me as a stranger in Thelonia. This is my true home. I have to protect it.'

'But the palimore would never recruit someone from the Waterlands.'

Lleu shrugged. 'My father is palimore. He met my mother here on a state visit.' Threon's stance relaxed. He was beginning to see the full picture. 'In another time, you might have been my king.'

A silent understanding fell between them. Lleu still needed to see the camp. He needed to know they were ready. Threon seemed to understand Lleu's concern without prompting. 'You want to see what we've got?' He inclined his head back to the camp. Lleu nodded and followed the prince as he picked his way through the forest. When they neared the edge of the clearing, Lleu stopped. 'Best I stay out of sight,' he said.

Threon inclined his head in agreement. 'We attack tomorrow. Tensions are high; I wouldn't want them to strike out at you.'

Through the leaves, Lleu could make out a sizable army. Ionese, Southlanders and Waterfolk, all gathered together. The Ionese were disciplined, a little brash with their scouting maybe, but the soldiers here bore themselves well. They were alert and shining in protective armour. The Southern men were less disciplined. They were animated, joking, sparring, some drinking, all showing a sheen of nerves for the battle ahead. And last was a scatter of scrawny Waterfolk. Thin, but muscled from hard years in the fields, they practised with the other soldiers. It was obvious they had never seen military training.

'So?' said Threon. 'What do you think?'

Lleu could already pick out the men and women who wouldn't live out the day tomorrow.

'It'll do,' he said, not knowing whether to believe his own words. If things went downhill, there was still a card he could play on the battlefield, but it would be a risk.

His ears pricked at a sound behind, and he raised his hands, turning around slowly. 'I'm not your enemy,' he said. A Bannvarian man confidently levelled a crossbow at him.

'Vituund,' said Threon, rushing to Lleu's side. 'This is Lleu. He's with us.'

Vituund held the crossbow steady, brows drawing together. 'A palimore in our camp, Threon?' He came a step closer, arrow still trailing on Lleu's chest. 'Who's to say he won't take intel back to his masters? We can't risk it so close to battle.'

Lleu kept quiet, allowing Threon to speak for him. 'He saved my life. We need him, Vituund.'

'How old are you, soldier?' Vituund addressed Lleu directly.

'One hundred and twenty-one,' he said, keeping his hands up, his features placid. He had a vial of vish at his neck. It would be enough to heal a wound as long as the Bannvarian missed his head and his heart. But if he drew the attention of the other soldiers... that would be a different story.

'At least a century with that army then? Must be like family to you.'

They were, that was true, but he wouldn't incriminate himself here.

'His silence confirms it. Blue eyes won't change the loyalties built by decades of fighting alongside the palimore. How many times have you broken bread together? How many times have you laughed? I bet you owe your life to more than a few of them.'

'Vituund, please,' Threon began. 'I trust him.'

'Did you never think that trust could have been manipulated to gain information? I won't let you risk everyone here, Threon. He knows too much.'

Threon stepped in front of the arrow. 'Leave him,' he said, and the two men's eyes met in a contest of wills. A small tremor on the crossbow. Anger darkened Vituund's face.

'Step aside,' he growled, coming forward. The arrow was inches from Threon's chest. He didn't move.

Lleu dropped his hands. The two royals kept eyes firmly locked on one another. Threon reached forward and took hold of the crossbow bolt. Vituund's grimace tightened as he did so, but he allowed Threon to direct the arrow out of harm's way.

'Go, Lleu,' said the prince. 'Be ready for us tomorrow.'

Lleu took the cue and backed away.

When he returned to the stallion, he reached between his eyes and scratched. 'You stay. Look after him tomorrow, boy. He's going to need all the help he can get.'

Threon had never seen battle before. As a child, he dreamt of being like the old heroes, earning a name for himself; having songs sung about him, rather than by him.

Battle tomorrow.

The thought excited and terrified him all at once. He and Vituund had made amends over Lleu's appearance. This close to battle, unity was essential. Together they relayed the news that they were to attack the next day. A nervous energy now filled the camp. At the fringes, the Ionese put up their tents, quiet and orderly. A strange aura of calm surrounded them, no doubt imposed by the presence of the Guardians.

The Bannvarians and Waterfolk were drinking by the fire to calm their nerves. Some sparred long into the night, sharing techniques in the hope that a few hours more practise might make the difference between life and death.

Threon joined Savanta by the fire. She had spent all day working on a wooden contraption which had started out as several panels of wood but now, with the help of two of Maraddah's old carpenters, had transformed into some kind of machine. She was making final checks now and had moved the thing closer to the fire so she could see better.

It was an oblong box that leaned on a diagonal angle. The face that angled towards the sky bore two dozen holes, each holding an arrow large enough that it could almost be called a spear.

'Looking good,' said Threon. 'Does it work?'

She gave him a look that told him he was foolish to ask. 'Of course it works. There was only time for two test runs before sunset, but she'll do the job.' She slapped the machine affectionately. Threon circled the contraption. 'It'll take two men to load it with any speed,' she said. 'Then it's just a case of pulling that crank until it's taut and releasing the lever.' Threon came to the front of the machine and ran a hand over one of the arrow heads. Even palimore would fall under the power of a weapon like this. Two dozen arrows would leave this box and rip into their army in a wall of ammunition.

'Shame you don't have the time to build more,' he said.

Savanta sat on a tree trunk that had been dragged over by the fire. Threon sat down beside her.

'Never saw myself building killing machines,' she said.

'Never saw myself leading an army.' He placed the jug of wine he had been carrying between them and handed her a cup.

'Are you stupid? Drink isn't going to improve your chances.'

He shrugged and poured. 'Might be our last chance to have a drink together. And Vituund's wine is pretty good.'

She sighed and clinked cups with him. 'Cheers, I guess.'

'To victory,' he said.

'This time tomorrow you could finally have your home back.'

He breathed in deeply. 'Home. It's been so long. Maybe I can finally ditch that vagabond title, eh?'

'Mm. What will you do if we win?'

'I'd like to rebuild my family's legacy. Rebuild the castle, replant the fields, help restore everyone's livelihoods…'

'But?'

'I fear more will come.'

173

Savanta stared into the fire. 'They will,' she said. 'Thelonian land doesn't exist anymore. We have mines, quarries, slums and lavish palaces. The only green land exists around the Imperial gardens. Without the raids, there is nothing to eat. Nothing to feed the soldiers, the peasants or the slaves.'

'Sounds rough.'

'It is,' she said. 'Your people who were taken for slaves, their life there…' she trailed off. 'I'm one of the lucky ones. I have a home, a family. We have enough to feed ourselves.'

'You've never talked about home before.'

'I can't go back. Not until this is over.' She smiled sadly. 'I have a daughter.' She sighed out a long breath. 'I miss her so much. What will she think when she sees me like this?' Her eyes glistened and she closed them tight, turning her face away so he wouldn't see her tears.

Threon put a hand on hers. 'You have a family. Be happy that you have someone to fight for.' He sipped his drink. 'Zenith doesn't want you to go home?'

She flinched at the mention of his name. 'I can't,' she said, holding out a grey hand in front of the fire. 'He has plans for me. Flying home now would be suicide. He follows me, always watching. I'm trapped.' She shrugged and drank some more.

They were silent for a while. 'I know it might not feel that way but being close to the gods could be a blessing. You have his protection.'

'You act as though you've never heard the old fables. I've heard you sing them! The Vyara choose those they wish to play with. Those who will fight for them, those who will be raped by them, those who will be sacrificed to them. My chest tightens every time you sing "Diana and the Blood of Trinity".'

A rumble of thunder sounded in the distance.

174

She looked down. 'We shouldn't be talking about this.'

Threon looked up in the direction of the rumble as a bolt of lightning ripped across the clouds. It sent a shiver down his spine. He gripped her hand. 'I'm sorry.'

She drained her wine and poured another. 'It is what it is.'

'I will pray to Athys for you.'

She laughed out loud. 'You really don't get it.' She let go of his hand, shaking her head. Threon stood, sensing she wanted to be left alone. 'Sorry, sorry. I'm fine, really.' She gave him a small smile and gestured for him to sit down again. 'You have his favour, you know. Zenith. He wants you to win.'

'Will you come with us tomorrow?'

'I'm no fighter. But I'll do what I can for you. If I can help from the air, count me in.'

'Good, thank you.'

Savanta put down her cup and stood. 'I'm going to bed. You should too. You've seen those soldiers. Fifty years of training and several of our lifetimes as a warrior. It's going to be bloody.'

With that she walked away into the darkness.

Threon remained at the fireside a while longer, talking quietly with the nervous farmers, offering them courage as best he could. They were not the skilled soldiers of Ionia or Bannvar. But they had fire in their blood. A will to regain their homes. And more. They wished to cross the sea. To free the slaves, and to wreak revenge on those who had stolen their lives.

A shadow fell over Threon and he woke, opening his eyes to see Vituund standing over him. He had fallen asleep by the fire and slept well beyond sunrise.

'I'm awake, I'm awake,' he mumbled.

Vituund helped him up. 'Come with me.'

Threon stood, rubbing his eyes. As he turned to follow the

Bannvarian, he could see that most of the rebel forces had gathered at the far side of the camp. 'What's going on?'

Vituund offered him a silent smile.

As they approached, the crowd parted to let them through. Vituund led him to a makeshift dais, made from firewood and woven willow. A chair was placed at its centre.

'Please,' said Vituund, gesturing to the seat.

Threon sat, looking around the faces of the crowd. They watched him expectantly.

'Vituund, what's going on?' he whispered out of the corner of his mouth.

'Your coronation.'

Threon couldn't help but laugh. 'Seriously?' But the mirth was quickly wiped from his face as Aya appeared before him holding a velvet pillow. On it sat the crown he had pulled from the ashes of the castle. It had been re-formed. The polished gold surface gleamed as it had during his father's reign.

'My Lord?' the queen said quietly, her face serious as stone. 'Are you ready?'

Threon was speechless.

'Well, you may not look the part, or even have words for the part, but king you are and king you'll be, whether we win or lose this battle. Lucky for you, I prepared a speech so you don't have to.' She gave him a sly wink, further creasing her heavily lined face.

She stepped onto the creaking dais and turned to face the gathered crowd. Lifting the crown above her head, she addressed them.

'We here gathered are united in support of this young man before us, who is tasked with the duty of leading a broken kingdom to a new freedom. It is a duty to which I know he has dedicated himself with much solemnity. He has behind him not only the splendid traditions and the annals of more than a thousand years, but the living strength and majesty of the people of the Waterlands. This coronation is not the symbol of a power and a splendour that are gone, but a declaration of our hopes for the future, and for the many years to come that Threon, gods willing, will reign in peace and prosperity.

'He has the blessing of all peoples of the Mainlands, as represented by you brave souls, gathered here to save them.'

She turned to Threon and slowly lowered the crown onto his brow. The metal was cool against his forehead, the weight of it solid, and reminded him of moments as a child when he begged his father to let him try it on.

Aya continued, 'Rise, Threon, first of his name, King of the Waterlands.'

He stood up. Cheers broke out across those gathered. His people. So this was what it felt like. He was a king.

Aya hissed at him, 'You'd better say something now.'

He fumbled for a few words and then shouted above the cheers. 'I thank you, brothers and sisters. I am here, ever at your service. Today we fight, not only for our kingdom, but for the kingdoms of our neighbours and friends.' He looked to Vituund and Aya. 'For the first time in four centuries, the Mainlands is united. Let today's victory mark a new chapter in our shared histories. And let today be the day the Waterlands is liberated.' He unsheathed his sword and raised it above his head as he cried, 'Water my blood!'

The cry was echoed by the Waterfolk. 'Water my blood! Water my blood! Water my blood!'

Several of them rushed forward and lifted him up, carrying him over the crowd.

King. He would go to battle as King.

Laughing, he tried to get down from their grasps while

holding his sword out of the way until eventually they set him back to the ground.

Azzania stood before him, wearing an amused smile. Threon straightened his robe and tried to smooth his hair. She reached a hand up to run her fingers over the crown. This was her victory as much as his. Without her, Threon would be trying to take back his home alone. Now they had an army. Now they had a chance.

She let her fingers drop down to trace his jawline. 'Congratulations, King,' she said, and kissed him softly on the lips. As she pulled away from him, she laughed. He must have been wearing a stunned expression. She cocked her head towards the gathered Waterfolk. 'They want to celebrate with you. Don't leave them waiting.' She moved away, leaving him to the cheering crowds. He stared after her, blinking in awe.

CHAPTER FIFTEEN

The day was dank and misty, rain veiling the landscape with grey.

The three armies stood in columns woven between trees in the forest. The outer formations were made up of disciplined Ionese warriors; beside them, the people of Bannvar and their armoured soldiers, and in the centre, the wild-eyed Waterfolk. Threon could see growing fear in them as they waited, hands on their weapons. These were mostly re-fashioned farm tools; sharpened scythes, mallets with nails beaten into the ends and riding crops rubbed with poisonous skullsbane. Savanta stood beside her machine on a ridge to the far right of the army.

Threon sat on Bloodbringer where the trees thinned. He had found the beast on the edge of camp and was thankful for the vantage the horse's height offered. He looked down on the sad remains of his home. Directly below, broken city walls and mounds of rubble marked the home he had been raised in. The fjord hugging the town still stood proud; the water kissed his face, and he imagined his city as it once was. Prosperous. Vibrant. Home.

He was flanked by the Queen of the East and the King of the South, each astride their horses, gleaming in armour.

'I've never fought in battle,' he confessed to them.

Aya laughed. 'Of course not. You're just a babe.' She punched his arm amiably. He frowned at her. 'Though I must confess, it has been many years for me. I was a naive young princess when the tribes began to fight in Ionia. But my mother and father made sure I would know how to crush my enemies. My army will do us proud.'

'They are impressive,' said Threon, hoping conversation would distract from his fear. 'Have they ever fought palimore?'

She avoided the question. 'They are strong, skilled warriors with Ionese hearts.'

'My men had a taste of palimore strength when we crossed a small handful of them during our journey,' said Vituund. 'We may outnumber them twelve to one, but I fear we will suffer heavy losses. If we lose too many, we won't be able to continue the fight…'

'Shut your nonsense,' said Aya. 'That is no talk before battle. We must have hearts of steel. I will not live to have this–' she waved an arm at the fallen city '–happen to my home.'

Vituund was silent then, shrinking back into himself, his eyes far away.

'Where are the Guardians?' asked Threon. He hadn't seen Azzania all morning.

'They come later,' she said. 'Fire in the blood is needed for battle. Their magic will suck the heat right from the flame. They will come when we need them.'

Threon nodded, pulling at his armour chest plate nervously.

'You intend to fight then?' Aya said.

'Of course.'

'You would be wiser to stay with us on the hillside.' She tutted. 'No heir, and a land in ruin. What will your people have if they lose you? Your kingdom will be nothing.'

'What will I have if I lose them? I can't stand here and watch them die.' He fiddled with his gauntlets.

'You fought well in the arena,' said Vituund. 'The spirit of Amel truly does live in you.'

Aya laughed heartily, slapping the flank of her mount. 'You threw him in the fighting pits?' Vituund blushed as she continued to laugh. She forced herself to stop and looked Threon in the eye. 'Battle is a very different thing. These are soldiers. Immortal soldiers. Not trained animals. Be sure that you know the danger you're committing to.'

'I know,' he said solemnly, remembering how he'd flung himself from the castle walls to escape them last time. His leg twinged at the memory.

She nodded approvingly. 'Good.'

Aya unsheathed the sword that hung at her waist. 'It has been many generations since our peoples came together. We make history today.' She brought the point of her sword up, and over the head of Threon's steed. 'Join swords with me.' The two men drew their swords. Threon laid his upon her blade. Vituund placed his on top of them both.

They looked at each other for a moment before she continued. 'Today we fight for freedom.'

All three lifted their blades to their faces, gleaming points to the sky in salute.

'For freedom,' said Threon.

'For freedom,' said Vituund.

Aya looked behind them to where the army stood, hidden between trees. Threon followed her gaze. They were all silent; some shuffled on their feet, others looked lost in prayer.

She smiled at Threon and raised an eyebrow. 'You wish to lead this dance?'

He took up the reins and trotted away from them, back to the army.

Sweat glistened on his forehead. His blood beat hot and fast.

A helmet rested on the pommel of his saddle. He tossed it aside, not wishing to compromise his vision. He pulled the gauntlets off too, giving a firmer grip of his sword hilt.

He knew he should say something. Make some speech. Build courage in the soldiers. Inspire them. But his throat was dry, his tongue stuck to the roof of his mouth. He could feel his eyes were wide, and they would see the nervous sweat that covered his brow if not for the rain.

Instead, he spurred Bloodbringer into a frenzy, cantering in small circles up and down the ranks. He raised his sword and thrashed it in the air, slicing through the rain. Moving made him feel better, more confident. His wild energy made them stand to attention. Hands reached for sword hilts, shields were braced, visors snapped down. His own people looked restless. They began to shuffle forwards, teeth bared, weapons clasped. For a moment, he thought they looked like wild bandits; farmers clutching foreign weapons, fear and vengeance in their eyes.

Threon felt like a coiled spring. He needed to release the energy. He turned his mount to face his home. Then spurred the horse on with a single cry.

'Charge!'

His command was echoed by the officers in the throng of soldiers. Bloodbringer danced down the hillside, flinging earth to the sky under hooves. A roar broke out behind, and Threon could see the furthest edges of the column charging out of the forest at the edges of his vision. He soared ahead of them on his steed, soon reaching the fallen wall.

The city alarm rang loud. Threon was blind to the arrows that clattered onto the stone around him. He charged on, up to the foundations of the castle, the stallion skipping over boulders, vaulting sections of shattered wall. He could see a group of men running towards him.

Five of them.

He wished he had more skill with a bow. As it was, he clutched his sword tight, praying they wouldn't shoot him before he reached striking distance. The speed of the horse brought him thundering towards them before he had finished the thought. He thrust his sword down in a loop to hit the nearest man.

He missed. The soldier ducked the blow and grabbed Threon's left leg in the process, jerking it out of the stirrup. He came off the horse backwards, landing heavily. His right foot was still caught in the other stirrup and he was dragged across the rocks for several paces.

Bloodbringer came to a stop.

By now, the army had caught up. They proved distraction enough to give him time to get to his feet.

More Thelonians were coming. He didn't have time to gauge their number before he saw a glint of steel flying at him. He brought his sword up to meet it just in time.

His opponent was built like the other palimore. Nearly a foot taller than Threon, with shoulders as wide as a horse and skin so tight over his muscles it looked like it would rupture.

The palimore was much stronger than him. He pushed Threon backwards and their swords slid together until they were hilt to hilt and only a few inches stood between the men's chests. The Thelonians had, mercifully, been caught unaware. This one wore no armour and carried no other weapons. Threon stepped backwards, wondering how much longer he could resist the pressure on his sword before he tripped in the rubble.

He stared into the soldier's dark eyes. A spark of anger was there but his overall demeanour was frightfully calm. In his peripheral vision, Threon could see men and women fighting all around him. Some had ploughed on further, getting closer to the enemy camp.

A cry burst out behind Threon, and a wounded woman fell sideways onto him.

The knock pushed him out of his attacker's way and the soldier staggered forward for a moment.

Threon took his chance and ducked deeper into the foray, away from his assailant.

Before him, three Waterfolk battled another soldier. The Thelonian swatted away their parries with methodical ease. The man nearest Threon caught a blow to his shoulder, and the palimore's blade sliced muscle from his arm. In the split second that the soldier's sword was embedded in flesh, Threon stabbed forward into the Thelonian's back. He pushed on his blade and saw the soldier look down in surprise as it burst from his stomach, blood seeping into his shirt. Threon pulled out the blade and watched the palimore fall as the man to his left collapsed, shaking, grabbing bloodily at his arm.

A growl behind him. Threon turned to meet the thrust of another's sword with his own. She was armoured, but slight in stature. She was shorter than most of the palimore men, a near match for Threon in size and strength.

They parried blow after blow. Threon tried to keep his breathing under control as he met her blade and watched his footing on the wet stones. Though she was small, her skill was beyond him. He was forced backwards.

An Ionese warrior ran to his aid. Together they thrust at her and she lost her advantage. But only momentarily.

In the next moment, she leapt forward at Threon. She swiped her sword at the Ionese man as she flew through the air. Threon was knocked to the ground. The Ionese soldier's head thudded to the floor beside him.

'Enough,' she said. 'You dare attack us unawares?'

Threon didn't have the breath to respond. She had both of his arms pinned beneath her knees. He tried to wrestle them out from underneath her, to bring his sword up into her back.

She brought her weapon above her, point directed at Threon's head. Blood dripped from her blade onto his cheeks.

He closed his eyes, unable to move. She drove the blade down.

It went dark. Threon felt the wind on his face. The pressure on his arms vanished.

He opened his eyes.

Savanta. Her dark wings cast a shadow over the duelling pair as she hauled the woman backwards. It was enough time for Threon to get to his feet before the soldier thrust her elbows into Savanta's ribs, forcing her to let go.

Savanta beat her wings, climbing higher, away from the foray. Threon was safe. For now.

She had abandoned her killing machine after the melee had truly taken hold. Her hands on the lever had been responsible for at least three palimore deaths. But when the two forces became one mass her fear of targeting the Mainlands soldiers made her leave the weapon behind and take to the skies instead.

Beneath her the scene was carnage.

The iron and animal smell of flesh rose up to her, like walking into a butcher's shop.

The castle stones were red with blood. In some places it pooled in vast puddles. Bodies piled up. Many men and women of the mortal army had fallen. Their bodies formed a fleshy carpet over the stones. Some now tripped over fallen allies, leaving them vulnerable to attack. The immortals made no such mistakes.

They moved swiftly, with a deadly grace. Even from such a distance she could see fear playing on the mortals. The raiders were calm, consistent, like they were running a drill that had been run a hundred times before. She had seen Threon injure one man, though he had crawled off, possibly to survive another day. She had counted three other Thelonians who had been killed, out of a force greater than one hundred.

She had never seen anything like it. She beat her wings, taking her higher and higher, away from those fighting. Away from their pained faces and bloody bodies. She rose so high that the people below looked like a swirl of colours, weaving in and out of each other, each one carrying a bloody trail behind.

They fought on for what felt like days. Her wings grew tired but she kept herself airborne, unable to look away. Eventually, she found herself drawn closer again, keeping her eyes on Threon all the while. She couldn't bear the thought of losing him.

He began to tire, stopping where he could to catch a breath, before being beaten into closer combat. She winced as she watched him pull off his body armour. The shirt beneath it was stained red-brown with blood. Palimore blood? His? She couldn't tell.

She flew closer, fear clutching her heart.

Even through the light rain she could see he was hot with exertion. Sweat covered his red face, his chest rose and fell heavily.

The sound of screams, of metal clashing, of bones breaking and flesh falling. He fought on, now more agile, lighter on his feet. More vulnerable.

Then she spotted another face she knew. Lleu was battling two Ionese soldiers just metres from Threon. Unlike many of the palimore, he was armoured, ready for battle. Her warning had served him well.

He parried the swords of the Ionese deftly, his attention elsewhere. He was holding back. His prowess was far greater than theirs, but he didn't strike them. He simply defended their blows.

His eyes flickered left and right. He was looking for something, or someone. She saw his eyes widen when they found his father. The commander was beating a fist into a soldier at the other side of the battle site. Lleu's attention returned to his opponents. He tried to push them backwards. She could see he wanted to make his way over to Khan but they blocked his path.

With an impatient thrust he brought his sword down heavily on one soldier, slicing him between his shoulder and neck. The first man fell. The second hesitated for a moment, watching his friend grasp desperately at the welt as he dropped down on weak knees. Lleu stabbed the second man in the stomach.

He didn't wait for him to fall. He pushed him aside to suffer on the ground and made his way through the throng, closer to his father.

Six more men and women died in his wake.

When Lleu reached the commander, he leapt to defend his back. He sidled up, so they were fighting all angles, shoulders touching.

'Son,' grunted Khan.

'We're not going to win this one,' panted Lleu. They were both shouting over the din of the battle.

He felt his father thrust forwards with his sword hand. A

loud cry as he hit his target. A man had launched himself at Lleu and he now engaged in a swordfight, trying to keep his attention on his father all the while.

'If you keep fighting like that we won't.'

Lleu's attention slipped for a moment and his opponent got through his defences. Briefly. The Mainlander brought his sword down on his shoulder. He felt the blow reverberate through his armour. A clump of his dark hair fell to the ground.

'My hair!' he swore, and beat his shield over the man's head, knocking him out.

He called over his shoulder again to Khan. 'Astor, Mante, Quaan. They're all dead.'

'Pregon too. And Vos. We can mourn them later.'

'We cannot mourn them if we too are dead.'

'I have never lost a battle.' Khan thrust forward again, twice. This time there was no scream. A body dropped to the floor and rolled into Lleu's view.

'Don't let your pride destroy us,' pleaded Lleu. Retreating now would offer the Mainlanders a chance.

'All's not lost yet.'

'No, but at what cost might we win? Keresan will have your head if you allow most of her raiders to be wiped out.'

Khan was silent, his anger spoken with violent cuts to anyone within a few feet.

'We've already lost several millenia's worth of skill. Vos was older than even you. Immortality makes you forget. Death comes to us all. Don't let it be like this. Taken unawares by farmers fighting with pitchforks, for fuck's sake.'

He felt his father's shoulders unstiffen. He turned so he could look Lleu in the face.

'If I call the order, you bear responsibility when we report to the Empress.'

'You're taking my advice?' His father never took advice from anyone. He suppressed a smile. 'I'll take responsibility, whatever the consequences.'

'Fine. I'll spread the order.'

Khan climbed up a segment of one of the fallen castle walls. 'Men! Retreat!'

The sound of swords clashing became less frequent. The screams fewer and further apart. Both Threon and his palimore opponent slowed their duelling and looked around to see what was going on.

Another palimore brushed by. He grabbed Threon's opponent by the shoulder with the words 'Come on'. The palimore wound out of the foray. Cries of 'Retreat!' began to echo across the battlefield.

Threon lowered his sword to watch in wonder as the raiders retreated to the harbour. Their faces were shocked, angry. As they went, they lifted the bodies of their dead and wounded.

The Mainlands' forces stood aside to let them pass. The few that didn't were met with swift retribution.

As they made their way down the hill, Threon's knees buckled and he collapsed to the floor. Around him, others fell or sat, or ran desperately to their fallen friends.

He closed his eyes, tired beyond exhaustion. His muscles burned, his injured leg screamed in pain, and his whole body was shaking with shock and the tail end of adrenaline.

He lay on the flagstones and ran fingers along the smooth floor. The old castle courtyard. Home.

The Guardians floated into the battlefield. They calmed those held in the grip of fear, assembled the dead and took pain from the dying. Azzania stood at the edge of the forest and watched them work, doing her best to cordon the fear that threatened to steal her focus. It had been two months since she set out from Ionia, leaving her home for the first time, to seek a champion to unite the Mainlands. The high altitudes were serene in their sparse population, where the cold landscapes often glistened under a mask of snow. The scene before her was a savage contrast. A ruined castle marred black by fire now gleamed wet with blood. Bodies scattered the landscape, and though the sounds of battle had died, she could hear a disgruntled retreat mingled with sobbing and the screams of the dying.

She turned at the sound of a horse approaching. 'A horrific sight,' said Aya.

'Yes,' said Azzania, forcing courage to her words. 'You must take solace in the void, Majesty.'

The queen gave her a pointed look. 'You too, Guardian.' Perhaps her fears were less thinly veiled than she had hoped. 'You worry for our champion?'

'I worry for them all.' The heightened sense of suffering that pressed heavily on her mind was easing under the work of the Guardians on the battlefield. She sighed.

'You should be with them,' Aya said, nodding to the Guardians. 'There's much work to be done.'

It didn't do well to be schooled by her queen. 'I only stayed behind to ensure your wellbeing, Majesty.' She didn't turn around as she spoke, staring ahead to the battlefield, eyes scanning for Threon.

'Well, I'm fine. Get on with it, girl. People need you.'

Azzania swallowed her irritation, drawing on the void to prepare herself for the work ahead.

As she walked down the hill, the scene came into sharper focus. Bloodied hands clutched at Guardian robes as the injured and dying pleaded for help. The iron smell of blood

190

was overpowering and the air hung heavy with trauma. She held herself straight, offering words of encouragement and command to subordinate healers, trying to maintain calm as she assessed the scene ahead. Most unharmed soldiers were helping to comfort their fallen comrades or were slumped to the ground, exhausted. She scanned the faces with a growing desperation. Where was Threon?

Overhead came the rhythmic hum of Savanta's wings beating the air. The Thelonian's eyes shone wide as she searched the bodies below. She circled the battleground and then paused abruptly in the air. 'Threon!' As she swooped down to the ground Azzania found herself running to join her.

Threon lay sprawled on his front, cheek to the ground, one arm thrown out to the side. Azzania rushed to him, and her horror vanished as she saw his fingers moving across the burnt earth. He was alive.

She rolled him onto his back and he opened his eyes. 'I thought you were dead,' breathed Azzania.

Savanta pushed past her and pulled him into a rash embrace. 'Threon!' His face flinched in pain, but he wore a smile.

'We won,' he said.

Savanta helped him to his feet. He looked around over the battlefield. The bodies of the dead were piled up high.

'How many dead?' he asked.

'Three or four hundred,' said Azzania 'We're still counting, and there are more on their way to death from injury.'

'They retreated,' he said numbly.

'I think it was Lleu,' said Savanta.

'We let them retreat.'

'They would have killed many more if you'd gone after them.'

'But they'll be back.'

'You can't fight again now. Just look around you.'

Threon cast his eyes around again at the devastation littering the castle grounds. Those who had survived lay weeping and wounded or were frantically helping those in need. 'The palimore will be clear of the harbour within the hour,' he said. 'They're loading the ships now, with a strong line of defence ready to meet us should we attack.'

The look of determination slipped from his face, replaced by exhausted resignation. 'We'll catch them up another time.'

'Come,' said Azzania. 'Vituund and Aya will want to see you safe.'

He shook his head. 'Not now.' He rolled his shoulders and touched fingers to a welt on his face as he looked out towards the harbour. 'I want to be alone.'

Azzania nodded in understanding. She watched as he half-dragged his bad leg, retreating from the carnage that troubled the site of the castle. It was a wonder to see the Thelonian horse catch up with him, and he swung himself up onto the steed's back. As he rode into the city, Threon's head hung slack with exhaustion.

By nightfall the death count had risen. Azzania knelt at the head of a dying woman, pressing against the edges of her mind to eliminate pain. The soldier's chest rose in short shallow breaths, eyes staring vacuous at the darkening sky. She had never used the void on so many people in such a short space of time. Her head pounded with excessive use. It was hard to remain focussed for so long, and the mental exhaustion brought with it fatigue and nausea. Anxiety gnawed at the edges of her calm. She would have to stop soon, before her body forced a sickly sleep on her. When the soldier fell back into unconsciousness she placed a kiss on her forehead and got up. Death would come soon.

Threon still hadn't returned to camp. Earlier, she had watched him ride the horse into the fields above the town, and he had sat there until the light sank beneath the sea's horizon. She wagered he was still there now and, keen to clear her head, made her way through the remains of the city, following his path.

She saw the stallion first, his outline a dark shadow on the blue-black sky. Her white robes must have made her more visible because Threon saw her first. 'Azzania?'

'Threon. Are you alright?' She struggled up the steep incline to join him, relieved to sink to the ground and regain her breath.

'You look exhausted,' he said.

'Our work goes on long after the battle.' She lay back on the grass and closed her eyes, bringing her hands up to massage her temples. 'You've been gone hours.'

'I needed some time. You know, to process.' She felt him lie back beside her. 'I watched the ships leave the harbour. My home is a burnt-out shell of its former self. The people I was born to serve are enslaved or changed forever or dead on the battlefield because of them.' His voice was level, any emotion he felt had been squeezed dry. She reached her fingers over the grass to his and clutched his hand. It felt good to touch him without the void; skin to skin, for simple human comfort.

She wanted to console him, to tell him that one day the Mainlands would be free from the threat of invasion, but exhaustion had sunk its claws in. Rolling onto one side, she forced her eyes open. She could make out Threon's outline, nothing more. He rolled his head to look at her. His hand reached over and fingers kissed her face. 'We should head back,' she whispered. 'They'll worry.' But already her limbs felt heavy and her breathing rhythmic with encroaching sleep. His fingers traced up to her eyes and she closed them.

Up here, the sounds of the army were secondary to the wind in the grass and the hiss of the sea. She let the peace of the moment swallow her, and soon fell into a deep and dreamless sleep.

CHAPTER SIXTEEN

Savanta beat her wings hard. The weight of the liquid strapped to her chest made it harder. The weight of her fear made it harder still.

Within half an hour she had the ships in her sight, their lights a foreboding glitter on the black water.

The palimore had escaped in two galleons. They moved sluggishly through the waves, sails limp. She dipped low and felt the sea spray cool her skin. From here she could see a name painted in bold, gold letters on the rear of the ship: *Abundance*. The ship ahead must be *Frostborn* then. She had watched the retreat and knew Lleu was aboard the latter. Only one ship would sink tonight; they needed him alive.

She beat higher into the air until she was level with *Abundance*'s topmast. She unscrewed the cap on the canister strapped to her chest. Most of the palimore's stores had been left behind during their rushed escape, and among them Threon had discovered a supply of liquid catchfire.

A small tip of her wings and the liquid poured down onto

the deck. Executioner's elixir. The few palimore stood on the ship were fatally oblivious, the waves hiding the sound as it splashed against the planks, just as the night hid her.

She reached for the matches in her belt. Lit one. Let it drop.

The ship came to life as flames erupted, hot gold spilling into the sea. She felt a rush of heat burst into the air and beat her wings in retreat.

She flew hard on her way back to port. The further she flew into darkness, the more deafening the screams of the dying echoed in her mind.

The stars disappeared behind thick black smoke and, in the distance, the sea was ablaze. Lleu's ship had swung around, heading back to save burning bodies that had plunged into black water.

He knew it was too late. They all knew it was too late. But they had to try. The same thought was on the minds of every soldier as they edged back, against the wind. It was over an hour before they reached the still burning remains of the other boat.

Some of the palimore pulled from the water were red and blistered, their skin charred, their voices lost to screaming. Most were already dead.

'A waste of life. These men deserved a better death.' The voice was his father's, spoken over his shoulder as he stared out at the fading flames.

Lleu didn't look back at him, and could think of nothing suitable to say.

The commander continued. 'We should have stayed and fought. I'll kill that winged demon if ever I see it again.' He didn't bring up Lleu's decision to free her, but his weary expression meant he didn't have to. Lleu's guilt burned afresh. His conflicted allegiances left him with constant remorse for all his actions.

Lleu turned away from the sea for a moment. The deck was lined with bodies. Some alive, some writhing in pain. Most of them had been his friends, his family, for over a century.

'Warriors like these deserve better,' he said.

His father started to walk away, then turned back to him. 'You'll answer for this. The Empress is not as forgiving as your foolish father.' He shook his head and walked away.

It was three days later when they arrived in Thelonia City, fighting the wind all the way. The journey had been arduous, morale in the gutter. The bodies they had brought home were rotting meat by the time they came to moor.

Khan and Lleu had borne the cold blame put on them by the other soldiers. Now Lleu approached the Empress's private dining chamber alone, a carefully worded report in his hands.

A guard stood outside the door. He stepped aside and let Lleu through.

Keresan stood at a window, looking out to the sea. Lleu cleared his throat. 'Your Eminence,' he said.

She didn't turn. 'I hear only one ship returned from the far side of the sea.' Lleu put his report on a nearby table and stepped further into the room. Sunshine glistened on the Empress's chestnut hair. 'Where is your commander?' she said, rounding to face him. She wore a white silk dress, a white fur cape hanging over one shoulder.

Lleu looked down. 'I came in his stead. The decisions that led to our demise were mine. I should be the one to answer for them.'

She stepped closer. 'You're his son, aren't you? The one born outside the breeding programme.'

He nodded. 'He acted on my suggestion to retreat. I'm not here to protect him.'

'Your report, then.' She sat down on a large wooden chair beside the table and began to pick at a platter of grapes.

He took a deep breath and sighed it out. 'Forgive me, My Lady, but you won't like what is to come.' She said nothing, watching him in cold silence until he continued. He shifted on his feet. 'A rebel force has become apparent in the Waterlands. Khan failed to slaughter all of their royal family. Threon Greenbrooke lives, and he has an army.' Keresan's eyes narrowed. He waited for her to say something but was only met with silence. 'They ambushed us. But they weren't alone. Ionese and Bannvarians joined them.'

'My army would crush a group of upstart peasants. Their finest warriors would be undone by our youngest recruits.'

'Ten of the raiding party were killed.'

Her expression darkened. 'You defeated them.' It wasn't a question.

'We retreated.'

Her body visibly tensed. There was a painful moment of silence as she stared at him, eyes fierce. 'My men do not retreat.' She stood and hurled the platter of grapes in Lleu's direction. It clattered to the floor at his feet.

She began pacing hotly, back and forth, muttering obscenities to herself.

'Should I continue, your Grace?' Lleu spoke to the ground.

'Yes, damn it.' She turned on her heel and marched up to him. She was far shorter than him, and slender. He could have snapped her body like a twig, but the power she held in her stance and the age that flickered in her eyes made her a frightful figure.

He tried to hold her gaze as he continued. 'We lost some of our best. Vos, Astor, Pregon.' He swallowed. 'We were hugely outnumbered and caught unawares. If we had stayed to fight many more would have died. I couldn't let you lose more of your raiders. It was on my recommendation that the commander gave the order to retreat.'

'I shared five centuries with Vos. Mother's balls! Greenbrooke will pay for this.'

Lleu held his hands behind his back as he spoke. He dug fingernails into palms as he continued.

'My Lady, you were right about the ships.' He took a slow breath to stop his voice from wavering. 'All men boarded the ships set to return home. We were far from shore when catchfire dropped from the sky and ignited the deck of the second ship. They tried to fight it, but the flames spread too fast. We turned around to save them, but for most it was too late…'

Her eyes had grown large, and for a moment he thought that she might cry.

'How many?'

'Forty-six soldiers.' He could no longer hold her gaze and let his eyes drop to the floor again.

She struck him across the face. The force of her blow made him stagger. He looked back at her, surprised. 'Your order to retreat killed more than if you had stayed to fight a thousand men.' Her voice shook with venom. 'And my Watcher? What of her? She never returned. An attack from the sky points to her wings.'

'I don't know, My Lady.'

'You don't know? You don't know! What use are you to me, except to cause the destruction of my forces? Guards!' The door opened and a guard appeared. Another followed soon after. 'Take him away.'

They moved to take Lleu's arms. He let them. His voice cracked as he said, 'They were my brothers, my sisters.'

The guards began to walk him backwards out of the door. Keresan slumped in her seat and gripped the chair's arms so tightly her fingers turned white. 'Wait,' she said. The guards paused but didn't let go. She was trembling with anger. 'Private Lleu, I rescind your access to vish'aad.'

He did not hear the words. He felt them in the pit of his stomach. It was no more than he had expected, no more than he deserved, but the blow fell like the executioner's axe.

CHAPTER SEVENTEEN

Savanta did not fly directly back to Maradah. Instead she flew beyond, to a wide fjord, and alighted on a cliff edge. She stared out over the dark landscape, numb, watching the reflection of the moon ripple in the water below. The men and women she had killed were in retreat. They were unprepared, and undeserving of such a death. She had been able to smell the fire on the wind on her return. She pictured burning bodies diving to the water, only to drown, vain efforts to put out a fire that would only grow like a monstrous god to take them all.

She hadn't cried a single tear for those who had fallen.

None of them had ever done her any harm. This was not her fight. But somehow she had allowed herself to become embroiled in a foreign war. Threon would tell her she had done the right thing. But surely killing those in retreat was unforgivable? She was a long way from the curious inventor living in Tannit. Blood on her hands, and a master on each side of the fight.

A hand touched her shoulder.

She sighed and turned around. Zenith stood behind. His

usually blond hair was now the colour of night. He sat down beside her and they stared out across the water in silence for some time before he spoke.

'They are the enemy, you know. Innocent individuals who aligned themselves to the wrong cause.'

'Please don't. I want to be alone.'

'Oh, my sweet. You are never alone. I am always with you.' His smile made her feel sick.

'You did me proud today.'

She pushed a pebble over the cliff edge and watched it fall into the water. 'Do I really deserve this?'

'The honour of sitting beside a Vyara? Probably not.' He laughed quietly to himself.

'You treat me like your pawn, your plaything. And for what? For building a machine that made you jealous?'

'All lives belong to the Vyara.' He took her hand. 'I can do with you as I please.'

Anger began to build in her, but she forced it down. She closed her eyes, remembering her lessons on the road. She summoned the void and began to feel a tingling sensation in the hand that he held.

She felt a breath of nothing wash over her. All anger, all sadness, all thoughts left her as the void stripped away her grey skin.

She could look Zenith in the face now. He tried to pull his hand away but she kept it firmly in her grasp. All humour left him in place of horror. 'No. You can't.'

Her natural skin slowly revealed itself as the void pushed back the grey, leading from her hand, up her arm, to her shoulder.

Zenith blinked; he looked in pain for a moment, and then broke free of her grasp, roaring in anger. 'Where did you learn that?' His figure began to grow larger. As he loomed over her, twice her size, dark clouds covered the moon.

A spark of fear broke through her trance, and Savanta lost control of the void. Her skin became grey again.

He stepped towards her. 'Do not resist me, mortal. I am your master. Do not forget it.' He stifled her next breath. Her chest struggled to rise. Panic rose in her as she fought for oxygen. Her heart pounded in her ears and she clawed at her throat, darkness creeping into her vision. She dropped to the floor, mouth gaping to draw breath, but none came.

'I've been lenient with you, Savanta. But your disloyalty goes too far.'

She stared at the grass under her hands as a burning heat built in her lungs.

As she neared unconsciousness, her body fell into survival mode. Her racing thoughts stopped. All focus was on the need for breath. It gave her a chance to latch onto the void again, and she took it.

This time she focussed on her lungs. They burned hotter.

She felt a thin stream of air trickle down her throat. She took a shallow breath. Then another. And another, until she was gasping in air.

She met the Vyara's eyes. He was looking at her as if for the first time.

She was coughing now, lightheaded, but far from suffocation. Staggering to her feet, she stared him down.

He was taken aback, now watching her in disbelief.

'Making an enemy of me is a big mistake, child.'

With that, he broke into a flurry of bats, flying away into the moonless night.

It was gone midnight in Maradah. The Mainlands' forces had made camp in the town, sheltering in houses, inns and canvas tents.

It wasn't until she was sure the camp was asleep that Savanta flew down to the city. She entered the tent that she and Azzania had been allocated. She picked up a fur and threw it around her shoulders against the cold night air, before creeping over to where the Guardian slept.

She placed a hand on Azzania's arm and her friend's eyes opened immediately.

'What's wrong?' she whispered.

Savanta put her finger to her lips and motioned her to get out of bed. She handed her a cloak, which Azzania swept around her naked body.

They left the camp in silence and Savanta led her down to the harbour.

When they were out of earshot, Azzania asked again, 'What is it?'

'I had an encounter with Zenith today. After the fire. I challenged him using the void.'

Azzania was impossible to read. Was that a look of reproach? Or admiration?

'That was foolish,' she said at last. 'What happened?'

'I don't know. It looked like my touch caused him pain. He cut off my air supply and when I managed to summon the void, his grasp on me faltered. I could breathe again.' Azzania looked impressed.

They had reached the harbour now. Azzania walked to the water's edge and looked up at the sky. The clouds had cleared and an atlas of stars shone down on them.

'The void is absence. It removes joy, sorrow, love, hate. It clears the mind, removes pain. The Vyara live on our emotions, our actions and our worship.' She looked back at Savanta. 'Removing these precious things threatens their existence. In Ionia we dedicate ourselves to the void for a reason. A strong Guardian presence there eliminates Vyaran power.'

'And your people travelling to Thelonia... They're not just going to heal the injured.'

'No, child.' She smiled sweetly. 'Threon's fight brings together something much bigger than the battle for his homeland. Challenging the Empire is a direct challenge to Deyar. He will become embroiled in this fight, and his siblings will either rally to his aid or stand against him in another Vyaran power struggle.

'You shouldn't have challenged Zenith today. You aren't strong enough to stand against him. He could have killed you for such defiance.'

'Maybe he has other plans for me.' She came to stand beside Azzania and looked out over the water. A wave of cold passed over her, and she shivered. 'Maybe he believes that a world without love, hate, joy and sadness is a world not worth living in.' A light wind circled the pair. 'Maybe he has plans for you and your kind.' Her last words came out like a winter wind. Savanta felt something inside her shrink, like her spirit had been pushed aside in favour of a darker power. The words she spoke were not her own. Zenith crowded her body and she was forced to play his living puppet.

Azzania went to say something but was cut off as Savanta hurled her into the shallow water below.

Both women landed in the icy water, legs sinking deep into mud. Azzania toppled backwards and Savanta leapt onto her with a strength that she had never known herself to possess.

Her fingers wrapped around Azzania's neck and she forced the woman's head under the salty water. Bubbles rose from cherry lips, and Savanta pushed harder against her throat, unable to stop herself.

The Guardian's body convulsed. Savanta shifted her weight, bringing her shins down on Azzania's legs, forcing them into the mud to prevent her kicking. Savanta mentally screamed at Zenith to release his control. She was helpless to stop his actions.

Azzania's hands were still free and she reached up as if to grab Savanta's throat in defence. Instead, the Guardian grabbed both her forearms and forced the void into her. Azzania stopped thrashing, and Savanta's old skin blossomed across her body with speed. She felt her wings grow shorter, pushing themselves back into her spine. Her hair, hanging wet about her face, changed from black to her natural red.

Something inside her ruptured, a feeling that started in her stomach and burst in her mind. Zenith was being ripped from her spirit. She cried out, feeling very naked. Very human.

Now she looked down, horrified. Azzania's arms had dropped, limp, and were floating in the lapping waves. Her eyes were open, red-rimmed through the water.

Savanta recoiled her hands from the woman's neck and got up, shaking. The body floated to the surface. Red marks at her neck, lips blue-tinged, accusatory eyes staring upwards.

She dragged her friend to shore in a trance. People were coming now, drawn by the noise. They were shouting, but she couldn't make out the words.

Numb, she hauled Azzania to the mud bank of the harbour. Tried to blow air into her lungs. Her lips were ice. She pressed up and down on her chest, tears streaming, shaking with cold and exhaustion.

Zenith would pay for this.

By the time a small group of Mainlanders reached them, she fell back, her arms too weak to continue the compressions.

There were shouts, and she was hauled up by two men and forced back up the hill. An Ionese man spat at her. She let her body hang limp as they dragged her away.

She must have passed out, because the next thing she

206

remembered was landing heavily on the cobbled floor of the gatehouse.

Imprisoned again.

Threon received news of the harbour incident at dawn.

He threw open the door to the gatehouse. 'What have you done?' His rage was quickly curtailed by the sight of a slender, naked girl curled up in one corner, sobs wracking her body.

She turned to look at him. Tan skin, red hair, wingless. 'Savanta?' Her green eyes were puffy and red-rimmed.

She turned away again, hiding her head between her knees, hugging them close to her body. 'I'm sorry.' The words shuddered out on a sob.

The Ionese soldier who had reported the incident stood behind him. He pushed past Threon and dragged Savanta to her feet. She stood meekly, shoulders slumped, arms wrapped around her chest. 'She's the one. We saw her change before our eyes. She did it just as she was drowning the Guardian, full of fury.'

Savanta said nothing. She looked weak, vulnerable, nothing like her previous terrible form.

'For gods' sake, cover her up,' said Threon to the soldier. He released her arm roughly and begrudgingly removed his cloak, tossing it at her. She pulled it around her shoulders, wiping snot and tears from her face.

Threon came closer, trying to keep the anger from his voice. 'I trusted you. Azzania trusted you. How did I get you so wrong?'

Savanta lifted her head to look at him. 'Threon, I swear it wasn't me. Azzania...'

'There are many witnesses, and all claim you're guilty.'

The Ionese man spoke up. 'What will you do with her?'

Threon didn't know how to answer that. 'Were your orders from the Empire? Why target the Guardians?'

'They weren't my orders – I don't know – I don't know what happened. I wasn't in control. Zenith—'

She was interrupted by the sound of the door opening. Azzania entered. She was wrapped in heavy furs, her skin still pale with cold and streaked with sea mud. He had never imagined she could look so vulnerable.

Threon looked from one woman to the other, unable to fathom what had happened between them. 'You should be resting.' He took Azzania's hand. She was cold. Her throat was red-purple, deep finger marks etched on pale skin.

She released his hand and walked further into the room. Savanta's eyes brightened. 'You're alive.' Honest relief flooded her features. She moved to embrace the Guardian, but the Ionese soldier grabbed her arm. 'Stay back, Islander.'

'Leave her,' said Azzania. 'It wasn't her fault.' The soldier looked to Threon, who nodded, before he released Savanta. He spat at her feet. 'She was under Vyaran influence,' Azzania reproached the soldier. 'Her actions were not her own. My strength with the void is what saved me. It was her weakness with it that undid her.'

'Azzania,' started Savanta, 'I'm so sorry—'

'You are a dangerous woman to know. A vessel for a powerful and savage god. I am sorry also. I underestimated Zenith's hold on you.'

'What now?' said the soldier. 'Under Ionese law, the sentence would be death.'

'Enough,' snapped Azzania.

Savanta looked so small and helpless now; her humour, confidence and strength ripped from her. Her gaze switched from Threon to Azzania and back again. Her pleading eyes implored compassion. Threon pitied her. They were her only friends and allies this side of the ocean, and now she looked at them both with fear.

'I won't kill an innocent woman for another's actions,' said Threon. 'But,' he swallowed, knowing how much the truth would hurt her, 'I can't endanger my people with your presence. The Guardians will come with us to Thelonia. I can't risk another episode like this.' He could no longer meet her eyes. 'You stay behind.'

Savanta's hope fell away. She stepped backwards to the wall and slumped down. Being left behind was tantamount to solitary confinement. The city would empty, and she would be left alone with no means to fly home.

The soldier grumbled in displeasure and left the room. Threon came to kneel beside her. She looked away from him, down to the cobbles. 'This breaks my heart,' he said. 'But you must understand.'

Her words were quiet, as if to herself. 'You choose to leave me here, stranded, to rot with my god.'

Threon couldn't find the words. Azzania took his hand and pulled him away. 'Leave her,' she said.

They left the room, and guilt tore at his heart as the Guardian bolted the door behind them.

CHAPTER EIGHTEEN

By the time he reached the barracks, word of Lleu's mortality had already swept before him. His fellow soldiers greeted him with pained looks. Some of them. Others were less than subtle in expressing their satisfaction at his sentence.

He went straight to his quarters without speaking to anyone. As the door slammed behind him, the walls of the small room shook. He slammed his fist on his desk; it refused to break, only causing him to cry out at the stab of pain.

He had resolved to weaken the Empire, but every step meant destroying the life and people he had grown up with. Perhaps that would stop now. Vish revoked, he would lose any respect he had built over the years. They might even cast him out. What good would he be to the resisting army then?

He kicked his desk chair and it splintered into three parts on the opposite wall. He grabbed its legs, thrashing them to crack against the floor, until he was running with sweat. Next the bed. The sheets tore easily, but the wreckage did nothing to satisfy. The room was sparse, with nothing left to destroy, so he resorted to beating the walls with his forearms and vocalising pain in a series of cries and curses.

The violent pounding broke a chain he wore at his wrist. It held a locket containing a strand of his wife's hair. As it clattered to the floor he stopped, still panting through gritted teeth, and bent to pick it up.

He brought it up to his lips to kiss it. Raikka. He missed her now more than ever. The soldiers had died for her, that's what he told himself. A small revenge for her capture. It was little comfort to the divided loyalties of his conscience.

'I'll find you,' he whispered, and collapsed back onto the bed, head in his hands, tearing at his hair.

He jerked upright as he heard the door latch slide backwards. His father came into the room. Solemnity and disappointment weighed down his features. 'You've heard?' said Lleu.

Khan nodded. 'I shouldn't have listened to you on the battlefield.'

Lleu shrugged. His father stepped over shattered wood to the side of the bed. He held out a hand. 'I've come for the last of it,' he said.

'Even my current supply?' His hand gripped protectively to the vial that hung at his neck.

'What difference will it really make? An extra two, maybe three days? I don't want to take it by force.' He kept his hand held out.

Lleu tugged on the vial and the chain snapped open, dropping from around his neck. He ran a finger over the glass, looking up at his father, hoping for empathy.

Khan reached out and took it from him. 'I'm sorry. I'd hoped we'd spend many more years together.'

Lleu's eyes widened. 'You can't make me leave.'

211

Khan looked away, avoiding his gaze. 'I can't watch you grow old. Watch you grow weak, wither, die.'

'Where do you expect me to go?'

'Go back to your mother's family. Live a mortal life with people on the same timescale. Staying here will drive you mad.'

Lleu had no idea Khan knew the rest of his family still lived. The surprise must have shown on his face.

'Of course I knew about your visits to them, about your strange obsession with your roots. Do you think I'm a fool?'

'You never said anything.' Did he know about Raikka too?

'To protect my son. Did you never think how dangerous it could be to keep that link with your old blood?' Lleu was silent. 'You thought you were fooling us all.' He sighed. 'You can have until the end of the week to settle your affairs.'

'No, wait. You can't. I'm still palimore.' He got to his feet. 'Don't waste a century of training. I can still fight. You expect me to farm?' He was on the edge of panic. How could they cast him out?

'You'll grow old. Or you'll be injured and we won't be able to use vish to heal you. In the Waterlands you can live the rest of your life in peace.'

'In peace. In poverty. In old age. And what will happen when you come for more slaves for the mines? No.' He grabbed his father's arm. 'Let me stay. Whether it's on the battlefield or on the training ground, leave me to bleed. I don't want treatment. Let me spend my last years here with you, and when age weakens me, let me die a quick death in combat.' He meant it. Not just for the sake of the rebellion, but for his own sake. Being palimore was all he had ever known. How would he cope on the outside?

After a century of taking vish, Lleu's body began to fall apart without it. The withdrawal was coming; he'd seen it happen before. Thirty years ago he witnessed a lieutenant's discharge. She endured it on the streets. At least Lleu had a roof over his head.

It began with a sickness in his stomach. His temperature rose and fell in hot and cold sweats. Then anxiety. His heart raced in his chest and his brain screamed out for more of the violet powder.

That first day, he had pleaded with soldiers for their supplies. Desperate. He blackmailed, threatened and begged. By the next day the pain built up, all over his body. His muscles tore as he moved. His eyes burned and leaked uncontrollably. Weakness confined him to his quarters, where he lay in bed until the mattress was sodden with sweat.

Night brought no relief with sleep. He lay awake, heart racing, limbs twitching. He buried his head into his pillow and bit down on it as he screamed.

The days blurred into one long stretch of hell. He was gifted with more of the same, and worse. Too weak to get up, he shat himself in bouts of diarrhoea that caused his guts to convulse and ache. The pain in his limbs was coupled with the sensation of needles repeatedly piercing his skin.

Once, he found the energy to get to the door, but found it locked.

Food and water appeared on his floor daily. Even the sight of food made him nauseous, and the water only prompted vomiting. He would dry heave until his throat was sore, until his face was slick with mucous and tears.

It could have been hours, days or weeks since his mortal sentence had been carried out – he couldn't tell – but at long last there came a day when he could eat again. The thin bowl of porridge sat heavy on his stomach. He felt sick, but it stayed down. By now he was dreadfully aware of the stench that filled his room. Vomit, sweat, piss, shit and shame.

That night, the door finally unlocked. His father greeted him, and he was led to a hot bath.

His body screamed as he stepped a foot into the hot water, skin oversensitive, but he pushed the pain to the back of his mind. Beneath his weakened muscles he could see ribs protruding. His father watched from the corner of the room as a slave sponged the filth caked to his skin.

'You'll be alright, Lleu,' his father said softly.

Lleu put his head in his hands, unable to hold back the tears.

CHAPTER NINETEEN

Threon had discovered cured meats, candied fruits, even wine, in the palimore stores. He had ordered everything to be laid out in a feast to celebrate their victory before setting sail for the island. Vituund's servants had set up rows of tables along the cobbled courtyard that opened out on the harbour. The sky had cleared and cold sunshine glanced off the calm sea.

Threon gorged himself, made ravenous by the exhaustion the last few days had brought. Vituund's attendants waited on the army, bringing drinks and fresh platters of food. Threon sat himself on a table of Bannvarian soldiers. One of Vituund's maids leaned over Threon's shoulder and filled his glass with wine. She smiled at him. 'I was rooting for you in the fighting pit,' she said. 'The king was right to pledge support.' Like most of Vituund's female servants, this woman wore a cerise robe with a matching headdress. Beads and circles of copper looped decoratively around her forehead and her eyes were lined with kohl. There seemed a marked contrast between those who had fought and those who had not. She was clean; clothes unsoiled and skin unmarked, and she was missing the look of fatigue that the soldiers wore.

Threon lifted the wine to his lips and a thousand memories flooded back. His mother had a fine palate for wine and collected vintages from far and wide. He wondered whether this might have come from her cellar.

He smiled back at her. 'You saw the fight?'

'I see all the fights. They're a great laugh, when I can get the time off.' She poured wine for the soldier sat next to Threon. 'I thought it would be a right buzz watching the battle yesterday. I snuck out of camp to see it from the edge of the forest. But it's really not the same. Just bodies flung together like worms in a pot. And all that noise! You must be exhausted.'

He shrugged in agreement. 'This helps to make up for it,' he said, indicating the spread on the table. 'Have you eaten?'

She shook her head. 'Nah, we have to serve others first.'

'There might not be any left by the time this lot have finished.' He looked around at the other soldiers, evidently as hungry as he was. 'Sit for a moment.' The girl didn't need telling twice. She grinned and stepped over the bench to seat herself close at his side.

'I've heard you sing,' she said. 'I used to drink in the Hawk when you played there. Heard you once or twice in the Bell too. You've a lovely voice.' She gazed at him intently, an edge of desire hanging on her words. Threon took a sip of his drink to break eye contact. 'You should sing tonight. Seeing as we're celebrating.'

Her hand found its way to his knee. He lowered the glass and was about to say something, but she leaned over and whispered in his ear, 'And you know, if there's any way I can help a soldier celebrate…' Her hand moved higher up his thigh. 'I love a man with blue eyes.' She squeezed his leg, and then something faltered on her face. Threon followed her gaze to see Azzania standing behind them.

'Azzania—' he started.

The maid stood and picked up her wine jug. She squeezed his shoulder as she turned to go. 'Hope to see you later, m'Lord.' He watched in disbelief as she sauntered to the next table. Her timing was damnable.

'Threon.' Azzania's tone chilled him. 'We need to make plans to sail. Aya and Vituund are waiting for us.' She strode away from him, in the direction of the ships.

'Shit, shit, shit.' He stood up and hurried to re-tie his sword belt.

One of the soldiers looked up from his food. 'In trouble there,' he smirked. Threon grunted in response and rushed to follow Azzania.

She was already across the jetty and climbing a gangway to a Thelonian ship; one of the three merchant galleons the palimore had left behind in their haste to escape.

As he stepped onto the jetty, something slowed his pace. He felt like someone was watching him. Then he heard a voice shimmer through the cold air. His ears pricked and he turned. The voice seemed to come from the water; a woman calling his name. A shiver ran down his spine. He went to take another step towards the ship. The voice came again. *Threon.* An ethereal whisper. His haste to catch up vanished with the sound. It compelled him to stop.

Down here, Threon.

He knelt down on the wooden jetty and peered over the side. There was nothing but the deep, dark water. The voice came again. *Threon.*

He knelt down to get a better look, and in doing so, felt a wave of vertigo sweep through him. He lost all sense of balance, of which way was up, which down. His body tilted forward and he fell head first into the water. The icy sea stung as he broke the surface. He felt himself being sucked under, deeper into the water. He was pulled down and down, much deeper than he knew the water level in the harbour to be. So deep that the dim light on the surface of the water almost vanished and he was consumed by black.

Eventually the pulling stopped. He tried kicking up to the surface but did not move any closer to it.

A shadow passed across the faint glow of the sun. It circled him, a mass of black silk swirling around him in the water. And then it stopped. The figure of a woman, dark hair and pale skin tinged with blue. She floated before him like a living corpse. Athys?

Threon let out a splurt of air as he tried to say something. His chest grew tighter and his eyes stung in the salt water.

She watched him passively as he struggled to kick back to the surface. Eventually, she spoke. 'You should have greater trust in me, Greenbrooke.' The words were muffled by water. No air left her lungs as she spoke.

He tried to speak again, only to watch precious oxygen ripple out of his lungs and up to the distant surface.

She cocked her head as she watched him struggle. She moved closer, and he could feel the black silk of her dress dancing around him. Her skin was sickly, translucent, her lips blue, her eyes sunken. He could see her veins, traced bold and black beneath thin skin.

He couldn't bear it much longer. He prepared to expel the last of his air and breathe in the cold water.

Moments before he could do so, she clasped him around the back of his head and kissed him deeply on the lips. He felt the need for air vanish instantly.

She pulled away from him and he stared at her, now certain

in the knowledge that he was in the presence of one of the Vyara.

'Better?' she said. This time the words were sharp and clear in his ears.

'Yes,' he said, attempting to bow. Speaking the word made him aware that water was now in his lungs, in his stomach, in his throat. The sensation was nauseating. 'Why am I here?'

'Threon Greenbrooke.' She spoke with a delicate deliberateness. 'It has been many generations since I last spoke to one of your line. Your reign, and your father's reign… they have not served the people well.'

'I'm doing my best.'

'You don't understand the world into which you tread. You think the immortal army will be your greatest challenge, but you're wrong. Thelonia is more intricately linked to Deyar than I am to the Waterlands. The Empress gained her power through an alliance with my brother. You fight against her, you fight against him. Vyara do not lose.'

'You don't want me to harm your brother?'

'My brother is an arrogant fool.' She snapped the words, then softened. 'Life can only be sustained with a balance of the three elements. All life needs water, air and earth. Deyar disrupts this balance by calling himself King; by controlling the populace; by weakening his siblings. In his wake, my power diminishes, as does that of Zenith.'

'And Zenith, does he agree?'

'Zenith is an even bigger fool. He thinks he can take on Thelonia with only his wits and that winged girl. Like all men, he desires power. He will use you for his own selfish ends, Threon Greenbrooke.'

'And where do you stand?'

'I make weather with one brother and carve mountains with the other. I crave unity. I want to restore balance to the

219

world. When the trinity are in equity, life thrives. I'm tired of these power struggles.

'I was once like them. I used to interfere in your world. I played with and manipulated your kind. But no longer. Not now Mother is gone. I watch my brothers now, squabbling like children. You must know you are not simply facing battle. The very land you stand on will be against you.'

'Will you help us?'

She closed her eyes. 'No.' He felt the word ripple towards him in the water. 'Millennia of Vyara squabbling for power. It ends now. I will not join my brothers' petty fight.' He was growing cold. He could feel the heat leaving his flesh and the icy water chilling him to his bones. She continued, 'I understand your desire for freedom, and welcome a world rid of Keresan. I will aid your passage across the sea and give you this warning. My brothers will come to blows on this. Do not stand in their way when they come to fight. Deyar's hold on the island only exists through the Empress. Break their link. That is the way.'

Threon's muscles had started to convulse. The cold had numbed his body.

'You're freezing,' she said. 'You must return.'

She brought her lips to his again. This time, he felt a violent force sucking the liquid from his lungs. His chest compressed as she drew out the kiss, and then she was gone.

He needed air.

Azzania had come running when she heard the commotion at the waterside. Someone said Threon had fallen in, and he'd been gone several minutes. She scanned the surface of the water. It was shallow enough to see the bottom, but there was no sign of him. The pain in her temples and a tightness in her chest told her the Vyara were at work. She lay on the jetty and dropped a hand down, fingers dipping into the water in an attempt to reach out with the void. The feeling that always came to her with such ease now felt like it was wrapped in a thick layer of damp wool. A Vyaran presence distanced her from her power. It was unnerving. She snatched back her hand before fear could take hold.

There was a gasp from those gathered as Threon broke through the surface. As the icy water broke around his head he breathed in deep, choking on damp air.

Azzania forgot her fear of the Vyara's presence and dived in. The cold stole her breath, but she swam to join him. He was an adept swimmer, but now splashed in panic and grabbed hold of her gladly. When they reached the edge of the jetty he tried to wave away her concerns and insisted on pulling himself out of the water without help. His arms shook as he did so and he collapsed panting on the wooden planks, body shuddering with cold. His teeth chattered, and he leant up against the jetty railings, likely to keep his legs from giving way.

Azzania put her hands on his chest. Forcing the void into him took all her concentration; the air of Vyara hung heavily on him. His face relaxed as she melted the cold from his mind. He breathed a sigh of relief and it took him a moment to notice her concern. 'Godstouched,' she said.

'I'm fine.'

She looked him in the eye, still holding him with the void. 'Be careful. The Vyara encroach on you. The void wanes under their power.'

He didn't seem to be taking her concerns seriously. 'Azzania, about earlier.' His teeth still chattered. 'It wasn't what it looked like.'

It never was what it looked like when it came to men. But she was surprised that he was so eager to show remorse, especially given his near drowning. 'Lucky for you, I'm

221

beyond the politics of jealousy.' A lie, but hurting him back wouldn't help things.

Vituund interrupted the moment, striding over to wrap his coat about Threon's shoulders. 'You had us frightened there, Threon. You Waterfolk have lungs of steel!'

There were few furnished rooms aboard the galleon, its chief purpose being to transport cargo. The three royals made their plans in the merchant's cabin. The room was all dark wood and richly adorned with foreign treasures. Paintings cluttered the walls and a large glass cabinet held an array of beautiful stuffed birds. The three monarchs sat around the merchant's desk, a map between them. They plotted their next move. Azzania leant against one of the portholes and watched their talk from a distance.

'One victory doesn't promise another,' said Vituund. 'Are we not wiser to rest our forces here? When more raiding parties come, we will be ready for them.'

Aya shook her head. 'The palimore are not finite in number. For every one of them who died on that battlefield, a new one will be recruited. And I'm not talking about the conscription of green young men. The vish'aad rations of each man and woman who died will be re-assigned to one of their soldiers-in-training. Fierce brutes, all of them.'

'She's right,' said Threon. 'We know they're more powerful. We can't sit and wait for them to return with a greater force. We need to remove not only the palimore, but the Empress herself. As long as her reign continues, they will continue to put mining ahead of agriculture, there will be hunger on the island, and they will continue to raid our lands.'

'We must strike fast, like a snake,' said Aya. 'They will not expect us to attack again so soon, especially on their land. Surprise is a powerful ally.'

222

Vituund shook his head. 'I understand, but the odds do not stack in our favour. Living in fear of them here is not desirable, but surely it is preferable to three kingdoms falling tomorrow on Thelonian soil. We cannot match their strength nor the healing offered by their vish'aad.'

Threon dragged his hands through his hair. 'What if our armies had vish too?'

'And how, my Lord, do you expect to achieve that?' asked Aya pointedly.

He looked at Azzania for backup. 'Lleu. He's disloyal to the palimore. He managed to call the retreat so must hold some sway. If he could help us get hold of some…'

Azzania perked up at his suggestion and came to stand beside him. 'If there was a way to reduce their supply, it would cause panic,' she said. 'Maybe even infighting if there wasn't enough left to go around.'

'It would give us an upper hand.'

Aya leaned back in her chair, nodding thoughtfully. 'No guarantees. But then, there are few certainties in war. If what you suggest is possible, we may indeed stand a chance of success.' She looked at Vituund and raised her eyebrows.

He sighed and brought his hands together in a steeple in front of him. 'How do we communicate with this soldier?'

Threon cursed their recent loss of faith in Savanta. Her speed and knowledge of the Empire would have proven invaluable. So instead he said, 'I'll go.' Athys had promised him swift passage across the sea. Perhaps this is what she had meant. Vituund frowned and Aya was about to say something, but he waved her down. 'He knows me. If we want to strike now, we can't risk sending someone he might not trust.'

'You can't go alone,' said Vituund. 'You're a king now. You have people to protect.'

Threon scoffed at the comment. 'I have nothing to lose. My people cannot rebuild until they are safe from the threat of raids. If this is the best chance they have at freedom, it's my duty to go for them.'

Azzania put a hand on his shoulder. 'I'll go with you,' she said. He met her eyes and smiled.

Aya clapped her hands together. 'A fine plan. I believe theft is better performed by two than by an army. You will travel more swiftly alone than with the full force. If you were to leave today, you should be able to reach the capital before we are ready to make sail.' She ran her hand across the map. 'This bay here, south of the city. It's in the Greylands and secluded enough to hide the arrival of an army. We will ready the troops and meet you here with the vish'aad.' She looked at Vituund and he nodded in resignation to her suggestion. 'Agreed?'

Threon spread his palms and smiled. 'Agreed.'

Threon and Azzania packed provisions and set sail on a small fishing boat. The sea was calm, the winds in their favour. Threon dangled his hand over the edge of the boat and watched his fingers trail a v in the water. Azzania was still looking back in the direction from which they had come, knees drawn to her chest.

'Don't look so worried.' She ignored him and continued staring back to shore. Maradah had vanished over the edge of the horizon before sunset and now a moon shone high above them. The boat sped through the water at an unnatural pace. She pulled on the void to dull her fear, feeling the influence of the Vyara on their journey.

'Do you think this is all Athys? Or is Zenith helping guide the wind?' He was teasing her, but she took his question literally.

'It's Athys.' Her words were short and sharp. She took a breath to calm her anxieties. The Vyara did not interfere with mortal lives in Ionia. She had never felt such a strong spiritual presence; like a powerful tide capable of guiding or drowning them. She felt out of control. For the first time her life was being steered by a power other than her own will. It struck her that this must have been how Savanta felt with Zenith ever at her shoulder.

'You can tell?' he asked.

'I can tell. I'm doing everything within my power to stop myself from forcing the void against her. Vyaran favours don't come without a price.'

'She wants to bring down the Empress as much as we do. There'll be nothing to pay for this.'

'Do you know nothing of Ionese history?'

Threon turned away from the water and leant up against the side of the boat. He shrugged. 'You know I never paid much attention to my tutors.'

'I see.' She returned to staring back out across the water.

Threon waited for her to say more, and when she didn't, said, 'Go on then. Enlighten me. It'll take your mind off things.'

Azzania frowned as she sat up to tell her story. Perhaps a history lesson would be of some use to him. 'You've never heard of Kyvo?' Threon shook his head. She tried not to roll her eyes. His knowledge was more patchy than she'd feared. 'Well, many generations ago there lived an Ionese knight named Kyvo. He was a great warrior, and a devout servant to the trinity. He would visit the temple morning, noon and night.

'A drought came to Ionia. The people prayed and prayed for Athys to bring water, but none came. Kyvo saw this to be a test and he held his faith, despite the failing crops and the deaths of the old and weak.

'In those days, we were known as the Sky People. We lived in the mountains, near the clouds. Most devoted themselves to Zenith. He came to Kyvo in a dream and told him that Athys had turned on the people; she was withholding her water and taking pleasure in watching the Ionese suffer. Zenith bade the knight draw together all the forces the land could muster to go against her. The loyal knight did as he was asked, and the pious people of the mountains responded to Zenith's call.

'It was all a game. Zenith led the people to the sea, and there he told them to destroy his sister. Some threw spears into the water, others fell to their knees and prayed for her to stop. And then the storms began. Zenith and Athys were fighting a battle all around them. Wind and rain soon became typhoon, hurricane, tsunami.

'Kyvo began to see that the Vyara he had spent his life worshipping were playing games with him, with his family, with all of his people.

'Bodies were broken in the wind, or were drowned, or were lost, never to be found again. Entire cities were destroyed. Thousands died. But Kyvo did not.

'The storm lasted fifteen days, and when it finally subsided he returned to his home to find it demolished, his wife and children dead, and no hope of the crops recovering. He realised he would soon starve, and die alone. He filled with anger. The betrayal had been too deep. He swelled with a desperate desire for revenge, and the energy he had always devoted in service of the Vyara was now pitted against them.

'He went to the temple; the only remaining building in his hometown. He demanded that Zenith show himself. When he did, the ensuing confrontation made history. Zenith sensed Kyvo had lost his faith and moved to kill him. But Kyvo's anger was so strong that when the Vyara touched him a shockwave split the temple in two. Both the knight and the god were propelled away from each other. When Kyvo landed he found that his anger had collapsed. He felt nothing. He got to his feet and walked to the god without fear. Zenith brought out his golden dagger to end the knight and Kyvo stood passively to receive the blow. But Zenith's weapon and arm passed through him as if they were made of cloud. Kyvo stood untouched, void of all feeling.

'Zenith retreated that day, and never returned. Kyvo was the first of the Guardians. He founded our way of life, and we have never trusted the gods since. Nor have they dared meddle with our lives.' She finished her story and looked to Threon for a response.

The teasing had left him. Something akin to understanding was written on his face. 'The gods can be cruel,' he said.

She sighed. 'The Vyara's power games cause so much grief for the living. Thelonia represents the epicentre of modern-day suffering. Huge divides in wealth, depletion of nature, unchecked slavery. Deyar has the power to make the people see the wrongdoing of their greed, and yet he encourages it.'

Threon got up and rummaged in a storage crate at the back of the boat. He pulled out two skins of wine and handed one to her. 'Here. Might help ease your mind.' She shook her head and waved it away. She envied his sense of calm but couldn't let her guard down until they were free of this sea spell. 'More for me,' he grinned. He pulled the cork of the skin off with his teeth and spat it onto the deck. He raised the wine in a toast. 'To a fairer future.'

She gave him a wan smile and continued to stare back towards land.

When they arrived on the island the next day, Azzania was exhausted. Threon had fallen asleep on the deck when the conversation had dried out and only woke again when he felt the hull scraping against sand.

It was late morning and a grey sky hovered above them, thick with dark cloud.

The fishing boat had beached itself a few feet from the shore. Azzania lowered herself into the shallow water, her white dress swirling in the grey waves. Threon vaulted over the side of the boat to land beside her.

The shoreline was speckled monochrome with pebbles that scraped against each other as the pair scrambled up the beach. As they moved away from the waves, a metallic noise grew, a scraping, chiselling sound. The pebbles rose up in a steep bank ahead of them, blocking their view. When they reached the top of the incline, they surveyed their new surroundings.

The dark skies were mirrored in the landscape. Before them, and stretching to the horizon, was an unnatural grey plain. Threon had never seen anything like it. The earth had been scorched, ripped and beaten. No vegetation could survive here. Piles of stone were man-made mountains. New caves had been scratched into the land's surface. And hundreds of men and women were throwing their weight into piercing the earth's skin with spades and pickaxes.

Even from a distance, Threon could see that they were emaciated. Sallow, sad faces, and a constant back-breaking rhythm striking the ground.

'Slaves,' said Azzania. 'All of them.' As she was speaking, Threon scanned the figures, searching for those he might know from home. 'Most will die of fatigue or be crushed in mining accidents. And if they survive long enough, the Empress imposes an early expiration. She doesn't want them to think they can take immortality for themselves by stealing the product they mine, so she insists that they are put to death after ten years' service. Why she thinks any of them would

228

wish to prolong their suffering is beyond me.' She motioned him to get lower to the ground. 'We should stay hidden.'

There were no walls hemming the workers in. Instead, large watchtowers rose out of the ground, patrolled by palimore. Threon couldn't see the crossbows but he knew they were there, trailing the innocents who had been torn from their homes.

They dipped back out of sight, below the pebble ridge. They trod north along the coast. The mine stretched on and on for many miles. The pair were soon exhausted by the drudgery of traipsing across pebbles. Threon took to wading through the shallow water where the land was flat with sand, while Azzania avoided getting sores and blisters by keeping her shoes on dry land.

Several hours had passed when a harbour town appeared in the distance. Threon quickened his pace, eager to explore the people of this new land and hungry for a hot meal. Azzania followed with renewed energy.

Despite the overcast sky, the rain held off. As they walked through the streets, dirty and dishevelled from travelling, they drew stares from the locals. Threon suddenly felt foolish for not making an effort to find new clothing. He again looked like a beggar in his stained southern rags. Azzania was still dressed in her white Guardian robes and drew even more attention than he did.

They walked through the harbour. Groups of children cleaned mussels with stones, plunging the clean shells into a large bucket of water. They watched the strange couple with large eyes. The fishwives hawked the day's catch in loud, brash voices. They quieted to a low mumble as the pair came into view. One cried out, 'Oi! Mainlands beggars.' Threon turned to the woman, but she was back laughing with her companions again.

As they neared the centre of town the smell of roast chicken found them and made hunger pains dig in Threon's belly. It came from a large tavern, The Mernad's Tail. The battered sign stuck out from the wall, the image of a fish's tail etched into old wood.

'Let's stop,' he said to Azzania. She looked as though she was about to protest, and then her face softened.

'Some food would be welcome.'

The barman gave a suspicious look when they handed him Ionese currency, but their well-rehearsed story about working for one of the Empress's chief merchants seemed to satisfy. A small amount of negotiation also bought them both a set of clothing in the local fashion from the inn's lost property box.

The place was packed. They sat down on a long table beside a grey-haired man with a thick beard. Both had bought a plate of steaming hot meat from behind the bar. Threon ate greedily, sucking the fat from his fingers when he had finished. Azzania picked slowly at hers.

'I don't eat meat,' she confessed. There was nothing else available.

'Well, if you don't want it…' He held out a hand.

'I didn't say that.'

The grey-haired man beside them stirred. 'Not from round 'ere, huh?' He gave her a broad smile. Several of his teeth were missing. 'You don't get many vegetarians in Porthallow.' He let out a hoarse chuckle.

She put down the chicken and returned his smile politely. 'No, we're not from around here. We work with the city merchants, and are trying—'

He didn't give her a chance to finish, striking Threon as the type who liked the sound of his own voice. 'The merchants, eh? There's rumours about that a whole ship of city folk drowned, coming back from the primitive side of the sea. Know anything 'bout that? You look pretty foreign to me.'

She went to respond, but he continued regardless. 'Say, what are you doing *here* anyway? Working with them merchants, you should be well clear of the Greylands. I'm going north myself tonight. Could do with the company. I could hang on another day or so to wait for you if you'd like a lift back to yer masters?'

Maybe fortune was on their side after all. Threon clapped the man warmly on the back. 'You're a gem. Tonight would be perfect.'

The old man talked constantly on the road. He had talked constantly in the tavern too, but there was still plenty to be said. He told them about his family, about the town, about the price of fish, the cost of war, the scheming of politicians, the dangers of travelling and how the young didn't know how good they had it. Threon had long since zoned out of his chatter, but Azzania still sat beside him at the front of the cart, nodding and occasionally chiming in. Threon sat in the back, surrounded by barrels of fish, tightly packed in water on their last journey to the kitchens of the Empire. He watched them writhe in intricate silver patterns.

They were driving along a road that went straight through one of the larger quarries. The road was smoother than any Threon had ever seen. No doubt made more comfortable for him and his companions at the expense of slaves.

The expanse of it astounded him. The man-made landscape spread to the horizon in all directions. The Greylands. An apt name. He wondered about his old stable hand. The boy was twelve. Had he ended up here? Here, to toil on stone until an untimely death, never to see the sweeping green slopes, or the calm blue expanses of the Waterlands again? He would be seventeen now, nearly a man. And the cook, his maid, the blacksmith and his two teenage girls… There were too many to count.

He let his body slump against the side of the cart, leaning his head back, and watched the landscape roll on by until sleep stole him away from it.

CHAPTER TWENTY

Savanta stood on the edge of the shore. The ships were growing smaller and less distinct in the misty air.

A stray dog had followed her up to the cliff. She was the only person left in the city now, and the skinny mutt was holding out on her charity. She kicked a stone at it and it slunk away, tail between legs.

A breeze rolled in from the ocean and she breathed in deep, arching her shoulders as if to fill her wings with the sea air. She cursed herself for it. She hadn't adjusted well to being flightless. Her old body made her feel naked. She was bound to the earth now. Helpless, stranded. Abandoned in a deserted city. Despite her pleas, none of the boats would take her. They had to forcibly remove her as she screamed at them about Erin. About how she needed to get home.

She sat on the wet grass at the cliff edge. It looked a long way down without wings. For a nauseating moment she contemplated throwing herself to the sea, feeling the air in her hair, for one brief horrible flight. She shuddered and pulled herself back from the edge.

She couldn't stay here like this.

Hoping against hope, she began to pray.

Threon took in the city with wide eyes. Slums gradually gave way to clustered stone buildings. Stacked one on top of another in some places, the crumbling walls only held together due to their tight proximity.

There were so many people. More than he had ever imagined could live in a single place. The cart waded slowly through the packed streets. Threon and Azzania had been tasked with keeping an eye on the barrels. The old man's desire for company became more transparent now; the pair were acting as his guards, protecting the cargo from thieves. Threon drew his sword in warning, but still hands reached up, trying to overturn the barrels. The courier continued to drone his stories, but it seemed now they were only for the benefit of the old horse.

The air thronged with sound. Chatting, laughing, shouting, babies crying, dogs barking, wheels turning. And the smell. Sewerage, meat, baking bread, beer, woodsmoke, people.

Azzania, too, looked around in wonder. Ionia was known for its small population. Threon could see the muscles in her neck and shoulders tense. The crowds were stifling.

They stayed with the cart for another hour as they picked their way through the bustling streets. Once the barrels reached the market safely, they handed the driver a silver coin for his trouble and wished him farewell.

The golden palace rose up above the slums in sleek splendour. They pushed through the crowds in its direction, stepping carefully over the many beggars who lined the pavements. Threon dropped coins for the thinner ones as they passed.

Trudging uphill, it wasn't long before they passed through a gate to the walled inner-city. Here, people dressed more grandly, the houses proud and decorated. Guards lined the streets every few feet and frequently cuffed pedlars and beggars, or anyone who seemed to get out of line. They kept their heads down and quickened their pace.

The barracks was in sight now. Sandy blocks of stone rose into high walls and turrets. Archways in the stone housed immaculate sculptures of men and women in palimore uniform. People were streaming in through the entrance gates, and a hawker nearby was calling out prices for tickets to today's fight. Threon nodded his head in the hawker's direction and Azzania shrugged in agreement. They paid him with their foreign currency without much qualm. Ionian coin seemed to be of value to the Thelonian merchants who travelled as far as the mountains. Tickets in hand, they followed the crowds into the barracks.

The people were finely dressed, poorer residents evidently outpriced by the cost of tickets. The queue was abuzz with jests and chatter as they walked the corridors that led to the arena seating.

Instead of following the crowds, Azzania pointed out a side door, cordoned off from the public. The people around them were too distracted by the evening of entertainment that awaited them and no one seemed concerned when the pair moved the barrier and stole through the door.

The noise of the crowds faded as the door closed behind. They were in another long corridor, lined with doors on either side. Each bore a name and a number. They were close enough together that the rooms behind each door could be single bedrooms. Threon looked at Azzania and grinned. Finding the soldier might be easier than they thought. Azzania read the names on the left of the corridor while

Threon checked the right. They reached the end of the corridor and turned a corner to find it snaked back on itself to reveal more rows of rooms. Another length of corridor, another corner, another row of doors… and then, there it was. Palimore 1839: Lleu Agnor.

Lleu hunched over his desk, whittling a pencil to a point using a knife. Focussing on shaving thin slivers of wood was helping to keep his mind from the cravings. He heard the door open behind him, and closed his eyes. He was not in the mood for company.

'Lleu.' His ears pricked at the sound of the prince's voice. He turned his head slowly. It really was him, and he'd brought an Ionese woman along too. Lleu's surprise at their arrival was dulled by a sudden wave of sickness, and he clutched his belly. Their expressions told him what he already knew; he looked like shit. He turned back to the pencil with a gruff expulsion of air. 'You shouldn't be here.' The writing desk was covered in wood shavings. The pencil he held was now only two or three inches long. He continued to attack it with his knife.

'Lleu. What happened? You look…' Greenbrooke trailed off. Lleu squeezed his eyes shut. If they'd come expecting to find a warrior, they were going to be disappointed.

'I've been made mortal,' he grunted, without turning around. 'For ordering the retreat.' He pressed his palms into his eyes. They were desert dry and a sharp pain was building behind them. 'What are you doing here?'

There was a tentative silence. He turned to look at the pair. The prince's face betrayed pity. He looked as though he was going to offer words of comfort, but they seemed to fall flat on his lips. He shook his head slowly. 'The army is coming. We need your help.'

Lleu gave no response. His mind felt as broken as his body. What help could he be to anyone?

The woman came closer and placed her hands on his shoulders. He shrugged them off in irritation. She withdrew her hands quickly, and then tried again. Lleu felt something melt through her into him. Tension dissipated from his body and he let his hands relax on the desk.

'You've Godsblood,' she breathed, closing her eyes, seeming to concentrate harder. He felt another ripple run from her fingers, out across his body. Her touch lifted the darkness that sat on his mind. The sickness was gone.

'Who are you? What are you?' His head felt clear for the first time in days. The heavy pit that had sat in his stomach lifted. He felt connected to her. He could sense her smiling, hear her words in his ears, and feel them in his soul. He turned to look at her. Her elfin features made him think of Raikka. 'You're Ionese?'

'Yes,' she said. 'I'm Azzania. A Guardian of the void.'

'A Guardian.' He spoke the words quietly. He frowned at Threon. It seemed he had turned to witchcraft to help his cause.

'We are not your enemy, Lleu. The void is nothing to fear. It cleanses us, purging human emotions that cause so much ill.'

He believed her. For a moment. And then she removed her hands from his shoulders and reality crashed back down on him like a mineshaft. The sickness and pain, the loneliness and angst. 'Leave me alone,' he said. 'I can't help you. Just look at me.'

Threon stepped forward. 'We can't win this fight without your help. You saved my life twice. Why risk your life for mine if it was all for nothing?'

'Think of your wife,' said Azzania.

He shot her a glance. 'You read my thoughts?' His hand reached instinctively to feel for the locket on his wrist that held a coil of her dark hair.

'I know you still love her,' the witch continued. 'The forces of the East are gathering and will be on these shores in days. Help us. We can bring down the Empress and close the mines. Your wife will go free. But we need your insider's knowledge.'

'Please go.' It was too much. Listening to them speak was making him feel nauseous, and anxiety was building fast. Raikka was probably already dead.

Azzania hesitated before she spoke again. 'We need vish'aad.' The word ignited a hunger in him. He clenched his fist tight. 'Thelonian forces vastly outnumber ours,' she continued. 'We need to keep our people alive. It's the only way.'

'I'd be shot down within a mile of the vault,' he said.

Threon flicked at the wood shavings on the desk. 'Any loyalty you felt for this place has to be gone now. They want you out. Help us turn the tables on them.'

He barely heard the words. His mind was reeling at the thought of vish. He wanted it. Needed it. He turned back to his pencil and began to slide slithers of wood from it again with his knife. His hands were trembling. He needed another dose. One more and he might feel in control again.

He stopped whittling and closed his eyes. 'We do this, and I get all the vish I need?'

'Of course,' said Greenbrooke.

Pushing his chair away from the desk, he stood, turning to his bed. 'I need to rest. Wake me before dawn and I'll take you to the vault.' He ploughed into the sheets, pulling them up over his head. 'Stay here. They might not let you in a second time.'

He felt the witch sit at the side of the bed. He flinched away when she reached to touch him again, and then relented. She rested a hand on his shoulder. He felt the pain dissolve and, mercifully soon, he slept.

With Azzania's foot butting his ribs, Threon groaned awake. His eyes blurred into focus. The darkness was broken only by a thin slice of light flickering under the bedroom door.

'Time to go,' she said.

He dragged himself up from the floor and stretched his aching muscles. 'Lleu,' he said.

Azzania reached out a hand and rocked the body hidden by mounds of blanket. Lleu grumbled beneath them and sat up, pressing his palms into his eye sockets. He swung his legs out from the bed and stood.

Without a word he motioned for the pair to follow him out of the door. Threon blinked against the torches burning in the corridors. Lleu put a finger to his lips and indicated down the corridor.

He picked up one of the lights and led them deeper into the barracks. They passed countless bedrooms, the biggest smithy Threon had ever seen, kitchens bigger than those of his castle, and training grounds that made him scream inwardly with envy. Given the opportunity, he didn't doubt his younger self would have relished the life of a soldier here.

Spiral stairs descended for several floors, taking them deep under the barracks.

'Here,' whispered Lleu. His voice hissed in echo around the high domed chamber. The room filled with light as a series of wall-mounted sconces burst into flame. Threon drew his sword and Azzania glanced about nervously. There was no one there.

'It's automatic,' said Lleu, his voice still low. Threon sheathed his weapon, gazing about the room.

Azzania was staring at a large ornate door set into the far wall. It gleamed gold, framed by drapes of heavy embroidered fabric. 'The other realm,' she breathed. 'That's where they keep the vish?'

'Vish is considered sacred,' said Lleu. 'It's guarded by Deyar's own sons and daughters. I had hoped your friend might have made it with you. If I'm not mistaken she has some link with the Vyara? Some divine intervention would prove handy.'

Lleu led them up to the door. As they neared, Threon could make out the intricate shapes of copulating couples embellished in the metal.

'It's where we meet the Children of Deyar to fulfil the requirements of the breeding programme,' said Lleu. 'Affectionately known as the rutting room.'

'The breeding programme?' said Threon, raising an eyebrow. 'Sounds fun.'

'Not really.'

'I can't go in there,' Azzania said to Threon. Her skin had paled and she wore a veil of fear that did not suit her usual composure. 'It reeks of the gods. I can smell it.' It was rare to see her so shaken. It put Threon on edge.

'I thought you said they'd shoot you down within a mile of the vault.' Threon watched the soldier closely. He was their only hope of tipping the odds against the palimore. Lleu was sweating again. From fear or withdrawal, Threon couldn't tell.

'They'll try.' The palimore shifted his weight from foot to foot, a nervous energy surrounding him. 'But you need this, right?'

'It will give us the best chance we've got.'

'You coming, or staying with the witch?'

Threon looked at Azzania. 'I'll be fine,' she said. 'You should go. Keep each other safe.' Threon nodded.

'What happens in there?' he asked.

'You stay out of sight. I try to call in some big favours.' Lleu drew his sword part way out of its scabbard and cut his thumb along its edge. 'You ready?'

Threon shrugged. Azzania caught his hand. 'Be careful.'

'Always.' He gave her a smile that he hoped wouldn't betray his nerves. Hers were clear as ice.

Lleu pressed his thumb up against the door and drew it down, smearing a crimson trail against the gold.

'Godsblood,' cursed Azzania, as she backed away.

The door cracked as it swung open, revealing deep darkness. Lleu disappeared into the black and Threon followed quickly at his heels.

The air changed texture. It grew thicker, heavier. He felt like he was moving slower, through a different timescale. Then light brought their surroundings into focus. They were in a grand yet gaudy room. Tall ceilings, hung with intricate glass chandeliers, heavy velvet drapes, gilded mirrors running from floor to ceiling. Not as otherworldly as he had expected; it looked more like an expensive brothel.

Threon went to say just as much but was hit by a wall of nausea. The thick air made his lungs hurt, and his head began to pound. He staggered back a step, nearly falling to the floor. Lleu grabbed him by the arm and manoeuvered him behind a wall of heavy curtains. He collapsed onto a bed of soft fur.

'Quiet,' hissed Lleu. 'We aren't alone.'

'My head,' he groaned. They were in a small room, just bigger than the bed he had fallen onto. It smelled of sweat and sex. 'Is this a fucking booth?'

Lleu ignored him. 'I forgot about the nausea. Your body needs to adjust to the other realm. The feeling will pass. Stay here.'

He disappeared through the curtains back into the main chamber.

241

Lleu had expected they would be alone at this hour in the morning, yet he could hear a couple moaning together behind a nearby set of curtains. He cursed them and stepped further into the room, aware that Threon was watching. She would be here soon.

A screen painted with erotic scenes divided the room and he hid himself behind it. Thankfully, the couple sounded decidedly engaged in each other's company and he hoped they wouldn't notice him. He sank down onto a bench and wiped at the sweat on his brow.

'I didn't think I'd ever be seeing you again,' said a female voice. Lleu looked up to meet Oxyara's eyes. A squat woman with copper skin and ruddy cheeks. She was one of the demigods – a daughter of Deyar and Keresan – charged with protecting the other realm, and a central part of the breeding programme. She looked pleased to see him. The first hurdle was over then. 'Come back for one last taste?'

Lleu pressed a finger to his lips, nodding in the direction of the soft moans emanating from behind them.

Ah, she said, her words flowing into his mind as she sat down beside him. *Trying to stay out of trouble? I'll be quiet as the grave.*

The silence was better, but he worried that her prying mind might see through to his true intentions. *I won't pry,* she promised. *We all have a right to our secrets. You most of all. Just look at you, Lleu. You've had a bad time of things, my love.* She ran a hand down his leg. He tensed slightly.

Not here for that, huh? Shame. It might help take your mind off things.

Unlike some of his fellow palimore, Lleu had never managed to master telepathy, an invaluable asset in battle. Most soldiers were the direct descendants of the demigods, but he was further removed, with too much of his mother in him to make much use of the little Godsblood he carried.

242

'I need to get to the Vault,' he whispered.

Well, of course you do, she cooed. *I can practically taste your need for vish. Such a shame to lose one like you to mortality. Condolences, my dear.* Great. He was already dead to her.

He closed his eyes. 'Please help me.' His hands were still shaking from withdrawal. She took them in hers, soft and warm.

You were always my favourite, you know. She tilted her head to one side and lifted his hands, kissing his fingers. *I know you never felt the same way about me, but that's okay. It's just part of the job, huh?*

He sighed. 'I'm married, Oxy.' No harm in telling her now. Marriage bans only existed for palimore. 'To a mortal. I'm going to find her, live a normal life. What's left of it.'

To her credit, the surprise left her face as soon as it arrived. *I should have guessed.* She smiled and nudged him playfully. *You're in love. That's delightful.* He managed to smile back. *I won't tell.* She was a good woman. It was a shame to deceive her like this.

'I just need some vish to get me out of here. It's a long way. I can barely walk in this state, let alone search the mines for her…'

The low moans coming from the couple began to rise higher, more frequent. They were nearly done. Oxyara pursed her lips, considering. If she refused, could he get past her alone?

Thankfully he didn't have to find out. 'Okay, come with me,' she whispered. 'A little rebellion is the least you deserve after what they put you through. Just don't you dare get caught.'

She walked with him to the far end of the room. Here they stood before another golden door, this time embellished with the image of people rising up in a pyramid. At the top shone the figure of Keresan, stood on the shoulders of the ancients, who stood on the shoulders of the palimore, who, in turn, stood on the shoulders of slaves. Oxyara pressed her palm against the door and it opened. Lleu glanced back to see the curtains twitch where Threon was poised, ready to go. He turned back and followed Oxyara through the door.

The other side of the door brought them to the square which lay before the golden palace. Or at least a version of it. Here all was grey, as if lit by silver moonlight, yet the sky was empty. Shadows of city locals skulked the cobblestones like ghosts, only half visible in this other realm. Just beyond the palace's shining walls lay an eternity's supply of vish. Lleu's heart began to pound. So close.

'You want me to go in and get some for you?' asked Oxyara.

Lleu licked his lips. Yes, yes he did, but that would never be enough. They needed it all.

'I'll go alone,' he said. 'No sense in you getting into trouble.'

'I might get into trouble if I get caught. You might end up dead. You should have more respect for the few years you have left now. I'll go.'

He was about to protest when an arrow clattered to the cobblestones at his feet. 'Oy!' a voice cried. To their right another demigod strode towards them, Threon pulled along at his side.

'Shit,' said Lleu.

'Get behind me,' said Oxyara. Lleu drew his sword and did as she asked. 'You dare to fire weapons at your sister, Torf?'

'Not at you. Just the dangerous company you keep. You know he shouldn't be in here.'

'What's this?' She nodded at Threon. 'A mortal? Looks like he's from across the sea.' Threon gave Lleu an apologetic grimace. Some backup he'd turned out to be.

'Looks like he's here to take what's ours. And I'll wager your treacherous friend there has something to do with it. How else would a mortal get in?'

'Lleu?' Oxyara looked back at him, the beginning of anger in her tone. Like a mother preparing to chastise her child.

'Blond hair, blue eyes; he's from the Waterlands. Seems too close a coincidence. An old relative of yours, Blue?'

'This isn't what it looks like,' began Lleu. 'I've never seen him—'

'You dare to betray my trust.' Oxyara turned around, her warm eyes now dark. Her voice dropped its usual playfulness, now grinding like steel. 'You came here to steal for the enemy?'

'No, I—' He was cut off again.

'You what? You thought good old Oxy would help you out without asking any questions? More fool me. I've grown too soft.'

'You let him in?' accused Torf.

'Leave it.' She waved him away. 'I'm dealing with it.' Her body started growing larger, until she towered above Lleu. 'I trusted you.' Before he knew what was happening her large hands closed about his neck and pulled him upwards, level with her face. His legs flailed in the air and veins pulsed on his forehead as he rasped in breath.

'Oxy…' he tried to say, but it just came out as a groan. Her grip tightened and he could feel his face swell. She was trying to kill him. He thrust his sword at her but it bounced off her skin as though she were made of stone. She squeezed harder and then propelled his body onto the cobblestones. He landed hard on his back and for a moment could do nothing but stare at the dark sky, heaving in winded breaths.

Threon soon landed beside him, sword clattering to the cobbles between them. Lleu began propping himself up, but

245

Oxyara pressed a massive hand on his chest and forced him back to the ground.

Lleu put his hands up in protest, still gulping in air. 'Oxy, please.'

'You betrayed my trust.' She kneeled over him, one knee either side of his chest, and pushed down. Lleu tried to speak again, but the pressure was too great on his ribs.

Threon managed to get to his feet and began backing away, but he was soon struck by Torf and staggered back to the floor under the power of the man's fist.

'I'm sorry,' wheezed Lleu.

'Bullshit. You came here with ill intentions. To steal eternity for yourself and – what – make your fortune selling the stuff to the enemy?' She placed a knee on Lleu's chest and turned to look at Threon as he flailed on the floor. There was a crack as she moved over Lleu's ribs. He let out a muffled cry. 'There, there my love,' she said. 'I thought you liked me on top.' A cruel smile. She turned back to Threon. 'You really thought you could steal from Deyar? And you thought this waste of space would be your best way in?' She stood up and Lleu rolled onto his side, coughing up blood. 'Sorry, but you made me look bad, baby.'

Torf had Threon by the throat now. 'Was it worth it?' he said. 'A glimpse of the divine in return for death? You made a wager for immortality. I'm afraid you lost.' He wrapped his hand around the prince's upper body and flung him across the floor. He tumbled over the cobblestones like a ragdoll and then lay still.

Lleu closed his eyes. It was over then. The whole damn thing was over.

CHAPTER TWENTY-ONE

Your friends need help.

Savanta woke with a scream. Her body convulsed and she threw herself out of bed, landing hard on the floor of the abandoned Maradah townhouse she had chosen as a temporary home. Her skin tightened and stretched, her body thrashing as something ripped at the flesh between her shoulder blades. She looked down at her body to see grey spread out from her chest and down her arms. She arched her back, gulping in breath as her wings burst from her back like a fist through a wall. She squeezed her eyes shut, breathing through gritted teeth as her heart raced.

Your prayers are answered, angel.

They had been thrown into a plunge cell. Steep walls rose around them in a circle, like they had been tossed to the bottom of a dry well. Not long after Threon and Lleu's capture, Azzania had been lowered and dropped into the cell to join them. She had been sedated with a venom dart, only half conscious.

Hours passed in the cold and dark. Apprehension of what was to come drew out time. Lleu had tried to sleep but the thundering in his chest kept him from rest.

After some time there was a sound above. 'Listen,' said Lleu. All three of them got to their feet, ready to meet their captors.

Blinding light spilled around the hatch as it opened.

He heard voices overhead. Danesh, Mit and Tanner, old friends from the raiding party. They chatted in hushed voices. Lleu picked out his name but couldn't make out what they were saying.

Lleu looked at his fellow prisoners. Both stood wide-eyed, muscles tensed in alarm. 'Get ready to move,' he said.

A thick rope spiralled into the room, throwing shadows on the wall as it fell.

'What's happening?' asked Threon.

There was a rustle from above and the silhouettes of the men appeared over the open hatchway.

'It's time,' said Danesh. 'Get your arses up here.'

'Start climbing,' said Lleu.

'Are you joking?' Threon nearly laughed at him.

'Do it,' urged the soldier.

'You better listen to him, Waterboy,' warned the voice from above. A bucket appeared in the hatchway and its contents emptied into the cell. Several large insects clattered to the floor. Creatures from the Empress's species bank. They were the size of a man's head with iridescent shells and a large stinger protruding from a scorpion-like tail. They moved quickly, scuttling on dozens of legs.

'Move!' commanded Lleu as he hoisted Azzania up onto the rope, pushing Threon after her.

He danced on his feet around the insects and risked kicking one against the wall when it got too close. The creatures encroached on the group, forming a circle that closed in around the rope.

Azzania was near the top but stopped to look down. Threon hadn't climbed high enough for Lleu to get off the ground. Lleu jumped up and grabbed the section of rope between Threon's hands and feet. He used his shoulder to force the prince up the rope.

When they reached the top, Azzania was already pushed up against a wall, her hands manacled at her back.

Mit grabbed both men by their wrists and pulled them out of the darkness. Lleu found his footing fast and swung at Mit's face. Mit's reflexes were too sharp. He caught Lleu's fist and kicked the back of his legs, forcing him to the floor. Threon was already on the ground beside him, manacles being clasped about his wrists. His face clenched in pain as Tanner pulled his shoulder back hard.

Lleu struggled against Mit. He managed to force himself to his knees and turned to take another swing. Mit blocked it and Lleu received a crack to his jaw in return.

'You could always best me in a fight,' said Mit, as he pinned Lleu down again, this time on his back. 'A few days without vish and you're ruined.' He looked him with pity. Lleu hated him then. He tried to break free again and Mit drew a knee sharply into his balls. 'You know there's no use. It won't help you in court.'

Mit turned him over. The manacles clasped around his wrists, heavy and cold. He took a sharp intake of breath as his cracked ribs pressed against the floor. Danesh helped Mit bring Lleu to his feet and the three prisoners were brought into a line.

Not taking any more chances, Mit produced a knife to escort Lleu to court. It nipped at his skin, tearing through his shirt as they walked.

Threon walked with his body at an angle, head stooped in pain. He had landed hard in the other realm. Lleu wouldn't have been surprised if he'd sustained a broken bone or two. Azzania strode purposefully, head held high. In the light, Lleu could see dried blood crusted on both of their faces.

He took in the sandstone walls as they walked. This had been his home for so long. He had always thought he would die in battle. Not like this.

He kept quiet on the way, his mind reeling, trying to find the words that might win freedom in court. His heart was beating fast. There was little hope. An ex-palimore soldier caught stealing from Deyar was bad enough. And if they recognised the prince...

They came to the court after several minutes. Danesh called through and the large wooden doors that stood before them opened. They climbed a steep set of stairs and emerged in the hexagonal courtroom. Sun streamed in through ornate stained-glass windows and the tall, black marble walls reflected a spectrum of colours.

Above them, dozens of ancients had gathered onto the gallery. They pointed and whispered as the three prisoners were brought forward. Their manacles were attached to a chain at the back of the room which forced them to face their expectant audience. In the centre of the gallery stood a stone pulpit bearing Deyar's sigil: the outline of an erupting volcano. Lleu's father gazed down at them from behind the pulpit, darkness etched on his face.

Lleu was the last to be shackled. Threon was beside him in the middle, and Azzania on the far side. She reached for Threon's hand from her manacles, and with a bit of effort they came close enough for fingers to touch. She closed her eyes and the pain seemed to melt from Threon's face. 'Thank you,' he whispered. They stayed like that, eyes only for each other, blocking out the gravity of their situation.

On either side of the commander sat a dozen senior officers. Lleu searched the gathered faces for friends. None had come to support him. Perhaps they simply didn't wish to watch him die. He met his father's eyes but couldn't read him. Was that sorrow? Disappointment?

Khan stood, and the men and women either side rose to their feet. As he spoke, his voice was lustreless, uttering words spoken a thousand times before. 'The three of you here stand today to be judged in the eyes of our Lord Deyar by the palimore he prescribes to hold the peace.

'The Ionese Guardian; you are charged with heresy of the highest order, of rebellion against the Vyara, and of involvement in the instigation of war.'

Lleu expelled a breath. They knew she was a Guardian. The Watchers had worked fast. Khan's voice wavered slightly as he continued.

'Lleu Agnor, ex-Palimore and Imperial Raider; you are charged with aiding and abetting enemy forces, of deceiving a demigod, of treasonous intent, and betrayal of your fellow soldiers.' Lleu dropped his head, pressing his nails into his skin in tight fists. It was agony to see his father finally understand his true intentions. As Khan spoke the charges, he looked straight ahead, avoiding Lleu's pleading eyes.

He continued. 'Threon Greenbrooke, deposed king of the Waterlands; you are charged with rallying forces against the Crown, of intent to steal vish'aad, of instigating a war, and of the war crime of destroying a retreating ship, and the murder of those on board.'

Dark murmurs broke out among those assembled.

Threon bristled, pulling forward against his chains. 'Maybe,' he said, still clasping Azzania's fingers. 'But what of

251

your crimes? Slavery, pillaging, murder.' Lleu tried to silence him with a glare, but he continued, voice rising in anger. 'You say I instigated a war. But you invade my land, abduct and kill my people. Destroy my father's army. Murder my family, my friends. You leave my people starving to feed your rich courts. Gods curse you all.' He spat the words, his eyes wide and fierce, anger pulling him forwards, taut against his manacles. 'You will suffer for what you have done. The Waterlands will have vengeance.'

Some of the palimore suppressed laughter in their stalls.

'I shall make this quick,' said Khan. 'The penalties for your crimes are clear. Practice of the void brings you to death, Guardian. And for your crimes, Water King, death also. For my son...' he faltered. A few lone cries of 'Death!' came from the gallery. Lleu held his father's gaze. If he would condemn him to death, he would do it staring Lleu in the face.

Azzania spoke then, before the Commander could continue. 'My understanding of the law in Thelonia is limited, but from what I grasp it is just. Threon and I understood we would suffer death for our actions if caught. I could not go peacefully to the grave knowing we had dragged an innocent soul with us.

'We took advantage of a wretch in the grips of withdrawal to meet our needs. If you were denied access to the very thing that gives you power, life, what would you do to get it back? We presented an opportunity for a taste of that substance that all you here have easy access to, and he took it. What addict hasn't lied or cheated to get a fix? Your son is sick. Blame the sickness, not the man.'

More murmuring broke out in the stalls, and the cries for death pitted out. A look of relief came over Khan, and perhaps even gratitude.

'But how can we be sure?' Mit was standing from his seat

in the stalls. 'Are these the words of a confessional heart before death, or the words of a conspiratorial ally, trying to save his skin?'

'Better regret his death, than find him leading an army into our midst,' came another voice.

And another, 'A father's judgement will always be clouded.'

'Silence,' roared Khan. He took a breath to steady himself and looked at Lleu. 'My judgment is this. The invaders will die. My son will be banished —' more noise from behind him '— but! But, as a test of character, my son will be the one to deliver the execution. Fail, and I promise you, all three will come to a swift end.'

Lleu looked desperately at his co-conspirators. Threon was wrestling with his manacles, pulling at them to escape. Azzania met his gaze with soft eyes. 'This wasn't your fault,' she said.

The whole room had broken into chatter. When he looked back to his father, he was speaking with two of the officers. They glanced over at the three captives, nodding and speaking in hushed tones.

When they had finished, Khan clapped loudly, regaining the attention of the room. 'Silence. It is decided. Lleu will administer a public execution in the arena at sunset.' He waved a hand at Mit, Danesh and Tanner. 'Take them away.'

Threon and Azzania were led down a different corridor to Lleu. After a brief walk, their captors locked them in a small torchlit cell. At least they hadn't been thrown back in the pit they had come around in. They were penned in by thick iron bars that flickered stark shadows against the stone wall behind them.

'Will he really kill us?' said Threon.

'If he has any sense. I don't think we're getting out of here, Threon.' She walked over and took his hand in hers. He wrapped his other arm around her waist and they stood in an embrace. 'Are you afraid?' she asked.

'Yes.' There felt little point in putting a brave face on things now. He felt her chasing away his fear as the void crept into his mind. 'No,' he said. The fear kept him sharp, and he wanted his wits needlelike. She eased away from him. 'We weren't ready. Why did we come here?'

'We had a chance.' She gave him a sad smile. 'There is still hope. My people are strong, and yours are fierce with a hunger for revenge. Together with Vituund, they stand a chance, whether we are there or not. Our involvement makes little difference now. We assembled the players and started the game. It's up to them now.'

'If they had the vish'aad though—'

'They will have to do without. My people can't heal, but they can ease pain and bring peace to the dying. Not one of them has signed up to this unaware of the risks.'

He took her hand again and drew her close, needing the comfort of another's touch. She sighed and lay her head against his shoulder. He reached a hand up to stroke her hair. Despite their impending fate, for the first time in a long time, he felt like he wasn't on his own. She wrapped her arms around his chest. He could feel her breath warm at his neck. He tilted her chin up and she leaned in, nuzzling her nose against his face. Their lips brushed. Threon closed his eyes and ran his fingers down her spine, breathing her in.

A clang on the bars. 'Enough of that.' The guards.

They'd come to take them away.

Lleu was taken to the back of the arena. He was shown to a small room used by the stadium's accountants and locked in,

254

alone. He paced back and forth, watching the sun crawl across the sky through a narrow window.

At mid-afternoon a plate of hot meat was pushed through the door. As he rushed over to it, the latch locked him in again. He devoured the tough cuts of beef and was dealt stabbing stomach pains for his efforts; it had been days since he had eaten properly.

The white light of the sun had deepened to orange when the door opened again. His father stepped into the room.

'Son.'

'Commander.'

The pair studied each other for a long moment, Lleu mirroring his father's frown. Khan looked worn. The silence was acrid, but Lleu wasn't going to be the first to break it. He waited with fists balled, muscles tensed, until Khan finally said, 'You've had a rough time recently.'

'Rough is one way to describe it.'

'Will you go back after this?'

'Back?'

'To the Waterlands. To your mother's line.'

He could have told him that they were probably all gone now, enslaved or dead, but he chose to say nothing.

'I should never have conscripted you to the raiding parties,' said Khan. 'Fighting your own kin – it was obviously too much for you. That one decision to retreat...' The Commander faltered, lost for words. Without that one decision Lleu would still be palimore, would never have lost his wits to withdrawal, would never have been caught in the other realm. But without his insistence of retreat, perhaps the palimore would have won that day, and it would have been over as soon as it began. Perhaps everything that had happened since really had been inevitable. Khan waited for Lleu to say something, but he remained silent.

'Don't let me down today. I'm choosing to believe that you were coerced into helping the foreigners. Whether that is the truth or not...' He sighed, looking suddenly old and drained, all of his usual presence gone in an instant. 'You must show the public that you see them as the enemy. Show no mercy, for your own sake. The snipers will be watching, should you hesitate. I don't want to scrape your body off the floor of the arena.' He expelled a breath. 'I've arranged a boat to take you into exile tonight. You'll find it by the crags of the fishing cove. This is the last time we'll ever meet.' He was holding a bundle of cloth under one arm. He handed it to Lleu. 'Your garb for the execution.' White tunic and trousers. They wanted it to get bloody, then. 'Have you nothing to say?'

'Thank you? Is that what you want? No, I have nothing to say.'

Khan looked down, disappointed. He turned to leave. 'Get dressed. We begin in an hour.'

When he had gone, Lleu looked back out of the window. News had travelled fast and the arena stalls were filling up. Executions were always inexplicably popular, benches filled with the appalled and the enthralled in equal measure.

He stripped and unfolded his new clothes. A glass vial clattered onto the floor out of the white fabric.

Lleu grabbed it and quickly emptied its violet contents onto the small windowsill. He could feel the bitter numbing at the back of his throat as he forced it up his nose. The tension eased in his body for the first time in what felt like a lifetime. The headache that had persisted for days disappeared. The pain in his ribs abated.

It felt like the first time. The vish gave him a dazzling high. The sun seemed brighter, he felt stronger and light on his feet.

He took a deep breath, turning his gaze back to the arena. There had to be a way out of this for them all.

But he didn't know how.

This time, the flight over the sea was much easier. Savanta was able to glide on swift winds for most of the journey. Zenith had explained what had happened to her friends and her brief time living in Thelonia City set her imagination on fire with the futures they faced. The Empress and her courts were never lenient. She knew capture would mean death for them.

Before leaving Maradah she had rushed to search through the remnants of military goods. The few dull blades and excess supplies that wouldn't fit upon Threon's ships. She picked up the three sharpest blades she could find and attached them to her belt, and found a barrel of catchfire that she looped around her neck with a cord. Taking off had been strenuous work under the weight of the weapons, but with the help of the wind she made it across the sea.

If the commander had reported her as a traitor she could be shot from the sky, so on arrival at the city she dove down to walk among the streets. She just needed to keep out of view of the palimore.

She alighted on the barracks road to find it near deserted. A few market holders sat idly with their wares, playing cards to pass the time. She approached a fruit seller. 'Where is everyone?' she asked.

He looked up and his eyes widened at the sight of her. She worried she already knew what he would say. 'The arena. Big execution today. You've not heard?'

One guard bound Threon's hands together in front of him. Another was tackling Azzania.

'Just don't touch her skin,' said the guard holding Threon. 'That's how she does her magic.'

'Way ahead of you,' the other guard replied, pulling on a pair of chainmail gloves. 'Come here, gorgeous.' He pushed her against a wall and bound her wrists. As he did so, he made a point of pressing his hips up against her so she was caught between his body and the wall. 'Such a waste,' he whispered into her ear. 'The pleasure house could do with more exotics.' She tried to escape his grasp but his strength was too much. 'Oh, I like it when they fight.' He thrust hard against her body, laughing, before forcing her forwards to join Threon outside the cell. Threon growled in anger, fighting against his captor's grip, but Azzania only trudged forwards, indifferent to the man's actions.

They were jostled down the corridor in the direction of the arena.

As they emerged into the cool evening air, the gathered crowd erupted in leers and they were pelted with curses, rotting food, and stones. The setting reminded Threon of the fighting pits in Bannvar, only much larger, and so much more hostile.

Two posts stood in the middle of the arena. Slender wooden headstones. This is where it ended then. Not quite how he had imagined his story would come to a close. Threon was jostled over to the nearest post, his arms forced above his head as he kicked out at his captors. They ignored his attacks and tied his wrists to a rope which connected to the top of the pole. The short rope allowed for a little movement and when the soldiers let go of him Threon swung his weight against it, forcing it to its limits in every direction, but it held fast.

They were waiting, apparently, for the audience to take their seats before the execution could commence. Threon's wrists were raw and bleeding from rope burn and his injured shoulder burned hot, but he didn't feel the pain. He needed to find a way out. He jerked down hard on his bonds again.

Beside him, Azzania stood calm, her eyes skyward. They had clothed her in a white dress marked with sigils of the Vyara. This inspired much amusement from the crowd, as did the crown of horseshit that they had plastered to Threon's head.

'This is it,' said Azzania, turning away from the sky to meet Threon's eyes. 'We've come to the end. Are you ready?'

No. No, he wasn't. There must be a way out. He had assessed all angles of the arena. Much like the one in Bannvar, there was one entrance, one exit. The stalls were high above them. It was as if they were in a sand-dusted hole. The arena walls would be tough to climb. But that didn't matter if he couldn't find a way out of the ropes. Lleu had saved his life twice. Would he really kill them?

'There's no way out, Threon. Don't give your last moments to fear.'

There must have been six hundred people watching. In the centre of the stalls was a large balcony. A richly jewelled woman, who must be the Empress, sat with a small circle of people. They chatted disinterestedly.

Above the arena's entrance door, drums began to beat in a rhythm like a heartbeat. An angular-featured man stepped forwards from the balcony to address the audience. He grinned at the gathered crowd from under a feather hat. 'Lords and ladies, we assemble here today to witness justice played out in glorious violence. The pair you see before you have committed grievous treason against our Empire.' Booing echoed around the arena. 'Before you stands Azzania of the Order of Guardians. She has defied our God, practiced heresy and sought to instigate a war against our people with the pretender, Threon Greenbrooke. Greenbrooke wants to destroy our trade links with his country, to bring our lands into a state of famine. He doesn't see the value of slavery for an elevated society.' Laughter. 'He is responsible for the murder of forty-seven of our protective palimore.' Outrage broke in the crowd. 'Together, they forced one of our men – once a soldier who vowed to give his life for this city – to break his oaths and steal from the King of the Gods.' People began to hurl stones again. 'Enough. Enough. Don't you want to give Lleu a chance at revenge?' A cheer. The heartbeat drumming looped faster and faster until it was in time with the pounding of Threon's own heart. 'Well, here… we…. go!' The crowd were in a frenzy by the time the gate cracked open and Lleu stepped into the arena.

Threon was expecting an axe, a sword, even a knife. But Lleu approached the pair barehanded. Threon pulled harder on his bonds. Azzania was looking at Lleu and inclined her head to draw him over to her.

'Are you ready?' she asked him. Threon could only just make out her words over the jeering crowd. The soldier's pupils were dark and vish wide.

'I don't know how to get you out of here,' Lleu whispered, panicked. His eyes darted to Threon who was still fighting against the rope ties. Threon pulled himself up with one arm and gnawed at the rope with his teeth.

'It was a good trade. Your life for ours. You will go to them, won't you? Your experience of the army will turn the tide for us, I know. Promise me quickly. I see snipers are watching you.' Four men with crossbows were positioned at each corner of the arena. They followed Lleu as he moved. Threon could see the soldier was shaking. His eyes flicked to the snipers and then back to Azzania. He didn't move to harm her and a restlessness sounded from the crowd. 'Your father offered you a chance to live,' said Azzania. 'Don't throw it away.'

260

'I'll go to them,' he said. 'I promise.'

'Make it quick?' Her lower lip was trembling gently. Tears threatened at the corners of her eyes but she blinked them back. He nodded. She leaned forward against the rope to offer him her throat. The crowd came to a hush, watching intently. His fingers shook as he took hold of her slender neck.

'You have killed a thousand people before me. You are trained to do this.' She kept her eyes locked on his.

Lleu squeezed his eyes shut and closed his hands around her throat.

Threon thrashed wildly beside them. He had no regard for the pain in his wrists and shoulders. He pulled, and bit and forced the rope until blood streamed down his arms. The crown they had made for him was shattered and in clumps, matted to his hair.

The crowd seemed to hold their breath, as if straining to listen for the snap of her neck. Threon pulled his body up off the ground and placed his feet against the post. With some effort he managed to walk vertically, straining to climb between the pole and the taut rope. Once he had gained some height, he plunged his body to the ground. There was a snap. A moment of panic, but Azzania still lived. Lleu still held her neck, hesitating. The rope that held Threon had snapped and hung loose at his feet.

Lleu turned, taken by surprise, just in time to receive the full force of Threon's furious body bowling into him. He could not stand by and watch Azzania be murdered. Threon smashed his fists and elbows into Lleu's face. He put his full fury into every blow. Lleu was taken aback and took the blows, shock on his face.

Blood poured from the soldier's nose and lips and mingled with the crimson flowing from Threon's wrists. The crowd began to heckle and cheer wildly. Threon had provided a show.

As he drove down his bound hands once more, Lleu met his fists with his palms. He twisted them and moved his arms so that Threon was forced off his body and onto the ground beside him. Lleu was on top of him quickly. He pinned Threon's arms down with his knees either side of his chest, just as Oxyara had done to him the previous day. He hit Threon square around the head with a fist. 'I didn't want it to be this way.'

It seemed Threon's attack had only served to strip the soldier of his previous hesitance. 'I won't go out easily.' Threon spat blood onto the sand.

'Can't you see, I don't have a choice.'

Azzania watched wide-eyed. 'Threon,' she called.

'She may be willing to give up,' said Threon. 'But I'm not. There must be a way out.'

'Death is the only way you will leave this stadium. I'm sorry. Don't make this harder than it already is.' An arrow dove into the ground beside them, a warning shot.

'Seems we're not killing each other fast enough for their liking,' said Threon.

Another fist across the right-hand side of his face. Threon blinked until his vision came back into focus. His fists were slick with his own blood and with a painful jerk he managed to get one hand free of the rope. In one swift move he took hold of the arrow at his side and dug it deep into Lleu's left thigh. The soldier cried out and the pressure eased enough on Threon's arm for him to roll free.

Lleu came to a stand and slowly pulled the arrow from his leg. The soldier was twice the size of Threon, with decades more experience in combat. And now they were both fighting for their lives.

'You owe me your life twice over, Greenbrooke. Why are you making this so hard?' Anger had replaced the fear and guilt that he had worn on entering the ring.

Lleu ran at him full pelt, throwing his weight into a tackle. The power of his shoulder on Threon's chest took the wind out of him. Lleu forced him up against the wall of the arena. Threon battled back, but his strength was incomparable to that of the soldier; a pup fighting a wolf. A sharp knee to his stomach brought him to a ball on the floor. Threon didn't get up again. The soldier crouched down and brought a hand to the back of Threon's neck. Threon grabbed at his wrist but could do nothing to move him.

The anger dropped from Lleu's face. He was in control now. 'I can make this really quick.' His tone was grave. 'Lie still and I'll break your neck. It's a clean death.'

Threon glowered as he looked up at the man with whom he had once been an ally. He was asking permission to end his life. Threon kicked out but Lleu pinned his legs to the floor.

As his last line of defence, Threon twisted his neck and sunk his teeth into Lleu's wrist.

It was at that moment that the arena boiled into fierce light.

Lleu let go of Threon to look around. Both men came to their feet to see the stadium alive with violent flames. The pit and the stalls burned red, orange, white. A wall of heat hit them hard and they both ducked to the floor, shielding their faces from the heat.

The crowd erupted, causing a stampede as several hundred people fled for the stall exits. Thick smoke blocked out the remaining daylight. Threon and Lleu looked at each other. 'What's going on?' gasped Threon.

'I don't know.'

'Azzania!' She was no longer tied to her post. A moment later she appeared out of the black smoke, running towards them.

'Are you both insane?' she said. She wrapped her arms around Threon and held him close.

263

The smoke began to shift, being moulded and sliced by something in the wind. A dark shadow passed overhead. It swooped low, rushing a breeze across the arena. A dark, winged figure dropped from the sky above them. She beat her great wings as she alighted, fanning the flames around them.

'Savanta,' breathed Threon, choking on the flames. 'How?'

'Enough. There's no time.' She dropped three short swords onto the sand before them. 'I've drenched most of the building with catchfire. Lleu, take them out through the slave entrance. You might come across soldiers on your way, but at least you won't fry.'

She beat her wings again. 'You can thank me later.' With that she flew into the smoke, the rising heat guiding her away from the volley of arrows that flew in her wake.

Threon put aside his astonishment and picked up the swords. He handed one to Azzania.

Lleu, still panting, held out a hand for the other.

'Give it to him, Threon,' said Azzania. Threon hesitated. The pain that Lleu had inflicted burned in his bones. The larger man was unarmed; the tables had turned.

'Threon,' cautioned Lleu, 'it's over. We don't need to fight. There's a way out for us. All of us.'

The fire caused the tension to break. The wind changed direction, forcing hot smoke upon them. Their eyes streamed and they choked on the black air. They needed to find a way out. Lleu might be their only chance.

'Come on,' cried Azzania. Lleu ran with them to the pit's exit, which was still free of flame.

Once inside, Lleu shut the door to the fire. They hunched over, hands on thighs, coughing as they regained their breath.

The two men eyed each other warily. Lleu wiped the blood from his face. 'I had no choice, Greenbrooke. You know that.'

Threon said nothing. Now that they were free of immediate danger, he could feel the pain rolling back in. His shoulder, his head, his bloody wrists, the stamp of Lleu's fists on every patch of his body.

'Enough,' said Azzania. 'You can sort this out between you later. Let's get out of here. We've a war to win.'

Savanta didn't stop flying until she was far from the city.

An arrow had pierced a hole in her right wing and made her flight uneven. Her right shoulder ached with the effort she put into keeping herself level. Despite this, she relished her return to the air. The days she had languished alone in Maradah had been long and bleak. Hours spent watching the horizon, watching and waiting, hoping against hope that the boats would turn back and come for her. The sense of abandonment had begun to tear at her soul. She began to believe that she would never see home again. And yet here she was. The right side of the sea.

She was high above the Greylands when she felt safe enough to stop. Gliding down to an abandoned open-pit mine, she lay on the cool ground, her chest rising and falling heavily as she caught her breath.

'Beautifully done.' Zenith. He was never far away.

She eased herself up onto her elbows. 'You're pleased, then?'

He had taken the form of a large owl in a nearby tree. The bird flew down from its perch and landed on the ground beside her.

'Of course. It was magnificent. Perfect timing, too. They were all on the edge of their seats as fire rained from above. Quite the spectacle.'

'I see your penchant for drama is as hot as ever.'

The bird cooed. Savanta came upright and sat cross-legged

265

before him. She felt an unfamiliar sense of gratitude towards him for the return of her wings. 'What happens now?'

'They'll escape. I'm keeping my other eye on them. They'll be out of the city within the hour. Then… I have faith that they will fall back into play. It won't be long until my brother is knocked from his high horse.'

She stretched out her damaged wing and ran her finger around the hole left by the arrow. The skin was thin so it didn't hurt much, but her muscles were sore from overcompensating in flight. She extended it to stretch it out. She wondered what Erin would think to see her now. Would she even recognise her?

'Will you let me go home now?'

'Home?' He preened his wing feathers.

'What more do you want from me? I've murdered a ship full of retreating men, set fire to a stadium of civilians and helped you start a war.'

She had expected him to laugh, or to shoot her request down with a sneer, but the bird simply cocked his head. He was considering it. 'Hm. You are looking a little worn, a little rough around the edges. You know, I think a short respite might do you good.'

Savanta was already on her feet. 'You won't stop me?'

'I won't stop you. But I won't promise that you'll find the peace you seek.'

Savanta wasn't listening. She was already on her feet, sprinting into the air.

CHAPTER TWENTY-TWO

Freezing white foam sprayed into the air as they ran into the water. Lleu untethered the small rowboat left for him by Khan and held it steady among the crags as Threon and Azzania hauled themselves in, wet and shivering. Lleu swung himself in to join them and angled the oars into the water.

'Where now?'

'South. There's a narrow bay in the Greylands. That's where our forces will be,' said Threon.

Threon's breath clouded in the air and his teeth chattered. He pulled Azzania close and rubbed her arms to warm her.

'I'm fine,' she said, but still allowed herself to be brought into his embrace. She coiled her fingers in his and her touch eased his shivering. Was that the void? He didn't think so, and the thought brought a small smile to his face.

Lleu cast the boat off into the water and took charge of rowing. Threon leant over the edge of the vessel and splashed his wounds clean. The sting of salt on open flesh bit sharp, but none of his wounds were deep enough to worry overly about infection. Once clean, he watched the soldier row in silence, oars sinking into the waves in rhythmic strokes. Azzania happily settled into Threon's arms as the soldier rowed the vessel south.

They came to shore shortly before dawn. All three collapsed on the rough sand beach, hungry, cold and beyond exhausted. Before they could rest, Lleu insisted they hide the boat from view. They built no fires and hid in a gorse thicket for cover. Threon had never felt so drained, so cold. He slumped to the ground shivering, too tired to build any kind of shelter for warmth. Azzania and Lleu dropped beside him, too tired to speak. Threon closed his eyes, willing on sleep to give him respite from the cold and the pain.

As he lay breathing into the sand a hand curled around his waist. He rolled over. Azzania was looking at him, her face pallid and solemn, still crusted with a little blood. She ran her fingers down his cheek and he pulled her close. She was soft and warm; holding her brought much needed comfort. She looked into his eyes and his lips met hers in a gentle kiss. They stayed like that a while, lips pressed, bodies held close, until she sighed and he felt her relax into sleep.

Threon pressed his forehead against hers and closed his eyes, following her into dreamless sleep.

Threon woke to the smell of blood.

He startled awake as a shadow crossed overhead. It was Lleu. The soldier dropped a pair of dead rabbits beside the embracing couple and Threon relaxed. Only rabbit blood.

'You two look pretty cosy,' said Lleu, giving them a wry smile.

Threon got to his feet slowly and helped Azzania up. His muscles ached, his skin was torn and bruised and he could barely move his shoulder. The morning sun shone bright and strained to ease winter's chill. 'Nice work on the rabbits,' he said. Lleu knelt on the sand, expertly ripping a short sword through one of the creatures. He wrenched the animal's guts out, and Threon suppressed a shudder. Given any more time yesterday, he could have very easily played the part of the rabbit in the man's hands.

'I set traps last night while you were sleeping.'

Threon's stomach growled at the sight of the meat as he tore the skin from the animal.

'Seems you were both too busy getting lost in each other's eyes to notice the ships?' Lleu added.

'Ships?' said Azzania.

Lleu pointed to the southern horizon. Seven dark marks were clearly visible on the sea.

'They're nearly here.' Threon felt a rush of adrenaline.

'It looks like they'll land less than a mile south of here. We should get moving. We'll have to eat these when they get here.'

They gathered themselves up and began to follow him down the beach. Azzania paced beside Threon and caught his hand as they walked. With every step his smile seemed to grow.

The night had settled a deep quiet on Savanta's hometown. Tannit's usually bustling streets were empty of people. As she alighted on her street a scavenging fox bolted for cover.

It felt strange to be back. She had seen so much, been through so much, since she had last laid eyes on this place. It somehow seemed so much smaller now.

She walked a few feet along the littered mud path to her home. It was a small house, squat and crowded by those around it. She had been born here, had given birth here, and

269

once thought she would die here too. She placed a hand on the familiar wooden door and exhaled fully before letting herself in.

Not much had changed. The cluttered living room was still warm from the glowing remains in the fireplace. She picked up the oil lamp that hung on the far wall and lit it. Half a loaf of her mother's bread had been left out on the table. She bit into it hungrily and a thousand memories of childhood rushed back. She fingered her old books which lay on the shelf, no doubt untouched since she left. Beside them sat a stuffed bear that belonged to Erin. Savanta's father had made it for her. Savanta had never much liked the thing; she found its lopsided eyes and sagging limbs oddly creepy, but Erin had always found comfort with the old toy. She picked it up and touched it to her cheek. It smelled of home. Of family. She carried it with her up the stairs.

There were two bedrooms. Her parents shared one; she and Erin shared the other.

She pushed open the door and her heart felt like it would burst. Her angel slept curled in a ball, as beautiful as the day she was born. Savanta slipped in silently and crouched beside the bed. She watched her little girl, so peaceful in sleep, and placed the ragged bear that she loved so much beside her.

She stroked her soft hair, which shone copper in the lamplight. Erin looked so peaceful, so angelic. Savanta almost feared touching her, as if waking her would shatter this perfect moment. A tear dropped down her face. She was home.

'Erin,' she whispered, running her hand down the little girl's arm. 'Mummy's home.'

The child half-awoke, grabbing hold of her hand. Savanta reached out to pick her daughter up. As she lifted her, Erin mumbled through dreams.

'It's okay, come here. I'm back.' The girl wrapped her arms around her mother, still lost in sleep. Savanta cradled her, holding her tight and burying her face in her daughter's hair. Tears ran freely down her face now. She hitched her daughter up on her hip to steady her and the little girl came awake. She yawned and her eyes blinked open. 'Erin, baby?' Their eyes met for the first time in what felt like a century. Time stood still.

And then Erin screamed.

Her face was a mask of terror. The old figure of her loving mother had been replaced by that of a creature of nightmares. Savanta snapped her wings in to make them seem smaller. Erin fought to get free and backed up against the bedroom wall.

'It's okay, it's only me. Can't you hear Mummy's voice?'

Erin was sobbing, confused, scared. Savanta took a step backwards, holding up her hands. Her heart jarred and a wave of nausea hit. Her knees felt weak, and she opened her mouth to say more, but no words came. The fear on Erin's face was torturous.

Savanta barely registered the commotion behind her; her whole world was falling apart in front of her.

'Get back from my girl.' Her father rushed into the room, a knife in one shaking hand.

Savanta took a step backwards, her hands held out in defence. 'Dad, it's me.'

'Erin, keep back,' he said. 'Deyar, protect us.' He made the sacred sign.

'Erin, sweetheart, it's me,' Savanta choked out the words, the tears insuppressible. 'Dad, please! You must know it's me.'

'Save it. The priests warned us about demons like you, carrying my daughter's voice. Get out of our house.' He jabbed forwards with the knife and she stepped aside to dodge it.

'Dad, it's me. Please.' Her mother appeared in the doorway behind him holding an axe. 'Mum, make him listen.'

'Oh Lord, it sounds just like her,' her mother's voice trembled. 'Gods help us, leave us in peace.'

She was backed up against a wall now, her father inching closer with the knife. She felt for the ledge of a window on the wall. 'Erin, sweetheart, it's me. Your mummy. Don't cry.'

'We buried your mother. Don't be taken in by it.' He backed her right up against the windowsill and pressed the knife to her throat. She looked into his eyes but all she could see was the pain of loss; there was no recognition to be found. 'Get out.' He pushed firmly on the knife and it began to cut at her skin.

'I'm not going anywhere. This is my home.'

'Leave.' He pressed the knife harder against her skin, teeth gritted, breathing hard through his nose. She had to make him see. Surely he wouldn't hurt her.

'Put the knife down, Dad. You can see it's me, under this skin.'

He withdrew the knife quickly, but her relief was short lived. He sprang the blade back at her, stabbing it into her belly. Her reflexes were quick, but they weren't quick enough. She moved just far enough for the blade to slice through her side. She stared down at the dark blood that poured from the wound. Her father held the knife tight, ready to thrust again. As he did, she pulled herself up to the windowsill and let herself fall, narrowly avoiding a second stab wound.

As she tumbled to the muddy street floor, the shutters closed on the window and she heard them latch shut. Beyond rose the sound of Erin breaking into tears. She looked down at her side. The gash was a finger's width deep, but she couldn't feel its sting yet. The pulse of fear and anger was overriding the pain.

An owl perched on the roof. 'You did this.' She screamed

the words, tears streaming uncontrollably. 'All I wanted was to hold her. I just wanted – I wanted to be home.' She fell back on the muddy street, sobbing. The owl flew down from the roof and appeared as Zenith's transparent outline.

'You haven't earned the right to your freedom, my dear,' he said coolly. 'Not yet. We've a long way to go.' She looked up to see him smiling. 'You kept asking to come home. It was getting rather repetitive. Are you satisfied now?'

'You're enjoying this.'

'As you said – I have a penchant for drama. Get up off the floor. You're getting filthy.'

She ignored him. 'You told the priests to warn them about me.'

'Oh, heavens, no. That wasn't me. That would have been my brother before you switched sides. He probably didn't want his gift to fly away home.'

'You're a manipulative piece of work.'

'Careful now.'

'They found a body.' She was incredulous.

'They needed closure. I gave it to them like the kind-hearted Vyara you all expect me to be.'

Savanta had had enough. She got up and sprinted down the street, choking down sobs as her bare feet pounded the dirt.

'You can't escape me,' he sighed. He appeared in front of her. She turned to run the other way, and there he was again. She ran at him, hoping to push past, but he held steady. She pummelled her fists against his chest. 'It's not fair.'

'There, there.' He circled his arms about her and she cried into his cold, translucent flesh. 'Let it out. It's for the best. You and I are a great team; I can't lose you just yet.' She sobbed into his chest, her hate for him rekindled. Would she never be free?

He stroked her back. 'I'll always be here for you. Always.'

CHAPTER TWENTY-THREE

Queen Aya was aboard the first galleon. They dropped anchor several dozen feet from shore and pushed through waves in a small rowboat to meet the trio who stood on the beach. Threon waded into the water to help the queen from the vessel. He offered his arm to her.

'Don't be ridiculous,' she said in greeting, batting him aside. She stood and jumped into the shallow water, causing the small boat to sway violently.

'Good to see you again, Majesty,' he said.

'Good to see you alive,' she said, still managing to look down her nose at him despite her diminutive height. 'You have their mineral?'

Threon gave a small shake of his head.

'Ah,' she said curtly. She waded past him to the shore. 'Azzania. So good to see you.' She extended her hands to the Guardian and they exchanged kisses on cheeks. 'What on earth are you wearing?'

'Execution dress.' Aya raised an eyebrow at that.

Lleu stood beside her. She eyed the man suspiciously as the rest of her companions from the rowboat came to shore, dragging the vessel behind them. He towered above her. 'A man this large must be our palimore rebel.' To her credit, she hid any misgivings she might have had about the soldier.

'This is Lleu,' said Azzania. 'He was born in the Waterlands; he lost everything he holds dear to the Empire. He has more reason than most to be on our side.'

Lleu gave a royal salute. 'It's a pleasure, ma'am.'

A satisfied smile touched the corners of her mouth. 'Always good to have an inside eye. Good to meet you, Palimore. At ease.'

A further two rowboats arrived on the beach. She turned to those assembled and clapped her hands twice above her head. 'Come now. I'm starved. Prepare lunch.'

An hour later Threon was sitting on the sand, his belly full, surrounded by his people. Spirits were high. A safe arrival, undetected. The bay was hidden by tall sand dunes and surrounded by miles of abandoned mining land. They would be safe here for now. The sound of laughter and mock fighting filled the air as Ionese soldiers taught farmers how to make battle. The sound reminded Threon of his days training with swordmaster Dann, and it brought a smile to his face.

All the ships had moored now, and Vituund had come over with a skin of wine to go with the fish prepared by the Ionese.

'Lessons in swordplay this close to the battle,' muttered the king. 'How much do you think those farmers will take in? It's too late for training now.'

Threon's smile fell as the Southerner began to pour a second cup of wine and handed it to him. He picked at the scabs that laced his wrists. 'What happened?' asked Vituund. 'You look terrible.'

Threon hadn't caught sight of his reflection yet, but he

275

could feel his face had swollen, and was probably as mottled with bruises as the rest of him. His eyes found Lleu, who was helping to unload the ships. He bore a thick split lip and still had crusted blood around his face.

'We ran into some trouble in the city,' said Threon. Vituund's eyes narrowed in suspicion as he followed his gaze to the soldier. 'It's fine, really. Nothing that won't heal.' Threon looked up as a shadow crossed the sands of the beach. Savanta glided over the camp, beating her wings to slow her descent. Several men cried out, pointing towards her in fear.

She landed, feet sinking into the sand as she hit the ground with force. Without saying a word she strode over to a platter of seafood laid out for the troops and took a large crab from the pile. A couple of Ionese guards drew swords to confront her but she ignored them and headed away from the crowd. 'Leave her,' called Threon.

She half ran up the pebble beach to a dune, where she sat and broke into her meal using a rock. Threon excused himself and made his way towards her. She didn't look up as he approached.

'Savanta.' He came to a stop a few feet downhill of her. 'You're back. Your body. Was it Zenith?'

She turned her face away from him, looking out to sea as she spoke. 'I know you don't want me here. I don't want to be here either. But it seems I have no choice.'

He felt for her. Forced into a monster's body, driven to a foreign land, and then abandoned by her only friends. She may have saved them, but he had to do what was right. 'You pose a danger to us here. I can't risk you attacking a Guardian again.'

She looked at him, her eyes hollow and bloodshot. 'It's not me who poses a danger.' She let out an exasperated laugh. 'You have no idea. You're getting involved in a war beyond the realms of men. You don't know the Vyara. He could use any of you to—' She stopped abruptly and the temperature of the air seemed to cool. A breeze stirred Threon's white clothing. The air seemed to hum, and then, before his eyes, Zenith appeared. Savanta sighed and gave Threon a look of resignation.

He was not what Threon had expected. Athys had been frightful, ensnaring, mythical. Before him stood what looked like a highly adorned courtier. His androgynous face was handsome, blond hair whipping about his shoulders. His cloak, etched with the night sky in silver thread, thrashed against the swirling wind.

'Threon Greenbrooke.' The Vyara beamed at him, voice like honey. 'We meet at last.'

Threon gave a cautious bow. 'It's an honour, my Lord.'

'Two gods in one week. He must be blessed.' He gave Savanta a wink. She ignored him, busying herself with sucking the meat from the crab legs. 'Most kings have a somewhat world-weary look about themselves. You're rather handsome, though. Even if you're a little rough around the edges. Don't you think, Savanta?'

She rolled her eyes. The Vyara stepped behind her and placed a hand on her shoulder. 'I know your witch tried to rid our poor Savanta here of me. She will need to be careful.' He looked pointedly at Threon. 'I don't like Guardians. I'm sure you'll understand.'

'With respect, I fear their feelings may be mutual.'

'You left this poor dear stranded, alone. She didn't want my help, but who else was there to turn to when her friends abandoned her?' He pouted, cocking his head to one side. Threon narrowed his eyes. They had only abandoned her after she had tried to murder Azzania. Under Zenith's control. If anyone was to blame…

'Yes, yes,' continued the Vyara, coming closer. 'I know. You

277

didn't like that little game in the harbour.' He stifled a laugh. 'That was just a bit of fun. Don't blame her. There are greater forces at work here. As I said; I don't like Guardians.' He met Threon's eyes, square.

'You want to help us?' he said. 'The Guardians fight with us too.'

'Of course. My brother's feelings about the witches are just as hostile. If they can help unsettle him, then I'm prepared to set aside my differences. For now. Besides, you are my army, my team, my side of this little quibble. And you, sir, are the unifying element behind this force.' He stepped away from Savanta and came closer, filling Threon's personal space. The Vyara towered over him, revealing a smile like a lizard. 'We should be friends.'

Threon looked to Savanta, but she was avoiding his gaze. The Vyara would be a powerful ally in the fight ahead. A dangerous one, too. But, what choice did he have? Could he dare refuse?

'It is an honour to have you as an ally, my Lord.' Behind Zenith, he could see Savanta shaking her head.

'Good.' Zenith drew out the word. 'Threon, my friend. It's been a long time since I worked with royalty in the living realm. I must have a bit of a soft spot for you.' He circled Threon, running a finger across his shoulders as he walked behind him. 'Do you want to see something out of this world?' The Vyara didn't wait for an answer. 'I know you failed in your little attempt to steal the Empire's vish supplies. Pitiful really. You ought to leave these things to the experts.'

'Like you?' Threon raised an eyebrow.

'Precisely.' He placed a hand on Threon's back and guided him over the dune. Just before they were out of sight of the camp, he turned and called to Savanta. 'Coming, my sweet?' She got up and followed mutely.

When they were out of sight, Zenith crouched on the sand and drew a large circle on the ground between them.

'We're going in again,' he said to Threon. 'To the other realm. The demigods can't stand in my way. You brought the party. It's only fair I supply the drug.' He flashed a white-toothed grin. 'They will descend into panic without vish. We will have a winning edge.'

Savanta joined them at the edge of the circle. Zenith placed his hand on the nearest half of the circle and pressed down. Threon crouched beside him to see what he was doing more closely. 'You like magic tricks?' the god asked. He kept his eyes on Threon as he pressed, his excited grin growing as Threon's eyes widened.

Sand filtered between his fingers as he pushed downwards, then the ground beneath his hand seemed to slip and give way. One half of the circle rose, and the side he was pressing on fell into the earth. There was a cracking sound, like the snap of dry bones, and Zenith released his hand. The circle he had drawn in the sand had become three-dimensional. It spun, seemingly on an invisible pivot, rotating around itself, scattering sand in all directions. It grew smaller and smaller as it spun, until it disappeared. What remained was a deep, blue hole. It looked like a pool of water with unimaginable depths.

'Ta-dah!' Zenith leaned back with a smile. Threon reached a cautious hand into it and a cool breeze licked his fingers.

He looked up, his eyes meeting those of the Vyara. 'This is my entrance,' said Zenith. 'Are you ready to go back to the other realm?' As he spoke the words, his form began to lose substance. His body became translucent and then melted into the air.

Threon looked at Savanta. She was nonplussed. 'Well?' she said.

'Well, what?'

'Now's your chance to try again.'

'But there's nothing there. I can't see a thing.'

'Get in the hole.' She shoved his shoulder with a hand. He caught himself before she could push him in and she suppressed a laugh.

He put his hand into the hole again. He could see nothing but blue space.

'I thought you trusted the gods?' Savanta's voice was tempered with malice.

Not one to be challenged, Threon swung his legs into the circle. It felt like slipping into cool water. He held Savanta's gaze, watching her face for fear as he lowered himself further into the blue. Sand trickled over the edge of the pit as his hands slipped in the earth.

'Time to let go, Kingy,' she said, moving one of his hands with her bare foot.

He lost his grasp of the land and slipped deeper, losing himself in blue.

There was no landing. He fell slowly, through blue skies, thick as honey. As he descended deeper, the heavens darkened, becoming a sea of stars. He stopped falling eventually and hung suspended in the air. Clouds drifted through an azure carpet below, and he seemed trapped between skies of night and day. The upper half emitted cool moonlight and the lower half shone rays of sunshine into the blue air. Where blue met black, at a horizon of sorts, a glowing globe hung.

'Zenith?' he called, voice faint in the vast space.

I'm here. Don't be frightened, boy. As the voice landed in his mind, a black-winged butterfly alighted on his shoulder. *This is my home. The sun and the moon, the day and the night, the wind in your hair, the air in your lungs. Few mortals have laid eyes on this sight. Breathe it in. The purest air you will ever taste. Isn't it delicious?*

It was. As he filled his lungs with it, he felt a sense of total clarity settling upon him. The air felt cleansing. His fatigue had lifted, the pain eased.

'I don't feel sick.' He had imagined he would be floored by nausea, like the last time.

Because you're here with my blessing. Last time you snuck in without permission. What did you expect?

'It looks so different.'

We're in the Vyaran realm. We'll have to delve down a tier to reach the home of the demigods. Head to the light at the horizon.

Threon found his body propelled slowly towards the half-sun, half-moon. He threw his arm over his eyes to shield them from the light as he neared the glowing orb.

The butterfly left his shoulder. It flew into the air and divided again and again until a thousand butterflies swarmed around each other. They pressed closer and closer until they formed the outline of a man. Zenith's body formed itself from their wings. He stepped in front of the light.

Ready?

He leant into the light and it shattered into dazzling shards. The air around them fell away and lost its clarity. Each breath tasted more stale than the last. Kaleidoscope colours infiltrated the edges of his vision.

A burst of light, and then darkness.

'We're here,' said Zenith, and it was a comfort to hear, rather than feel, the words. 'Part of my brother's realm.'

Threon's eyes took a moment to adjust to their dim surroundings. They stood on a cobbled path. The same cobbled path that he had been captured on with Lleu. In front of them stood the golden palace, the ghosts of nobility scurrying about their business in its shadow, oblivious to the god and his companion.

'This way.' Zenith inclined his head towards the main

gate. 'Deyar's children have created their own version of the palace here to fit their needs. My brother assumes the safest place for his dear love's vish is in the home their children sleep in. It's unfortunate for him that he underestimates my ambition.'

Threon marvelled at the height of the gates as they passed through them, ornately decorated, and shining silver in the grey light.

'Where are the guards?'

'Staying out of my way, if they know what's good for them.'

'Do your children live here too?' Threon again cursed the days he'd spent as a youth hiding from his lessons with the high priest. A king was supposed to be wise. There was so much he was ignorant of.

'My children? Heavens no. My offshoots live in your realm. Free to tease and please humanity as they will. It's only Deyar who chooses to keep his offspring tied down, employed as menial guards. A demigod deserves better.'

'You have many children?'

'A few. I'm picky when it comes to human breeding. Though your friend, Savanta, may have merit... She has spirit.'

'You think she would be up for that?' Threon laughed nervously.

Zenith raised an eyebrow. 'You think that matters?' His tone sent a shiver down Threon's spine. 'You've a lot to learn about religion, my boy.'

Threon changed the subject. 'Where's the light coming from? How come I can see?' There were no stars and no moon, yet he could see the outline of the golden palace as if it were a full moon night.

'You think my brother would have a sky in his realm? No.

282

Your mind creates the light, allowing you to see what you need to see. And avoid seeing what you shouldn't.'

They reached the large gilded doors. 'Remember, you're only here for a taste of adventure. Stay out of trouble and let me lead.' He touched a finger to the heavy doors and they swung open silently.

Inside, the air was warm and thick with moisture. Mosaics of gold, copper and silver covered the entrance hall walls. They didn't shine, their colours muted by the strange light. The smell of wet earth and decay tempered the air.

He heard a growl ahead. An enormous cat appeared, striped black and white. It seemed to emerge from a solid wall and its image wavered, as if it was pacing through a heat shimmer. It paused, looked at them, and let out a deep growl. After a moment, the creature leapt at the opposite wall and disappeared into the dull metal tiles.

Zenith continued to stride down the hall, his heels clicking against the ebony floor. Threon reached out a hand to touch the wall. It felt solid enough. And cold. It felt like ice against his fingers despite the cloying heat of the room.

At the end of the hall stood a large stone door. The plain grey rock was thickly veined with streams of violet. Vish'aad. Threon held out a hand to touch the vessels of the life-giving substance, but a loud crack sounded and the door swung open.

A warm fog poured out of the room ahead. Light hung in the moisture-laden air, making it glow. Before they could pass through the doorway, a voice spoke.

'Zenith.' The voice was deep, male. The shadow of a figure emerged from the fog. The man was a similar height to Threon, with darker skin and large black eyes. His face and arms were intricately painted with filigree patterns of copper. He wore light summer clothes of Thelonian design. Behind him four figures, similarly dressed, lingered in shadow.

283

'Nephew.' Zenith greeted him with false warmth. 'It's been too long.'

'What are you doing here?'

'Oh, I think you know.'

'Is this the boy who's come to challenge Mother?' He advanced towards Threon. 'I could break him right now.' Threon could feel his breath on his face. He pushed back, shoving his chest hard with both hands. He instantly regretted it. Despite his slight appearance the demigod didn't move. His chest felt like it was made of stone. Threon received a sharp punch to the stomach in return and doubled over in pain.

'Massa. Leave him.' Zenith's words were sharp, an elder chiding an over-boisterous child. Massa's attention was deflected for a moment. 'Massa, my dear boy. We're family. Let's not start a fight.'

'You are the one trespassing in our home.'

'Trespassing? And I thought you'd be pleased to see me.' He pouted, a gleam of misdemeanour in his eyes. 'I'm hurt.'

'If you're here for the vish, you can forget it.'

The shadowy figures in the mist encroached closer. Threon made out Oxyara, another woman, and two men who appeared to be twins.

'Ah, children, but you can't stand in my way. I mean, physically, it's impossible. You will lose. Respect your elders. I'd hate it if we came to blows. Family shouldn't fight.'

Oxyara glowered at Threon. 'That's the one,' she said. 'He tried to break in before. Cost me the world of trouble.'

All five demigods came forward to surround the two intruders, forming a circle around them. Threon kept his eyes on Zenith, not sure what move to make next. He felt naked without his sword.

Zenith took a step forward. Massa and Oxyara backed

away as he advanced in their direction, a level of uncertainty in their eyes. The Vyara's cloak billowed out around him, making him appear even larger. Threon came closer, keeping step with Zenith as he advanced.

They reached the grey stone doors. Oxyara paused and her quick glare at Massa brought him to a stop too. They barred the entrance and the other three closed in from behind. Zenith didn't slow his pace. As Oxyara and Massa stood hand in hand in the doorway their figures grew larger until they filled the space, barring the entrance to the next room. In the corners of his eyes, Threon could see the figures behind also growing larger.

Zenith chuckled to himself, and then sighed. 'Shame. Fight we must.'

He took the edge of his cloak in one hand and whipped it in their direction. A blast of air propelled the pair backwards. Zenith walked into the next room and Threon followed, looking over his shoulder all the while.

An ethereal glow hung in the room's warm air, like a sunbeam caught in a cloud of dust. The room was cavernous. Tall ceilings held up by marble pillars. At the back of the room, a circle of marble rose up out of the ebony floor. It looked like a grander version of a water well. Behind them, the three upright demigods walked purposefully towards Zenith.

As Zenith turned to face them, the twins and their sister began to sprint towards him in unison. They drew knives from their belts and one of the twins held up a spear. As they reached the Vyara he opened his arms wide, baring his chest. They drew back their weapons and made to stab him. As the metal hit his flesh, it shattered. They were now level with him, blunted instruments falling to the ground at their sides.

Zenith tipped his head to one side. 'Really?' A flash of blinding light shredded across the room. Lightning branched across the ceiling. A rumble of thunder accompanied Zenith's words as he spoke to them. 'I've never tried this on a demigod.' As he spoke, Threon could see the three on the ground begin to panic. Their eyes widened, they clawed at their throats and began to turn red in the face. Zenith smiled. 'Well, it seems to be working. Does my glory take your breath away, little children? I wonder, could this *kill* you?' He seemed to ask the last question to himself, his face a mask of cold curiosity as he watched them writhe on the floor.

Threon hadn't noticed Oxyara approach. It was only when her towering shadow loomed over him that he spun around. Too late. She was twice his height. Using a knee, she shoved him backwards and he slid across the polished floor. She, too, had a knife on her belt and drew it before charging towards him. Her massive body leapt at him and knocked him sideways, just short of pinning him to the floor. Threon scrambled backwards, trying to escape, but she caught one of his legs and pulled him back towards her.

'You dare to come back here,' she said, 'to steal what you failed to steal before.' She ran the knife up and down his torso, where it caught on his shirt, ripping the fabric and nipping his skin. 'We may not be able to harm *him*, but you, my friend are a different story. Where first? Here?' She hovered the knife over his navel, smiling. 'Here?' His heart. 'Here?' His throat. Threon swallowed.

He could hear Zenith laughing at the other side of the large room. Threon called out to him and he turned briefly. 'In trouble already?' he snapped, irritated. Pressing his index finger against his thumb, he made a flicking motion at Oxyara. She was propelled across the room. Threon stood quickly and rubbed a hand against his neck, looking just in time to see Oxyara disappear into the marble well at the back of the room.

Zenith gave a grunt of satisfaction. He was still toying with the twins and their sister, and somehow Massa had been ensnared under the same grasp. Threon ran to see what had become of Oxyara. He peered over the edge of the marble well to see she was pulling herself up a ladder set into the curved, tiled walls. But she couldn't hold Threon's attention for long. The large woman was dusted all over in vish. And beneath her lay a deep hoard of the mineral. The earthy smell of it rose up to where Threon stood. Clouds of violet dust swirled below him, rising up from her body's imprint.

'Zenith,' he called. 'It's here.' He was shaking with nervous excitement. A grin burst across his lips, despite the danger.

'Keep out of trouble, boy. I'll be over shortly.' He hadn't killed the demigods, but they were in evident pain. One or two of them made pleading sounds, begging the Vyara to let them go.

Oxyara emerged from the hole. Anger filled her stance, but her face writhed with confusion and fear. Threon took a step backward towards Zenith, and the flailing bodies of the other demigods fell into her eyeline. He could see her think twice. A moment of hesitation, and then she sprinted away, down a corridor that led off the main room until she was out of sight.

Threon glanced back at the Vyara before taking hold of the ladder and lowering himself into the well. Disturbed clouds of the substance caught sharply at the back of his throat and the peat smell grew stronger as he descended.

When he had climbed down a dozen rungs his foot hit the powder, bringing another swirl of violet smoke into the air. He cautiously stepped off the ladder with the other foot and sank into the drug as if it were snow. He wetted a finger and knelt down to dip it into the substance.

He still remembered the rush of the last time. The instant pain relief. The dizzying high. The strength it brought.

He touched the vish to his tongue.

His heart quickened, his vision sharpened. The fear that had held him just moments before fled. He felt alive.

He scooped up a small heap of the powder in both hands. The cost of this handful alone would have kept a family living well for a lifetime. And there was so much *more*. He threw his arms up in the air and let the powder settle on his hair and shoulders. He felt his grin widen as he relaxed and fell backwards, arms spread wide. He landed softly among flurries of violet and watched the particles dance in the air. The soft sounds of pain inflicted by Zenith now felt distant enough to be coming from across the ocean. He bit his lip as he breathed in deeply, feeling the mineral course through his veins.

It was some time before he noticed the sounds of pain had abated. Then a crash, like a battering ram beating stone walls. The ground shook. He bolted upright. The sound shook the chamber a second time. 'Zenith?'

The Vyara appeared at the lip of the well. 'Time to go, friend. I don't think you'll want to be around when my brother breaks through.' He tittered a nervous laugh.

'Deyar is here?'

'I've locked him out.'

'Of his own realm?'

'It won't last long. Quick now. Get out.'

Threon leapt up and scaled the ladder. As he climbed, the particles of violet that hung in the air became more dense. Zenith's hand extended out towards the well, but not to aid Threon's exit. The vish rose up through the air towards him, as if he were urging it to stream skywards.

The crashing became louder, more incessant.

Threon scrambled up the last steps of the ladder before he was totally enveloped in what was now a gushing stream of violet. He hauled himself out and turned around. The vish

288

tumbled up through the well in a torrent that continued vertically. The colour was mesmerising.

'Brother!' The word came from beyond the doors, dark and heavy. A smug smile crossed Zenith's lips.

There was so much of it. A deluge of the mineral cascaded up from the well. 'This isn't the only access point,' said the Vyara. 'It's one of several deposit sites in the palace. There's a vast chamber full of the stuff beneath us.'

It sped towards a new opening that had appeared in the ceiling. The demigods had all vanished, no sign of their bodies on the ground. Presumably they had fled like Oxyara.

The room continued to tremble with the hammering on the door.

'I can't keep him out for long. Hopefully we'll have just long enough,' said Zenith. 'Hopefully.'

The hiss of violet air grew louder, faster, but no sound could drown out Deyar's anger. A shattering crack and the stone doors through which they had entered fell in on themselves. Threon flinched as they slammed against the floor. There was no battering ram. Just an enormous figure of a man, dark skinned, muscular, and brutally angry.

The stream of violet stopped abruptly. The vish that was still mid-air pattered to the floor like a cloudburst. Zenith turned slowly to face him. 'Brother. It's been too long.' He spread his arms wide in a welcoming gesture.

Deyar stood over twenty feet tall. He reached Zenith in three strides. 'This is your greatest betrayal.' He spat as he spoke, towering over the sky god. His voice was deep enough to verge on hypnotic. 'You trespass here, you steal from my wife, and you torture my children.' Something had changed in Zenith's eyes. A deep-set resentment that spoke of ancient conflict. 'I have done you the favour of casting a blind eye these last two centuries. It ends now. You have declared war.'

Zenith grew larger, until he was eye to eye with his brother. Though they matched in height, the resemblance ended there. Deyar's skin dark as earth, and Zenith's pale as cloud. The sky god was lissome, beautiful even, while his brother was heavy with muscle, features like chiselled rock. 'Deyar, my dear.' Zenith smiled over threatening eyes. 'That was the point.'

Threon looked about for somewhere to run. He heard a voice from above. Savanta peered over the edge of the hole that had opened in the ceiling. Behind her was the blue sky of the beach. She lowered a rope down to him. 'Climb up.'

The Vyaras' eyes were locked on each other as if engaged in some mental combat. He grabbed hold of the rope and began to climb, hoping the gods would remain distracted. The rope dropped a few inches as Savanta struggled to hold Threon's weight. Her face strained with effort. 'Hurry up!'

The floor and walls began to shake, and then Deyar threw himself at Zenith. They both fell with force against a wall. It shattered under their weight. Blocks of marble scattered across the ground and the room shook heavily. A wind began to whip through the room and caught Threon on the rope. He began climbing with renewed vigour. A wave of heat rose from below. Together air and earth could spark fire, said scripture. And beneath him was the proof. A bright blaze of blue flame where the gods had stood, and the room began to fill with smoke. The Vyara had both vanished from sight. He heard their wild cries of anger and felt the room shake as he imagined them careening against the building.

He reached for Savanta's outstretched hand. She pulled him up, arms shaking with effort.

Threon tumbled up onto the sand, blinking in the bright daylight of the beach. 'Thank you,' he panted.

'You owe me twice now.'

'I won't forget it.'

The hole he had emerged from began to shrink again, until it was nothing but sand. He put his hand where the circle used to be and pressed down. Nothing. He dusted the sand from his palms, still reeling from the experience.

Savanta stood up. 'Are you beginning to understand what you're involved with now?' The ground beneath them rumbled. They froze, eyes flicking back to where the hole had once been. After a moment, Threon allowed himself to breathe again, and took her proffered hand to come to his feet.

'I knew it would be risky,' he said.

They turned to look back at the camp. Beyond the reach of the tide, a mountain of vish'aad had appeared. Soldiers gathered around it and on top of it. They crammed the stuff into their pockets, into tankards, into chests, into anything they could find. He could hear laughter. It had felt like a long time since they had had anything to celebrate.

Aya was shouting commands, trying to control the situation, and failing. The soldiers were too elated to listen. This stuff would save lives. It would heal and strengthen in battle. It would change their fortunes. Threon grinned.

'If Zenith has always hated his brother, why didn't he do this before?' he asked. 'The ancients will be crushed without their supplies.'

'If you're going to piss off Deyar, timing is crucial. He's been waiting for you, Threon. Your army is his key to winning power. He can't take Deyar's place as king without the support of a people. Without their belief, worship, sacrifices, what would he be? He needs the people of the Mainlands to support his claim.'

'Well, if he helps us win freedom...'

She shrugged and gave him a sad smile. 'We are all pawns in a game between gods. We can only hope we're being manipulated by the winning side.'

'Enough of this now.' Threon was feeling way too good to dwell on dark possibilities. The vish. It was amazing. Like gold flowing through his veins. 'You look like you could do with a pick-me-up.' He inclined his head down the slope to the chaotic celebrations below.

'Let's join the party.'

Aya's attempts to control the soldiers evaporated when Threon arrived and climbed to the summit of the mineral pile. He threw armfuls of vish over his head, a wild grin on his face. 'Armies of the East. Tonight we celebrate!' A cheer roared from those around him. A small victory, at last. It was so good to see a ripple of joy diffuse around the camp.

Savanta cautiously picked her way up the mound on foot. It seemed that the soldiers had briefly forgotten their distrust of her in the festive atmosphere.

'Your first step to freedom.' She gave Threon a smile, the first he had seen on her in a while.

'*Our* first step.' He flashed a wicked grin and threw the vish in his hand at her. She squealed, shielding her eyes, and then pushed him over. He pulled her with him and they fell together, rolling and giggling in the rising violet dust.

Around them, the soldiers began to do the same, pupils wide. Throwing the stuff, rubbing it in each other's hair and boisterously claiming their share. It felt good to play. Playing like children in a coloured mound of sand.

Threon stopped when he registered Aya's look of disapproval trailing him. He sat and slid down the mound on his backside.

'Do you call this regal behaviour, Greenbrooke?'

'Lighten up, Aya.' He put an arm around her shoulder to lead her away from the jubilant soldiers. She shrugged him off, irritated.

'Was this you? Where did this come from?'

'You haven't tried it yet? You should. It'll wipe that grimace off your face.' He laughed. Her frown only deepened. 'Guess who's just been on another trip to the other realm?'

'You?' She was incredulous.

'Zenith took me on a little adventure.'

She took a moment to compose herself, her features flicking between curiosity, suspicion and satisfaction. She seemed to settle for the latter. 'Well, well. I don't waste my time on religion, but I'll give my thanks to the sky god today. This is a small step to victory.'

'The ancients will be plunged into chaos,' said Savanta who had come to join them. 'This stuff is amazing. I feel like I could take on the world.'

'We shouldn't be so frivolous with such a vital resource,' snapped Aya. 'This is medicine that can heal our sick. And the wounded are going to pile up higher than Threon's ego.'

'Aya,' countered Threon, 'look at your men. They look like they've already won. Confidence and strength like that is what we need for the battles ahead. We need fierce fighters. Men and women who believe they can bring down a warrior with two centuries under his belt.'

She nodded slowly and opened her mouth to respond, but Threon's attention had been caught elsewhere. Behind her, he spied Lleu talking to Azzania. The palimore looked different. He held himself better, his shoulders seemed wider, chest high. Threon excused himself from Aya and wandered over to them, Savanta in tail.

'You're high,' was Azzania's cool greeting. Threon just grinned at her.

'Lleu, you look a few shades brighter,' said Threon.

'I feel myself again. Gods, it's good to have access to the stuff again. Did you do this?'

293

'This is Zenith's work,' said Savanta. 'Don't expect this gift to come without a price.'

Threon dusted some of the vish off his shoulders and sucked it off his fingers. 'If that price is helping him topple Keresan, I'm happy to pay it.'

The rest of the day was spent in high spirits. The ships were unloaded of their goods, and the horses made ready with carts, loaded high with vish crates and military supplies. Azzania was called away to council the queen. Back in Ionia, Azzania was the monarch's tutor in the void and the queen's lessons had lapsed during her time away.

She held hands with Aya now, coming to the end of a guided meditation. She released the queen and both women opened their eyes. Aya released a slow breath, her face washed in contentment. 'Better?' asked Azzania. Both women had abstained from taking vish'aad, preferring to take comfort in the void.

'Much. Thank you, child.' The queen rolled her shoulders and rang a small bell that sat on the table before them. Her wall tent had been one of the first to be erected and offered privacy enough for the lesson. A servant entered at the sound of the bell. 'Tea,' she ordered. 'And let some air in, please.' The servant bobbed his head and pulled open the fabric door of the tent to reveal the busy scene on the beach. It was a wonder to see the three nations working so good naturedly together. A special kind of bond developed between people who risked death to fight alongside each other.

It was a strange fusion of cultures. The Guardians were serene in white, and the red-clad Ionese soldiers efficient in their discipline. The Southerners were more at ease, bright in their blue robes. The Waterfolk were uncertain of themselves – citizens, not soldiers. Threon seemed to take something from each of them. He was as at home with the Southerners as with his own people, and now she watched him sparring with one of her kinsmen, mimicking the foreign swordplay.

'You have eyes for that one,' said Aya, leaning back in her chair.

Azzania looked away from Threon, holding onto a thread of the void to avert the heat she felt rising in her cheeks. Aya was a perceptive woman; there was little point in denying it. 'I see hope in him.'

The queen looked pleased. 'Good. If there's one thing we all need, it's hope.' The servant returned with a tray of tea. He poured two cups and left the women to their conversation. 'And does this hope extend to something between the two of you?'

Aya wasn't merely prying. There would be ramifications if she entered into a formal relationship. Senior members of the order pledged to put their duties above all else; love was too strong an emotion. It was seen to get in the way of their work.

Azzania sipped her tea, unsure how to answer. 'If we succeed here. When we return…'

'Yes, as promised. You can take office as High Priestess.'

'And my mother?'

'She will be demoted. You will take her place, but I won't cast her out. Your politics is your own to deal with. I'm not getting involved.'

'She tried to poison me.'

Aya had heard all this before. 'Perhaps she'll try again. She will not take kindly to you taking her position as priestess.' She picked up her tea. 'Or perhaps you'll deal her the same disservice when you take her place.' She raised a questioning eyebrow.

Azzania ran her hands through her hair. She had not missed the dangers of working for the Order. Competition among the higher ranks could be lethal and her ambition had made her a target.

She looked back out at the beach. Threon had roped a couple of Waterfolk into his sparring session. They laughed together as he gave them tips on how to beat the Ionese soldier. He caught her watching and smiled at her.

Despite all recent hardships, it had felt a relief to escape the callous power games of the Order. She felt freer than she had in a long while. Leading the Order was her lifelong ambition, but recent encounters put that in perspective. She smiled back at Threon. Perhaps there was another path for her.

Savanta had spent several hours carrying rations to shore and began to tire as the sun came to rest on the horizon. She heaved the chest she was carrying onto the back of one of the carts. Before securing it in place, she opened the lid and looked inside. Perfect. She picked out a slab of cheese and a nondescript bottle that she hoped was wine. Concealing them under a wing, she walked away from the party, up a steep dune.

'I could do with a break too.' Lleu took her by surprise, following close behind.

'You? You're made of muscle.'

'Okay, maybe I don't *need* a break… but a drink?'

'You saw?'

'I see everything. Cheese too?' He grinned.

She sighed. 'Come on then. At least you're not afraid of me like the rest of them. I could do with a conversation that doesn't start with "devil woman" after today.'

'Ha. They haven't quite worked me out yet either. Should I be feared, or bribed into being a personal bodyguard?' He laughed.

Savanta stopped and lowered herself onto the sand. Lleu collapsed beside her and stretched his arms above his head.

She slid the cork out of the bottle and took a sip. 'Ooph. That'll keep us warm.' She handed the drink to Lleu, who glugged at the bottleneck.

'Brandy. Excellent.'

'So it looks like you're firmly on the opposite team now?'

'So it would seem.'

'Last time I saw you, you were about to kill Threon.'

'When faced with his own death, a man will do many an unpalatable thing to survive. I never fully aligned myself to the Empire. The things they've done to the people here… to the people across the sea. To my family, my wife…'

'You're married? I didn't think palimore were allowed. What with the breeding programme and everything.'

He dug a heel into the sand and grunted sadly. 'They took her. She's a slave now. For all I know, she could be dead already.'

'That's terrible. I'm sorry.'

He took the bottle from her and sank several large gulps. 'I'll find her. I plan to leave tomorrow. Now Threon is back to lead his people, I figure I can go. The palimore will be told to come down hard on the mines. With the vish gone, they'll need more, and fast. Many slaves will die.'

'Do you know where she is?'

'She could be anywhere in the Greylands.' He stared blindly into the sand as he spoke, seeming smaller to her now.

'I lost my family too,' she said. 'My mother, father. Little Erin.' As she spoke the name, Erin's face flashed into her mind; round cheeks and smiling eyes. The look of fear on her face as she saw her winged body. She closed her eyes tight for a moment to force back the tears. 'And yet, somehow I'm fighting on the same side as the bastard who drove them away from me.'

'Life rarely deals us the hand we desire.'

She sighed. 'Where will you go tomorrow?'

'I'll start west of here. The Pullman mines, then Tanmar.'

They sat in silent reflection for a while. Savanta unwrapped the cheese from its paper and broke off a chunk to graze on. So many had lost so much, Islanders and Mainlanders alike. Even palimore suffered under the Empire. She came to a decision. 'Lleu, I'd like to help you. If I can.'

'Help me?'

'I lost my family, but maybe I can help you find yours. You put yourself at risk to save me from captivity in Maradah. I owe you this at the very least. From the air, I can scan a thousand faces in moments. I might be able to help find her.'

He scratched his chin thoughtfully. 'That's a very generous offer, but it could be dangerous. You mean it?'

'As long as *he*,' she looked up at the sky, 'doesn't stop me. I mean it. I would rather free slaves than go to war.'

Lleu pushed the bottle deep into the sand and gripped her shoulder. 'It would mean the world to me. Thank you.'

She pulled her wings in tight and leaned back against the sand, content in her decision. The lives she had taken on the boat still haunted her. Maybe freeing a slave could go a little way to atonement.

CHAPTER TWENTY-FOUR

They left early the next morning, without saying goodbye. The sun was yet to rise and their breath fogged in the cold air. Roads lacerated the land between mines, and they followed one west to the Pullman site. The road was deserted and they could enjoy walking an easy path as the morning sky blushed into colour at their backs.

In all his years as a soldier, Lleu had never fought alone. They had always worked as a unit, and he was glad of the company now. He could tell Savanta was tired but she didn't grumble. Lleu, on the other hand, felt better than he had in weeks. He'd eaten well, slept nearly a full night, and the gnawing desire for vish had finally abated. It was a liberation for both mind and body.

'Tell me about her,' said Savanta. She was asking about Raikka.

'She's…' He sighed, breathing out a steam cloud into the cold air. Language seemed a poor tool with which to convey the woman who meant so much to him. 'She didn't see me the way others do. When people meet one of the palimore they react instinctively with either fear or respect. She had neither.' He smiled at the memory of how they had first met. He had been visiting his Waterlands family when she knocked on the door, peddling silks. She invited herself in, helped herself to his lunch and laughed as she took hold of his bicep when he wasn't looking. She had been bright and curious and talked to him with a familiarity he only received from other soldiers. 'Being with her feels like escape.' He clutched at the locket on his wrist. 'She's Ionese. Long black hair. Short. Slim. Always wears a beautiful silk dress… though I expect they'll have her in mining garb now.' As he spoke, her image flared in his mind. Bright eyes. Infectious smile. And the memory of the last time he saw her, bound in chains, unable to help…

'Ionese? At least she shouldn't be too hard to spot among the other slaves.'

'There are over five thousand of them,' he said. 'This won't be easy.' He instinctively touched a hand to his sword hilt, a comfort to feel it at his side. He had furnished himself with a set of Ionese weaponry, stolen the night before. 'She's a survivor. She'll have found a way to keep on. When I find her, I'm going to return home. Back to the Waterlands. Back to my family home. We'll farm and grow old together.'

'Grow old together? If Threon wins, we'll all be offered immortality.'

'No we won't.' He shook his head. 'There isn't enough vish to sustain an entire population. Why else would the Empress be so restrictive with it? There's a strict limit on the number of ancients. When I was struck off, one of the palimore-in-training will have gained my quota. If the battle is won, the mines will have to close, the supplies be destroyed.' He only hoped that Threon had the willpower to go through with it.

If they kept the vish, the formation of another ancient elite seemed inevitable. 'When immortality can be bought, injustice and corruption thrive.' The thought of going through withdrawal again filled him with dread. But perhaps, he reasoned, he'd be caught in the mines and killed long before that ever became a problem.

Savanta walked on, seeming deep in contemplation. He wondered if she had ever thought about a life beyond the Empire, a new kind of society. Probably not.

It was a day's walk to the mine. Savanta grew bored of pacing and took to the air at midday. Lleu watched her with a little envy. She soared across the sky, free as the wind. He was relieved to see that Zenith was evidently content with her decision to join him.

The scenery grew flatter, more industrial. In place of hills, slag heaps and pits filled the landscape. It was deathly quiet. This area had been cleared of vish and abandoned. No slaves worked, no trees grew and other than the occasional bird, no animals lived here. With Savanta in the air and his strength returned, Lleu picked up the pace. It was raining now and the cool water refreshed him as he jogged the path. The dusty road turned to a grey mud as he ran.

When they grew near, he whistled to call Savanta's attention. She swooped down.

'We're nearly there. Let's go on foot for now. I don't want them to spot you and raise an early warning.'

He knelt down beside a puddle that had formed in the road. The sides of it were thick grey clay. He scooped it up and rubbed it along his arms, legs and face and dirtied the white linen he was wearing.

'That's a good look,' said Savanta with a wry smile. His skin was a lighter echo of her own under the clay.

'Come on, let's get off the road.'

It wasn't long before the sounds of metal biting rock met their ears. They trod carefully, using slag heaps and abandoned old buildings for cover as they neared.

A few slaves passed them but paid little attention. They were listless, lacking the energy to engage with the strangers. 'Do you know Raikka?' Lleu asked the question of every slave who passed. 'Have you seen an Ionese slave?' They only recoiled from him, exhausted with fear. A filthy palimore and a winged demon. He couldn't blame them for backing away.

'We need to get rid of the guards,' said Lleu. He couldn't know for certain that Raikka was on this site, but the search would be impossible with soldiers nearby. 'See that building over there with the lamplight?' She nodded. 'That's the guard base. Those men around it are palimore. How are you with a bow? From the air you should be able to pick them off fairly easily.'

'I've never used a bow.' She must have read the astonishment on his face. 'What? I'm an engineer, not a soldier.'

'It's a crossbow. Easier to master. You crank back the handle like this.' He began to show her, but she took it off him and after running her eyes over the weapon's mechanism managed to load it herself.

'Like this?'

He nodded, impressed. 'Think you can do that while flying?'

'Yes. But they'll start shooting back.'

'Stay high. Looking up into the rain will obscure their view and give you a slight advantage. I'll do my best down here with the longbow – though it's quite a distance.' He handed her the crossbow. 'Make your first shot count. Catching them unawares is our only advantage here.' Lleu took the longbow from his back and strung an arrow. He took a steadying breath, willing his fingers to stop shaking as he drew the

302

bowstring back. 'Ready?' He hoped she was. A contingent of palimore guards was a tall order to face alone.

'Let's find out.' She ran a few steps and took to the air, flying higher and higher. Lleu stepped out from his cover, crouching low to the ground. He hurried over to a mine shaft and pressed himself up against an old storage building, out of sight. The sound of rain and mining gave good cover, drowning out his footsteps.

There was a shout. Savanta's first arrow had landed in the ground several feet from one of the soldiers. Lleu cursed under his breath. The alarm had been raised. They gathered together, searching about for the attacker. There were six men and one woman in total. A relatively small number of guards for a mine this size. Lleu waited until their eyes were away from his position, then stepped out and released. His arrow shot through a soldier's eye. He fell dead to the floor. Another of Savanta's arrows fell. Closer this time. And another, in quick succession. This time she caught one of the men in the shoulder. He cried out and looked up.

'There. There! That thing in the sky.'

A volley of their own arrows launched towards Savanta. Lleu saw her beating higher as he stepped out into full view. He loosed two arrows. Another head shot left the woman dead. And another injured one of the men in his side.

It took seconds for them to ascertain the direction of his attack. Now, their arrows came at Lleu. He dived to the floor and rolled to avoid them. Around him, the slaves had stopped what they were doing, fixated on the scene unfolding before them.

Two of the palimore continued to fire arrows into the sky at Savanta, as the other three drew their swords and charged at Lleu. Lleu managed one more arrow – another man down – before he had to drop his bow and draw his sword to meet their attack.

As they neared he picked out their faces. Robb and Talyn.

Robb was the first to meet his sword. The metal clashed and slid until they were hilt to hilt. Robb's eyes burned into Lleu's. 'You.'

Behind him, the injured Talyn called to the archers. 'It's Khan's boy. The traitor.'

Robb's face was close enough that Lleu could smell the tobacco that stained his beard. 'Why, brother?' Robb's eye twitched with anger at this betrayal. 'Why?'

Lleu kicked him in the stomach, forcing Robb back a step and giving himself space to parry Talyn's next blow. The arrow to his shoulder had impaired the man's sword arm. Good. 'It's nothing personal,' growled Lleu, drawing his shortsword to defend Robb's next blow. Fighting two soldiers was a common training exercise. Always difficult, but not impossible to win. He gripped the two swords tightly, eyes flicking from man to man, trying to calculate their next moves. More of Savanta's arrows rained from the sky, with frightening inaccuracy.

Robb's voice grew shrill. 'We've known each other for more than a century.' He pulled his sword back and jabbed in tandem with Talyn. Lleu had to step backwards to avoid a lethal blow. Robb advanced. 'I trained you.' Another blow clashed against Lleu's shortsword. 'Taught you everything I know.' Another blow. 'We've shared women, shared blood.' And another. 'Why would you turn on us?' His face was flushed and a vein pulsed at his forehead.

Lleu pushed hard on his sword to force Robb back a step, just in time to block Talyn's next blow. He retreated further until he was backed up against the storage shed that he had been using for cover, preventing either from trying to attack from behind.

He ought to have ignored the taunting, conserved his

energy to focus on the fight. But a rage was building in him. Being back in the mines made the images of what his wife must be going through all the more real. 'Are you blind to what the Empire stands for?' he cried. 'What the palimore do? We plunder the Mainlands, forcing thousands into starvation. We drive slaves to death. We fight and we drink and we fuck in our merry little bubble, while we create a living hell for the world around us.' Lleu gripped tighter around his sword hilts, feeling his body shake with anger. 'Are you proud of what you've achieved in your many years?'

The other two soldiers had started running his way. Mar and Sidan. He risked a quick glance at the sky. Savanta was nowhere to be seen. His stomach lurched, but there was no time to worry about her fate now. They had all reached him. A tight wall of angry soldiers. He parried blows from all sides. This was easy work for them. Mar had already had one opportunity to strike at his right arm but hadn't taken it. They were toying with him.

Sweat beaded on his forehead and he panted for breath as he forced their blades away, his feet dancing to avoid the strikes to his legs. His opponents seemed to relax into a routine. They were reassured by their numbers. Lleu couldn't beat them while they worked together. The verbal taunting continued from all sides. Opportunities for killing blows were ignored. Lleu's arms grew heavy with effort. Every attack he attempted was foiled by the need to defend. Even offering a glancing blow to the injured soldiers felt beyond him now. The soldiers grinned maliciously as they fought. They were trying to wear him down. They were waiting for him to give up.

Movement in the sky caught Lleu's eye. Savanta. She was safe. The sight of her gave him hope and a spur of energy. He ducked to avoid one blow and, as he stood again, arced the shortsword over his head. It was a risk, exposing his left-hand side to attack. But it proved worth it. His shortsword planted itself in Talyn's forehead. It bit into his skull and Lleu lost hold of the weapon as the soldier fell backwards, eyes rolling.

Then he saw more reason for hope. Guided from above by Savanta, a group of around twenty slaves ran towards them. Looking fearful, but angry and determined, they wielded pickaxes. Lleu's killings had made them see an opportunity for escape.

Lleu held the attention of his attacking soldiers. They didn't notice the slaves until they were nearly on them. Mar spotted them first and cried out. All three turned, startled. The palimore lurched at their fresh attackers, leaving Lleu to fall back against the hut, exhausted.

He had seen slave uprisings before. He had quashed them too. Slaves were abused, sleep-deprived and emaciated. When they had the courage to attempt an uprising, they never stood a chance. No uprising had been successful in Lleu's lifetime, and the cruel examples made of any survivors were a sure way of deterring future attempts.

Now the palimore tore through this band of slaves. They didn't hold back with the same levity with which they had tackled Lleu. Several bodies fell almost immediately. The ground beneath them was soon red with blood. Savanta had doubled back on herself and Lleu could see her shouting to other slaves, commanding them to move forward. Several dozen other slaves had downed tools to watch the scene unfolding in front of them. Lleu forced himself upright and called to them. 'Take up your pickaxes. Freedom is in reach. Help them!' They looked warily at him, but when he ran to join the melee a few followed. As more joined the fray, more and more slaves found courage. The palimore were hugely outnumbered.

A massacre. The bodies of slaves kept falling, thin bodies crumpled to the ground, faces frozen in pain. Over the sound of the rain came the sound of death. As the bodies piled up, the slaves climbed over each other with a fatal determination to reach the soldiers. The injured crawled from the scene, some screaming, some silently clutching at their wounds. Despite the bodies mounting on the ground, the slaves fought on, attacking their masters with a desperate fury. Lleu forced his way through the battling slaves. He couldn't see the soldiers; they were heavily surrounded. One of these pickaxes would break through soon. They were going to win this.

More noise came from behind. Lleu turned to look. Another wave of slaves sped across the landscape. They held up scraps of metal, axes, beams of wood – all primitive weapons – but the bloodthirst in their cries sent a chill down his spine. And above them, like a demon in the night, flew Savanta. She led them to the fight and doubled back again in the air.

Lleu was pressed forward by those joining the fight, squeezed together with the slaves, but with no clear route to reaching the palimore. Pushing into the foray had been a mistake. Not all those who fought had seen Lleu's attempts to liberate them. To them, he was a palimore. To them, he was the enemy. Now he struggled to move. He could neither reach the enemy nor escape the growing crowd of slaves.

He didn't know what hit him, but it hit him hard. Lleu felt the trickle of blood down his neck before falling to the floor. A ringing in his ears, darkness, and a cloying warmth clasped him as he fell.

Lleu woke to someone shaking his body.

He bolted upright, hands grasping for his sword.

'Lleu?' That soft voice.

The sword clattered to the floor. It was her.

Raikka flung her arms around him. 'You found me.'

Lleu struggled for words. He wrapped his arms around her and held her tight, burying his head in her tangled hair. He could feel the hollows between her ribs. Her spine protruded from her back and she smelled of blood and fear. Tears fell on his shoulder where she lay her head. He couldn't hold her tight enough, breathing her in, never wanting to let go. 'You're alive.' His throat tightened as he spoke. 'I thought I might never find you.'

'I knew you would.'

'Raikka.' He kissed her paper-dry lips, her sallow cheeks, ran his hands through her hair. 'You look like you've been through hell.'

'It's over now.' Her eyes danced all over him as she stroked his face. 'You're hurt, Lleu.' Her fingers gently brushed the bulge at the back of his head where he had been knocked out. 'I had to drag your body out from under the others. I thought you were dead.' Tears welled in her eyes again.

'I'm fine, I'm fine.' He glanced about him and saw the pile of bodies heaped by the guardhouse. Slaves pulled their friends and family from the mound. All around, people sat weeping. 'The palimore are dead?'

She nodded and looked around, her expression blind to her surroundings. 'This angel of death called us to arms. She said you'd come to free us. It's the first time I've seen hope in these people since landing on this hellish island.' It was a high price to pay for freedom. He estimated that the dead numbered nearly four dozen. It said something of the poor health of the slaves that so many had had to die to overcome three guards.

'I'm so glad you're okay.' He pulled her close again. They lay on the wet ground, lost for words, but finding comfort in each other's arms.

Their privacy was broken when a shadow came across the

light. Lleu sat up to find Savanta standing over them. 'The angel of death?' he said.

She smiled. 'We all need a good epithet. This must be your lovely lady.'

Raikka stood and bowed her head. 'Thank you. You've given us our freedom.'

She pulled Raikka close and kissed her on the cheek. 'You earned freedom for yourself. Those bastards got what they deserved.'

Lleu picked himself up slowly and rubbed his head. The pain could have been worse. He wrapped his arms around his wife again. He didn't want to let her go. They had found each other. His dreams of a simple, happy life felt within reach.

'The slaves want to help,' said Savanta.

'Help?'

'They want to join Threon's army. They want revenge.' She seemed almost excited. 'Just think, if the other slaves want to fight too – the Mainlands' army would more than double in size.'

'I only set out to rescue my wife. Going to the other mines...' He looked at Raikka. 'It's too risky.' He wouldn't gamble away their chance of a life together, not now.

Savanta didn't hide her disappointment. 'I thought this was what you wanted? Down with the Empire?'

He shrugged, not knowing what to say to her. 'Well, I'm going to carry on,' she said. 'What we did here was incredible. Nine hundred people have their lives back. We could save more.'

Lleu began to shake his head. He was done. 'Savanta, we're going home.'

She was about to protest again when Raikka stepped forwards, out of his arms. 'I'll help.'

'No.' Lleu took her hand. 'We've only just found each other.'

She looked into his eyes. 'My time here has been short. But some of the people I've met here have been slaves for years. They've been taken away from loved ones. Some have watched their children die. I've seen people beaten and starved to death. If I can help bring down the Empire, I will.'

Lleu reached a hand up to her face and wiped at the tears falling down her cheeks. 'If we run – who's to say they won't come after us again?' she pleaded. 'If we can help this Threon defeat the Empire, I side with him. I'd rather die than face the chance of a second enslavement.'

'I can see why you like her,' said Savanta. She was smiling. 'There are only two more mines in operation. Please. We can do this.'

He had been holding onto thoughts of peace, of a life away from chaos. Now they slipped away. He sighed and looked at his wife. 'If you're sure this is what you want, I'm with you.'

'Thank you. We won't lose each other again. I promise.'

They tore down the guardhouse that day. The liberated slaves built a pyre for their dead loved ones with the debris. Raikka and Lleu helped clean the bodies before they were carried away to be laid on the wood.

Forty-seven dead.

Tears flowed that day, but Lleu could feel a palpable resolve in the air. There was an eagerness to fight back. His eyes lingered on Raikka as she worked, mopping blood from the corpses, straightening their clothes, combing tangled hair with her fingers. They worked close together, not moving out of arm's reach. They shared small smiles as their hands brushed each other, happiness tempered only by the dead.

Raikka would fall into silence as she worked on some of the bodies. Lleu guessed they had been friends but was unsure whether to ask. When they pulled one woman out, Raikka had cried out and fallen into his chest in tears. He held her tight and they watched two teenage boys wash the blood from the body. When they had finished, Raikka knelt beside her friend's corpse, hands shaking. She kissed her forehead and then nodded to the boys to take her to the pyre.

When the pile of bodies had been reduced, Lleu caught sight of the palimore. He walked over to get a closer look.

Their bodies had been mutilated beyond recognition. He knelt down in the blood pooled beside their remains. One had been scalped, another's eyes had been pulled from their sockets. Shit smeared the open chest of another. He recognised Robb, but only by the bloody tufts of beard that protruded from his swollen and blackened face. He had been stripped naked, his manhood removed.

Lleu closed his eyes. Raikka appeared behind him and laid a hand on his shoulder.

'They did terrible things here,' she said.

'No one deserves a death like this.' He shook his head sadly. This could easily have been him. 'I want to bury them.'

'You can't.'

He looked at her. 'They were my brothers once.'

She pursed her lips and was silent a moment before speaking. 'I never understood what it meant to be palimore.' She spoke softly. 'You would tell me stories about your work and they sounded like the old songs of heroes. I thought you were all above us. Immortal, powerful, strong. I know the truth now.' He forced himself to hold her gaze, a sinking feeling in his stomach. 'Palimore beat and abuse. They find pleasure in power. They rape and they kill. I've seen three people who survived a ten-year stint in hell rewarded with one of their knives in the back. They deserve worse. They deserve a lifetime of pain. We are merciful to grant them such a swift death.'

She turned away from the bloody sight. Lleu caught her hand and held her close. She shook gently in his arms, crying into his chest. 'It's okay,' he said. 'It's okay. It's over.'

'The whole time I was here.' She choked on the words through her sobs. 'The whole time, I kept thinking, my husband is palimore. Lleu, you are those men on the floor. You've worked in these mines. You've killed the innocent. You've tortured—' She stopped and pushed away from his embrace. 'Can I forgive that?'

Her words were the barest whisper, but they hit like a dagger to the heart. 'I—' He faltered, not knowing what to say. 'Rai, I'm not like that.' She stepped back from him, watching him closely as he spoke. Her sobs had stopped. Silent tears streamed down her face.

'Palimore destroyed my homelands; they enslaved my wife. I'm doing everything I can to stop them.'

'You wanted to run away.'

'You matter more to me than anything in the world. I want to run with you. I want to keep you safe, get you as far away from all of this as possible. But if you chose to stay, I stay too. And I promise I will make up for everything I've done.' He stepped towards her. She didn't back away, and let him take her in his arms again. 'I've caused you so much pain, it breaks my heart.'

She stood limply in his embrace and closed her eyes. 'Where do we go from here?'

CHAPTER TWENTY-FIVE

Unloading the boats had taken too long. The last one had been cleared of goods and weapons by sunset, and Aya insisted that they rest the night before beginning their march in earnest.

Threon paced out his frustration on the sand. With the vish gone, the Empire would be preparing a hasty retaliation. While most men slept he drew on a bottle of wine, cursing their lack of progress. The whole army were on the beach now. Their numbers swelled across the landscape like a small city. An army this size could never move at speed. And delay could cause catastrophe. He took another glug at the bottleneck, wiping at his face as the wine licked down his chin. He found himself outside the royal accommodations. Vituund and Aya had retreated to their tents after sunset. Both slept in enormous, opulent structures that had taken several men half a day to erect. A waste of man hours and another bloody thing for them to carry on the road. He nearly tripped on one of their many tent pegs as he passed by. His shelter was set up beside theirs. After many nights sleeping under the stars, Threon had no need of the tent that Vituund had provided. It was simpler, but still too large for his liking. The canvas door parted slightly in the breeze and he pulled it open. Azzania stirred as he did so, lifting her head from the bed and rubbing sleep from her eyes. 'I thought you'd be awake,' he apologised.

She sat up and pulled the blanket around her bare shoulders, shivering. Her breath fogged in the cold air. 'Why are you still up?'

He shrugged. 'Go back to sleep.' He let go of the tent flap and walked in the direction of a nearby fire. It had been left unattended for a couple of hours and had reduced to glowing embers. Still, he was glad of its modest warmth. He pulled his cloak hood up against the cold and breathed into his hands, his vision unfocussing as he watched orange sparks spit into the darkness.

Threon found his thoughts returning again and again to his encounters with the palimore. Their aptitude in battle surpassed anything he had ever seen. Despite the best efforts of those around him, none would ever match up to an immortal soldier. They had centuries of experience in battle, and godsblood in their veins...

'You look miserable.' Azzania interrupted his thoughts, coming to sit beside him. She held his hand and he felt the void spread through his body, taking the drunken edge away, restoring clarity. He shook his hand free and the inebriation swept back.

'I drink for a reason, you know. I enjoy feeling this way.'

She shook her head, amused. 'Suit yourself. But it's making you dismal.' Their situation was dismal. What did she expect?

A shadow passed overhead. Azzania pointed out Savanta's circling figure.

'How long has she been up there?' he asked.

Azzania shrugged and waved up at the Thelonian. After a moment Savanta arched towards them and spiralled down, alighting on the other side of the fire. She stretched her wings out and rubbed her shoulders. 'I'm surprised to find you awake,' she said.

'Dark thoughts are keeping him up,' said Azzania reproachfully. 'He should be resting.'

'Two nights and a day you've been missing.' Threon slurred the greeting. 'Didn't think to tell us you were leaving?'

'I've been busy,' she said. She looked energised, brighter than Threon had seen her in weeks. 'And I have good news. Lleu and I liberated the Pullman mines.'

'What?' He nearly fell forwards as he pushed himself to his feet.

'A push in the right direction and the slaves revolted. They're free now. Most of them are Waterfolk. They want to help. Can you spare weapons for another nine hundred?'

Threon was incredulous. He stood and gripped her by the shoulders, a grin spreading across his face. 'How on earth did you manage that?'

'Slaves have a fierce capacity for vengeance. We were simply the catalyst that drove them to action.'

'Where's Lleu?' asked Azzania.

'With his wife.' Savanta smiled. 'They're on their way to Tanmar, then to Alman to free the rest. I'm going to join them, but I wanted to share the news with you first.'

'It's very welcome news. How will the slaves find us?'

'Go to them. The swiftest route to the capital is from Pullman. They've started moving slowly towards the city. The couriers will arrive at the mine soon to pick up the next load of vish and discover what's happened; they want to reach the city before news of their uprising spreads. They're a day ahead of you so you'll need to move quickly to catch up. Lleu says you'll be safe travelling the road to Pullman if you leave now.'

Threon nodded and turned to Azzania. 'Sober me up. We've got to get moving.'

Threon grasped the excuse to leave camp with enthusiasm, eager to be doing something, to be helping, to be moving. He woke Vituund and insisted that the camp move out at dawn. The Bannvarian was elated at the news of more support and had leapt out of bed grinning. He walked with Threon now, wrapped in a heavy coat, as they marched out of camp to where the animals were tethered.

It didn't take long to spot him. Bloodbringer's coat shone in the moonlight, his muscular frame dwarfing the surrounding horses. As they neared he raised his head and whinnied, snorting a cloud of breath towards the pair. 'I couldn't leave him behind,' said the old king.

Threon reached a hand out and rubbed the stallion between the eyes. 'Thank you,' he said to Vituund.

'If there was ever a beast to get you there in good speed,' said Vituund, patting the horse on the flank.

'You'll make sure Aya's people are ready at first light?'

'Of course. Leave it to me. It's better to leave that woman to her sleep. She doesn't take kindly to interruptions.' He chuckled silently. 'She'll be delighted. We'll be at your heels within hours.'

Threon nodded. 'Good.'

'You must be excited to see your people?'

'Nine hundred of them! And potentially more coming.' Threon beamed. Savanta and Lleu had achieved what he hadn't even considered a possibility until after the battle.

Vituund helped him tack the horse, and Threon was

316

pleasantly surprised at the ease with which the king did so. During their time on the road together, Vituund had proved more practical than most nobles. As they finished, Azzania appeared over a dune. She had packed provisions. She carried blankets, water, a small amount of food, and weapons. 'You ready?' she said. He didn't need to ask whether she was coming with him. He pulled himself into the saddle and offered her a hand. She took it and swung up to sit behind him. Vituund gave them both a warm smile. 'Ride well, friends. We'll follow in your wake.'

'Don't take your time about it,' said Threon with a smile, nudging Bloodbringer past the king. 'We'll see you soon.'

'Soon,' said Vituund, calling after them as they sped down the beach.

It was nearing midday when they caught sight of the liberated slaves. Threon felt drained with lack of sleep, but the sight of the men and women ahead of them renewed his energy. Azzania clung to his waist as he nudged Bloodbringer to a gallop.

There were close to a thousand men and women clustered together, resting in a makeshift camp. As the sound of drumming hooves reached them he could see some people rise to their feet, grabbing weapons. A group of half a dozen men began to run towards them with a bloodthirsty cry. He reined Bloodbringer in and both he and Azzania dismounted, hands up in defence. An axe was thrown at them, only narrowly missing Azzania before impaling itself in the ground.

'We're not palimore,' she shouted, but the men continued to run at them until they were inches from the pair. Threon took a small step backwards, warily watching the pickaxe and iron mallet poised ready to smash into his body. Not the welcome he had hoped for.

317

'We're from the Waterlands,' he said calmly.

The oldest man in the group wrinkled his nose. 'This one looks like he's from home, lads. The woman's Ionese, I'd wager.' Faces softened, shoulders relaxed, and the weapons were lowered. 'You don't look like you've been working mines.' They didn't. The miners were grey with built-up layers of dirt, rakishly thin, but with shoulders and arms like those of an ox. Threon and Azzania were clean and recently fed, hands uncalloused and bodies unchanged by half a decade of slavery.

'We've come to help,' said Threon, extending a hand. 'Name's Threon.'

The old man clasped it. 'Like the old prince, eh? I'm Bran.'

'I'm Azzania,' said the Guardian, stepping forwards. 'And he *is* your prince.'

Bran laughed, but stopped when he saw she wasn't joking. 'Threon Greenbrooke?'

Threon smiled and shrugged. 'Guilty as charged.'

'The winged woman said you lived. I didn't believe it. We were damn sure they killed you.'

'They're going to wish they had. When they see the ferocity of you lot, they're going to be crying for their mothers.'

The old man chuckled, and went to pat Threon on the back, but looked unsure of himself. Behind him, one of the men started to bow to one knee. 'None of that, friends,' said Threon, waving the man back to his feet. 'We're each as worthy as the next man.' They relaxed again, and Bran gave him a grin.

'Let's catch up with the rest. Folks will be dying to meet you.'

The majority of those assembled were blue-eyed Waterfolk. Threon's heart broke to see what they had been reduced to: threadbare clothes, sullen eyes, malnourished bodies. As word spread of his arrival, they stopped walking, keen to glimpse their king. He and Azzania were soon surrounded by a large crowd. He saw hope begin to shine in their eyes. An army was coming to help. Revenge was close.

A woman pushed through the crowd that had gathered to question the pair. 'It's true,' she called, charging forward towards him. 'Threon.' She ran into him, wrapping her arms around his chest in a tight embrace, then stepped back, seemingly embarrassed by the gesture which showed so little deference. 'Our king!'

It took him a moment to place her face. 'Lena?' She looked different. Her cheeks had lost their colour, her wrinkles lay deeper and her plump figure had been reduced to bones. He embraced the woman again. The castle chef; the woman who had snuck him sweets as a child, the woman behind every meal of his young life, a constant smiling figure in the days before the raids.

'It's good to see you, Threon. For too long we thought you were dead.'

'It's good to see you in one piece too.'

She patted him on the arm. 'We can get sentimental later.' She nodded her head towards the crowd. 'You're like a ghost from the past to this lot. We've been waiting too long for hope like this.' The look in her eyes made it clear that she wanted him to make some sort of address.

He let go of her and turned to those gathered. By now, even those at the furthest end of the travelling column had noticed the disruption and were walking back to get a better look. He climbed onto Bloodbringer's back to gain height. Nearly a thousand pairs of eyes watched expectantly.

He took a breath and began to speak. 'The Thelonians stole you away from your homes and I can't even begin to imagine what you've all been through. I want to put an end

319

to the inequities of the Empire. But this is not my fight alone. This is yours. I fight with you; for you; for our freedom. And the freedom of our children and their children after. The ancients have shackled our nation and we must destroy the force that tries to collar us.' As he spoke, he saw people stand taller, grim determination setting on their faces. 'We march on the city. And we are not alone. Bannvar and Ionia join us. The Mainlands will be free of this terror.' A few people nodded, others puffed their chests with pride, then an excited mumbling broke out. These people wanted to fight.

A voice rose from the crowd. 'Lead the way, King.' Threon allowed himself a smile.

He glanced at Azzania. She grinned and took his hand as he helped pull her up to join him on the back of the horse. He spurred Bloodbringer on and trotted into the assembled crowd. They fell in behind him, grinning from thin faces, and travelled on, every step taking them closer to the city.

As the excitement of finding his people began to fade, Threon's exhaustion took over. His head lolled as they rode. Azzania poked him sharply in the back and did her best to rouse him with the void. His weariness was nothing compared to the trials of those around him, and not wishing to look the cosseted royal, he dismounted in favour of walking. Azzania joined him on the ground and offered the horse's back to a man injured in the uprising. Threon trudged on through the day. By the time they set camp his left leg was aching from walking on the old injury.

The camp was made up of clusters of men and women around small fires. No tents or kitchens. A handful of pit ponies were tethered with a few supplies packed into their carts. They were woefully undersupplied. The slaves had brought oats with them and they all shared a meagre supper of porridge. They slept under the stars, settled between campfires. Threon gave the cheese and saltfish Azzania had packed to a group of young boys who barely looked old enough to be called teenagers.

He sat with her now on the hard stone ground, idly playing with the thin porridge he had been handed.

Lena approached and smiled in greeting. 'Here,' she said as she neared, scattering crushed green leaves on his food. 'This will give it a bit of flavour. It's no substitute for salt or sugar, but it'll help.' She stretched her back out. 'We must be getting out of the Greylands now. The greenery is starting to build up.'

'It's been so long since I've seen a familiar face from home,' said Threon. 'Sit with us, please. Everyone else seems to be giving us a wide berth.'

She laughed and eased herself to the ground. 'You're their king. The old etiquette still stands; they're simply keeping a deferential distance.'

'Hah. I'm dressed like a beggar. And smell worse. Deference is the last thing I should have coming my way.'

'I think you'll make a very different king to your father.' She gave him a smile.

'A king without a kingdom. That is different.'

'Yes. But one who united the Mainlands, and convinced thousands to stand up for their freedom. And a beautiful bride at your side, too.' Azzania blushed; a rare sight. Lena continued before either of them could correct her. 'You've grown up fast.' She put a weathered hand on his. He thought back to the days before the raids, to the Threon she used to know. The days before he'd travelled further than thirty miles from home, before he'd spent time imprisoned, before he'd lived on the streets, before he'd killed. A lot had changed.

321

'Tell me what happened on the day of the raid,' he said. 'Did anyone else from the castle survive?'

'You really want to hear about that? It'll spoil an otherwise beautiful night.'

Threon met her eyes steadily. 'Tell me.'

She sighed, looking out over camp for a moment before telling her story. 'It was a cruel day. I can only tell you what I saw, and what I've heard from others since.' She looked down, rubbing her chin thoughtfully. 'I woke up when little Gareth broke into my room. Do you remember him? The pot washer.' Threon shook his head. 'Sweet boy. I don't think he made it. He woke me up to say there was a fire in the city near my daughter's house. By the time we were outside the castle walls it was clear what was going on. We could hear swords clashing and people screaming. I could see the raiders coming up the road in formation. We ran together and hid in the ditch beside the west wall.

'I couldn't face fleeing. Others did, but so many were falling with arrows lodged in their backs. We didn't move. We stayed hiding there and when they came, I didn't know what to do. Gareth started throwing stones at them. I tried to fight them off me, but by the gods, the strength on them. I was loaded onto a cart crammed with people. They trailed arrows on us and shot at anyone who moved.' She paused to run a blade of grass through her fingers. When she spoke again, her voice was quiet, ashen. 'I never saw Gareth or my daughters again. Smithy Jim was on the same cart as me. He survived the journey here but died only weeks after when a mine shaft collapsed on him.'

Threon shook his head. Jim had been a monster of a man, stronger than most of Maradah's soldiers. It was a poor way to go.

Lena continued. 'It was my job to bring the carts in, filled

322

to the brim with stone waste. They're heavy as hell. I've got calves like a goat and a bald patch from pushing them to and fro with my head.' She bowed her neck so Threon could see, and shrugged. 'Much longer there would've broken my back. Sometimes I'd stop, I couldn't help it. Crying like a baby. But those palimore would always be on us. They usually threatened death. And they weren't idle threats. I saw it happen. Sometimes it was whips.' She pulled back her sleeve. The tail-end of a red welt flared against her pale skin. 'Neal from the stables, Hannah from the library, the butcher's son Harry, they all died. Your handmaid too, I'm sorry to say. I know you were fond of her.'

Threon tensed. He and Lydia had been good friends as well as clumsy lovers. He'd known she was likely dead, but hearing the words felt like ripping the scab off a wound.

The list carried on. 'Jon the stable master wound up in Pullman. He stood up to one of the palimore and was executed in front of everyone. Aeryn the falconer – I won't go into what they did to her – she's at peace now. The list is a long and sorry one. I'm sure you needn't hear more.'

Threon looked out over the camp. People were settling down to sleep, many lying down together in groups for warmth. He could only imagine how their experiences must have drawn them closer during their time as slaves. It was a relief to look on so many survivors when hearing about so much death.

'You didn't mention my parents.' He spoke slowly, curiosity and dread hanging on the answer to his unspoken question.

She inhaled and huffed the air out. 'I heard rumours, nothing more.'

'I'd like to know.' He felt Azzania clasp his hand and he squeezed it, grateful to have her near.

'Alright.' She plucked the blade of grass she had been playing with and rolled it between her fingers. 'The queen was asleep, I hear. They broke into her room and her screams were silenced mercifully quickly. Your father tried to fight, of course. You know what he was like. One of the guards made it to Pullman. He said he watched them taunt the king. He fought back as best as he could, but not even kings can best those soldiers.'

Threon had imagined their deaths a thousand different ways. He had hoped that they would be together at the end, that his father would have cut through dozens of palimore like a figure from legend before the end. But their deaths had been just as brutal as every other sorry story to come out of Maradah.

'Thank you for telling me.' He put down his unfinished porridge, no longer hungry. Lena went to say something, but then seemed to think better of it. 'We should rest now. We'll be at the capital tomorrow and I haven't slept in two days.'

She looked relieved to be excused from sharing further bad news and stood, giving him a sad smile before returning to her campfire.

As they lay down to sleep, Azzania curled up beside him. The pair looked back along the route they had travelled. He knew she was looking for the same thing. A sign of the Mainlands army.

'They'll come soon,' she said. 'Don't worry.'

He took her hand and stroked her skin. She kissed him and closed her eyes, falling into an easy sleep. Threon kept his eyes on the horizon, watching and listening for the sign of horses, until at long last sleep overcame him.

The next morning Threon woke early. It was cold and a mist had settled around the camp. He stood up and rubbed his side where bruises threatened from sleeping on the rocky ground. Most of the camp was still asleep, bodies as still as corpses across the cold landscape.

A group of teenage boys had risen and sparred together on a brow that overlooked the camp. Threon cricked his neck and rubbed his arms for warmth, then made his way up towards them. They faltered in their game as he approached, looking nervous. One of them bowed and a couple of others followed suit. Threon cringed inwardly. 'No need, lads,' he said as he joined their circle. There were four of them and he could see now they were older than he had first thought. Each wore a scruff of beard. Young men, though they were small for their age; lacking height and bearing frames of those denied nutrition through their growing years. 'Practising for the fight ahead?'

'Yessir,' said one.

'Ever had a sword lesson?' The lad shook his head and Threon unsheathed the sword Azzania had chosen for him. 'Well, it's never too late. Stand like this.' He stepped back with one foot and raised his sword, holding the pommel at his side. The men picked up their weapons and mimicked him. They were armed with a mix of spades and pickaxes. The point of Threon's sword dropped. What defence could he teach using a spade? He fought to hide his concern. 'Okay, show me what you've got.'

The young men looked at each other nervously, before one of them plucked up the courage to mount an attack. He ran towards Threon, pickaxe raised, eyes tight shut. He swung blindly and Threon stepped out of the way, before the young man came to a stop when he tripped over the weight of the fallen pickaxe. He turned to look at Threon.

'Lesson one. Keep your eyes open.' His assailant blushed. 'You know your weapon. You've used these tools for years.

You understand its weight, but now you need to control the way it moves in the air. You're not throwing its weight against stone now. You need to keep control of it. Keep it aloft, don't let it fall. Let it become an extension of your arm. You want it to feel natural.' He tried to keep encouragement in his voice, but his heart sank as he watched the men swinging their mining tools through the air.

He stayed a while longer, giving pointers on footwork and how to block an attack until they all tired. Before leaving them to rest he said, 'There's a whetstone in my saddle pack. Make sure your weapons are sharp.' Would a sharp-edged spade make a difference?

That day's march led them into greener landscapes. Grass and trees unfolded around them and birdsong returned to the skies. Confined to the mines during their enslavement, Threon's companions took on a new life in the verdant scenery.

Threon began to worry. The vegetation indicated that they were close to the city. The army had to catch up soon. He had given a young boy the reins of his horse that morning and ordered him to scout behind for a sign of Vituund and Aya. He still hadn't returned.

He walked with Azzania at the rear of the troop. 'Stop looking back,' said Azzania. 'You'll make them nervous.' But perhaps they *should* be nervous.

'They should have caught up by now,' he said. 'We're putting ourselves in danger being so close.' He looked ahead at the swathes of liberated slaves. They had picked up a new confidence since walking into this new landscape. And no wonder. After years with nothing but rock and ash, seeing this vegetation must have felt a little like a return home. Ahead he could see hedges and dry-stone walls that marked the boundary of farms. Crops and cattle broke up the

326

landscape in a patchwork of fields. And in the far distance stood the beginning of the city slums. A disarray of roofs and wooden buildings. They could be spotted soon. 'I'm going to order them to turn around. This is too dangerous. We have to wait for the army.'

The furthest end of the column was a long way ahead. They seemed to have quickened their pace. Threon inclined his head to Azzania and the pair jogged to catch up and spread the message to turn back.

Another pyre burned, spitting spears of flame into the evening air. Lleu wrapped his arm around Raikka, skin warmed by the orange glow. He placed a kiss on her forehead.

'It might seem romantic under different circumstances,' she said.

'Mm,' he agreed. They were both exhausted from the effort of liberating the Tanmar slaves. Their numbers had doubled. Nearly two thousand free, but the celebrations were again subdued by the number of dead. Several scores of innocent lives crackled in the flames. His stomach gave an involuntary rumble at the smell of burning flesh. There hadn't been enough food for everyone.

Raikka shifted in his arms and brushed against a fresh wound. He flinched and she lurched away from it. 'Sorry.'

'It's alright. It's not deep.'

She pulled his shirt open to examine the lesion again. There were only enough first aid supplies for the palimore who staffed the mines; there were never meant to be provisions for the slaves. There hadn't been nearly enough to go around the wounded. 'Could do with a stitch or two, but I'll live without. Just means another scar.'

'I like your scars,' she said. 'They all tell stories. And this is a good story to tell. We did a good thing today.'

327

'We did.' He pulled her back into his arms, forcing away the memory of how he'd stabbed Gwyn in the back, and the surprise on Hern's face when she saw it was him who had betrayed them.

'Is she alright?' asked Raikka, nodding across camp. Beyond the fire, he could see Savanta seemingly engaged in conversation with herself.

'She belongs to Zenith. He speaks to her sometimes.'

'I forget the Vyara can be so direct. They don't come to Ionia.'

'So I hear.' He hadn't told her his father was born in the breeding programme, though she might have guessed. Did she know godsblood flowed in his veins? 'Must be peaceful.'

'I can't wait to take you back there. You'll love the mountains. A perfect retreat for the retired soldier.'

He smiled into the fire. 'Sounds idyllic.'

'Marvellous work, my sweet.' Zenith was standing above an old mine adit and counting out the miners with a finger. 'Too many to count. Wonderful. And they'll all give thanks to me for this victory.' He stretched his arms over his head and sat down, legs hanging over the mouth of the mine.

'Yes, because it was all down to you.'

'Wasn't it? Were the miners praying to you and the soldier, or to me, when faced with danger?'

'I thought Waterfolk were loyal to Athys.'

'For now. But when they see you, my herald in the sky, and feel the wind at their backs... things change.' He kicked his boots against the rock. 'When I held sway in Ionia, they would leave maidens for me on the snowy slopes of the mountains. What happened, Savanta?' He sighed dramatically. 'But not to worry. I'll have it all back soon. The island will be mine.'

'I'm thrilled for you.'

'I knew you would be.' He bared his teeth at her and jumped down to the ground. He looked out over the flames and she followed his gaze. 'Sweet, aren't they?' He was watching Raikka and Lleu, nestled together by the fire.

'They've been through a lot to find each other.'

He nodded. 'He's still young enough to have his humanity. Mortals will fight each other for eternal life, but they don't understand how it destroys them.' He sounded sombre as he spoke, genuinely sorry for a loss Savanta couldn't understand. 'We who live too long forget true loyalty, true courage, true love.' He raised a hand and a cool breeze rolled through the camp. Lleu pulled Raikka closer and rubbed her arms for warmth. Zenith cocked his head to one side with a sad smile. 'In the end, meaning to life ceases. Experience too much and nothing can ignite a spark. My brother thinks he loves Keresan. She thinks she loves him. A false reality.'

The Vyara's usual mischief was gone, leaving him with an air of wistfulness, and a touch of sadness. He must have sensed her watching him because he turned back with a forced smile and a huff of air. He clapped his hands together. 'We'll put an end to that though, eh?'

CHAPTER TWENTY-SIX

Threon and Azzania called to the miners nearest, telling them to turn back. They slowed but didn't stop. All eyes were on the farm ahead. Those marching at the front of the column had broken into a run, making for the fields.

'Stop,' cried Threon, but they were too far ahead to hear. Years of starvation drove them forward on impulse. The crops in the field were too much to resist. 'Wait!'

Those who had slowed on his command looked uncertainly at him. He could see the hunger that implored them to follow. 'You think fresh food won't be guarded in this place?' he snapped. 'You want to draw the palimore out to us?' That stopped them. But this group only made up a handful of their full force. More than half of them had been too far ahead to hear him. 'Wait here,' he called to them, and the command in his voice made for obedience. 'We need to turn back to join our army.'

Azzania was already sprinting to the farm, calling out to the men and women ahead. Threon rushed to follow her and as they ran he saw the first few miners climb over a low wall and run into a field of root vegetables. More followed. He ran faster, shouting all the while to draw them back, but there was little use. Even if they could hear him he doubted they would obey with food in such close reach.

'Oh no,' said Azzania, slowing to a jog. Threon caught up with her and slowed to match her pace. She pointed to where guards filed out into the fields from their watches across the farm. Thirty or so broad men dressed in leather armour drew crossbows and advanced on the looters. With food so precious here, it was no wonder the farms were well protected. A bell rang, raising an alarm. Any hopes of a surprise attack on the city vanished. News of their arrival would soon spread.

'We have to help them,' said Threon. He turned around and waved to those who had stopped on his command. 'They need help.' A nervous clamour as they clutched weapons and began to move forwards. The alarm bell stirred barking dogs which raced across the fields towards the intruders.

As Threon ran to help he saw the first guard take a shot at the looters. They were spread out in groups of twos and threes, picking at different parts of the field. A young man bent over double as the arrow thudded into his abdomen, and then he fell to the ground. The first shot inspired the other guards to take aim, and nine more looters fell.

But Threon's people vastly outnumbered these guards. By the time he had vaulted the stone wall, half of their force was in the field. More than four hundred angry men and women ran at the guards. Their crossbows did little to hold them back. They swarmed around the guards and destroyed them, leaving behind only tatters of flesh and bone.

The alarm bell was still ringing. They had to get out of the fields. Threon screamed orders but this was not a disciplined army. There were no sergeants to relay orders, and he had no horse. From the ground and without help, he could only shout to those within earshot.

He looked around, panicked. Some of the troop clustered together, weapons raised and ready to defend themselves from further attack. Others succumbed to hunger and pulled fistfuls of carrots from the ground. If the bell was still ringing, it was ringing for a reason. More would come to defend this farm.

He continued to shout orders until his throat was raw. He found Azzania bent over the body of one of the dying looters, her palms pressed to either side of his forehead. Blood soaked the man's shirt where the arrow had hit. She whispered soothing words and had her eyes closed in concentration. Threon watched her until the man rasped a last breath and she took her hands from his head.

'What do we do?' she asked. Threon looked around at the chaos. They would be assigned to experienced soldiers when the army caught up. Split into smaller groups, under experienced leaders, these men and women had the potential to act as part of a disciplined army. But with Threon in command alone, it seemed impossible to implore them to act as one.

A thunder of hooves from behind. They both turned, expectantly. Had the army caught up?

Azzania caught Threon's hand and stepped closer to him. The horses that appeared on the horizon weren't from the Mainlands. These beasts were Thelonian.

'The palimore,' she whispered. A force of around fifty scouts, easily strong enough to overwhelm them given the way they were currently scattered.

Everyone in the fields turned at the sound. A wave of silence fell over them. Followed by the sound of panic. 'Ready your weapons,' commanded Threon, but his voice was lost to the clamour around him. They began to retreat across the field. Slowly at first, and then with speed. A few people pointed to the slums at the edge of the city as possible shelter.

The palimore advanced at a relaxed trot. These soldiers were unlike the raiders they had faced in Maradah. These gleamed in armour and were prepared for an assault. They spread out into a horizontal line: a wall of soldiers ready to catch any who might try to retreat away from the city.

Threon squeezed Azzania's hand. 'They're trying to herd us closer to the slums,' he said. 'We'll be trapped in narrow streets there. Easier to pick off.'

'It looks like it's working,' she said, looking back at the mass of people running in fear.

Threon kicked at the soil and cried out in frustration. 'Stand your ground. Stand your ground!' But it was no use. He longed to have his horse back. From up high he would be more prominent. They would see him. He would have the speed to relay orders across a swathe of people. Now he was just one foot soldier shouting into a troop in chaos.

'We have to go with them,' said Azzania.

'It will be slaughter.' He couldn't believe this was happening. The Mainlands army couldn't be far behind. This timing was damnable. It was bad odds, but they would still stand a better chance if they fought here, in the open. He looked back again. The miners were running for the slums now. 'Damn it,' he spat. 'We better catch up with them.'

As expected, the palimore held back until Threon's force had run the road into the slums. A ramshackle of wooden buildings crammed together to provide meagre shelter to local families. The streets ran with sewage and were piled high with scavenged materials. Slum residents disappeared into their homes at the sight of their approach. They heralded trouble.

Threon ran with Azzania at his side, both panting to keep up with the retreating force.

Then those ahead came to a sudden stop. The pair pushed forwards to see why.

Another score of palimore had appeared ahead of them. They were trapped between two walls of soldiers with a sprawl of buildings and narrow streets to each side. Just as the palimore had planned.

The volley of arrows hit before any of them could take a breath to shout in warning. Threon dived to the floor, pulling Azzania down with him. His fall to the ground was matched by twenty dead, arrows lodged in their throats and chests. Beside him, a woman choked on her own blood, eyes wide with panic as she gaped at him. Her face locked in an eerie grimace as life left her moments later.

More arrows sped towards them. 'Fight!' he shouted. Threon rolled to one side and got to his feet as men and women around him charged forward. More fell, arrows snatching the life from them. Another volley hit and another twenty fell before the first man reached the small group of palimore.

Threon drew his sword, charging over the dead as he followed the miners' fury. The slums made a poor battlefield. The miners bottlenecked between buildings as they clamoured to reach their attackers. The enemy easily blocked their path, even though they were so few in number. The sounds of anger, of metal on metal, of screaming, all filled the air. More miners died. Threon had thought their odds were bad in Maradah, but here, exhausted and with bad weapons, the miners were being broken down like carcasses on a butcher's table. The bodies piled up high before the palimore, forming a grotesque wall of the injured and the dying. Threon pulled himself up and over the dead. He reached the top, standing side by side with a dozen miners. He swung his sword lightning fast as one of the Thelonians bore down on him. He met the soldier's blade and got a good look at her face. There was no anger; she fought with a calculated precision, but he could see sweat on her brow, a darkness about her eyes. The beginnings of withdrawal perhaps? The thought distracted him and he was overpowered, forced backwards. As he fell onto the growing pile of dead, he saw the mounted palimore had caught up behind them and were now drawing back bow strings. The fortune of his fall shielded him from the next volley of arrows. Two score of men and women fell under their force and Threon fought to get to his feet as the bodies piled around and on top of him.

The fear in the air was palpable. Some of the miners made to run back the way they had come but they were surrounded. It seemed hopeless. Threon gasped for breath, taking in the horror unfolding around him. The palimore were encroaching on them, forcing the Mainlanders closer together. This would not end well. Their only hope would be to escape down the narrow alleys. 'Run,' he called. 'Retreat!'

He caught sight of Azzania. She was in a side alley, crouched over an injured body, lost in the void. Threon ran to her, narrowly avoiding the next volley of arrows.

'Zan,' he shouted. 'Leave him. We've got to get out of here. This is a slaughterhouse.'

She looked up coolly from the body. 'We all deserve to die in peace,' she said, letting go of the man's head. His eyes rolled up into his skull. Another volley of arrows. More people fell amidst the screams.

The miners began breaking into slum buildings, climbing on top of them, hiding behind them. The urge to flee blazed among the freed slaves. An older woman was pushed over in the commotion and Threon saw her trampled to death. The palimore moved forwards, cutting through anyone in their path. People were hauled to the ground as they tried to scramble up buildings. Blood flowed in the gutters. They were being butchered like lambs.

Azzania pulled his hand. The palimore were nearing. 'Run,' she said.

He glanced back at the oncoming soldiers. To return to the fight would be suicide. He allowed her to drag him further down the alleyway. They ran through the filthy streets, outpacing other fleeing miners. The young and old lagged behind. Threon tried to close his ears to the sounds of death rising behind him. He didn't look back again.

They ran until his lungs burned. By now they were far from the site of battle. Azzania stopped and leaned against the makeshift walls of one of the slum buildings. Threon closed his eyes, pulling in air and trying to ignore the pain building in his leg. The old break burned hot. He could still hear the chaos of killing. They still weren't safe.

He scrambled up the wall Azzania was leaning against. The roof was made of woven willow; it creaked under his weight. Another taller building backed onto the one he had climbed. He scaled this too, and Azzania followed.

From here they had a better view of the slums. He could hear the screams and clash of metal coming from all directions now. The palimore were filtering through side alleys, cutting down miners as they ran.

'We have to hide.' Azzania panted to regain her breath.

Threon bent at his waist, blinking against the dark patches that crossed his vision as he gasped in air. 'This is my fault,' he murmured. 'We should've turned back. It was damn foolish to continue without the army.' Was this it then, had they lost? With no sign of Vituund and Aya, or Lleu and Savanta, they were waiting for the end of a massacre. There would be no happy ending, no revenge or glory, just a wash of blood and a mountain of bodies.

Threon knelt and began ripping at the willow beneath their feet. They could keep out of sight here until the army arrived… or the palimore found them. As he tore the roof apart it became apparent that there were people inside. The family within began to scream. They didn't look like much of a threat and he ignored them. When the gap was big enough he offered his hand to Azzania to help her down.

'Please, please, be quiet,' he said to the family. The woman and her three children continued screaming. She had grabbed a panel of wood to defend herself. 'Please. I don't want to have to hurt you.' He pulled his sword halfway from its sheath. At the sight of the metal the woman stopped screaming, and instead began to cry quietly. She pulled the children towards her protectively and they cowered in a dark corner.

Azzania began to lower herself into the room when Threon heard something. He froze.

'What is it?' she asked.

He pulled her back out onto the roof and looked out in the direction of the noise.

Horses and an Ionese war chant.

'Couldn't they have got here an hour ago?' snapped Threon. Azzania could see his anger came from the same disappointment she felt. The army had been so close behind. If they had caught up only an hour sooner they could have met the palimore with their full force, been protected by soldiers and weapons, and healed by vish.

So many had died.

Threon drew his sword, ready to join the fray again. 'The Guardians will be following behind. I'll go with you to keep you safe.'

Azzania shook her head. 'No, I'll go alone. I know how to keep out of trouble. You don't belong in the heat of battle this time.' His brow furrowed. 'For an Empire to fall, first you must remove the head.' Understanding dawned on him. 'Go to the palace. Keresan must be killed.'

The army were encroaching on the slums now, neat formations of Ionese warriors, flanked by Bannvarians and Waterfolk. Threon's eyes lingered on them. She could see that he wanted to be with them, to support them. She took his hand. 'You have proven time and again that you are as willing as any of them to lay down your life for this cause. They will not miss you. One more body in that army will make little difference. You can make a bigger impact alone. Removing a leader is the job of a lone assassin, not a vast army. Don't you want to face the one who ordered the raids?'

He tore his eyes away from the soldiers. She could see he saw sense in her words. His time on the streets would have taught him how to stay out of sight. If he could reach the Empress unchallenged, there was a chance... 'You're right,' he said as he undid the belt that held his shortsword. 'Please take this if you're going alone.'

'My hands and heart are my greatest weapon,' she said. 'But if it'll keep your mind at ease.' She took the blade from him. 'Be safe. Channel the void. I'll see you when this is over.' She kissed him on the lips and turned to go.

'Wait.' He caught her hand and pulled her close. Running his hands over her face, he kissed her deeply. She succumbed to his taste, his scent, his rough skin. His touch made her heart beat faster. Her hairs stood on end, every sense wanting to absorb a part of this man. Her training with the Guardians

338

had taught her to push away from the strength of emotion. Emotions like this could only build up to then be broken, leaving behind two damaged individuals. She shoved the thought aside. This felt right. She squeezed his hand and returned his kiss with fervour. Their intimacy felt like waves of honey and electric.

He pulled back and she opened her eyes again. 'What if something happens to one of us?' he said. It was a thought she had avoided dwelling on. It was at that moment, seeing the anxiety the question caused him, that she made her decision. When all this was over, she didn't want to return to the order. There was a deeper happiness to be found in wild emotion. A deeper happiness to be found in spending her life with this man.

She placed his palm against her chest. 'We will always hold a piece of each other.' She ran a hand down his cheek and gave a sombre smile. 'The Guardians don't advocate love, but you've changed the way I see such things.' She held onto her feelings for him as she drew on the void. The void clashed with the heat of her affection, opposing forces vying against each other. Threon's eyes widened as he felt it too. It was nothing like the void. The void brought clarity, peace, tranquillity. This felt like fever and flame. A warmth and satisfaction washed over them both. This love-tempered void stole away their anxiety and turned it to ardour, and all fear faded. She had never felt anything like it.

She stepped back, and as his palm left her chest they both smiled at each other. She could feel him still, as if an invisible thread of emotion ran between them. 'What was that?' he breathed.

'I don't know,' she said. She felt like something had unlocked within her.

'It feels like we're still joined,' he said.

The sounds of battle pulled her attention again. Her heart longed to explore this new feeling with him… and perhaps there would never be another opportunity. His eyes traced back to the army too. 'We should hurry,' she said, regretting every word. His smile dropped and he nodded.

He squeezed her hand. 'Stay safe.'

'You too.'

He stepped back and then turned, making his way to the edge of the rooftop. He gave her one last glance before facing the palace and heading towards the glare of gold on the horizon.

Her heart ached to watch him leave.

Savanta dove down, landing with such speed that she tumbled to the floor. She shook herself off and ran to Lleu.

'It's started.' She panted for breath, her wings and shoulders aching with exertion. The holes in her wings caused by palimore arrows made the journey that much harder.

'It's started?'

'The army have reached the capital. There were so many bodies, Lleu. The slum roads are piled high.'

'The palimore are winning?'

'The miners seem to be pitted against a small number of them. Only twenty or so, but it doesn't look good. It won't be long until reinforcements arrive. We've got to hurry.'

The soldier looked back at the mass of freed slaves pacing behind. 'The strongest can march harder. Anyone who can't keep the pace should give up their weapons and be prepared to tend the wounded when they reach the city. Tell them to follow my pace.' He nodded to those who were within earshot. 'Let's move.' He set off at a jog and they quickened their pace to keep up.

Savanta beat her wings until she was airborne again. She glided low over the swathes of liberated slaves. All three mines had now been emptied, and the numbers following Lleu outnumbered the Mainlands' combined forces. She shouted down to them, and as the news spread their speed doubled. Chants rose and a bloodthirst boiled in the air. Thousands of men and women raced to death or vengeance.

Exhausted, Savanta turned around and flew back to the capital. Lleu and the others were three miles away. They'd reach the slum in less than an hour. She would be there in minutes.

Her mind was ablaze. The smell and sight of so much death was overwhelming. She found herself mentally calling out for Zenith. He hadn't come to her since they had liberated the last mine. She thought his silence would bring her peace but instead it filled her with anxiety. Had something happened to him? Now, more than ever, they needed the wind to blow in their favour.

As she sped on she could see dark plumes of smoke rising in the distance. The slums were on fire. The smoke-laden air forced her lower to the ground.

She followed the trampled scrubland and disturbed gravel that lay in the wake of the Mainlands army's path. As she neared, the sun smeared a deep red across the smoky air. She focussed on the sound of the wind passing over her wings to drown out the growing noise of battle.

A small group of nobles were gathered under a canopy at the edge of the city. Vituund and Aya sat astride horses, surrounded by neat, unscathed servants. She glided down to the ground, not waiting to catch her breath before approaching.

The king and queen looked out over the burning city, their faces drawn. She came before them and bowed low.

341

'Watcher,' said Vituund, nodding his head to her. His face was drawn with worry but he hid any fear from his voice. 'You bring us news?'

'Where's Threon? And Azzania?' she asked.

'I hoped you might be able to tell us,' said Aya solemnly. 'They left ahead of us to join the Pullman miners two days ago.'

'They went ahead? But the Pullman miners have been all but wiped out.' The sight had been far worse than anything she had witnessed in the battle for Marradah. She felt a chill run down her spine.

Aya nodded sadly. 'So we hear. You haven't seen them?'

'No…' She resolved to find them both. They deserved better than a death in the dirt of the slums.

'What are you doing here?' asked Vituund. 'Tell us you were successful in the other mines.' He busied himself in adjusting his armour as he spoke, perhaps to hide his nerves; she could sense how keenly he anticipated her response.

'We were. Most will be here within the hour.' Raised eyebrows at that. And a small breath of relief.

'How many?'

'Two thousand? Maybe three. There wasn't time to count. What about the battle? Tell me how I can help.'

'The palimore's full force has descended on us,' said Aya, taking a smoke pipe from one of the men beside her. 'We need all the help we can get. Our force needed rest but got none before the call to battle. There have been many casualties from what we can tell, but the riders reporting to us can't get a good picture of what's going on. My Guardians are doing what they can for the injured. Seek them out if you are in need of vish.'

Savanta was keen to get away, to find Threon and Azzania. She began to pace backwards, bowing as she did so. 'I'll scout

342

for you. Eyes from the sky may prove an advantage over your riders.'

She stretched her wings out ready to depart. Vituund cleared his throat and she paused. 'And what of Zenith? How will he help our plight?'

Savanta shook her head, trying to think of something comforting to say, but could not. 'I'm sorry, my Lord, I don't know.'

The upper city was in chaos. The wealthy citizens of Thelonia were barricading themselves inside their homes or packing their belongings and preparing to flee.

Threon pressed himself up against the walls of a coach house as a band of palimore charged onto the street. Streams of enemy soldiers had made their way through the upper city to the slums. The numbers were in the thousands.

He wiped the sweat from his brow and steadied his breathing, ready to make another dash towards the palace. He stuck to the shadows and took advantage of the evolving turmoil which was keeping watchful eyes distracted. Soldiers clamoured in confusion, shouting orders, recalling old invasion drills.

The palace was in sight. Another three dashes in and out of shadows and he found himself at the gates. The handful of guards there were gripped in the panic of the battle below. They swapped posts and several of them abandoned their positions altogether to fetch weapons. Fights broke out between several men and women who clawed at vish'aad vials around each other's necks.

Threon took advantage of their distraction and dove for cover behind an abandoned cart beside the gates. He watched there, waiting for the opportune moment. A tussle broke out, and as the guards wrestled on the ground he took his chance and ran through the gates. He found himself in the royal garden. The immaculate formations of extraordinary flowers would normally have taken his breath away, but there was no time for wonder. He could hear a victor emerging from the guards' clash. A rosebush etched thin, red scratches on his skin as he dove for cover again.

Two thick box hedges ran between the bush and the main palace entrance. The foliage was tightly packed and offered good cover. He forced his way slowly along one of the hedges, crawling on his belly beneath its branches. Twigs cracked under his feet and hands, but the sound was muffled by the surrounding chaos.

When he reached the far side he was covered in scratches. He paused to remove a couple of thorns that had embedded in his knees. He was a mere three strides from the gold walls of the palace. The ornately jewelled gates of the building stood open and unguarded. But only slightly ajar. It was impossible to see far beyond them. They opened into darkness.

Threon crouched silently for a long while, straining for any sound that might come from beyond those doors, but he could hear nothing. Sprinting through would be running into the unknown.

More palimore had arrived and a squad had taken to targeting Lleu's recruits, shooting bows from the cover of slum buildings. Arrows fell on the miners as they ran to grab weapons from Vituund and Aya's stockpile. They were old, the blades dull and the bow strings loose, but they were better than shovels and axes.

Lleu ordered his new troops forwards in groups of thirty or forty to select a weapon, keeping the rest out of firing range. Five were shot dead and the stockpile ran dry before a third of them had a chance to grab a weapon.

344

They were woefully unprepared. The liberated slaves were half-starved. They were farmers, shopkeepers and fishermen turned slaves, turned soldiers. They lacked the skills to fight. Against the palimore they didn't stand a chance. Lleu led them on, instilling confidence in them with his calm command. They were padding. Another body to throw at the Empire. Expendable lives sacrificed for a greater cause.

'Let the fire of your vengeance drive us to victory!' His words roared above the miners. Their eyes were wide with fear but the air thronged with energy. They wanted this.

Raikka stood beside him. He had chosen a light shield for her and given her one of his swords. He had pleaded with her the whole way to go to safety, to stay behind, but his pleas had fallen on deaf ears. A spark of pride fought to beat down his fear as she stood ready to fight. 'Stay close,' he said. 'Don't leave my side.'

She bobbed her head in acknowledgement. The shield she held dwarfed her slim body.

Lleu turned to the army. 'Forward march. Death or deliverance!'

In his youth he had dreamed of leading a force of this size, and now he could hear his father's voice ringing through commands. Onwards into the path of falling arrows, into the smoke and heat, into the slums.

Bodies piled in the streets. The iron smell of blood mingled with burning flesh. The full palimore force was against them now, he wagered.

The narrow streets forced the band of miners to lose formation. He lost control of their positions. Some ran head on into the fray. Others froze at the sight of it. They were soon scattered sparsely throughout the slums, battling against small groups of palimore. Raikka kept pace with him, nervously watching his every move.

Deep growling could be heard ahead. Through the thick smoke, Lleu could make out the ghostly outline of animals of war. Two tygers and half a dozen wolves hunkered low to the ground, ready to fight. Lips curled back, teeth bared.

'Get behind me.' Raikka was taking steps backwards. Lleu's words brought her back to his side. She positioned herself in his shadow.

The tygers came forward and the wolves slunk around to block the path behind them. Lleu tightened his grip on his sword hilt, the blade held high, ready to strike. He had seen men torn in two under the pressure of those jaws.

Not giving the creatures a chance to pounce, Lleu ran at them, bringing his sword down on the head of the first tyger. The blade pierced the flesh and glanced off the skull. The animal screeched in pain and veered to the side, falling disorientated to the floor. Lleu caught the second tyger as it launched itself through the air at him. His sword hit the animal's shoulder, but not before the beast had knocked him flat on his back. It dug its razor claws into his chest, rancid breath hot on his face as the creature opened its jaws.

But the animal did not bite. It screamed as Raikka's sword burst through its side. It thrashed in pain, ripping still more at Lleu's chest. He cut up into its belly with his sword and warm blood poured out over his hands. The tyger rolled off and slunk into the shadows, tail between its legs.

Lleu got to his feet, automatically reaching for the vial at his neck to heal the wounds, but there was nothing there.

He looked around for his wife but she was gone. The wolves were on her tail, hurtling past him. He sprinted after them.

'Lleu.' The voice came from a side alley. He glanced in its direction but saw only shadow, and forced himself faster after the wolves. Three steps later he was on the ground again, an

346

arrow buried deep in his calf. He cried out, reaching for his injured leg. A pair of rough hands grabbed him by the shoulders and hauled him onto his back.

'Son,' growled Khan, his hand reaching for his sword.

CHAPTER TWENTY-SEVEN

The palace was cavernous, cold and overly lavish. Darting through the doors brought Threon into a dim courtroom. High ceilings, walls adorned with vast mosaics depicting vibrant scenes of Thelonia, and a chandelier the size of a temple dome. At the centre of the room towered a statue of Deyar, his milk-white eyes taking in the room.

Threon breathed a sigh of relief when he saw the disorder that held sway here. There were no guards, only crying servants running from room to room, panic-stricken. Just how his court must have looked moments before the raiders slaughtered everyone. It seemed unlikely that the guards would leave the palace unattended for long. He had to move quickly.

A young serving boy ran within Threon's reach and he grabbed him by the scruff of his collar. The boy yelped as he came to an abrupt stop, startled eyes trailing up to Threon's.

'The Empress. Where is she?' he growled. The boy's lower lip quivered at his tone, eyes welling as he stared dumbly up at him. 'Now, quickly.' Threon moved his free hand to his waist and drew his sword a few inches. The boy glanced down and began to move his mouth, tongue stumbling over the words. He lifted a finger and pointed to a corridor that ran off to their right.

'The t-t-tower,' he said, before bursting into tears. Threon let go of him and the boy stumbled as he ran to increase the distance between them.

The corridor led to another walled garden. Threon stuck to the dense borders of wildflowers, keeping cover, though there were still no guards in sight. The tower stood in the very centre of the garden, smaller than he would have imagined, at only two storeys tall. In marked contrast to the outer walls, the tower was not plated with gold. Its smooth marble surface looked grey under the smoke-gorged sky.

Looking around, he darted across the open grass to the tower's door. It stood ajar, a carving of Deyar smiling out from its dark wood. Gas lamps flickered at the walls inside, illuminating spiralling stairs leading both upwards and down into the ground. He could hear voices now. Male voices, coming from below. Their composure gave them away as soldiers rather than panicking house staff. Guarding her room perhaps? He began his descent.

The lower levels of the palace were chiselled into the rock like a network of caves, walls as smooth as the surface of a lake. The lamps cast dancing shadows around him. He took a steeling breath, the voices growing louder with every step. If he wanted to get past, he would have to face them.

There was a break in their conversation.

'You hear that?' Swords ripped from sheaths, boots against several steps and then they were standing before him. Two palimore. Both nearly a foot taller than him, and twice as broad. But there was a nervous quality to them. A thin sheen

349

of sweat on their foreheads, dark circles below their eyes. They held themselves with an anxious bearing.

Threon's heart pounded hard. He couldn't take two palimore alone, even with their withdrawal beginning to seep to the surface. He raised his arms in surrender and gave them a nervous smile. 'Gentlemen,' he greeted them. 'Please, there's no need for weapons —'

And then he was up against a wall, sword against his neck.

'Looks like he's from across the sea,' said one.

'How did you get in here?' said the palimore holding him against the wall.

'The door was open.' Threon did his best to keep his voice level. 'You would do well not to slaughter the Mainlands' peace envoy.' They both shifted slightly at his words, but the sword remained at his throat. His eyes flicked further down and he could see the door they were guarding. It was carved with a dozen creatures from myth and legend. As the guard saw him look, the sword inched closer. So she was in there, then.

The one with the sword eyed him closely, coming near enough that Threon could feel his breath against his face. He was grateful that they hadn't seemed to recognise him from the arena. He kept his eyes down in deference and bowed his head to them. 'Gentlemen, please. The slums are running with blood. I must entreat your Empress with our terms.'

'Terms?' They both laughed. The sword pressed harder against his neck.

'Really, gentlemen, I'm sure there's no need —'

'We'll be the judge of that. Take his weapons.' The other guard obliged.

A click from below. All three turned to see the door they had been guarding open. The Empress emerged. She rested a hand high on the door frame and eyed the trio with a frown.

She looked different to the last time he had seen her, in the arena. She seemed shorter, her clothing a simple green dress, her face painted with the barest makeup. She was slight of form and walked barefoot, seeming innocuous, fragile even. How could such a woman have caused so much pain?

The guards stood to attention without moving the sword from Threon's neck. Her eyes met his and she looked him up and down.

'It was good of you to come yourself, Threon,' she said. 'I've been looking forward to meeting you properly. Come.' She let her fingers drop from the frame and turned back into the room. The guard brought the sword out of harm's way.

Threon bobbed his head. 'Thank you, gentlemen.'

He followed her, and the door closed behind him. They were alone.

Where are you?

There was no answer to Savanta's calls. She swept through the air, her stomach turning at the sights and smells from below. The air was crowded by a wake of circling buzzards. When the living moved far enough from the dead, they would dive down, ripping out eyes and throats, tearing corpses apart with their talons.

She searched desperately for familiar faces but could find none. Threon, Azzania, Lleu. All lost in a sea of bloodshed.

Zenith. Please.

The fearless anger of the miners was gone, their desire for vengeance wiped out after the first few hundred had fallen. They tried to retreat, but she could see so many running lost, pelting deeper into the city as they tried to escape down narrow streets. The palimore would follow, and they would be cut down like wheat.

We need help.

She descended, following the plight of two Waterlands

351

women as they ran from battle. 'You're going the wrong way,' she shouted, but they didn't hear. 'It's a dead end.' One of them looked up and saw her. Savanta gestured wildly for them to turn around, but the woman didn't understand. Both women fell to the floor in an instant, arrows deep in their chests. A palimore soldier emerged from a side street. Savanta started and beat her wings down hard to gain altitude, narrowly avoiding an arrow herself.

Zenith!

She forced herself higher and higher, out of reach of further arrows, out of reach of the smell. The wind sighed in her ears, taking away the screams that roared below. She closed her eyes and for a moment imagined she was somewhere else. Away from the horror. When she opened them again and looked down, she found she only had a wider perspective of the carnage. The streets writhed with conflict, leaving behind a snail-trail of blood as the battle moved across the city.

We need you. Please.

The wind's temperature changed, and a gust of warm air rolled over her.

I'm here, he said.

The room was vast, stretching out well beyond the boundaries of the tower above. It was devoid of natural light, cave-like walls lit with flickering, golden candles that reflected on the floor's iron tiles. Metal bars ran around the circumference of the room, and it felt like they had stepped into an expansive cage. In reality the bars were there to protect them. Between the bars and the walls, dozens of exotic animals were caged. Big cats, vibrantly coloured reptiles and birds, wolves, a bear, and other strange creatures Threon couldn't put a name to. Most slept. He wondered how they survived underground in the dark like this.

Keresan paced ahead of him. He followed, expecting to be tackled by guards at any moment, but as he reached the centre of the room it seemed they truly were alone.

She swung herself into a chair at the head of a long, dark table, kicking her legs over its arms. A plump-looking fox appeared from underneath it and came to sit beside her. She dropped a hand down and it nuzzled her affectionately. 'Have you come to kill me, Threon?' Her dark eyes looked up slowly to meet his.

She wouldn't have let him get this far without being sure she had the upper hand. He scanned the room for threats. The animals were all secured behind their bars and she didn't appear to be armed. He stepped closer cautiously. 'It would only seem fair. Your people tried to kill me.'

She licked her lips. 'I don't like people standing in my way. If you had stood to one side you could have continued your merry little life as a busker. Instead, you show up at my home with pretences of being a king. Did your parents' deaths teach you nothing?'

'It taught me there are some evils in the world worth going to war for.'

She laughed. 'You call this war? Peasants with pitchforks?' Her face dropped back to stone. 'I have lived longer than any history book your country has to offer. You couldn't count the number of rebellions I've thwarted. I always win.' She leant over the table and poured a large glass of wine from a decanter, then reached for the second glass. 'Care to join me?'

'I'm not stupid.'

'Don't trust me? Suit yourself.' She leaned back in her chair and took a sip. 'Mmh. A beautiful vintage. My raiders brought this back from your mother's wine cellar. I hear she was famed for her palate.' Her eyes flicked up to his. She was looking for a reaction.

Threon lost patience trying to work out the game she was playing. He sprinted across the room and grabbed her by the throat. The wine arched through the air before the glass shattered on the floor. He stood over her, the rage of his past pouring into a tightening grip.

'Foo-lish boy.' Her words croaked through her narrowing throat. Her face swelled and reddened but she did not fight back. He waited for the guards to burst in and shoot him, alarmed by the shattered glass. But they didn't come. As a smile drew across her lips it dawned on him that he might have played right into her hands. But how?

He reached for the spare wine glass, but as he brought the vessel down hard towards her face, pain burst from his leg.

The fox wailed. It had leapt at Threon and dug its teeth deep into his right thigh. The shock was enough to cause the glass to slip from his fingers. It shattered against the iron floor.

The animal's body began to mutate, jaws still firmly clamped on his leg. Its eyes bulged. Its shoulders broadened, and its back sprouted upwards in a steep hump. Its skull split. Its fur was torn into shreds as it expanded from within. The fleshy expanse exceeded Threon in height and he let go of her neck, retreating a few steps. As he did so, the torn husk of its skull fell away from his leg.

The monstrous form beside him grew to the rough shape of a man. It reached forward with a slick pink stump that might have been an arm and knocked Threon to the floor. He scrambled to his feet and grabbed one of the chairs, not sure whether he intended to use it as a shield or a weapon.

Within seconds the fox flesh twisted and contorted more, forming fingers, feet, a face. A large dark-skinned man stood naked before him. His eyes were milky-white.

'Deyar.' Threon shrunk away from him, walking backwards

into a wall of cages. The animals within woke: growling, screeching, flapping.

Keresan stood up beside the Vyara, smoothing the red marks on her throat. 'Threon. You threaten me, you threaten our god.'

'This one serves my brother.' Deyar's brow creased as he spoke, voice as deep as hell's drums. He took his empty eyes from Threon for a moment and turned to Keresan. 'My love.' He bent down to kiss her neck and the red marks vanished. Threon edged around the wall of cages, searching for a weapon or a way out.

Keresan smiled as she rubbed her neck. 'What shall we do with him, Lord?'

'He tried to hurt you.' Deyar rolled his head from side to side as if considering. 'He will spend eternity in my underworld.' He was looking at Threon again, his voice steady and certain. 'Earth will clog your lungs, fill your veins and block your sight. No light, no sound, no water or air. You will suffer though all the ages of man and beyond the end of time. Your slow death will feel sweet compared to the eternity that awaits you.'

Threon took a deep breath to focus his mind. This is why the guards hadn't broken in to save her. He smashed the chair against the cage bars behind him. The shrieks of wild animals flared through the room. He was left holding a single chair leg, easier to brandish and sharply pointed.

Keresan cocked her head to one side. 'Sad, isn't it?' she said. 'He thought he could march in here and kill me. I almost feel sorry for him.' She stroked a finger absentmindedly up and down Deyar's arm. 'How should he die?'

'That I leave to you. You've always been more creative in that department.' Deyar kissed her on the lips and then lifted a finger to beckon Threon towards them. He stepped forward, unable to stop himself, the force as strong as a magnet on iron. His grip tightened on the chair leg despite his growing fear that it would do little to protect him. When he was a foot away from the Vyara, Deyar put his hand up in a signal to stop. Threon stopped. He gritted his teeth, trying to regain control of his movements.

The ground directly beneath his feet began to shift. The iron floor liquified below him. He wanted to leap to more solid ground but it was as if his muscles no longer belonged to him. His feet sank slowly into the floor and iron danced upwards in streams, adhering itself to his legs.

It felt like ice. A chill rushed up his spine. His skin screamed with pain at the intensity of the cold. He groaned as it crept higher, his eyes wide, his jaw tight. It stretched up and he felt the metal wrap around his hands which hung immobile at his side. When the iron had risen up to encase him as far his hips, it solidified.

'All yours,' said Deyar to Keresan. He pulled up a seat at the table, dwarfing the chair with his huge body, and brought the decanter to his lips.

Threon's eyes flicked to Keresan. She paced closer. He could move his upper body again but his legs were immobile, held tight by the metal.

'That's better.' Her voice was flat, calculated.

She skirted the cages on the surrounding walls, stopping at a section to his right. The cages were smaller here. Some were made of glass. He made out fat spiders, brightly coloured frogs and coils of snakes. One of the containers held a scorpion the size of a small dog.

'Who's coming out today?' She spoke to the animals, running her hand across their enclosures. She paused to open a cage and pick out one of the spiders. It climbed onto her hand and ran circles as she rotated her palm up and down in time with its motion. Not satisfied, she returned the creature and paused at another glass box.

'You.' She reached both hands in slowly, her eyes lighting up as she smiled. In one hand she brought out a small snake, clasping it behind the head. It shone iridescent, flowing through the colours of a rainbow. With the other hand she picked up a metal pipe. 'The Ionese silvertail. You've heard of it?' He had, and his stomach dropped as she spoke. She strode over to him.

'You're not bringing that thing anywhere near me.'

'Just try to relax. This is the way things are.' She tilted her head as she stepped closer.

She shifted the pipe in her hands to get a better grip and brought it around with a hum of air. Threon didn't feel the bar hit his face. One moment, he was staring at her, and the next, there was nothing.

'Do something!'

All in good time, my dear.

'People are dying. Help them.'

People die all the time. Most of the time it's a dull, drawn-out affair. These people have a spectacular opportunity to die as heroes.

'They're being slaughtered by the palimore.'

Did you expect anything different?

'I thought you wanted to win. Help them. Please!'

I can't get too distracted. I'm waiting for the right moment.

'The right moment? Much longer and there won't be an army left.'

If you could only hear the prayers, the promises they're making for me down there as they fight for every breath. This, all of this, is a bountiful feast.

'You've got to be fucking joking. These are people's lives.'

357

And I'm afraid this is only the appetiser. The real fight is still to come.

Threon came to slowly. He was slumped backwards, his hands and legs still clasped in an iron mound that encased him up to his hips. As his eyes focussed, he realised he was looking at the ceiling. Then he made out a thick dark line leading down to his mouth.

He panicked. Something was choking him. The pipe that had knocked him out was at the back of his throat. He retched as his body fought uselessly to expel it.

Keresan stood over him, holding the pipe upright. She moved it slowly from side to side and he was forced to move his head with her. His nose ran wildly and tears streamed down his face.

His spine arched backwards. He could feel blood pumping fast around his head and longed to stand fully upright. The pressure at the back of his throat offered him little to no movement unless she allowed it. He tried to speak but only a gargled cry escaped.

Her expression was passive as she studied his face, the snake draped around her shoulders.

'I'm sorry for your sake that it has to be this way,' she said. 'You were meant to die in the arena. It would have been swifter.' Her eyes lowered to look at the snake. 'But you see, you brought a war to my home. I need a decent distraction while my palimore crush the rebellion.' She circled him, and Threon retched as the pole moved with her. As she pushed down on it, he was forced to arch backwards until his back screamed in pain. Sweat beaded on his forehead. He coughed and gagged, and the thought occurred that he might choke to death on his own spit.

'I haven't done this for a couple of hundred years,' she said.

'We used to hold public executions using the method that you're about to experience, but they were deemed too barbaric. Mortals can be squeamish like that.' She shifted the pipe again and Threon gagged more. He could feel his throat convulsing to repel the metal. He thrashed his arms, hoping to break loose.

With one hand still on the pipe, Keresan reached up to her shoulder and picked up the snake. It coiled comfortably around her hand. 'She's very beautiful, don't you think? Her venom isn't strong enough to kill. Not straight away. But that's the point.' A small smile touched her lips. 'She will slide down this tube and be forced into your throat. As she hits the stomach acid, she will lash out in fear, desperately fighting her way out. It's a sorry death for her too, but I can spare one animal from my collection for such an occasion.' She leant closer and whispered into his ear. 'Don't fear it. Death comes to all mortals. Why put off the inevitable?'

She lifted the snake up and used a finger to bob its head into the mouth of the pipe. Threon cried out, wrestling his shoulders back and forth in an attempt to dislodge the tube. It cut into his throat and he could taste blood. It made no difference. Keresan held the pipe firm.

'Goodbye, Vagabond King.'

Azzania raced through the streets, a group of Guardians following close behind. She could feel Threon. She had never felt connected to anyone without the power of touch before, but she could feel him now. He was in trouble. They had to hurry.

Thirty of her order had banded together as soon as she arrived at the battle line. They ran behind her now; she could feel his fear growing with every stride.

The palace reared up ahead of them. They were at the gates. The sight of the approaching Guardians forced the four quarrelling soldiers to stop what they were doing. Arrows streamed through the air towards the group. Several dived to the floor to avoid being hit. Azzania ran forwards. They were so close now.

She let Threon's sword hang at her side. Peace and serenity would be her weapons. She launched herself at one of the men. He raised his sword but she clasped her hands to his face before he could reach her. The heat and stress of war melted from his features in an instant. His sword hand relaxed, but he didn't put it down.

She had never touched an ancient before. His mind stretched on and on. So many experiences, so much love, so much pain. She cleared it in an instant.

He blinked at her. 'Feel that?' she said. 'This is peace. It bests war every time. You don't need to kill me.'

'Those are my orders.' His voice was a soft whisper. In her peripheral vision she could see that the other soldiers had been subdued by the remaining Guardians.

The man's sword twitched as he tightened his grip slightly. 'You are in the void,' she said. 'Absorb the quiet. Here you only need do your own will. Let us pass in peace.'

His face flickered with a momentary frown. He was fighting it. He lifted the sword higher. 'Please. Stay with me. I don't want to have to drill deeper.'

His face twitched again. His biceps tightened. 'Don't,' she said.

He cried out and brought the sword down fast towards her head. She broke through his subconscious, driving deep into his mind. She expunged it. Centuries of memories and emotion negated. She voided his soul.

Azzania let go and stepped away from the soldier. The man gazed back at her through empty eyes. He sank slowly to the floor and began to weep.

360

Three of her fellow Guardians were still engaged with the remaining soldiers. She motioned to the others. They sprinted through the palace and past lush gardens towards a squat stone tower.

'Here,' she panted.

Ianoff, a leader among her order, hesitated. Several others held back, too. 'Vyara,' he said. 'I can feel it; they are here. We must tread carefully, sister.'

Her desire to help Threon had blinded her from the truth of his situation. She pulled on her inner serenity. Calm, cold logic muted her heightened emotions. She saw it now. She couldn't risk taking the order inside.

'Forgive me, brother,' she said. 'I see clearly now.' She had a plan. 'Circle the tower. We won't risk entering, but perhaps we can shield him from the Vyara's influence.'

'It's never been done before.'

'It hasn't been tried since the days of Kyvo, but it can be done. Will you try with me?' She scanned those gathered. They were calculating the risk, and the possible gain.

Ianoff nodded. 'I will.' His voice was joined by many of the others. They positioned themselves around the tower. Azzania took the space in front of the door. She placed her hands on the shoulders of the two Guardians either side of her, and they did the same until they formed a circle around the tower.

They were joined.

Time slowed. Azzania felt every heartbeat. She felt the spaces between each beat. Her breathing slowed and deepened. Her vision unfocussed as she turned her attention to Threon. The void amassed between them.

'Father.' Lleu tried to pull himself free, but Khan had him pinned. Lleu lifted his head in time to see the last wolf's tail disappear behind a corner, following Raikka. 'Let go of me.' He struggled again, but to no avail. As he kicked out the arrow twisted deeper into his leg and he cried out in pain.

The commander glowered at him. His face was smeared with sweat, soot and blood. His chest rose and fell heavily. 'You betrayed me, son.' His grip loosened and Lleu hauled himself backwards out of his father's shadow. He stood shaking, glancing momentarily down at the arrow that protruded from his left leg, then back in the direction in which Raikka had fled. 'I should have known not to trust your water blood.'

Lleu held his hands up defensively, still gripping his sword in one hand. 'I don't want to fight.'

Khan laughed, his eyes wild. 'You don't want to fight?' He swept his arms out to indicate the scenes unfolding around them. 'You led invaders into your own home. Stole from your god. Destroyed the mining industry that keeps us *alive*. Hundreds of your brothers and sisters are dead. Because… of… you.' He ran his palm along the flat of his sword. 'You were meant to kill Greenbrooke. One death could have saved us all from this living hell.'

Khan advanced on him. Lleu stepped backwards, avoiding bodies as he did so. 'I grew to watch my Waterlands family buckle under our greed,' he said. 'They were enslaved, stolen from, starved and murdered. So we could live under a fucking golden palace on the other side of the sea. We live beyond our years, but without purpose. We exist to protect the elite who wage inequities on all around them. It's not right.' He was now holding his sword at the side of his chest, poised ready to fight.

'I gave you everything, boy. You would have died half a century ago, an old and frail man on a squalid Mainlands farm. Instead you've grown to see the world, to lie with the

362

children of the gods, to surpass the strength of mortal men. I gave you a life others would kill for.'

Lleu stopped retreating. Khan stepped forwards and their swords touched. The two men were inches from each other. The commander's eyes were red-rimmed and wild. Sweat streaked through the blood and soot that covered his face.

'The things I've done for the palimore haunt me. I hate the man you made of me.' Lleu felt the pressure on his sword increase. He pushed back.

'You ungrateful brat.' Khan slid his sword to the tip of Lleu's blade to free himself from their deadlock. He stepped back and swung the sword down over Lleu's head.

'Do you know the symptoms of the silvertail's venom?' Keresan reached out a hand, stroking Threon's cheek. He tried to flinch back from her but the pipe held him firmly in place. 'The venom is a form of saliva, highly modified to inflict excruciating damage on the victim. The toxins will begin to slowly destroy your central nervous system.'

Deyar picked up a candle from the table and moved over to her, wrapping an arm around her waist. She took the candle from him and let go of the snake's body. The creature slid down the tube. Threon fought to keep his throat closed. He imagined its forked tongue slipping past the back of his mouth. 'You'll feel your breath labour, your heart struggle, you'll lose control of your limbs, your bladder, your bowels. Then your body tissues will start to break down.' Threon was drenched in sweat. He retched involuntarily and closed his eyes tight, worried the constriction of his throat would cause the animal to bite. 'Your blood will haemorrhage, your muscles will waste. It will burn through your limbs, taking every last part of you, until you can take no more, and your body gives up, leaving behind a vein-streaked, blood-swollen corpse.'

Keresan moved the candle flame directly beneath the metal pipe. 'The poor creature doesn't want to slide down your neck.' She moved the flame up and down the pipe. 'But when faced with deadly heat…'

The snake began to writhe, forcing itself against the back of Threon's throat. His breath quickened through his nose, his heart thundering in his chest.

Then something caught his attention. A sensation like a mental tug. The thread of emotion that hung between Threon and Azzania pulled taut and surged with feeling. She was coming.

A ripple of void, like a cool breeze, rolled through the room.

Keresan's face wavered. She felt it too. Her eyes flicked to Deyar. His body tensed, and pupils snapped into existence in the milk of his eyes.

Azzania. Threon could feel her. And behind her, a powerful force. He reached out to her mentally. If he could tap into the void…

The force hit like a wall. The power of a dozen Guardians flooded into him through his link with Azzania. Calm flushed the room. Panic left him.

He met Keresan's eyes.

Lleu raised his sword to block his father's attack. The commander was one of the strongest men in the army. Lleu felt the full force of his muscle driving down against his sword. His calf burned and throbbed as he was forced down under the weight of the attack. Lleu broke free by dropping to the ground and rolling away. As he did so, the arrow caught on the uneven street and snapped, sending a dizzying wave of pain to his head. Khan's sword slammed into the floor. He growled and charged at Lleu, wrestling him to the ground and landing a blinding punch to the side of his head.

As the world blinked back into focus, Lleu found his face pushed hard against the cobbles. He could taste the blood that lined the streets and feel it seeping through his clothes and hair. The pressure on the side of his face was immense; Khan could crush his skull if he chose to do so. The palm against his cheek began to shake. The commander was sobbing. He brought his hand up in a fist and smashed it down, striking the ground beside Lleu's head. He grabbed his son by the left shoulder and swung again, this time catching him square on the jaw. Lleu felt something crack and his vision exploded.

'You reduce me to this,' croaked Khan. 'No man should have to kill his son.' Lleu kicked and flung his fists back up at the man, but Khan easily caught his wrists and held him firm. There were tears in the man's eyes, but his face was tight with anger. 'I will make it quick.' His voice was a whisper. 'There are many who would hate me for it. You deserve worse.' He released one of Lleu's wrists to reach for his sword, which had been cast to the cobblestones.

It was a reckless mistake, perhaps influenced by the start of his descent into withdrawal. Perhaps he thought his son would yield to him. Lleu seized the opportunity, and struck out with his free hand, driving it into Khan's abdomen. His father reeled, but only for a moment. In that split second, Lleu rolled from underneath him, snatching up his sword. He kicked Khan to the floor and angled the weapon down at his father's chest. The older man held his hands up, letting out a mad, deep chuckle. 'Nice move, son, but you wouldn't kill an unarmed man,' said Khan. He didn't sound convinced.

'Not usually,' said Lleu. 'Maybe today's different. This is war, after all.' Khan's fingers extended upwards slightly. Lleu stamped a boot over his hand before it could reach the arrows protruding from his quiver. 'I've watched you fight my whole life. I know your moves.'

'If you're not going to give me a fighting chance, just do it. Kill me.'

Lleu brought the sword point over Khan's chest and rested it directly above the heart. Khan panted beneath him. He looked pitiful; a brute of a man reduced to submit to his son's will. 'I don't want to do this,' said Lleu. Khan's eyes were like fire. 'You don't have to die.' Emotion welled up inside him as he spoke. 'Join our fight. Help us bring down the Empire.' Even as he spoke the words he knew they held no hope.

'Join you? You're destroying everything and everyone I ever held dear.' Khan reached up and grabbed Lleu's blade with both hands. Blood ran red over his fingers. 'I should have killed you when I had the chance. Do it, if you have the balls. We can't keep playing cat and mouse, boy. One of us must die.'

Lleu's hands went white under his grip on the sword. He was shaking. The blade gave away his fear as it trembled over his father's chest.

Khan smirked at him. 'This wasn't how it was meant to end for me.' Blood ran freely down the end of the sword as Khan gripped tighter. Tears threatened to blur Lleu's vision. 'Killed by my own blood. I hope you live to regret this.'

Khan pulled the blade down sharply. Lleu watched in slow motion as the blade sank into his father's heart.

He let go of the hilt. The sword stood upright, deep in his father's flesh. Khan let go of the blade and his arms fell open. His body convulsed and he gave a last, grotesque smile. Blood pooled at the corners of his mouth and ran down his cheeks.

Lleu knelt at his side and pulled out the sword to hasten his passing. Blood bubbled up from the wound and soaked the ground beneath them. He held his father's head and kissed it. 'I'm sorry. I'm so sorry.' He let loose tearless sobs as

366

the life left Khan's eyes. 'I'm sorry. I'm sorry.' The words were just a whisper now.

With shaking hands he closed Khan's eyelids and wailed to the sky.

'Where's Threon? Shouldn't you be helping him?'

It's regrettable that I can't help the boy. I planned to put him to good use when this was over.

'You're a Vyara. What could possibly stop you from helping him?'

If the boy dies, you have those damn witches to blame.

Keresan met Threon's gaze. Her eyes had widened. The void was a new sensation for her, but it did not slow her down. She held the candle closer to the pipe, though he noticed a slight tremble in her hand.

He closed his eyes and let the feeling flow through him. The void surrounded him, embraced him. He imagined it surging out of every part of his body to fill the room. When he opened his eyes again Deyar was glaring at him. He could feel the Vyara's power. Millennia of prayers granted and ignored. The devotion, the despair. The weight of millions of lives all crying out for help. The intensity of faith.

The Vyara roared with rage and Keresan took a step away from him, making sure to keep hold of the pipe. Deyar swung towards him, shoulders shaking with rage.

'You are with the witches,' he hissed.

Latching onto the void, Threon steeled himself. Azzania was with him now. He could feel her. He embraced the peace that channelled through the room and felt it radiate back out through him. He focussed on his ice-cold legs. The void spread down through his body to warm them, probing the Vyara's hold on him.

Deyar's eyes burned with venom. He gripped his fists tightly and began to move slowly and deliberately towards Threon.

The iron encasing Threon's hands began to shift. The feeling spread down from his hips. The sensation of liquid running down his legs. The casing slipped further.

It cracked.

Threon fell to the floor just as the god was within striking distance. The iron around his legs restored itself to flat tiles, the void freeing the metal of Deyar's command. As he fell, the pipe ripped from Keresan's hands and clattered to the ground.

He wrenched his head forwards, throwing the snake out of his mouth. Its back end coiled up defensively, head reared high. Threon had no time to spit and retch to soothe his throat.

He turned around to face the god, feeling the void radiate out of him like heat from a burning coal. Deyar dropped to his knees. A look of alarm passed across Keresan's face. 'Deyar?' The Vyara screamed with rage, pressing his palms tight against his ears.

Avoiding the snake, Threon dove to grab the pipe where it lay on the floor beside her.

The scream came to an abrupt end, and when Threon looked up the Vyara was gone. Keresan's eyes scanned the room for a sign of the god. She was visibly trembling, her chest rising and falling in panicked breaths. She was on her own. Deyar had been forced from the room by the void.

Threon didn't hesitate.

He swung the pipe at the back of her head with force. She was still searching the air for her absent god.

The blow didn't knock her out. She turned around, blinking in mute surprise. She took one step towards him, then staggered. He swung the pipe again. It crashed into her face. This time her body fell to the floor. This time she didn't get up. Blood poured from her crushed nose and ruined right eye. It bubbled around her mouth with her shallow breaths. 'You thought you could live forever,' he whispered.

The void had left him. Anger welled up instead.

Threon brought the dented pipe down on her face again. And again. And again, until he was pummelling fragments of skull against wet tiles. With each blow he thought of those he had lost, of those who were dying outside the walls, and of his murdered family. Tears of anger tempered the blood that spattered his face. When his arms grew too heavy he fell to his knees and dropped the pipe. Panting with exertion and shaking with adrenaline, he stared blankly at the corpse.

The Empress was dead.

CHAPTER TWENTY-EIGHT

The room began to shake. Animals cried out from their captivity as plaster crumbled from the ceiling. A heavy shudder from under his feet sent Threon sprawling forwards onto his hands. He pulled himself back up from the glaze of blood that washed the floor. Letting out a shuddering breath, he grabbed the pipe again and made for the door.

Clutching the makeshift weapon, he was ready to lash out at the guards. Screaming in rage, ready to fight, he kicked down the door.

The hallway was empty.

The guards had abandoned their post. Another quake forced Threon to grab hold of the wall to steady himself. A large crack appeared above the doorway. He grabbed his sword and bow from where the guards had thrown them to the ground and hurried to exit the shaking building.

The light outside had dimmed under heavy cloud. Sheets of rain fell thick and heavy. Flashes of light illuminated dark swathes of cloud. He could see figures beyond the doorway, static silhouettes in the bursts of light.

He notched an arrow before emerging into the open. The rain soaked through to his skin and slicked his hair flat. He tasted Keresan's blood as the rain washed it across his lips.

He held the bow up, ready to loose. Another crack of lightning revealed those around him with a roar of thunder. Figures garbed in white. Guardians.

'Azzania!' His voice strained against the pelting rain. She had been so close, but he could no longer feel her. The ground heaved again and he fell to his knees. The Guardians were scattered, seeming lost and confused. He grabbed one of the women by her dress as she passed. 'Where's Azzania?' Her blue eyes widened as she recognised him. 'What's going on?'

She moved her lips to speak and then shook her head. She pointed to her right and ran. His gaze followed her finger to a white-clothed figure, immobile on the grass. Threon staggered to his feet and ran. As he neared, he recognised the white robes as Azzania's execution dress. He half fell as he rushed to her side.

Fresh blood stained her clothes, and an arrow impaled her breast.

A man with a crossbow stood several feet away. One of the Guardians had the assailant in some sort of trance. He would die for touching her.

Azzania was on her side, head turned into the wet ground. He put a hand to her cheek and lifted her face gently. Her eyes opened a slit. 'Threon.' Her voice was a whisper. He stroked the wet hair from her eyes. 'You're alive,' she said.

'Shh, shhh. It's okay.'

'I'm not in pain.' She smiled weakly. 'The void protects me.' He put his head to her chest. Her breathing gurgled. The arrow had punctured a lung.

'I'll get you out of here, hold still.' He took the arrow shaft in two hands and snapped it as close to the body as he could manage.

She held up a pale hand to meet his. They were both shaking. 'It's okay. I don't fear death.'

Threon felt his lip tremble. His eyes welled up and he swallowed hard. 'I won't let you leave me.'

'Death is just the next chapter…' The rest of her words were drowned out by thunder. Another tremor. Her body rocked from side to side in the force of the quake. He tried to keep her still. 'The Vyara are angry. Listen to the earth and the sky. The brothers have finally come to battle.'

'I killed her,' said Threon. 'I felt you. I felt the void.'

'Yes. You channelled the void. A natural.' She smiled wanly. 'I'm proud.' A cough racked her chest for a long moment, longer than Threon felt he could bear. When she had finished, blood reddened her lower lip and spilled over her chin. He pulled her up and held her close.

'Why did you come here? You were meant to stay back—' He bit his lip, stopping before the hurt and anger poured into his words.

'It's nearly over.' She paused for a moment, closing her eyes. He could hear the liquid mounting in her lungs as she breathed. 'Deyar will rage. We prevented him from saving his love. He will seek vengeance for her murder. Let the Guardians protect you. And the air god, if you must.'

'They will pay for what they've done to you. For what they've done to everyone.'

Another quake. A large section of the palace wall thundered to the ground. One of the bigger stones rolled to Threon's feet as the shockwaves continued.

'Be careful,' she said. He ran his hand through her short hair. She was shivering with cold. He brought his lips down

372

to meet hers in a bloody kiss. She slipped into unconsciousness and he held her in his arms as the world shattered around them.

Savanta was thrown through the air. The winds were picking up. She beat hard against the storm, struggling to gain her bearings. The rain quenched the fires below, causing torrents of black smoke to clog the sky. She held her breath as she was thrown through a cloud of it. The hot, sooty air made her eyes water. She closed them and fought to fly out of the smoke. *Zenith, please stop.*

Another gust of wind sent her sprawling sideways. Unable to regain control, she fell earthwards and spiralled into a chimney stack. Pulling her wings in tight to protect them, she slid to a stop on the ridge of the house's roof. She came to a crouch, holding onto the tiles with her hands. The ground was as perilous as the sky. It shook violently. Tiles clattered down the roof to smash on the corpse-strewn street below.

She was in the upper city and from here she had a clear view of the slums. They had been devastated. The wooden shacks had kindled on the smallest flame. When the wind rose, people couldn't run fast enough to outpace the blaze. Soldiers, civilians and rebels gave up their fight and burned together with nowhere left to run. Now, as the fires damped down in the rain, she could make out the charred bodies of the dead piled together on the streets.

She stared wide-eyed at the scene before her. Buildings fell as the earth heaved with tension. Sections of the ground had fallen away altogether, pulling homes down into shadowy depths. Rainwater flooded the streets and the wind ripped trees from their roots.

At least the sound of the storm dimmed the screams.

Another rumble. It built and built. The roof she perched on

collapsed. She opened her wings in fright and was pulled upwards by a timely gust of wind. She let the storm carry her, watching the city crumble beneath as the rain streamed over her wings.

Then an explosion. Rising above the city, Mount Ariad erupted. Day turned to night as black petals of ash bloomed into the sky. The left side of the mountain fell away under a great force. The shock of it nearly startled her from the air. She had to get away. Fresh terror seemed to unfold with every passing second. There was nowhere to hide from it.

Heading towards the ocean, her heart pounding in her chest, she flew blindly through the storm, dashed from one wind to another. The mountain's ash filled the sky, flashing with wild fronds of light. Her lungs burned with smoke inhalation as dizziness threatened to send her plunging down. She began to lose altitude. Beneath her, a few surviving soldiers brawled, nigh on oblivious to the apocalypse unfolding around them.

She fought to control her breathing and focussed on beating her wings steadily against the wind. She began to rise again.

Something halted her progress. She slowed and turned to look back.

Lleu.

He was alive, and engaged in battle with another palimore. He looked exhausted, throwing poor attacks at his assailant. The street had turned to thick ashen mud in the rain. He staggered as the earth moved beneath his feet. He was struggling. She looked seaward, then back at Lleu, cursing her generous nature. Swooping down to a nearby pile of rubble, she picked up the heaviest stone she could manage. Her back and wing muscles screamed as she brought the rock higher and higher into the air. The extra weight was agony. She hovered above the melee, angling herself above Lleu's

374

foe. The stone began to slip from her fingers in the rain. She let go.

The stone caught the palimore on the shoulder. He fell backward and Lleu leapt on him, driving an axe into his head.

Savanta swept down. 'Lleu!'

He looked up and swung his axe back in defence. She held her hands up, settling on the muddy ground.

Soot, sweat and blood marbled his skin. His whole body heaved as he puffed in breath. He let out a scream of rage and threw the axe. Savanta flinched as it sped past her and buried itself in the ground.

Lleu dropped to his knees and folded over, his head on the earth, fists gripping at mud. His body shook violently.

'Lleu?'

Savanta took a careful step towards him. He was sobbing.

She placed a hand on his shoulder. He reared up, flinging his arms wide, knocking her to the ground. He turned to look at her, the whites of his eyes bloodshot. Tears formed rivulets down his face.

Savanta picked herself up, keeping her eyes on him.

'Lleu, what's wrong?' It was only then that she noticed the body. The Commander was soaked with blood, eyes vacant. He lay a few feet from Lleu.

The sky flashed bright again, capturing the grieving soldier in a frozen moment in time. 'Lleu, did you…?' Killing a parent. She couldn't even begin to comprehend what he was going through. 'I'm so sorry.'

'Have you seen Raikka?' His eyes were red-rimmed with pain.

Savanta shook her head. So many of the miners had died. If Raikka hadn't had Lleu at her side for protection… 'You were separated?'

'Wolves tailed her. I have to find her.' There was a

hysterical edge to his voice. He stalked over to the axe and picked it up.

The smell of sulphur grew as more ash billowed into the sky. The house behind Savanta began to crumble as another quake rocked the earth and sent her sprawling into the mud. She got to her feet to find Lleu was already running. At every house he passed, he threw the door open and called Raikka's name. Searching a city this size for one individual would be impossible at the best of times, but to do so now was madness. She took to the air to follow him

She tried to keep her voice gentle as she called down to him. 'Lleu, we have to get out of here. It's not safe in the city.' He didn't hear her. The tremors weren't stopping. Panic built inside Savanta. 'Lleu?' Another explosion from the mountain. Reflex forced Savanta to draw her wings in, hands over her ears. She nearly tumbled out of the sky. Lleu didn't even flinch. He flung open another door then wailed Raikka's name down a narrow alley. He would never find her.

Savanta dropped to the ground in front of him. 'We have to get out of the city. It's not safe,' she screamed. He pushed past her.

'Save yourself,' he growled over his shoulder. 'I'm not leaving without her.'

She ran to catch up with him. 'Lleu, this is madness! How do you expect to find her? I can help lead you out of here, but you have to come *now*.' She grabbed his shoulder in an attempt to slow him.

His head snapped back towards her. He pushed her hard against a building. 'I said I'm staying. Now leave me!' There was something alarming in his tone. This was a man who had been driven to the brink.

She recoiled from him as soon as he let go. She stepped backwards, away from the desperate man. The sky was growing darker still. The rain fell black with ash, dappling her skin. If she waited much longer flight would be impossible.

With a sad last glance at Lleu, she ran forwards, spreading her wings to embrace the storm.

CHAPTER TWENTY-NINE

When the Vyara fought, they lost all care for the living. *We're destroying the city,* spoke the wind.

The earth rumbled. *I would watch it burn rather than see you take charge.*

Deyar and Zenith tumbled through realms, smashing through dimensions as they fought. The pillars of the earth shook as they brawled. They drew on the power of blood, fear and prayer from the warring human world. A potent tonic.

The stars glittered in anticipation of a new alignment, a new order, a new king. More endless than space and time, more powerful than imagination and memory, more cunning and cruel than any beating heart, they were gods, and they were ageless, and they did not fight like the living.

With fists of fire they collided like great ships. Their fight was a mirror to reality. When Zenith roared in battle, reality thundered. Ice rained from the clouds; winds danced and twisted and tore up the city; day turned to night and the air pressed down with the weight of vengeance, dark and thick and heavy.

When Deyar roared in battle, reality quaked. Great heaving coughs shook the ground; liquid fire burst from the mountain, fearless and feral in its dark ascent to suffocate the sky. The earth tore buildings to tatters as it growled, opening its jaws to swallow homes in a convulsion of fury.

Give in, Deyar. The battle is ending. Give up now and save your remaining subjects.

I would sacrifice them all to see you pay for what you've done.

You're a fool to fall for a woman. You thought she could live forever? Vyara should never stoop so low.

Another eruption on earth. They fought on, pinballing between stars.

The Vyara were made as shepherds, not warriors, but when the crook is tossed aside, so goes any care for the living. Gods are ageless, timeless, eternal forces. Their futile efforts to destroy each other would end in death for neither of them. Instead, it would rip the world asunder.

Zenith wrestled and beat and stormed the land, and the living fell like toy soldiers in a battlefield that held no sanctuary. The ground moved and swelled and slipped and tore. The sky made blind, made choke, made ice from bones. The living screamed, the living bled, the living ceased.

You've held power for too long, brother. Let the sky have its day. Give in to me.

Never.

I'm winning this fight. The palimore are dying. Keresan is gone. The Mainlanders won't worship you for centuries after what your followers have done to them.

Another eruption shook the stars and they fell away into darkness.

Hurricane winds sucked up the city.

The ground split.

The mountain heaved another breath of ash.

Stars fell from the sky.

An eternity of existence had given the Vyara an unearthly grasp of human emotion; and millennia with a woman – a living, breathing, warm-blooded creature – had impossibly tied Deyar's heart to her. The grief seeped through every crack and fibre of his being: contaminating, violating, breeding rot through the god, through the land. It sucked the fight from him. The rumble of shaking earth began to quell. It quivered like the shuddered breath of grief. Deyar was tiring. The ground gave a last death-rattle.

Only the sound of the wind and the rain remained.

You surrender?

I will give you the Empire, brother. On one condition. Give me the boy. Give me my vengeance.

That's not the deal. I have plans for him.

Then more will die.

The sound of the earthquake rumbled louder again as Deyar threw himself at his brother.

CHAPTER THIRTY

When the earth stood still, Threon raised his head from Azzania's shoulder. The ground was black with ash, mirroring the sunless sky. 'It's stopped,' he whispered to her. She was still breathing, but unresponsive.

He tried again to reach her with the void, attempting hopelessly to latch on to the feeling that had come to him in the tower. There was nothing.

His concentration broke as words hissed into his mind.

I will give you the Empire, brother. On one condition. Give me the boy. Give me my vengeance.

The words made his blood run cold. He looked down at Azzania. Her eyes fluttered beneath their lids, breath bloody and ragged. He squeezed her hand and laid a kiss on her lips. As their mouths met his tears fell on her face, running down her ash-stained cheeks.

'I love you,' he whispered.

He took a deep breath and stood. Tearing his eyes away from her caused a knot in his stomach. He swallowed hard and walked to the palace walls, climbing up the fallen rubble. The fighting had come to an end. Palimore and Mainlanders had given up arms to find shelter. There had been no victory here for men and women. This was a war of gods, and the living were destined to lose.

From the top of the wall Threon could see the city below. In the falling rain the screams seemed muffled. The slums were gone. In their place, smouldering ash. How many had burned alive? Buildings in the upper city were in ruins. Homes had collapsed on their owners. Wide cracks had formed where the city had fallen beneath the earth. Rain washed blood through the streets and parted around countless bodies, piled high.

The damage was far greater than any the raiders had inflicted on his home.

Threon closed his eyes, taking in a shaking breath. There was no one left who he cared for. His family, his household, were gone. Did this avenge their death? Would his parents be proud? His people were destroyed. This war had killed more of them than anything the Thelonians had inflicted. Lleu and Savanta were lost in the hell that lay before him. Azzania was dying.

No kingdom. No people. Only the weight of death to bear.

The earth began to move again. The screaming grew louder. Cracks grew wider and more houses fell.

He reached out to Deyar with his thoughts.

I'm coming.

The doors to Deyar's temple stood open. Stairs descended beneath the palace to a deep cavern that made the Vyara's place of worship. Rain had flooded the chamber, a couple of inches of water covering the floor.

Threon swallowed, flexing his wrists to stop his shaking. At the bottom of the stairs he paused to remove his sword and bow. The torches still burned in the temple and the earth felt settled here, the quakes reduced to a gentle shaking.

He stepped down into the chamber and watched the ripples spread from his footsteps as he paced to the centre of the room. There he lowered himself onto the wet stone floor. He stared up at the cave-like ceiling and closed his eyes.

'I'm ready, my Lord.'

Darkness. And cold.

Earth smothered him. Immobilising as it pressed against his body. It filled his nose, his mouth, his lungs, his stomach. His heart was still, his veins ice.

Welcome to your penance, Threon Greenbrooke.

He could feel the weight of Deyar's pain. The anger and sadness of an eternal god. How long had he been here? A lifetime. More than a lifetime. Empires crumbled, oceans dried up and stars died as time consumed itself here.

His corpse had been left to rot on earth and Deyar had imagined a new vessel for him. One whose sole purpose was to perpetuate suffering. His body could not move for the weight that bore down. His eyes would not open for the earth that pressed hard against them. His chest would not rise for his lungs were compacted.

You will try to hold onto the memories of your loved ones, of yourself, of your world. The words rang in his skull. He strained to hold on to memories of life. Of friends, of family, of enemies... *But, given enough time, everything fades. Time will erase your name, your life, but you will never be free of this body.*

The urge to breathe, to see, to move, screamed out from his soul, the insuppressible need to function like the living. His senses were buried under the weight of a continent. His body bound and entombed, sealed in the dark.

He would be earth, and suffering. Alone. Forever.

He would never leave this place.

CHAPTER THIRTY-ONE

The storm ceased. The earth was still.

Savanta turned back to the city. She was exhausted. Her flight across the sea would have proven suicidal, ending in a watery grave. She needed to get back to land, to rest.

The sky began to brighten. The winds had picked up and whipped ash away from the city. She allowed herself to be carried on the breeze. Zenith had won. Tears welled in her eyes. It was over.

The palace was still standing: the only building to remain untouched by the destruction of the storm. She glided there on the fresh wind. As she reached land she could see streams of people making their way towards the miraculously untouched building.

White dots marked out the Guardians, who moved between the littered bodies distributing vish and easing the passage of death. A crowd had gathered at the main palace entrance. Vituund and Aya were at its head. She dived down to join them.

Aya was speaking to the crowd. Her clothes were torn and dirty, the lines of her face exaggerated by soot-covered skin, but she still held herself with the bearing of a queen. As Savanta came down to land, she noticed a few palimore soldiers had joined the crowd. They sat in the mud beside their enemies, all bloody, all exhausted. She caught Vituund's eye as she alighted and he broke away from the crowd to join her.

'Where's Threon?' she asked.

Vituund shook his head slowly. She caught her breath. 'We found his body in the temple. I'm sorry.'

She shut her eyes tight, expelling a slow breath. 'Have you seen Lleu?'

'The palimore? No.' He shook his head again. 'It will take days to account for the dead and wounded.'

She cursed herself for not staying with him. He had grown careless in his grief. Anything could have happened.

'Azzania?'

'The Guardians are tending to her wounds.'

'Where's Threon now?'

'We brought his body into the palace. He rests in the throne room.'

Trancelike, Savanta made her way through the palace doors. The first room she came to was lined with the injured. Guardians fluttered from person to person, whispering in hushed voices to one another. The occasional low moan was silenced by the touch of the void.

They paid no mind to her as she passed through. Halfway across the room she spotted Azzania. She lay still, eyes closed, as if she were sleeping. Three Guardians busied themselves around her. One held a compress to her head and another stitched a bloody hole in her side while a third held her hand;

he had his eyes closed and whispered softly under his breath. Savanta hovered over them, wanting to help. A curt glance from the woman doing the stitching told her she was not welcome. She backed off, leaving them to their work.

She took the stairs to the throne room slowly, trying not to picture Threon's death, hoping that somehow Vituund was wrong.

A pair of Ionese soldiers stood guard outside the room. They bristled as she approached, reaching for their spears.

'Let me through,' she said.

'The queen commands we let no man enter.'

She was tired and bitter. Spreading her wings to their full, she hissed the words, 'By Zenith's command, let me pass.' The pair backed away as her wings cast them in shadow.

'The angel of death,' one whispered. They stepped aside and she walked in, closing the door behind her.

The room was cold, dark and captivating. There were no windows. A handful of candles burned on the floor, their wax spilling over the tiles. The flickering light illuminated ornately carved stone walls, studded with gems. The throne was positioned in the centre of the far wall. It was huge, comprised of clay and metal and stone and bone. It wasn't beautiful, but it exuded power.

At its feet lay Threon.

Vituund's rich blue cloak was laid over his body. His eyes were closed and his head rested to one side, facing Savanta. She bit her lip. Kneeling at his side, the orange light flickered ghastly shadows across his face. She thought it would look as though he were asleep, but it was quite different. His features sagged, all colour had left his skin. The man was gone and all that was left was flesh and bone.

She tore a section of her dress off and folded it into a small cushion which she placed under his head to stop it from lolling to the side. A short intake of breath as she lifted his head. His skin was cold as stone.

How had he died? No blood seeped through the cloak and only minor cuts and bruises showed on his face.

She was too tired to cry. Too drained by war. She felt empty.

Leaning over, she planted a kiss on his forehead. 'You did it, Threon,' she said. Her words echoed back to her in the empty room. 'The Empire has fallen. Zenith won. Your people are free to rebuild their home.'

She stopped. Her words jarred against the silence. After the cacophony of war, the quiet felt alien. The silence felt too sacred to disturb.

She sat back on her haunches. It was all over. It was time to go home.

Drawing on the peace of the throne room, she reached out for the void as Azzania had taught her. A gentle tingle in her fingers grew. It rippled back her grey skin, revealing pale fingers, then freckled arms. She let her mind go blank, letting go of the hurt, of her memories, of herself. The void reached her shoulders, touching at the tips of her wings. She was ready to say goodbye to flight. This body did not belong in her future.

'What do you think you're doing?' There was an icy touch of humour to Zenith's voice.

Savanta froze. Her mind returned to her surroundings and she suppressed a sob. The grey flooded back into her flesh.

He was standing behind her. His shadow danced across the walls in the candlelight.

She closed her eyes. 'You won your fight. Am I not free to go?'

He walked around her and came to stand in front of Threon's body. 'Such a shame.' He shook his head. 'He was destined to be a great king. I had high hopes for him. You were a fool to give yourself up, Threon.' He sighed. 'Who shall I use as my puppet now?'

'Can't you bring him back? Like you did for Astor in the stories?' A moment of hope tugged at her.

'No. He's in a place even I can't reach. Still,' he clapped his hands, 'we must go on. I have an empire to build.' He skipped up the steps and swung himself onto the throne.

'You're King of the Gods now.'

'Marvellous, isn't it?' He flashed her a grin. 'Deyar will be sulking for decades. I'm free to roam the lands here unhindered; to tear down his temples and inspire more worship. We'll have sky shrines, solstice rites and festivals of the stars.'

'You destroyed the capital.'

He shrugged. 'The city needed to go. Clean slate. It will make the transition less painful. Aligning to a new god is often easier when people are desperate.'

'And the people who died?'

'More will be born.' He raised an eyebrow at her, and she held back from saying more.

He got up from the throne and came to stand before her. He offered her his hand and she took it, coming to her feet. They held each other's eyes for a long moment. Savanta was the first to tear her gaze away.

'Despite your insolence, you've served me well, my dear.' He ran his fingers down one of her wings, pulling it out to splay the leathery flesh caught between the bones. 'You've played a big part in this adventure.' He paused for effect. 'I'd like to reward you.'

She stiffened slightly. Dare she trust a reward from the Vyara?

He circled her, coming around to admire her other wing.

'How shall we reward you? Mm? A constellation? A royal

388

title? Maybe you would like to bear one of my children?' His smile sent a chill through her.

'Why tease me like this? You know what I want.'

'Oh, Savanta. I was hoping you might have developed a bit more imagination.' He sighed dramatically. 'You want to go home.'

She met his eyes again. Was he playing with her? She kept silent.

'Fine,' he said.

'Fine?'

'You can go home. I'm a generous god, after all.'

Her heart quickened. Did he really mean it?

'You're sure you want your old body back?'

She nodded, unable to hold back a smile. 'Yes. I want life as it was before.'

'You'll miss these wings. It's a long road to home.'

'Please. I want this. I need it. I miss my little girl.'

He gave her a sideways glance and then placed his hand on her chest. She braced herself for the feeling of his fingers pushing through her skin. They were warm. Nausea built as he pushed past her lungs and heart. And then a strong sense of suction. The bones of her wings retracted into themselves, and into her spine. Her skin blistered back into flesh. She felt her body become heavier, her hollow bones filling again. Her hair changed from black to flame red.

As he withdrew his hand she fell on all fours, hyperventilating.

Her body felt alien. Instinctively, she tried to pull her wings about her for protection. They were gone.

She reached behind. Two small stumps remained at her back where once she had wings. She looked up at Zenith, wide-eyed.

'This is only temporary,' he explained. 'You're primed to

sprout back those beautiful wings on my command. I'll be calling on you again.'

'You said I was free.' She couldn't hold back the anger.

'I said you could go home. Really, you must *listen*. You will never be free. I've granted you a fine gift. Go, be with your family. But never forget, you will always belong to me.'

He looked back down at Threon, head tilted to one side. 'Such a waste.'

With that his body slipped into opacity and vanished.

Savanta ran her hands along her arms and through her hair. She rolled her shoulders, adjusting to the loss of her wings. She was trembling.

It was time to go home.

Savanta found Lleu in one of the courtyards that had been made into a temporary hospital. The injured were thickly strewn around the site. Guardians bustled around the soldiers, administering vish and easing pain with the void.

She was relieved to see that Lleu wasn't hurt. He knelt on the soot-stained paving beside one of the injured. It was Raikka. Savanta rushed over to him.

'You found her,' she beamed. Then, more tentatively, 'Is she going to be alright?' Raikka lay still, eyes closed in deep sleep.

Lleu turned at the sound of her voice, his brow furrowed. He didn't recognise her. Savanta came to crouch beside him on the ground. She twitched her back muscles, instinctively trying to draw in the wings she no longer possessed.

Lleu looked terrible. He was filthy; caked with mud and soot and blood. His face was drawn and tired, but he managed a wan smile when recognition dawned. 'Savanta?' he said.

She smiled. 'Zenith gave me my body back. I can go home.' She looked at Raikka. One of her legs had been neatly wrapped in a bandage that had soaked through with blood. 'What happened?'

'The wolves. She managed to escape them, but not before they attacked her leg. She made her way to the palace and avoided getting caught up in the worst of the quakes and fires.' He nodded to a clay cup beside her head. 'She's had vish on the wound and some redseed tea to help her sleep. She'll be alright.' He took Raikka's hand in his and spoke to the ground. 'I'm sorry for how I treated you earlier… You were only trying to help me.'

Savanta shook her head. 'There's nothing to apologise for. I'm glad you're both safe.'

'What about Threon? Azzania? Have you seen them?' When she hesitated he looked at her and her expression must have betrayed her grief. Lleu closed his eyes and his posture slackened. He expelled a long breath. 'After everything they worked for…'

Savanta ran her fingers through the ash on the ground. It painted her fingers grey and she was relieved to think that she would no longer wake every day to that unnatural skin tone. 'They set us free,' she said. 'What will you do now?'

'Raikka always wanted to show me her home. Perhaps we'll travel to Ionia. Maybe buy a farm… grow old together.' The tiredness left his eyes for a moment as he spoke about the future. 'And you?'

'I'm going home.' Saying the words brought an unbidden smile. Home. At long last.

CHAPTER THIRTY-TWO

In the deep quiet of the throne room, something began to stir. A pulse awoke. A finger twitched. Two blue eyes opened.

Threon's chest rose. Cool air flooded his lungs. He let the air go again and drew another breath. He was alive.

His heart felt like a storm, beating for the first time after returning from the abyss. The candlelight blinded his vision. Blinking the brightness away, the room slowly came into focus.

He pushed himself up to sit. Cold permeated his body. The warmth of his flesh had bled out with death. Violent chills shook him and he rushed with stiff hands to bring the cloak that covered him closer to his chest. His teeth chattered, his whole body felt numb.

It took several minutes before he could rise, shaking, to his feet. He fell forwards immediately. The noise drew attention and the door to the throne room opened.

Guards rushed to wrap their cloaks about Threon and held him up, one under each arm. Their speech was fast and loud, incomprehensible.

Descending the stairs was painful. With each step, more nerves fired to life. He tried to help them support his weight but only managed to drag one foot in front of the other by the time they reached the bottom.

The light outside took his vision away again. Then: voices and clamouring; hands taking hold; furs about his shoulders; hot water at his lips. It could have been hours or minutes, he couldn't tell. His mind woke again, and he was sitting beside a blazing fire. He held a cup of hot tea, his hands still shaking.

A man in blue sat beside him. 'Threon?' he said.

Threon swallowed. He looked at the man and a memory pulled itself from the fog. 'Vituund?' His voice was barely audible, his mouth parched, lips dry.

A wide smile broke across the man's face. 'You're back. By some curse or blessing, you're back.' A hand slapped between Threon's shoulder blades.

Threon looked down at the tea. He lifted it up, breathing in bitter steam. He looked back to Vituund. 'I died,' he said.

'What was it like?' The man was grinning white teeth at him.

'Cold. And dark. I – I don't remember.' He tried to force the memories. There was nothing.

'Drink your tea.'

Threon lifted the cup to his lips and took a sip. The liquid warmed his insides.

'What were you doing in the temple?'

'The temple?'

'Your body was found in the temple. Not a mark on you. What happened?'

Threon shook his head. 'I don't know.' He stared down at the ground, then another memory hit. 'Where's Azzania?'

393

'We'll talk about that another time. You need to recover first.'

A feeling of dread crept over him. 'Tell me.'

Vituund's shoulders dropped. 'She's alive.' He was choosing his words carefully. 'Her wound is deep. Her kin are caring for her.'

Threon stood, spilling hot liquid over his hands. Vituund reached for his arm and pulled him back down with remarkable ease.

'Recover first,' said Vituund. 'She won't even know you're there.'

'I feel wretched.'

'You've come back from the grave. Drink. Valerian root and henbane. It will help you rest.' A bed of furs had been thrown before the fire. Vituund nodded to it. 'I'll keep watch while you sleep.'

Threon didn't remember finishing the tea. He didn't remember crawling into the furs. He only remembered watching the shadows of flames flicker behind closed eyes.

When he woke, Vituund was gone. The fire dwindled and the sun shone warm on his skin. His muscles ached. From death or battle, he couldn't tell.

In Vituund's place sat a half-familiar woman. She plaited her red hair and hadn't noticed him waking. He pushed himself up onto his elbows and winced as his tight muscles stretched with a tearing sensation.

Startled, she stopped what she was doing.

'Threon!' Her eyes lit up when she saw him. She leapt from her seat and threw her arms around him. He groaned as she pressed against his aching shoulders. 'Sorry, sorry.' She pulled away. 'I'm so glad you're okay.'

She had tanned, freckled skin and large, green eyes. 'Savanta?'

She nodded, a huge smile drawing across her face. 'Zenith gave me my body back. I can go home. Did he save you too?'

Threon furrowed his brow. 'I don't think so.' His head felt clearer. The shaking has stopped. But the last of his memory was still unaccounted for.

'You died. Zenith said he had plans for you.'

Plans. Yes, that felt familiar. There was more, but he couldn't grasp the thought. He shook his head to clear it.

'I need to stretch my legs. I feel like shit.'

She reached a hand down to him, and he let her help him to his feet. She slipped her arm around his waist and he was grateful that she allowed him to lean on her without needing to ask. They moved away from the fire and he looked around at his surroundings. They were in the rose garden, flowers all dark with ash. The few people who weren't lying injured were busily running to and fro. Rubble was being cleared, supplies were being salvaged from buildings.

Threon rolled his neck and shoulders, easing the stiffness. The ache in his muscles was a comfort more than a pain. He felt human again.

'Take me to Azzania,' he said. 'I'd like to see her.' Savanta halted. 'What?' he asked.

Savanta avoided his eyes. 'She died.'

His stomach dropped. He felt his legs give way and she caught him before he could fall. 'I'm so sorry, Threon.'

He closed his eyes. 'Where is she?'

'There's to be a mass funeral tonight. She'll sit with the Ionese on a pyre. Your people are to be taken out to sea. The Bannvarians and Islanders are digging pits for their kin.'

'How many dead?'

Her fingers intertwined with his. She squeezed his hand. 'Too many.'

'I want to see her.'

Savanta sighed and led him towards the palace doors.

Even in death, she was beautiful.

Threon crouched at her side and clasped her hand in his. She was cold. Her stillness sent a chill through him. Her eyes were closed, her lips gently parted as if waiting for a kiss. The Guardians had dressed her in fresh white.

She was meant to be invulnerable. A power against the gods. She made her own fate. How could she be gone?

As the sun bled into night, the sky filled with smoke and sparks. Threon stood on a section of palace wall, between the sea and the pyre. Three ships sailed with his kin. The farmers and slaves had paid the heaviest price among the dead. Hundreds of bodies slid from the ships into the water, weighed down by stone.

'Ranar ardell,' he said, sending a prayer to Athys for their souls. He wasn't sure what good it would do them, but a familiar prayer brought him a little comfort.

The fire behind him blazed hot against his back. He hadn't wanted to watch the bodies kindle under the first flames. He didn't want to see her skin blister and blacken. Now the fire roared. He turned around to a wall of orange heat, bodies indecipherable in the dancing flames. The fire had carried her spirit away. She would be at peace in the void. Nothing could hurt her now.

Aya and Vituund stood either side of him. The queen gripped his shoulder. 'The dead don't wish us to mourn. They transcend, and we must go on living.'

He didn't respond, staring deep into the flames.

The three monarchs watched long into the night. It was nearing dawn when the last ship returned, when the last soldier was buried, when the last ember cracked.

'It feels a hollow victory,' said Threon to Vituund. 'I'm sorry that I ever asked you to come.'

'Don't be a fool, boy,' snapped Aya. 'These people gave their lives for the freedom we have won. Do not call their sacrifice a hollow victory.'

'You are free to rebuild now,' said Vituund.

'Yes.' Threon sighed. 'My people can rebuild. But I can't go home. Not yet.' Vituund frowned. 'You both have kingdoms to rule, people that depend upon you. I have a handful of farmers who have proven themselves more resilient than I thought humanly possible. But I have no household, no family, or lineage. I don't even have four walls I can call home in Maradah.'

Aya tried to say something. He silenced her with a wave of his hand. 'If we leave now to return home, the ancients and the palimore who survived will take power and revert back to the old order of things. The mines will reopen, and eventually the raids will start again. Slavery will return and our descendants will curse our names for not finishing what we started here.'

'Threon, you can't—' Vituund began, but Aya cut across him.

'He's right. Someone must remain to maintain the peace.' She put a hand on Threon's shoulder. 'This is a huge sacrifice.'

'I'll miss the mountains, and the rivers. But I have nothing else waiting for me at home. The Waterlands will be a republic. The people don't need me there.'

They returned to watching the embers. 'You will be remembered as the hero in this tale, Threon,' said Vituund.

It didn't feel that way. He watched the spitting fire die, wishing he could turn back time to a day before any of this happened.

CHAPTER THIRTY-THREE

Three days passed. They blurred into each other as the Mainlands' forces arranged to leave, Thelonians grappled with a new leadership, and people from all sides grieved.

Threon found Lleu in the harbour, preparing to depart with Raikka. Savanta already stood on the jetty, watching as he unfurled the sails of a small fishing vessel.

'Lleu,' called Threon. 'You're leaving?'

The palimore looked up and gave him a smile. 'Afraid so, my friend.'

'There's a place for you here if you want it, you know. You can help me build a new island. I need someone who knows these shores, knows the old systems.'

The palimore shook his head. 'I'm not your man.' He sat down beside his wife on the far side of the boat. It swayed in the water. He put a hand on her uninjured leg. 'I want to live a normal life. We're going to Ionia.'

'Look after him, now,' said Savanta to Raikka. 'Make sure he keeps out of trouble.'

The Ionese woman grinned at Lleu. 'I will.'

'I'm glad for you both,' said Threon. 'I wish you well.' He stepped off the jetty onto the boat and embraced the ageless soldier. 'I brought this, just in case…' He handed Lleu a bag he had been carrying. 'The rest will be destroyed, but I thought we could make an exception.' Lleu opened the drawstring. The bag was full of vials of vish. The soldier laughed and handed it back.

'Destroy it with the rest,' he said. 'It's time for me to live an honest life. I've had more than my fair share of years. If I can spend the ones I have left with this one,' he threw Raikka a smile, 'I'll be a rich man.'

Threon hitched the bag over his shoulder and held a hand out to Lleu. 'Maybe, someday, we'll meet again.'

'When we're old and grey,' conceded Lleu with a small smile. He clasped Threon's hand. 'I'll know where to find you.'

Threon returned his smile. 'Safe travels, brother.'

Lleu bowed his head. 'Rule wisely, Greenbrooke.'

Threon stepped back onto the jetty. Savanta caught his hand. 'I'm going too.' He frowned. 'Home. To my family, to my daughter. I can have my life back now.'

'You've done so much, suffered so much for Zenith… I owe you more thanks than I can give. I abandoned you when it wasn't your fault, and in return you saved my life.'

'I know.' Her smile told him he was forgiven. He reached out both hands to her. She batted past them and embraced him, speaking into his ear. 'Threon, don't ever forget what you did here. The slaves are free. The mines are closed. We can reclaim the land and make it green again.' She stepped back from the embrace.

'If you ever need anything,' he said. 'You, or your family, you must let me know.'

'Are you sure you want to stay?'

'I can't go home. Not yet. I have to finish what I started.'

'You're a noble man under that shabby exterior.' She tugged at a frayed corner of his shirt. 'I hate goodbyes.' She sighed and began walking backwards, away from them both. 'It's been quite an adventure.' With that she turned on her heel, raising a hand in farewell. Threon felt a knot of sadness as he watched her leave.

Lleu freed his boat from its mooring, tossing the rope into the hull.

'Good luck, Lleu,' Threon said as the soldier pushed the vessel away from the jetty.

'You too. Until next time.'

Threon turned and walked away, his footsteps taking him into deeper solitude.

The ships were loaded.

Threon stood beside Aya and Vituund as they supervised the loading of troops, food and precious metals. A light rain fell.

'They're pleased to be going home,' said Vituund. 'As am I.' He sighed as he said this, revealing a deep weariness.

'We have a duty to keep each other,' said Aya. 'For our children, and our children's children. Our kingdoms must remain united in peace.'

The two men nodded. 'We have lost so much to gain a sense of peace,' said Vituund. 'I hope, out of this sorrow, a new bond has been forged between kingdoms.'

'Indeed,' she said. 'Threon, you have two hundred of our soldiers who have volunteered to remain behind with you. Should the ancients form an uprising that could surpass them, you must send word to us.'

'I will.'

'And I will arrange for my royal architect to visit Maradah with his men. Your people deserve their city back.'

'Thank you. I hope to see it again when order is restored here.'

'You will.' She gave him a hearty slap on the back.

Men hoisted sails on several of the ships. 'We should go,' said Aya. She turned to Threon and took him by the shoulders. 'Thank you doesn't begin to cover it. If you require anything at all, just send word.'

Vituund inclined his head in a bow. 'You truly live up to the legend of Amel. Threon the Valiant. It has been a pleasure to call you friend.'

Threon watched them board and sat on the dock. He stayed until he was soaked through with rain and the ships were motes on the horizon.

The walk to the palace was silent. The past few days had been so busy with making arrangements and saying goodbyes that Threon hadn't had a moment alone. Not since he first awoke in the throne room.

The courtyard where Azzania had died lay empty. Straps of bloody fabric and empty vials of medicine littered the floor. His footsteps echoed as he walked.

He took the stairs to the throne room slowly. This was his new home. It couldn't feel further from it.

Zenith was waiting for him at the door.

He leant casually against a wall. 'Threon, welcome home.' His eyes were narrow, his voice implying anything but welcome.

'Zenith.' Threon moved to pull open the door but the Vyara's hand slammed onto the wood, keeping it shut.

'My brother let you go,' he hissed. 'Why?'

Threon met his eyes. 'Why do you Vyara insist on interfering in the lives of mortals?'

401

The Vyara pressed off the wall and leaned close. He breathed in deeply, as though he were smelling him, his eyes dancing over Threon's face. 'He's planted something in you. I can feel it. Remember, I brought you here. You belong to me.' He slid his hand away from the door. 'Don't betray me, boy. It won't end well.'

Threon kept his eyes on the god. As he pulled open the door, Zenith evaporated into the air.

A handful of candles flickered at the bottom of their wicks. It was dark and cold and reminded him of death.

He ascended the steps to the throne and sat. This is how it felt to be a king. The price of war brought nothing but death and a regal chair.

Several small chests of vish were stacked beside the throne. He flipped open the lid of the nearest.

So much suffering for this. He dragged his finger through the powder. It was due to be cast to the sea.

It would be a shame to waste it. The thought was his own, and not his own. It reached out from something placed deep inside him.

He brought his finger up into the flickering candlelight. It was dusted with the drug. He closed his eyes and touched the bitter substance to his lips.

ACKNOWLEDGEMENTS

I couldn't have completed this book without the generous support of so many wonderful people. I am lucky to have them in my life. Thanks to Harry Robbins, Marcus Burnham and Siân Stocks who set first eyes on the story and helped me shape it.

Ty Newydd writing centre played a big part in improving my confidence as a writer and making that all-important introduction to my publisher. This book wouldn't have happened without the incredible team at Parthian Books and my special thanks to Rich Davies, Carly Holmes and Molly Holborn for making it a reality.

I was very fortunate to meet a wonderful group of writers as I came to the end of writing *The Vagabond King*. Thank you to Samuel Hulett, Jafar Iqbal, Ross O'Keefe, Caragh Medlicott and Thomas Tyrell for sharing your stories with me, and for listening to mine.

Huge thanks go to my loving husband for giving me the space, time and encouragement to finish the novel.

And thank you to you, dear reader, for taking the time to step into my story.

Parthian Books: Recommended Fiction

The Blue Tent
Richard Gwyn
ISBN 978-1-912681-28-0
£9.99 Paperback

'One of the most satisfying, engrossing and
perfectly realised novels of the year.'
– *The Western Mail*

"This book is itself a sort of portal, where the
novelist-as-alchemist builds us a house
in the hills and then fills it ... with a
convincing magic.'
– *Nation.Cymru*

'A mysterious, dream-like story, delicately-
written and with a disturbing undertow,
The Blue Tent is in the best tradition of
modern oneiric fiction.'
– Patrick McGuinness

The Levels
Helen Pendry
ISBN 978-1-912109-40-1
£8.99 Paperback

'...with all the tension and plot twists and
turns that you would expect from a gripping
crime novel, makes an unsettling,
compelling read.'
– *Morning Star*

'...this is an assured novel and marks Helen
Pendry as an important new literary voice.'
– Kirsti Bohata, *Wales Arts Review*

'This is an elegant, wise and warm story that
stays with you long after finishing it.'
– Mike Parker

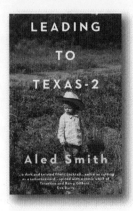

Leading to Texas-2
Aled Smith
ISBN 978-1-912109-11-1
£8.99 Paperback

'Aled Smith has mixed a dark and
twisted filmic cocktail.'
– Des Barry

Zero Hours on the Boulevard
ed. Alexandra Büchler
& Alison Evans
ISBN 978-1-912109-12-8
£8.99 Paperback

'A book about friendship, community,
identity and tribalism...'
– *New Welsh Reader*

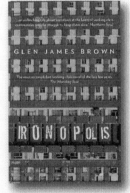

Ironopolis
Glen James Brown
ISBN 978-1-912681-09-9
£9.99 Paperback

'The most accomplished working-class
novel of the last few years.'
– *Morning Star*

'...nothing short of a triumph.'
– *The Guardian*